August 2011

Dear Friends,

Rain is a fact of life in the Pacific Northwest. Washington isn't known as the Evergreen State for nothing! It has a reputation for prodigious amounts of rainfall (although it's really not as bad as that sounds). During the winter months in particular, we get far more drizzle than rain; in fact, anyone carrying an umbrella is automatically identified as a tourist. Seattle, Washington, is where *Marriage Wanted,* the first of these stories, is set. *Laughter in the Rain,* however, is set in Minneapolis, which gets its fair share of precipitation, especially in summer (which is when this story takes place).

I want to point out that *Out of the Rain,* the title for this two-in-one volume, has a figurative and emotional meaning, as well as the obvious literal one. I believe that we all need to belong to someone, the *right* someone, and for most of us, love—in the form of marriage and family—is how we achieve that. Love and marriage provide shelter from the storm, a way to find warmth, security and comfort, to get *out of the rain.*

These two romances, *Laughter in the Rain* and *Marriage Wanted,* were originally published in 1986 and 1993 respectively. The world is an entirely different place now, thanks to cell phones, iPods, Twitter, Facebook and the like. The airport and flying experience has been completely transformed, to take another example. So have various slang terms, cultural references and so on. I know that jarringly dated material can distract readers from the story, so my editor, Paula Eykelhof, and I have done our best to refresh and update these books without changing them in any significant way.

When these books were first published, *Marriage Wanted* was dedicated to Theresa Scott, who's still a dear friend. *Laughter in the Rain* was dedicated to Tami Sahli, who as a teenager babysat our four children. She, too, remains a family friend.

My hope is that you'll curl up with this book some rainy afternoon, a hot cup of tea in hand, and become engrossed in these stories.

As always I enjoy hearing from my readers. You can connect with me on my website at www.DebbieMacomber.com or write me at P.O. Box 1458, Port Orchard, WA 98366.

Debbie Macomber

DEBBIE MACOMBER

Out of the
RAIN

MIRA®

ISBN-13: 978-0-7783-2988-6

OUT OF THE RAIN

Copyright © 2011 by MIRA Books

The publisher acknowledges the copyright holder of the individual works as follows:

MARRIAGE WANTED
Copyright © 1993 by Debbie Macomber

LAUGHTER IN THE RAIN
Copyright © 1986 by Debbie Macomber

For questions and comments about the quality of this book please contact us at Customer_eCare@Harlequin.ca.

www.MIRABooks.com

Printed in U.S.A.

Also by Debbie Macomber

CONTENTS

To Randall Toye
who has supported and encouraged me
for twenty-eight wonderful years.

MARRIAGE WANTED

One

Savannah Charles watched the young woman wandering around her bridal shop, checking prices and looking more discouraged by the moment. Her shoulders slumped and she bit her lip when she read the tag on the wedding gown she'd selected. She had excellent taste, Savannah noticed; the ivory silk-taffeta dress was one of her own favorites. A pattern of lace and pearls swirled up the puffed sleeves and bodice.

"Can I help you?" Savannah asked, moving toward her. Startled, the woman turned. "I… It doesn't look like it. This dress is almost twice as much as my budget for the whole wedding. Are you Savannah?"

"Yes."

She smiled shyly. "Missy Gilbert told me about you. She said you're wonderful to work with and that you might be able to give Kurt and me some guidance. I'm Susan Davenport." She held out her hand and Savannah shook it, liking the girl immediately.

"When's your wedding?"

"In six weeks. Kurt and I are paying for it ourselves. His two younger brothers are still in college and his parents haven't got much to spare." Amusement turned up the corners of her mouth as she added, "Kurt's dad claims he's becoming poor by degrees."

Savannah smiled back. "What about your family?"

"There's only my brother and me. He's fifteen years older and, well…it isn't that he doesn't like Kurt. Because once you meet Kurt, it's impossible not to love him. He's kind and generous and interesting.…"

Savannah was touched by Susan's eagerness to tell her about the man she wanted to marry.

"But Nash—my brother—doesn't believe in marriage," the young woman went on to explain. "He's an attorney and he's worked on so many divorce cases over the years that he simply doesn't believe in it anymore. It doesn't help that he's divorced himself, although that was years and years ago."

"What's your budget?" Savannah asked. She'd planned weddings that went into six figures, but she was equally adept at finding reasonable alternatives. She walked back to her desk, limping on her right foot. It ached more this afternoon than usual. It always did when the humidity was this high.

Susan told her the figure she and Kurt had managed to set aside and Savannah frowned. It wasn't much, but she could work with it. She turned around and caught Susan staring at her. Savannah was accustomed to that kind of reaction to her limp, the result of a childhood accident. She generally wore pants, which disguised the scars and disfigurement, but her limp was always noticeable, and more so when she was tired. Until they knew her better, it seemed to disconcert people. Generally she ignored their hesitation and continued, hoping that her own acceptance would put them at ease.

"Even the least expensive wedding dresses would eat up the majority of the money we've worked so hard to save."

"You could always rent the dress," Savannah suggested.

"I could?" Her pretty blue eyes lit up when Savannah mentioned the rental fee.

"How many people are you inviting?"

"Sixty-seven," Susan told her, as if the number of guests had been painfully difficult to pare down. "Kurt and I can't afford more. Mostly it's his family.… I don't think Nash will even come to the wedding." Her voice fell.

Despite never having met Susan's older brother, she already disliked him. Savannah couldn't imagine a brother refusing to attend his sister's wedding, no matter what his personal views on marriage happened to be.

"Kurt's from a large family. He has aunts and uncles and, I swear, at least a thousand cousins. We'd like to invite everyone, but we can't. The invitations alone will cost a fortune."

"Have you thought about making your own invitations?"

Susan shook her head. "I'm not very artsy."

"You don't need to be." Opening a drawer, Savannah brought out a book of calligraphy. "These are fairly simple and elegant-looking and they'll add a personal touch because they're individualized." She paused. "You'll find other ideas on the internet."

"These are beautiful. You honestly think I could do this?" She looked expectantly at Savannah.

"Without a doubt," Savannah answered with a smile.

"I wish I could talk some sense into Nash," Susan muttered, then squared her shoulders as if she was ready to take him on right that minute. "He's the only family I have. We've got aunts and uncles here and there, but no one we're close to, and Nash is being so unreasonable about this. I love Kurt and nothing's going to change the way I feel. I love his family, too. It can be lonely when you don't belong to someone. That's Nash's problem. He's forgotten what it's like to belong to someone. To be in a relationship."

Loneliness. Savannah was well acquainted with the feeling. All her life she'd felt alone. The little girl who couldn't run and play with friends. The teenage girl who never got asked to the prom. The woman who arranged the happiest days of *other* people's lives.

Loneliness. Savannah knew more than she wanted to about long days and longer nights.

"I'm sure your brother will change his mind," Savannah said reassuringly—even though she wasn't sure at all.

Susan laughed. "That only goes to prove you don't know my brother. Once he's set on something, it takes an Act of Congress to persuade him otherwise."

Savannah spent the next hour with Susan, deciding on the details of both the wedding and the reception. With such a limited budget it was a challenge, but they did it.

"I can't believe we can do so much with so little," Susan said once they'd finished. Her face glowed with happiness. "A nice wedding doesn't mean as much to Kurt as it does to me, but he's willing to do whatever he can to make our day special."

Through the course of their conversation, Savannah

learned that Kurt had graduated from the University of Washington with an engineering degree. He'd recently been hired by a California firm and had moved to the San Francisco area, where Susan would be joining him.

After defying her brother, Susan had moved in with Kurt's family, working part-time and saving every penny she could to help with the wedding expenses.

"I can hardly wait to talk to Kurt," Susan said excitedly as she gathered her purse and the notes she'd made. "I'll get back to you as soon as he's had a chance to go over the contract." Susan paused. "Missy was right. You *are* wonderful." She threw both arms around Savannah in an impulsive hug. "I'll be back as soon as I can and you can take the measurements for the dress." She cast a dreamy look toward the silk-and-taffeta gown and sighed audibly. "Kurt's going to die when he sees me in that dress."

"You'll make a lovely bride."

"Thank you for everything," Susan said as she left the store.

"You're welcome." It was helping young women like Susan that Savannah enjoyed the most. The eager, happy ones who were so much in love they were willing to listen to their hearts no matter what the cost. Over the years, Savannah had worked with every kind of bride and she knew the signs. The Susans of this world were invariably a delight.

It was highly unlikely that Savannah would ever be married herself. Men were an enigma to her. Try as she might, she'd never been able to understand them. They invariably treated her differently than they did other women. Savannah assumed their attitude had to do with her damaged leg. Men either saw her as fragile, untouchable, because of it, or they viewed her as a buddy, a confidante. She supposed she should be flattered by the easy camaraderie they shared with her. They sought her advice, listened politely when she spoke, then did as they pleased.

Only a few men had seen her as a *woman,* a woman with dreams and desires of her own. But when it came to love, each of them had grown hesitant and afraid. Each relationship had ended awkwardly long before it had gotten close to serious.

Maybe that wasn't a fair assessment, Savannah mused sadly. Maybe it was her own attitude. She'd been terrified of ever falling in love. No matter how deeply she felt about a man, she was positive that her imperfection would come between them. It was safer to hold back, to cling to her pride than risk rejection and pain later on.

A week later, Susan came breezing through the door to Savannah's shop.

"Hello," she said, smiling broadly. "I talked to Kurt and he's as excited as I am." She withdrew a debit card from her purse. "I'd like to give you the down payment now. And I have the signed contract for you."

Savannah brought out her paperwork and Susan paid her. "My brother doesn't believe we'll be able to do it without his help, but he's wrong. We're going to have a beautiful wedding, with or without Nash, thanks to you."

This was what made Savannah's job so fulfilling. "I'll order what we need right away," she told Susan. Savannah only wished there was some way she could influence the young woman's unreasonable older brother.

She knew his type—cynical, distrusting, pessimistic. A man who scoffed at love, who had no respect for marriage. How very sad. Despite her irritation with the faceless Nash, Savannah couldn't help feeling sorry for him. Whether or not he realized it, he was going to lose his sister.

There were just the two of them, so she didn't understand why Nash wouldn't support his sister in her decision. Luckily Susan had Kurt's parents. Undoubtedly this was something her brother hadn't counted on, either.

Susan left soon afterward. What remained of Savannah's day was busy. The summer months used to be her overburdened time, but that hadn't held true of late. Her services were booked equally throughout the year.

Around five-thirty, when Savannah was getting ready to close for the day, the bell chimed over her door, indicating someone had entered the shop. She looked up from her computer and found a tall, well-dressed man standing by the doorway. It had started to rain lightly; he shook off the raindrops in his hair before he stepped farther inside. She saw him glance around and scowl, as if being in such a place was repugnant to him. Even before he spoke she knew he was Susan's brother. The family resemblance was striking.

"Hello," she said.

"Hello." He slid his hands in his pockets with a contemptuous frown. Apparently he feared that even being in this place where love and romance were honored would infect him with some dread disease. It must take a good deal of energy to maintain his cynicism, Savannah thought.

"Can I help you?" she asked.

"No, thanks. I was just looking." He walked slowly through the shop. His expensive leather shoes made a tapping sound against the polished hardwood floor. She noticed that he took pains not to touch anything.

Savannah nearly laughed out loud when he passed a display of satin pillows, edged in French lace, that were meant to be carried by the ring bearer. He stepped around it, giving it a wide berth, then picked up one of her business cards from a brass holder on a small antique table.

"Are you Savannah Charles?" he asked.

"Yes," she replied evenly. "I am."

"Interesting shop you have here," he said dryly. Savannah had to admit she found him handsome in a rugged sort of way. His facial features were strong and well-defined. His mouth firm, his jaw square and stubbornly set. He walked in short, clipped steps, his impatience nearly palpable. Naturally, she might be altogether wrong and this could be someone other than Susan's brother. Savannah decided it was time to find out.

"Are you about to be married?"

"No," he said disgustedly.

"This seems like an unusual shop for you to browse through, then."

He smiled in her direction, acknowledging her shrewdness. "I believe you've been talking to my sister, Susan Davenport."

So Savannah had been right. This *was* Susan's hard-nosed older brother. His attitude had been a dead giveaway. "Yes, Susan's been in."

"I take it she's decided to go through with this wedding nonsense, then?" He eyed her suspiciously as if to suggest his sister might have changed her mind except for Savannah's encouragement and support.

"It would be best if you discussed Susan's plans with her."

Nash clasped his hands behind his back. "I would if we were on speaking terms."

How he knew his sister was working with her, Savannah hadn't a clue. She didn't even want to know.

"So," he said conversationally, "exactly what do you do here?"

"I'm a wedding coordinator."

"Wedding coordinator," he repeated, sounding genuinely curious. He nodded for her to continue.

"Basically I organize the wedding for the bride and her family so they're free to enjoy this all-important day."

"I see," he said. "You're the one who makes sure the flowers arrive at the church on time?"

"Something like that." His version oversimplified her role, but she didn't think he'd appreciate a detailed job description. After all, he wasn't interested in her, but in what he could learn about his sister and Kurt's plans.

He wandered about the shop some more, careful not to come into contact with any of the displays she'd so carefully arranged. He strolled past a lace-covered table with an elegant heart-shaped guest book and plumed pen as if he were walking past a nest of vipers. Savannah couldn't help being amused.

"Susan hasn't got the money for a wedding," he announced. "At least, not one fancy enough to hire a coordinator."

"Again, this is something you need to discuss with your sister."

He didn't like her answer; that much was obvious from the way his mouth thinned and the irritation she saw in his eyes. They were the same intense blue as his sister's, but that was where the resemblance ended. Susan's eyes revealed her love and enthusiasm for life. Nash's revealed his disenchantment and skepticism. She finished up the last of her paperwork, ignoring him as much as she could.

"You're a babe in the woods, aren't you?"

"I beg your pardon?" Savannah said, looking up.

"You actually believe all this…absurdity?"

"I certainly don't think of love and commitment as absurd, if that's what you mean, Mr. Davenport."

"Call me Nash."

"All right," she agreed reluctantly. In a few minutes she was going to show him the door. He hadn't bothered to disguise the purpose of his visit. He was trying to pump her for information and hadn't figured out yet that she refused to be placed in the middle between him and his sister.

"Did you ever stop to realize that over fifty percent of the couples who marry in this day and age end up divorcing?"

"I know the statistics."

He walked purposely toward her as if approaching a judge's bench, intent on proving his point. "Love is a lame excuse for marriage."

Since he was going to make it impossible for her to concentrate, she sat back on her stool and folded her arms. "What do you suggest couples do then, Mr. Davenport? Just live together?"

"Nash," he reminded her irritably. "And, yes, living together makes a lot more sense. If a man and woman are so hot for each other, I don't see any reason to muddy the relationship with legalities when a weekend in bed would simplify everything."

Savannah resisted the urge to roll her eyes. Rejecting marriage made as much sense to her as pushing a car over a cliff because the fender was dented. Instead she asked, "Is this what you want Susan and Kurt to do? Live together indefinitely? Without commitment?"

That gave him pause. Apparently it was perfectly fine for other couples to do that, but when it came to his little sister, he hesitated. "Yes," he finally said. "Until this infatuation passes."

"What about children?"

"Susan's little more than a child herself," he argued, although she was twenty-four—and in Savannah's estimation a mature twenty-four. "If she's smart, she'll avoid adding to her mistakes," he said stiffly.

"What about someone other than your sister?" she demanded, annoyed with herself for allowing him to draw her into this pointless discussion. "Are you suggesting our society should do away with family?"

"A wedding ring doesn't make a family," he returned just as heatedly.

Savannah sighed deeply. "I think it's best for us to agree to disagree," she said, feeling a bit sad. It was unrealistic to think she'd say anything that would change his mind. Susan was determined to marry Kurt, with or without his approval, but she loved her brother, too. That was what made this situation so difficult.

"Love is a lame excuse to mess up one's life," he said,

clenching his fists at his side with impotent anger. "A lame excuse."

At his third use of the word *lame,* Savannah inwardly flinched. Because she was sitting behind her desk, he didn't realize *she* was "lame."

"Marriage is an expensive trap that destroys a man's soul," Nash went on to say, ignoring her. "I see the results of it each and every day. Just this afternoon, I was in court for a settlement hearing that was so nasty the judge had to pull both attorneys into chambers. Do you really believe I want my little sister involved in something like that?"

"Your sister is a grown woman, Mr. Davenport. She's old enough to make her own decisions."

"Mistakes, you mean."

Savannah sensed his frustration, but arguing with him would do no good at all. "Susan's in love. You should know by now that she's determined to marry Kurt."

"*In love.* Excuses don't get much worse than that."

Savannah had had enough. She stood and realized for the first time how tall Nash actually was. He loomed head and shoulders over her five-foot-three-inch frame. Standing next to him she felt small and insignificant. For all their differences, Savannah could appreciate his concerns. Nash loved his sister; otherwise he wouldn't have gone to such effort to find out her plans.

"It's been interesting," Nash said, waiting for her to walk around her desk and join him. Savannah did, limping as she went. She was halfway across the room before she saw that he wasn't following her. Half turning around, she noticed that he was looking at her leg, his features marked by regret.

"I didn't mean to be rude," he said, and she couldn't doubt his sincerity. What surprised her was his sensitivity. She might have judged this man too harshly. His attitude had irritated her, but she'd also been entertained by him—and by the vigor of their argument.

"You didn't know." She finished her trek to the door, again surprised to realize he hadn't followed her. "It's well past my closing time," she said meaningfully.

"Of course." His steps were crisp and uniform as he marched across her shop, stopping abruptly when he reached her. A frown wrinkled his brow as he stared at her again.

"What's wrong?"

He laughed shortly. "I'm trying to figure something out."

"If it has to do with Susan and Kurt—"

"It doesn't," he cut in. "It has to do with you." An odd smile lifted his mouth. "I like you. You're impertinent, sassy and stubborn."

"Oh, really!" She might have been offended if she hadn't been struggling so hard not to laugh.

"Really."

"You're tactless, irritating and overpowering," she responded.

His grin was transformed into a full-blown smile. "You're right. It's a shame, though."

"A shame? What are you talking about?"

"You being a wedding coordinator. It's a waste. With your obvious organizational skills, you might've done something useful. Instead, your head's stuck in the clouds and you've let love and romance fog up your brain. But you know what?" He rubbed the side of his jaw. "There just might be hope for you."

"Hope. Funny, I was thinking the same thing about you. There just might be a slim chance of reasoning with you. You're clearly intelligent and even a little witty. But unfortunately you're misguided. Now that you're dealing with your sister's marriage, however, there's a remote possibility someone might be able to get through to you."

"What do you mean?" he asked, folding his arms over his chest and resting his weight on one foot.

"Your judgment's been confused by your clients. By their anger and bitterness and separations. We're at opposite ends of the same subject. I work with couples when they're deeply in love and convinced the relationship will last forever. You see them when they're embittered and disillusioned. But what you don't seem to realize is that you need to see the glass as half-full and not half-empty."

He frowned. "I thought we were talking about marriage."

"We are. What you said earlier is true. Fifty percent of all married couples end up divorcing—which means fifty percent of them go on to lead fulfilling, happy lives."

Nash's snort was derisive. He dropped his arms and straightened, shaking his head. "I was wrong. There's no hope for you. The fifty percent who stay together are just as miserable. Given the opportunity, they'd gladly get out of the relationship."

Nash was beginning to irritate her again. "Why is it so difficult for you to believe that there's such a thing as a happy marriage?"

"Because I've never seen one."

"You haven't looked hard enough."

"Have you ever stopped to think that your head's so muddled with hearts and flowers and happy-ever-afters that you can't and won't accept what's right in front of your eyes?"

"Like I said, it's past my closing time." Savannah jerked open the shop door. The clanging bell marked the end of their frustrating conversation. Rarely had Savannah allowed anyone to get under her skin the way she had Nash Davenport. The man was impossible. Totally unreasonable...

The woman was impossible. Totally unreasonable.

Nash couldn't understand why he continued to mull over their conversation. Twenty-four hours had passed, and he'd thought about their verbal sparring match a dozen times.

Relaxing in his leather office chair, he rolled a pen between his palms. Obviously Savannah didn't know him well; otherwise, she wouldn't have attempted to convince him of the error of his views.

His eyes fell on the phone and he sighed inwardly. Susan was being stubborn and irrational. It was plain that he was going to have to be the one to mend fences. He'd hoped she'd come to her senses, but it wasn't going to happen. He was her older brother, her closest relative, and if she refused to make the first move, he'd have to do it.

He looked up Kurt Caldwell's parents' phone number. He resented having to contact her there. Luck was with him, however, when Susan herself answered.

"It's Nash," he said. When she was little, her voice rose with excitement whenever he called. Anytime he arrived home, she'd fly into his arms, so glad to see him she couldn't hold still. He sighed again, missing the child she once was.

"Hello, Nash," Susan said stiffly. No pleasure at hearing from him was evident now.

"How are you doing?" That was the purpose of this call, after all.

"Fine. How about you?" Her words were stilted, and her stubbornness hadn't budged an inch. He would have said as much, then thought better of it.

"I'm fine, too," he answered.

The silence stretched between them.

"I understand you have a wedding coordinator now," he said, hoping to come across as vaguely interested. She might have defied him, but he would always be her big brother.

"How do you know that?"

"Word, uh, gets around." In fact, he'd learned about it from a family friend. Still, he shouldn't have said anything. And he wouldn't have if Savannah hadn't dominated his thoughts from the moment he'd met her.

"You've had someone checking into my affairs, haven't you?" Susan lowered her voice to subzero temperatures. "You can't rule my life, Nash. I'm going to marry Kurt and that's all there is to it."

"I gathered as much from Savannah Charles...."

"You've talked to Savannah?"

Nash recognized his second mistake immediately. He'd blown it now, and Susan wasn't going to forgive him.

"Stop meddling in my life, Nash." His sister's voice quavered suspiciously and seconds later the line was disconnected. The phone droned in his ear before he dejectedly replaced the receiver.

Needless to say, *that* conversation hadn't gone well. He'd like to blame Savannah, but it was his fault. He'd been the one to let her name slip, a stupid error on his part.

The wedding coordinator and his sister were both too stubborn and naive for their own good. If this was how Susan wanted it, then he had no choice but to abide by her wishes. Calling her had been another mistake in a long list he'd been making lately.

His assistant poked her head in his door, and he gave her his immediate attention. He had more important things to worry about than his sister and a feisty wedding coordinator who lived in a dreamworld.

"What did my brother say?" Susan demanded.

"He wanted to know about you," Savannah said absently as she arranged champagne flutes on the display table next to the five-tier wedding cake. She'd been working on the display between customers for the past hour.

"In other words, Nash was pumping you for information?"

"Yes, but you don't need to worry, I didn't tell him anything. What I did do was suggest he talk to you." She straightened, surprised that he'd followed her advice. "He cares deeply for you, Susan."

"I know." Susan gnawed on her lower lip. "I wish I hadn't hung up on him."

"Susan!"

"I… He told me he'd talked to you and it made me so mad I couldn't bear to speak to him another second."

Savannah was surprised by Nash's slip. She would've thought their conversation was the last thing he'd mention. But from the sound of it, he didn't get an opportunity to rehash it with Susan.

"If he makes a pest of himself," Susan said righteously, "let me know and I'll...I'll do something."

"Don't worry about it. I rather enjoyed talking to him." It was true, although Savannah hated to admit it. She'd worked hard to push thoughts of Nash from her mind over the past couple of days. His attitude had annoyed her, true, but she'd found him intriguing and—it bothered her to confess this—a challenge. A smile came when she realized he probably saw her the same way.

"I have to get back to work," Susan said reluctantly. "I just wanted to apologize for my brother's behavior."

"He wasn't a problem."

On her way out the door, Susan muttered something Savannah couldn't hear. The situation was sad. Brother and sister loved each other but were at an impasse.

Savannah continued to consider the situation until the bell over the door chimed about five minutes later. Smiling, she looked up, deciding she wasn't going to get this display finished until after closing time. She should've known better than to try.

"Nash." His name was a mere whisper.

"Hello again," he said dryly. "I've come to prove my point."

Two

"You want to prove your point," Savannah repeated thoughtfully. Nash Davenport was the most headstrong man she'd ever encountered. He was also one of the handsomest. That did more to confuse her than to help. For reasons as yet unclear, she'd lost her objectivity. No doubt it had something to do with that pride of his and the way they'd argued. No doubt it was also because they remained diametrically opposed on the most fundamental issues of life—love and marriage.

"I've given some thought to our conversation the other day," Nash said, pacing back and forth, "and it seems to me that I'm just the person to clear up your thinking. Besides," he went on, "if I *can* clear up your thinking, maybe you'll have some influence on Susan."

Although it was difficult, Savannah resisted the urge to laugh.

"To demonstrate my good faith, I brought a peace offering." He held up a white sack for her inspection. "Two lattes," he explained. He set the bag on the corner of her desk and opened it, handing her one of the paper cups. The smell of hot coffee blended with steamed milk was as welcome as popcorn in a theater. "Make yourself comfortable," he said next, gesturing toward the stool, "because it might take a while."

"I don't know if this is a good idea," Savannah felt obliged to say as she carefully edged onto the stool.

"It's a great idea. Just hear me out," he said smoothly.

"Oh, all right," she returned with an ungracious nod. Savannah might have had the energy to resist him if it hadn't been so late in the day. She was tired and the meeting with Susan had frustrated her. She'd come to her upset and unhappy, and Savannah had felt helpless, not knowing how to reassure the younger woman.

Nash pried off the lid of his latte, then glanced at his watch. He walked over to her door and turned over the sign so it read Closed.

"Hey, wait a minute!"

"It's—" he looked at his watch again "—5:29 p.m. You're officially closed in one minute."

Savannah didn't bother to disagree. "I think it's only fair for you to know that whatever you have to say isn't going to change my mind," she said.

"I figured as much."

The man continued to surprise her. "How do you intend to prove your point? Parade divorced couples through my wedding shop?"

"Nothing that drastic."

"Did it occur to you that I could do the same thing and have you meet with a group of blissful newlyweds?" she asked.

He grinned. "I'm way ahead of you. I already guessed you'd enjoy introducing me to any number of loving couples who can't keep their hands off each other."

Savannah shrugged, not denying it.

"The way I figure it," he said, "we both have a strong argument to make."

"Exactly." She nodded. "But you aren't going to change my mind and I doubt I'll change yours." She didn't know what kept some couples together against all odds or why others decided to divorce when the first little problem arose. If Nash expected her to supply the answers, she had none to offer.

"Don't be so sure we won't change each other's mind." Which only went to prove that he thought there was a chance he could influence her. "We could accomplish a great deal if we agree to be open-minded."

Savannah cocked one eyebrow and regarded him skeptically. "Can you guarantee you'll be open-minded?"

"I'm not sure," he answered, and she was impressed with his honesty. "But I'm willing to try. That's all I ask of you."

"That sounds fair."

He rubbed his palms together as though eager to get started. "If you don't object, I'd like to go first."

"Just a minute," she said, holding up her hand. "Before we do, shouldn't we set some rules?"

"Like what?"

Although it was her suggestion, Savannah didn't really have an answer. "I don't know. Just boundaries of some kind."

"I trust you not to do anything weird, and you can count on the same from me," he said. "After all—"

"Don't be so hasty," she interrupted. "If we're going to put time and effort into this, it makes sense that we have rules. *And* something riding on the outcome."

His blue eyes brightened. "Now there's an interesting

thought." He paused and a smile bracketed his mouth. "So you want to set a wager?"

Nash seemed to be on a one-man campaign to convince her the world would be a better place without the institution of marriage. "We might as well make it interesting, don't you think?"

"I couldn't agree more. If you can prove your point and get me to agree that you have, what would you want in exchange?"

This part was easy. "For you to attend Susan and Kurt's wedding. It would mean the world to Susan."

The easy smile disappeared behind a dark frown.

"She was in this afternoon," Savannah continued, rushing the words in her eagerness to explain. "She's anxious and confused, loving you and loving Kurt and needing your approval so badly."

Nash's mouth narrowed into a thin line of irritation.

"Would it really be so much to ask?" she ventured. "I realize I'd need to rely on your complete and total honesty, but I have faith in you." She took a sip of her latte.

"So, if you convince me my thinking is wrong on this marriage issue, you want me to attend Susan's wedding." He hesitated, then nodded slowly. "Deal," he said, and his grin reappeared.

Until that moment, Savannah was convinced Nash had no idea what he intended to use for his argument. But apparently he did. "What would you want from me?" she asked. Her question broke into his musings because he jerked his head toward her as if he'd forgotten there might be something in this for him, as well. He took a deep breath and then released it. "I don't know. Do I have to decide right now?"

"No."

"It'll be something substantial—you understand that, don't you?"

Savannah managed to hold back a smile. "I wouldn't expect anything less."

"How about home-cooked dinners for a week served on your fanciest china? That wouldn't be out of line," he murmured.

She gaped at him. Her request had been generous and completely selfless. She'd offered him an excuse to attend Susan's wedding *and* salvage his pride, and in return he wanted her to slave in the kitchen for days on end.

"That *is* out of line," she told him, unwilling to agree to anything so ridiculous. If he wanted home-made meals, he could do what the rest of the world did and cook them himself, visit relatives or get married.

Nash's expression was boyish with delight. "So you're afraid you're going to lose."

Raising her eyebrows, she said, "You haven't got a prayer, Davenport."

"Then what's the problem?" he asked, making an exaggerated gesture with both hands. "Do you agree to my terms or not?"

This discussion had wandered far from what she'd originally intended. Savannah had been hoping to smooth things over between brother and sister and at the same time prove her own point. She wasn't interested in putting her own neck on the chopping block. Any attempt to convince Nash of the error of his ways was pointless.

He finished off his latte and flung the empty container into her garbage receptacle. "Be ready tomorrow afternoon," he said, walking to the door.

Savannah scrambled awkwardly from the stool. "What for?" she called after him. She limped two steps toward him and stopped abruptly at the flash of pain that shot up her leg. She'd sat too long in the same position, something she was generally able to avoid. She wanted to rub her thigh, work the throbbing muscle, but that would reveal her pain, which she wanted to hide from Nash.

"You'll know more tomorrow afternoon," he promised, looking pleased with himself.

"How long will this take?"

"There are time restrictions? Are there any other rules we need to discuss?"

"I… We should both be reasonable about this, don't you think?"

"I *was* planning to be sensible, but I can't speak for you."

This conversation was deteriorating rapidly. "I'll be ready at closing time tomorrow afternoon, then," she said, holding her hand against her thigh. If he didn't leave soon, she was going to have to sit down. Disguising her pain had become a way of life, but the longer she stood, the more difficult it became.

"Something's wrong," he announced, his gaze hard and steady. "You'd argue with me if there wasn't."

Again she was impressed by his sensitivity. "Nonsense. I said I'd be ready. What more do you want?"

He left her then, in the nick of time. A low moan escaped as she sank onto her chair. Perspiration moistened her brow and she drew in several deep breaths.

Rubbing her hand over the tense muscles slowly eased out the pain.

The phone was situated to the left of her desk and after giving the last of her discomfort a couple of minutes to ebb away, she reached for the receiver and dialed her parents' number. Apparently Nash had decided how to present his case. She had, too. No greater argument could be made than her parents' loving relationship. Their marriage was as solid as Fort Knox and they'd been devoted to each other for over thirty years. Nash couldn't meet her family and continue to discredit love and marriage.

Her father answered on the second ring, sounding delighted to hear from her. A rush of warm feeling washed over Savannah. Her family had been a constant source of love and encouragement to her through the years.

"Hi, Dad."

"It's always good to hear from you, sweetheart."

Savannah relaxed in her chair. "Is Mom around?"

"No, she's got a doctor's appointment to have her blood pressure checked again. Is there anything I can do for you?"

Savannah's hand tightened around the receiver. She didn't want to mislead her parents into thinking she was involved with Nash. But she needed to prove her point. "Is there any chance I could bring someone over for dinner tomorrow night?"

"Of course."

Savannah laughed lightly. "You might want to check Mom's calendar. It'd be just like you to agree to something when she's already made plans."

"I looked. The calendar's right here in the kitchen

and tomorrow night's free. Now, if you were to ask about Friday, that's a different story."

Once more Savannah found herself smiling.

"Who do you want us to meet?"

"His name's Nash Davenport."

Her announcement was met with a short but noticeable silence. "You're bringing a young man home to meet your family? This is an occasion, then."

"Dad, it isn't like that." This was exactly what she'd feared would happen, that her family would misinterpret her bringing Nash home. "We've only just met...."

"It was like that with your mother and me," her father said excitedly. "We met on a Friday night and a week later I knew this was the woman I was going to love all my life, and I have."

"Dad, Nash is just a friend—not even a friend, really, just an acquaintance," Savannah said, trying to correct his mistaken impression. "I'm coordinating his sister's wedding."

"No need to explain, sweetheart. If you want to bring a young man for your mother and me to meet, we'd be thrilled, no matter what the reason."

Savannah was about to respond, but then decided that a lengthy explanation might hurt her cause rather than help it. "I'm not sure of the exact time we'll arrive."

"No problem. I'll light up the barbecue and that way you won't need to worry. Come whenever you can. We'll make an evening of it."

Oh, yes, it was going to be quite an evening, Savannah mused darkly. Two stubborn people, both convinced they were right, would each try to convert the other.

This was going to be so easy that Nash almost felt guilty. Almost... Poor Savannah. Once he'd finished with what he had to show her, she'd have no option but to accept the reality of his argument.

Nash loved this kind of debate, when he was certain beyond a shadow of a doubt that he was right. By the time he was done, Savannah would be eating her words.

Grabbing his briefcase, he hurried out of his office, anxious to forge ahead and prove his point.

"Nash, what's your hurry?"

Groaning inwardly, Nash turned to face a fellow attorney, Paul Jefferson. "I've got an appointment this evening," Nash explained. He didn't like Paul, had never liked Paul. What bothered him most was that this brownnoser was going to be chosen over him for the partnership position that was opening up within the year. Both Paul and Nash had come into the firm at the same time, and they were both good attorneys. But Paul had a way of ingratiating himself with the powers that be and parting the waters of opportunity.

"An appointment or a date?" Paul asked with that smug look of his. One of these days Nash was going to find an excuse to wipe that grin off his face.

He looked pointedly at his watch. "If you'll excuse me, Paul, I have to leave, otherwise I'll be late."

"Can't keep *her* waiting, now can we?" Paul said, and finding himself amusing, he laughed at his own sorry joke.

Knotting his fist at his side, Nash was happy to escape. Anger clawed at him until he was forced to stop and analyze his outrage. He'd been working with Paul for nearly ten years. He'd tolerated his humorless jokes, his conceited, self-righteous attitude and his air of superiority without displaying his annoyance. What was different now?

He considered the idea of Paul being preferred to him for the partnership. But this was nothing new. The minute he'd learned about the opening, he'd suspected Stackhouse and Serle would choose Paul. He'd accepted it as fact weeks ago.

Paul had suggested Nash was hurrying to meet a woman—which he was. Nash didn't bother to deny it. What upset him was the sarcastic way Paul had said it, as though Savannah—

His mind came to a grinding halt. Savannah.

So she was at the bottom of all this. Nash had taken offense at the edge in Paul's voice, as if his fellow attorney had implied that Savannah was, somehow, less than she should be. He knew he was being oversensitive. After all, Paul had never even met her. But still…

Nash recalled his own reaction to Savannah, his observations when he'd met her. She was small. Her dark, pixie-style hair and deep brown eyes gave her a fragile appearance, but that was deceptive. The woman obviously had a constitution of iron.

Her eyes… Once more his thoughts skidded to a halt. He'd never known a woman with eyes that were more revealing. In them he read a multitude of emotions. Pain, both physical and emotional. In them he saw a woman with courage. Nash barely knew Savannah and yet he sensed she was one of the most astonishing people he'd probably ever meet. He'd wanted to defend her, wanted to slam his colleague up against a wall and demand an apology for the slight, vague though it was. In fact, he admitted, if Paul was insulting anyone, it was more likely him than Savannah….

When he reached his car, Nash sat in the driver's seat with his key poised in front of the ignition for a moment, brooding about his colleague and the competitiveness between them.

His mood lightened considerably as he made his way through the heavy traffic to the wedding shop. He'd been looking forward to this all day.

He found a parking spot and climbed out of his car, then fed the meter. As he turned away he caught sight of Savannah in the shop window, talking to a customer. Her face was aglow with enthusiasm and even from this distance her eyes sparkled. For a reason unknown to him, his pulse accelerated as joy surged through him.

He was happy to be seeing Savannah. Any man would, knowing he was about to be proven right. But this was more than that. This happiness was rooted in the knowledge that he'd be spending time with her.

Savannah must have felt his scrutiny, because she glanced upward and their eyes met briefly before she reluctantly pulled hers away. Although she continued speaking to her customer, Nash sensed that she'd experienced the same intensity of feeling he had. It was at moments such as this that he wished he could be privy to a woman's thoughts. He would gladly have forfeited their bet to know if she was as surprised and puzzled as he felt. Nash couldn't identify the feeling precisely; all he knew was that it made him uncomfortable.

The customer was leaving just as Nash entered the shop. Savannah was sitting at her desk and intuitively he realized she needed to sit periodically because of her leg. She looked fragile and confused. When she raised her eyes to meet his, he was shocked by the strength of her smile.

"You're right on time," she said.

"You would be, too, if you were about to have

home-cooked meals personally served to you for the next week."

"Don't count on it, Counselor."

"Oh, I'm counting on it," he said with a laugh. "I've already got the menu picked out. We'll start the first night with broiled New York sirloin, Caesar salad and a three-layer chocolate cake."

"You certainly love to dream," she said with an effortless laugh. "I find it amusing that you never stopped to ask if I could cook. It'll probably come as a surprise to learn that not all women are proficient in the kitchen. If by some odd quirk of fate you do happen to win this wager, you'll dine on boxed macaroni and cheese or microwave meals for seven days and like it."

Nash was stunned. She was right; he'd assumed she could cook as well as she seemed to manage everything else. Her shop was a testament to her talent, appealing to the eye in every respect. True, all those wedding gowns and satin pillows were aiding and abetting romance, but it had a homey, comfortable feel, as well. This wasn't an easy thing to admit. A wedding shop was the last place on earth Nash ever thought he'd willingly visit.

"Are you ready to admit defeat?" he asked.

"Never, but before we get started I need to make a couple of phone calls. Do you mind?"

"Not in the least." He was a patient man, and never more so than now. The longer they delayed, the better. It wasn't likely that Paul would stay late, but Nash wanted to avoid introducing Savannah to him. More important, he wanted her to himself. The thought was unwelcome. This wasn't a date and he had no romantic interest in Savannah Charles, he reminded himself.

Savannah reached for the phone and he wandered

around the shop noticing small displays he'd missed on his prior visits. The first time he'd felt nervous; he didn't know what to expect from a wedding coordinator, but certainly not the practical, gutsy woman he'd found.

He trained his ears not to listen in on her conversation, but the crisp, businesslike tone of her voice was surprisingly captivating.

It was happening again—that disturbing feeling was back, deep in the pit of his stomach. He'd felt it before, several years earlier, and it had nearly ruined his life. He was in trouble. Panic shot through his blood and he felt the overwhelming urge to turn and run in the opposite direction. The last time he'd had this feeling, he'd gotten married.

"I'm ready," Savannah said, and stood.

Nash stared at her for a long moment as his brain processed what was going on.

"Nash?"

He gave himself a hard mental shake. He didn't know if he was right about what had happened here, but he didn't like it. "Do you mind riding with me?" he asked, once he'd composed himself.

"That'll be fine."

The drive back to his office building in downtown Seattle was spent in relative silence. Savannah seemed to sense his reflective mood. Another woman might have attempted to fill the space with idle chatter. Nash was grateful she didn't.

After he'd parked, he led Savannah into his building and up the elevator to the law firm's offices. She seemed impressed with the plush furnishings and the lavish view of Mount Rainier and Puget Sound from his twentieth-story window.

When she'd entered his office she'd walked directly to the window and set her purse on his polished oak credenza. "How do you manage to work with a view like this?" she asked, her voice soft with awe. She seemed mesmerized by the beauty that appeared before her.

After several years Nash had become immune to its splendor, but lately he'd begun to appreciate the solace he found there. The color of the sky reflected like a mirror on the water's surface. On a gray and hazy morning, the water was a dull shade of steel. When the sun shone, Puget Sound was a deep, iridescent greenish blue. He enjoyed watching the ferries and other commercial and pleasure craft as they intersected the waterways. In the last while, he'd often stood in the same spot as Savannah and sorted through his thoughts.

"It's all so beautiful," she said, turning back to him. Hearing her give voice to his own feelings felt oddly comforting. The sooner he presented his argument, the better. The sooner he said what had to be said and put this woman out of his mind, the better.

"You ready?" he asked, flinging opening a file cabinet and withdrawing a handful of thick folders from the top drawer.

"Ready as I'll ever be," she said, taking a chair on the other side of his desk.

Nash slapped the files down on his credenza. "Let's start with Adams versus Adams," he muttered, flipping through the pages of the top folder. "Now, this was an interesting case. Married ten years, two sons. Then Martha learned that Bill was having an affair with a coworker, so she decided to have one herself, only she chose a nineteen-year-old boy. The child-custody battle lasted two months, destroyed them financially and ended so bitterly that Bill moved out of town and hasn't been heard from since. Last I heard, Martha was clinically depressed and in and out of hospitals."

Savannah gasped. "What about their sons?" she asked. "What happened to them?"

"Eventually they went to live with a relative. From what I understand, they're both in counseling and have been for the last couple of years."

"How very sad," she whispered.

"Don't kid yourself. This is only the beginning. I'm starting with the *A*s and working my way through the file drawer. Let me know when you've had enough." He reached for a second folder. "Anderson versus Anderson... Ah, yes, I remember this one. She attempted suicide three times, blackmailed him emotionally, used the children as weapons, wiped him out financially and then sued for divorce, claiming he was an unfit father." His back was as stiff as his voice. He tossed aside that file and picked up the next.

"Allison versus Allison," he continued crisply. "By the way, I'm changing the names to protect the guilty."

"The guilty?"

"To my way of thinking, each participant in these cases is guilty of contributing to the disasters I'm telling you about. Each made a crucial mistake."

"You're about to suggest their first error was falling in love."

"No," he returned coldly, "it all started with the wedding vows. No two people should be expected to live up to that ideal. It isn't humanly possible."

"You're wrong, Nash. People live up to those vows each and every day, in small ways and in large ones."

Nash jabbed his finger against the stack of folders. "This says otherwise. Love isn't meant to last. Couples are kidding themselves if they believe commitment lasts beyond the next morning. Life's like that, and it's time the rest of the world woke up and admitted it."

"Oh, please!" Savannah cried, standing. She walked over to the window, her back to him, clenching and un-clenching her fists. Nash wondered if she was aware of it, and doubted she was.

"Be honest, Savannah. Marriage doesn't work any-more. Hasn't in years. The institution is outdated. If *you* want to stick your head in the sand, then fine. But when others risk getting hurt, someone needs to tell the truth." His voice rose with the heat of his argument.

Slowly she turned again and stared at him. An almost pitying look came over her.

"She must have hurt you very badly." Savannah's voice was so low, he had to strain to hear.

"Hurt me? What are you talking about?"

She shook her head as though she hadn't realized she'd spoken out loud. "Your ex-wife."

The anger that burned through Nash was like acid. "Who told you about Denise?" he demanded.

"No one," she returned quickly.

He slammed the top file shut and stuffed the stack of folders back inside the drawer with little care and less concern. "How'd you know I was married?"

"I'm sorry, Nash, I shouldn't have mentioned it."

"Who told you?" The answer was obvious but he wanted her to say it.

"Susan mentioned it…."

"How much did she tell you?"

"Just that it happened years ago." Each word revealed her reluctance to drag his sister into the conversation. "She wasn't breaking any confidences, if that's what you think. I'm sure the only reason she brought it up was to explain your—"

"I know why she brought it up."

"I apologize, Nash. I shouldn't have said anything."

"Why not? My file's in another attorney's cabinet, along with those of a thousand other fools just like me who were stupid enough to think love lasts."

Savannah continued to stare at him. "You loved her, didn't you?"

"As much as any foolish twenty-four-year-old loves anyone. Would you mind if we change the subject?"

"Susan's twenty-four."

"Exactly," he said, slapping his hand against the top of his desk. "And she's about to make the same foolish choice I did."

"But, Nash…"

"Have you heard enough, or do you need to listen to a few more cases?"

"I've heard enough."

"Good. Let's get out of here." The atmosphere in the office was stifling. It was as though each and every client he'd represented over the years was there to remind him of the pain he'd lived through himself— only he'd come away smarter than most.

"Do you want me to drive you back to the office or would you prefer I take you home?" he asked.

"No," Savannah said as they walked out of the office. He purposely adjusted his steps to match her slower gait. "If you don't mind, I'd prefer to have our, uh, wager settled this evening."

"Fine with me."

"If you don't mind, I'd like to head for my parents' home. I want you to meet them."

"Sure, why not?" he asked flippantly. His anger simmered just below the surface. Maybe this wasn't such a brilliant idea after all….

Savannah gave him the address and directions. The drive on the freeway was slowed by heavy traffic, which frustrated him even more. By the time they reached the exit, his nerves were frayed. He was about to suggest they do this another evening when she instructed him to take a left at the next light. They turned the corner, drove a block and a half down and were there.

They were walking toward the house when a tall, burly man with a thinning hairline hurried out the front door. "Savannah, sweetheart," he greeted them with a huge grin. "So this is the young man you're going to marry."

Three

"**D**ad!" Savannah was mortified. The heat rose from her neck to her cheeks, and she knew her face had to be bright red.

Marcus Charles raised his hands. "Did I say something I shouldn't have?" But there was still a smile on his face.

"I'm Nash Davenport," Nash said, offering Marcus his hand. Considering how her father had chosen to welcome Nash, his gesture was a generous one. She chanced a look in the attorney's direction and was relieved to see he was smiling, too.

"You'll have to forgive me for speaking out of turn," her father said, "but Savannah's never brought home a young man she wants us to meet, so I assumed you're the—"

"Daddy, that's not true!"

"Name one," he said. "And while you're inventing a beau, I'll take Nash in and introduce him to your mother."

"Dad!"

"Hush now or you'll give Nash the wrong impression."

The wrong impression! If only he knew. This meeting couldn't have gotten off to a worse start, especially with Nash's present mood. She'd made a drastic mistake mentioning his marriage. It was more than obvious that he'd been badly hurt and was trying to put the memory behind him.

Nash had built a strong case against marriage. The more clients he described, the harder his voice became. The grief of his own experience echoed in his voice as he listed the nightmares of the cases he'd represented.

Nash and her father were already in the house by the time Savannah walked up the steps and into the living room. Her mother had redecorated the room in a Southwestern motif, with painted clay pots and Navajo-style rugs. A recent addition was a wooden folk art coyote with his head thrown back, howling at the moon.

Every time she entered this room, Savannah felt a twinge of sadness. Her mother loved the Southwest and her parents had visited there often. Savannah knew her parents had once looked forward to moving south. She also knew she was the reason they hadn't. As an only child, and one who'd sustained a serious injury—even if it'd happened years before—they worried about her constantly. And with no other immediate family in the Seattle area, they were uncomfortable leaving their daughter alone in the big city.

A hundred times in the past few years, Savannah had tried to convince them to pursue their dreams, but they'd continually made excuses. They never came right out and said they'd stayed in Seattle because of her. They didn't need to; in her heart she knew.

"Hi, Mom," Savannah said as she walked into the kitchen. Her mother was standing at the sink, slicing tomatoes fresh from her garden. "Can I do anything to help?"

Joyce Charles set aside the knife and turned to give her a firm hug. "Savannah, let me look at you," she said, studying her. "You're working too hard, aren't you?"

"Mom, I'm fine."

"Good. Now sit down here and have something cold to drink and tell me all about Nash."

This was worse than Savannah had first believed. She should have explained her purpose in bringing him to meet her family at the very beginning, before introducing him. Giving them a misleading impression was bad enough, but she could only imagine what Nash was thinking.

When Savannah didn't immediately answer her question, Joyce supplied what information she already knew. "You're coordinating his sister's wedding and that's how you two met."

"Yes, but—"

"He really is handsome. What does he do?"

"He's an attorney," Savannah said. "But, Mom—"

"Just look at your dad." Laughing, Joyce motioned toward the kitchen window that looked out over the freshly mowed backyard. The barbecue was heating on the brick patio and her father was showing Nash his prize fishing flies. He'd been tying his own for years and took real pride in the craft; now that he'd retired, it was his favorite hobby.

After glancing out at them, Savannah sank into a kitchen chair. Her mother had poured her a glass of lemonade. Her father displayed his fishing flies only when the guest was someone important, someone he was hoping to impress. Savannah should have realized when she first mentioned Nash that her father had made completely the wrong assumption about this meeting.

"Mom," she said, clenching the ice-cold glass. "I think you should know Nash and I are friends. Nothing more."

"We know that, dear. Do you think he'll like my pasta salad? I added jumbo shrimp this time. I hope he's not a fussy eater."

Jumbo shrimp! So they were rolling out the red carpet. With her dad it was the fishing flies, with her mother it was pasta salad. She sighed. What had she let herself in for now?

"I'm sure he'll enjoy your salad." And *if* his anti-marriage argument—his evidence—was stronger than hers, he'd be eating seven more meals with a member of the Charles family. Her. She could only hope her parents conveyed the success of their relationship to this cynical lawyer.

"Your father's barbecuing steaks."

"T-bone," Savannah guessed.

"Probably. I forget what he told me when he took them out of the freezer."

Savannah managed a smile.

"I thought we'd eat outside," her mother went on. "You don't mind, do you, dear?"

"No, Mom, that'll be great." Maybe a little sunshine would lift her spirits.

"Let's go outside, then, shall we?" her mother said, carrying the large wooden bowl with the shrimp pasta salad.

The early-evening weather was perfect. Warm, with

a subtle breeze and slanting sunlight. Her mother's prize roses bloomed against the fence line. The bright red ones were Savannah's favorite. The flowering rhododendron tree spread out its pink limbs in opulent welcome. Robins chatted back and forth like long-lost friends.

Nash looked up from the fishing rod he was holding and smiled. At least *he* was enjoying himself. Or seemed to be, anyway. Perhaps her embarrassment was what entertained him. Somehow, Savannah vowed, she'd find a way to clarify the situation to her parents without complicating things with Nash.

A cold can of beer in one hand, Nash joined her, grinning as though he'd just won the lottery.

"Wipe that smug look off your face," she muttered under her breath, not wanting her parents to hear. It was unlikely they would, busy as they were with the barbecue.

"You should've said something earlier." His smile was wider than ever. "I had no idea you were so taken with me."

"Nash, please. I'm embarrassed enough as it is."

"But why?"

"Don't play dumb." She was fast losing her patience with him. The misunderstanding delighted him and mortified her. "I'm going to have to tell them," she said, more for her own benefit than his.

"Don't. Your father might decide to barbecue hamburgers instead. It isn't every day his only daughter brings home a potential husband."

"Stop it," she whispered forcefully. "We both know how you feel about marriage."

"I wouldn't object if you wanted to live with me."

Savannah glared at him so hard, her eyes ached.

"Just joking." He took a swig of beer and held the bottle in front of his lips, his look thoughtful. "Then again, maybe I wasn't."

Savannah was so furious she had to walk away. To her dismay, Nash followed her to the back of the yard. Glancing over her shoulder, she caught sight of her parents talking.

"You're making this impossible," she told him furiously.

"How's that?" His eyes fairly sparkled.

"Don't, *please* don't." She didn't often plead, but she did now, struggling to keep her voice from quavering.

He frowned. "What's wrong?"

She bit her lower lip so hard, she was afraid she'd drawn blood. "My parents would like to see me settled down and married. They…they believe I'm like every other woman and—"

"You aren't?"

Savannah wondered if his question was sincere. "I'm handicapped," she said bluntly. "In my experience, men want a woman who's whole and perfect. Their egos ride on that, and I'm flawed. Defective merchandise doesn't do much for the ego."

"Savannah—"

She placed her hand against his chest. "Please don't say it. Spare me the speech. I've accepted what's wrong with me. I've accepted the fact that I'll never run or jump or marry or—"

Nash stepped back from her, his gaze pinning hers. "You're right, Savannah," he broke in. "You *are* handicapped and you will be until you view yourself otherwise." Having said that, he turned and walked away.

Savannah went in the opposite direction, needing a few moments to compose herself before rejoining the others. She heard her mother's laughter and turned to see her father with his arms around Joyce's waist, nuzzling her neck. From a distance they looked twenty years younger. Their love was as alive now as it had been years earlier...and demonstrating that was the purpose of this visit.

She scanned the yard, looking for Nash, wanting him to witness the happy exchange between her parents, but he was busy studying the fishing flies her father had left out for his inspection.

Her father's shout alerted Savannah that dinner was ready. Reluctantly she joined Nash and her parents at the round picnic table. She wasn't given any choice but to share the crescent-shaped bench with him.

He was close enough that she could feel the heat radiating off his body. Close enough that she yearned to be closer yet. That was what surprised her, but more profoundly it terrified her. From the first moment she'd met him, Savannah suspected there was something different about him, about her reactions to him. In the beginning she'd attributed it to their disagreement, his heated argument against marriage, the challenge he represented, the promise of satisfaction if she could change his mind.

Dinner was delicious and Nash went out of his way to compliment Joyce until her mother blushed with pleasure.

"So," her father said, glancing purposefully toward Savannah and Nash, "what are your plans?"

"For what?" Nash asked.

Savannah already knew the question almost as well

as she knew the answer. Her father was asking about her future with Nash, and she had none.

"Why don't you tell Nash how you and Mom met," Savannah asked, interrupting her father before he could respond to Nash's question.

"Oh, Savannah," her mother protested, "that was years and years ago." She glanced at her husband of thirty-seven years and her clear eyes lit up with a love so strong, it couldn't be disguised. "But it *was* terribly romantic."

"You want to hear this?" Marcus's question was directed to Nash.

"By all means."

In that moment, Savannah could have kissed Nash, she was so grateful. "I was in the service," her father explained. "An Airborne Ranger. A few days before I met Joyce, I received my orders and learned I was about to be stationed in Germany."

"He'd come up from California and was at Fort Lewis," her mother added.

"There's not much to tell. Two weeks before I was scheduled to leave, I met Joyce at a dance."

"Daddy, you left out the best part," Savannah complained. "It wasn't like the band was playing a number you enjoyed and you needed a partner."

Her father chuckled. "You're right about that. I'd gone to the dance with a couple of buddies. The evening hadn't been going well."

"I remember you'd been stood up," Savannah inserted, eager to get to the details of their romance.

"No, dear," her mother intervened, picking up the story, "that was me. So I was in no mood to be at any social function. The only reason I decided to go was to make sure Lenny Walton knew I hadn't sat home mooning over him, but in reality I was at the dance mooning over him."

"I wasn't particularly keen on being at this dance, either," Marcus added. "I thought, mistakenly, that we were going to play pool at a local hall. I've never been much of a dancer, but my buddies were. They disappeared onto the dance floor almost immediately. I was bored and wandered around the hall for a while. I kept looking at my watch, eager to be on my way."

"As you can imagine, I wasn't dancing much myself," Joyce said.

"Then it happened." Savannah pressed her palms together and leaned forward. "This is my favorite part," she told Nash.

"I saw Joyce." Her father's voice dropped slightly. "When I first caught sight of her, my heart seized. I thought I might be having a reaction to the shots we'd been given earlier in the day. I swear I'd never seen a more beautiful woman. She wore this white dress and she looked like an angel. For a moment I was convinced she was." He reached for her mother's hand.

"I saw Marcus at that precise second, as well," Joyce whispered. "My friends were chatting and their voices faded until the only sound I heard was the pounding of my own heart. I don't remember walking toward him and yet I must have, because when I looked up Marcus was standing there."

"The funny part is, I don't remember moving, either."

Savannah propped her elbows on the table, her dinner forgotten. This story never failed to move her, although she'd heard it dozens of times over the years.

"We danced," her mother continued.

"All night."

"We didn't say a word. I think we must've been afraid the other would vanish if we spoke."

"While we were on the dance floor I kept pinching myself to be sure this was real, that Joyce was real. It was like we were both in a dream. These sorts of things only happen in the movies.

"When the music stopped, I looked around and realized my buddies were gone. It didn't matter. Nothing mattered but Joyce."

"Oh, Dad, I never get tired of hearing this story."

Joyce smiled as if she, too, was eager to relive the events of that night. "As we were walking out of the hall, I kept thinking I was never going to see Marcus again. I knew he was in the army—his haircut was a dead giveaway. I was well aware that my parents didn't want me dating anyone in the military, and up until then I'd abided by their wishes."

"I was afraid I wasn't going to see her again," Savannah's father went on. "But Joyce gave me her name and phone number and then ran off to catch up with her ride home."

"I didn't sleep at all that night. I was convinced I'd imagined everything."

"I couldn't sleep, either," Marcus confessed. "Here I was with my shipping orders in my pocket—this was not the time to get involved with a woman."

"I'm glad you changed your mind," Nash said, studying Savannah.

"To tell you the truth, I don't think I had much of a choice. It was as if our relationship was preordained. By the end of the following week, I knew Joyce was the woman I'd marry. I knew I'd love her all my life, and both have held true."

"Did you leave for Germany?"

"Of course. I had no alternative. We wrote back and forth for two years and then were married three months after I was discharged. There was never another woman for me after I met Joyce."

"There was never another man for me," her mother said quietly.

Savannah tossed Nash a triumphant look and was disappointed to see that he wasn't looking her way.

"It's a romantic story." He was gracious enough to admit that much.

"Apparently some of that romance rubbed off on Savannah." Her father's eyes were proud as he glanced at her. "This wedding business of hers is thriving."

"So it seems." Some of the enthusiasm left Nash's voice. He was apparently thinking of his sister, and Savannah's role in her wedding plans.

"Eat, before your dinner gets cold," Joyce said, waving her fork in their direction.

"How long did you say you've been married?" Nash asked, cutting off a piece of his steak.

"Thirty-seven years," her father told him.

"And it's been smooth sailing all that time?"

Savannah wanted to pound her fist on the table and insist that this cross-examination was unnecessary.

Marcus laughed. "Smooth sailing? Oh, hardly. Joyce and I've had our ups and downs over the years like most couples. If there's anything special about our marriage, it's been our commitment to each other."

Savannah cleared her throat, wanting to gloat. Once more Nash ignored her.

"You've never once entertained the idea of divorce?" he asked.

This question was unfair! She hadn't had the opportunity to challenge his clients about their divorces, not that she would've wanted to. Every case had saddened and depressed her.

"As soon as a couple introduces the subject of divorce, there isn't the same willingness to concentrate on communication and problem-solving. People aren't nearly as flexible," Marcus said. "Because there's always that out, that possibility."

Joyce nodded. "If there was any one key to the success of our marriage, it's been that we've refused to consider divorce an option. That's not to say I haven't fantasized about it a time or two."

"We're only human," her father agreed with a nod. "I'll admit I've entertained the notion a time or two myself—even if I didn't do anything about it."

No! It wasn't true. Savannah didn't believe it. "But you were never *serious*," she felt obliged to say.

Marcus looked at her and offered her a sympathetic smile, as if he knew about their wager. "Your mother and I love each other, and neither of us could say we're sorry we stuck it out through the hard times, but yes, sweetheart, there were a few occasions when I didn't know if our marriage would survive."

Savannah dared not look at Nash. Her parents' timing was incredible. If they were going to be brutally honest, why did it have to be now? In all the years Savannah was growing up she'd never once heard the word *divorce*. In her eyes their marriage was solid, always had been and always would be.

"Of course, we never stopped talking," her mother

was saying. "No matter how angry we might be with each other."

Soon after, Joyce brought out dessert—a coconut cake—and coffee.

"So, what do you think of our little girl?" Marcus asked, when he'd finished his dinner. He placed his hands on his stomach and studied Nash.

"Dad, please! You're embarrassing me."

"Why?"

"My guess is Savannah would prefer we didn't give her friend the third degree, dear," Joyce said mildly.

Savannah felt like kissing her mother's cheek. She stood, eager to disentangle herself from this conversation. "I'll help with the dishes, Mom," she said as if suggesting a trip to the mall.

Nash's mood had improved considerably after meeting Savannah's parents. Obviously, things weren't going the way she'd planned. Twice now, during dinner, it was all he could do not to laugh out loud. She'd expected them to paint a rosy picture of their idyllic lives together, one that would convince him of the error of his own views.

The project had backfired in her face. Rarely had he seen anyone look more shocked than when her parents said that divorce was something they'd each contemplated at one point or another in their marriage.

The men cleared the picnic table and the two women shooed them out of the kitchen. Nash was grateful, since he had several questions he wanted to ask Marcus about Savannah.

They wandered back outside. Nash was helping

Marcus gather up his fishing gear when Savannah's father spoke.

"I didn't mean to pry earlier," he said casually, carrying his fishing rod and box of flies into the garage. A motor home was parked alongside the building. Although it was an older model, it looked as good as new.

"You don't need to worry about offending me," Nash assured him.

"I wasn't worried about you. Savannah gave me 'the look' while we were eating. I don't know how much experience you have with women, young man, but take my advice. When you see 'the look,' shut up. No matter what you're discussing, if you value your life, don't say another word."

Nash chuckled. "I'll keep that in mind."

"Savannah's got the same expression as her mother. If you continue dating her, you'll recognize it soon enough." He paused. "You *are* going to continue seeing my daughter, aren't you?"

"You wouldn't object?"

"Heavens, no. If you don't mind my asking, what do you think of my little girl?"

Nash didn't mince words. "She's the most stubborn woman I've ever met."

Marcus nodded and leaned his prize fishing rod against the wall. "She gets that from her mother, too." He turned around to face Nash, hands on his hips. "Does her limp bother you?" he asked point-blank.

"Yes and no." Nash wouldn't insult her father with a half-truth. "It bothers me because she's so conscious of it herself."

Marcus's chest swelled as he exhaled. "That she is."

"How'd it happen?" Curiosity got the better of him,

although he'd prefer to hear the explanation from Savannah.

Her father walked to the back of the garage where a youngster's mangled bicycle was stored. "It sounds simple to say she was hit by a car. This is what was left of her bike. I've kept it all these years as a reminder of how far she's come."

"Oh, no…" Nash breathed when he viewed the mangled frame and guessed the full extent of the damage done to the child riding it. "How'd she ever survive?"

"I'm not being facetious when I say sheer nerve. Anyone with less fortitude would have willed death. She was in the hospital for months, and that was only the beginning. The doctors initially told us she'd never walk again, and for the first year we believed it.

"Even now she still has pain. Some days are worse than others. Climate seems to affect it somewhat. And her limp is more pronounced when she's tired." Marcus replaced the bicycle and turned back to Nash. "It isn't every man who recognizes Savannah's strength. You haven't asked for my advice, so forgive me for offering it."

"Please."

"My daughter's a special woman, but she's prickly when it comes to men and relationships. Somehow, she's got it in her head that no man will ever want her."

"I'm sure that's not true."

"It is true, simply because Savannah believes it is," Marcus corrected. "It'll take a rare man to overpower her defenses. I'm not saying you're that man. I'm not even saying you should try."

"You seemed to think otherwise earlier. Wasn't it you who assumed I was going to marry your daughter?"

"I said that to get a rise out of Savannah, and it worked." Marcus rubbed his jaw, eyes twinkling with delight.

"We've only just met." Nash felt he had to present some explanation, although he wasn't sure why.

"I know." He slapped Nash affectionately on the back and together they left the garage. When they returned to the house, the dinner dishes had been washed and put away.

Savannah's mother had filled several containers with leftovers and packed them in an insulated bag. She gave Savannah detailed instructions on how to warm up the leftover steak and vegetables. Attempting brain surgery sounded simpler. As it happened, Nash caught a glimpse of Marcus from the corner of his eye and nearly burst out laughing. The older man was slowly shaking his head.

"I like the coyote, Mom," Savannah said, as Nash took the food for her. She ran one hand over the stylized animal. "Are you and Dad going to Arizona this winter?"

Nash felt static electricity hit the airwaves.

"We haven't decided, but I doubt we will this year," Joyce answered.

"Why not?" Savannah asked. This was obviously an old argument. "You love it there. More and more of your friends are becoming snowbirds. It doesn't make sense for you to spend your winters here in the cold and damp when you can be with your friends, soaking up the sunshine."

"Sweetheart, we've got a long time to make that decision," Marcus reminded her. "It's barely summer."

She hugged them both goodbye, then slung her purse

over her shoulder, obviously giving up on the argument with her parents.

"What was that all about?" Nash asked once they were in his car.

It was unusual to see Savannah look vulnerable, but she did now. He wasn't any expert on women. His sister was evidence of that, and so was every other female he'd ever had contact with, for that matter. It looked as though gutsy Savannah was about to burst into tears.

"It's nothing," she said, her voice so low it was almost nonexistent. Her head was turned away from him and she was staring out the side window.

"Tell me," he insisted as he reached the freeway's on ramp. He increased the car's speed.

Savannah clasped her hands together. "They won't leave because of me. They seem to think I need a baby-sitter, that it's their duty to watch over me."

"Are you sure you're not being overly sensitive?"

"I'm sure. Mom and Dad love to travel, and now that Dad's retired they should be doing much more of it."

"They have the motor home."

"They seldom use it. Day trips, a drive to the ocean once or twice a year, and that's about it. Dad would love to explore the East Coast in the autumn, but I doubt he ever will."

"Why not?"

"They're afraid something will happen to me."

"It sounds like they're being overprotective."

"They are!" Savannah cried. "But I can't force them to go, and they won't listen to me."

He sensed that there was more to this story. "What's the *real* reason, Savannah?" He made his words as coaxing as he could, not wanting to pressure her into telling him something she'd later regret.

"They blame themselves for the accident," she whispered. "They were leaving for a weekend trip that day and I was to stay with a babysitter. I'd wanted to go with them and when they said I couldn't, I got upset. In order to appease me, Dad said I could ride my bicycle. Up until that time he'd always gone with me."

Nash chanced a look at her and saw that her eyes were closed and her body was rigid with tension.

"And so they punish themselves," she continued in halting tones, "thinking if they sacrifice their lives for me, it'll absolve them from their guilt. Instead it increases mine."

"Yours?"

"Do you mind if we don't discuss this anymore?" she asked, sounding physically tired and emotionally beaten.

The silence that followed was eventually broken by Savannah's sigh of defeat.

"When would you like me to start cooking your dinners?" she asked as they neared her shop.

"You're conceding?" He couldn't keep the shock out of his voice. "Just like that, without so much as an argument? You must be more tired than I realized."

His comments produced a sad smile.

"So you're willing to admit marriage is a thing of the past and has no part in this day and age?"

"Never!" She rallied a bit at that.

"That's what I thought."

"Are *you* ready to admit love can last a lifetime when it's nourished and respected?" she asked.

Nash frowned, his thoughts confused. "I'll grant

there are exceptions to every rule and your parents are clearly that. Unfortunately, the love they share doesn't exist between most married couples.

"It'd be easy to tell you I like my macaroni and cheese extra cheesy," he went on to say, "but I have a feeling you'll change your mind in the morning and demand a rematch."

Savannah smiled and pressed the side of her head against the car window.

"You're exhausted, and if I accepted your defeat, you'd never forgive me."

"What do you suggest, then?"

"A draw." He pulled into the alley behind the shop, where Savannah had parked her car. "Let's call it square. I proved what I wanted to prove and you did the same. There's no need to go back to the beginning and start over, because neither of us is going to make any progress with the other. We're both too strong-minded for that."

"We should have recognized it sooner," Savannah said, eyes closed.

She was so attractive, so…delectable, Nash had to force himself to look away.

"It's very gentlemanly of you not to accept my defeat."

"Not really."

Her eyes slowly opened and she turned her head so she could meet his eyes. "Why not?"

"Because I'm about to incur your wrath."

"Really? How are you going to do that?"

He smiled. It'd been so long since he'd looked forward to anything this much. "Because, my dear wedding coordinator, I'm about to kiss you."

Four

"You're...you're going to kiss me?" Savannah had been exhausted seconds earlier, but Nash's words were a shot of adrenaline that bolted her upright.

"I most certainly am," he said, parking his car behind hers in the dark alley. "Don't look so scared. The fact is, you might even enjoy this."

That was what terrified Savannah most. If ever there was a man whose touch she yearned for, it was Nash. If ever there was a man she longed to be held by, it was Nash.

He bent his head toward hers and what resistance she'd managed to amass died a sudden death as he pressed his chin to her temple and simply held her against him. If he'd been rough or demanding or anything but gentle, she might've had a chance at resisting him. She might've had the *desire* to resist him. But she didn't. A sigh rumbled through her and with heedless curiosity she lifted her hand to his face, her fingertips grazing his jaw. Her touch seemed to go through him like an electrical shock because he groaned and, as she tilted back her head, his mouth sought hers.

At the blast of unexpected sensation, Savannah buckled against him and whimpered, all the while clinging to him. The kiss continued, gaining in intensity and fervor until Savannah felt certain her heart would pound straight through her chest.

Savannah closed her eyes, deep in a world of sensual pleasure.

"Savannah." Her name was a groan. His breathing, heavy and hard, came in bursts as he struggled to regain control. Savannah was struggling, too. She finally opened her eyes. Her fingers were in his hair; she sighed and relaxed her hold.

Nash raised his head and took her face between his hands, his eyes delving into hers. "I didn't mean for that to happen."

An apology. She should've expected it, should've been prepared for it. But she wasn't.

He seemed to be waiting for her to respond so she gave him a weak smile, and lowered her gaze, not wanting him to guess how strong her reaction had been.

He leaned his forehead against hers and chuckled softly. "You're a surprise a minute."

"What do you mean?"

He dropped a glancing kiss on the side of her face. "I wouldn't have believed you'd be so passionate. The way you kissed me…"

"In other words, you didn't expect someone like me to experience sensual pleasure?" she demanded righteously. "It might shock you to know I'm still a woman."

"What?" Nash said. "What are you talking about?"

"You heard me," she said, frantically searching for her purse and the bag of leftovers her mother had insisted she take home with her.

"Stop," he said. "Don't use insults to ruin something that was beautiful and spontaneous."

"I wasn't the one—"

She wasn't allowed to finish. Taking her by the arms, he hauled her toward him until his mouth was on hers. Her resistance disappeared in the powerful persuasion of his kisses.

He exhaled sharply when he finished. "Your leg has nothing to do with this. Nothing. Do you understand?"

"Why were you so surprised, then?" she asked, struggling to keep her indignation alive. It was almost impossible when she was in his arms.

His answer took a long time. "I don't know."

"That's what I thought." She broke away and held her purse against her like a shield. "We've agreed to disagree on the issue of love and marriage, isn't that correct?"

"Yes," he said without emotion.

"Then I don't see any reason for us to continue our debate. It's been a pleasure meeting you, Mr. Davenport. Goodbye." Having said that, she jerked open the car door and nearly toppled backward. She caught herself in the nick of time before she could tumble headfirst into the alley.

"Savannah, for heaven's sake, will you—"

"Please, just leave me alone," she said, furious with herself for making such a dramatic exit and with him for reasons as yet unclear.

Because he made her *feel,* she guessed sometime later, when she was home and safe. He made her feel as if she was whole and without flaws. As if she was an attractive, desirable woman. Savannah blamed Nash for pretending she could be something she wasn't and the anger simmered in her blood long after she'd readied for bed.

Neatly folding her quilt at the foot of her bed, Savannah stood, seething, taking deep breaths to keep the tears at bay.

In the morning, after she'd downed her first cup of coffee, Savannah felt better. She was determined to put the incident and the man out of her mind. There was no reason for them to see each other again, no reason for them to continue with this farce. Not that Nash would *want* to see her, especially after the idiotic way she'd behaved, scrambling out of his car as if escaping a murderer.

As was so often the case of late, Savannah was wrong. Nash was waiting on the sidewalk in front of her shop, carrying a white bag, when she arrived for work.

"Another peace offering?" she asked, when she unlocked the front door and opened it for him.

"Something like that." He handed her a latte, then walked across the showroom and sat on the corner of her desk, dangling one leg, as though he had every right to make himself comfortable in her place of business.

Savannah hadn't recovered from seeing him again so soon; she wasn't prepared for another confrontation. "What can I do for you?" she asked stiffly, setting the latte aside. She sat down and leaned back in the swivel chair, hoping she looked relaxed, knowing she didn't.

"I've come to answer your question," he said, leg swinging as he pried loose the lid on his cup. He was so blasé about everything, as if the intensity of their kisses was a common thing for him. As if she was one in a long line of conquests. "You wanted to know what was different last night and I'm here to tell you."

This was the last thing Savannah expected. She glanced pointedly at her watch. "Is this going to take long? I've got an appointment in ten minutes."

"I'll be out of here before your client arrives."

"Good." She crossed her arms, trying to hold on to her patience. Their kisses embarrassed her now. She was determined to push the whole incident out of her mind and forget him. It'd been crazy to make a wager with him. Fun, true, but sheer folly nonetheless. The best she could do was forget she'd ever met the man. Nash, however, seemed unwilling to let that happen.

"Well?" she pressed when he didn't immediately speak.

"A woman doesn't generally go to my head the way you did," he said. "When I make love to a woman I'm the one in control."

"We weren't making love," she said heatedly, heat flushing her cheeks with instant color. Her fingers bit into the soft flesh of her arms as she fought to keep the embarrassment to herself.

"What *do* you call it, then?"

"Kissing."

"Yes, but it would've developed into something a whole lot more complicated if we hadn't been in my car. The last time I made love in the backseat of a car, I was—"

"This may come as a surprise to you, but I have no interest in hearing about your sexual exploits," she interjected.

"Fine," he snapped.

"Besides, we were nowhere near making love."

Nash's responding snort sent ripples of outrage through Savannah. "You overestimate your appeal, Mr. Davenport."

He laughed outright this time. "Somehow or other, I thought you'd say as much. I was hoping you'd be a bit more honest, but then, I've found truth an unusual trait in most women."

The bell above her door chimed just then, and her appointment strolled into the shop. Savannah was so grateful to have this uncomfortable conversation interrupted, she almost hugged her client.

"I'd love to continue this debate," she lied, "but as you can see, I have a customer."

"Perhaps another time," Nash suggested.

She hesitated. "Perhaps."

He snickered disdainfully as he stood and sipped from the take-out cup. "As I said, women seem to have a hard time dealing with the truth."

Savannah pretended not to hear him as she walked toward her customer, a welcoming smile on her face. "Good morning, Melinda. I'm so glad to see you."

Nash said nothing as he sauntered past her and out the door. Not until he was out of sight did Savannah relax her guard. He claimed she went to his head. What he didn't know was that his effect on her was startlingly similar. Then again, perhaps he did know....

The woman irritated him. No, Nash decided as he hit the sidewalk, his stride clipped and fast, she more than irritated him. Savannah Charles incensed him. He didn't understand this oppressive need he felt to talk to her, to explain, to hear her thoughts. He'd awakened wishing things hadn't ended so abruptly between them, wishing he'd known what to say to convince her of his sincerity. Morning had felt like a second chance.

In retrospect, he suspected he was looking for help himself in working through the powerful emotions that had evolved during their embrace. Instead, Savannah claimed he'd miscalculated her reaction. The heck he had.

He should've realized she was as confused as he was about their explosive response to each other.

Nash arrived at his office half an hour later than usual. As he walked past his assistant's desk, she handed him several telephone messages. He was due in court in twenty minutes, and wouldn't have time to return any calls until early afternoon. Shuffling through the slips, he stopped at the third one.

Susan.

His sister had called him, apparently on her cell. Without further thought he set his briefcase aside and reached for the phone, punching out the number listed.

"Susan, it's Nash," he said when she answered. If he hadn't been so eager to talk to her, he might have mulled over the reason for her call. Something must have happened; otherwise she wouldn't have swallowed her pride to contact him.

"Hello, Nash."

He waited a moment in vain for her to continue. "You called me?"

"Yes," she said abruptly. "I wanted to apologize for hanging up on you the other day. It was rude and unnecessary. Kurt and I had a…discussion about it and he said I owed you an apology."

"Kurt's got a good head on his shoulders," he said,

thinking his sister would laugh and the tension between them would ease. It didn't.

"I thought about what he had to say and Kurt's right. I'm sorry for the way I reacted."

"I'm sorry, too," Nash admitted. "I shouldn't have checked up on you behind your back." If she could be so generous with her forgiveness, then so could he. After all, Susan was his little sister. He had her best interests at heart, although she wouldn't fully appreciate his concern until later in life, when she was responsible for children of her own. He wasn't Susan's father, but he was her closest relative. Although she was twenty-four, he felt she still needed his guidance and direction.

"I was thinking we might have lunch together some afternoon," she ventured, and the quaver in her voice revealed how uneasy she was making the suggestion.

Nash had missed their lunches together. "Sounds like a great idea to me. How about Thursday?"

"Same place as always?"

There was a Mexican restaurant that was their favorite, on a steep side street not far from the King County courthouse. They'd made a point of meeting there for lunch at least once a month for the past several years. The waitresses knew them well enough to greet them by name.

"All right. See you Thursday at noon."

"Great."

Grinning, Nash replaced the receiver.

He looked forward to this luncheon date with his sister the way a kid anticipates the arrival of the Easter bunny. They'd both said and done things they regretted. Nash hadn't changed his mind about his sister marrying Kurt Caldwell. Kurt was decent, intelligent, hardworking and sincere, but they were both too young for marriage. Too uninformed about it. Judging by Susan's reaction, she wasn't likely to heed his advice. He hated to think of her making the same mistakes he had, but there didn't seem to be any help for it. He might as well mend the bridges of communication before they became irreparable.

"Is something wrong?" Susan asked Savannah as they went over the details for the wedding. It bothered her how careful Susan and Kurt had to be with their money, but she admired the couple's discipline. Each decision had been painstaking.

"I'm sorry." Savannah's mind clearly wasn't on the subject at hand. It had taken a sharp turn in another direction the moment Susan had shown up for their appointment. She reminded Savannah so much of her brother. Susan and Nash had the same eye and hair color, but they were alike in other ways, as well. The way Susan smiled and her easy laugh were Nash's trademarks.

Savannah had worked hard to force all thoughts of Nash from her mind. Naively, she felt she'd succeeded, until Susan had come into the shop.

Savannah didn't know what it was about this hard-headed cynic that attracted her so strongly. She resented the fact that he was the one to ignite the spark of her sensual nature. There was no future for them. Not when their views on love and marriage were so diametrically opposed.

"Savannah," Susan asked, "are you feeling okay?"

"Of course. I'm sorry, my thoughts seem to be a thousand miles away."

"I noticed," Susan said with a laugh.

Her mood certainly seemed to have improved since their previous meeting, Savannah noticed, wishing she could say the same. Nash hadn't contacted her since their last disastrous confrontation a few days earlier. Not that she'd expected he would.

Susan had entered the small dressing room and stepped into the wedding gown. She came out, lifting her hair at the back so Savannah could fasten the long row of pearl buttons.

"I'm having lunch with Nash on Thursday," Susan announced unexpectedly.

"I'm glad you two have patched up your differences."

Susan's shoulders moved in a reflective sigh. "We haven't exactly—at least, not yet. I called him to apologize for hanging up on him. He must have been eager to talk to me because his assistant told me he was due in court and I shouldn't expect to hear from him until that afternoon. He phoned back no more than five minutes later."

"He loves you very much." Savannah's fingers expertly fastened the pearl buttons. Nash had proved he was capable of caring deeply for another human being, yet he staunchly denied the healing power of love, wouldn't allow it into his own life.

Perhaps you're doing the same thing.

The thought came at her like the burning flash from a laser gun, too fast to avoid, and too painful to ignore. Savannah shook her head to chase away the doubts. It was ridiculous. She'd purposely chosen a career that was steeped in romance. To suggest she was blocking love from her own life was ludicrous. Yet the accusation repeated itself over and over....

"Savannah?"

"I'm finished," she said quickly. Startled, she stepped back.

Susan dropped her arms and shook her hair free before slowly turning around to face Savannah. "Well?" she asked breathlessly. "What do you think?"

Although she was still preoccupied with a series of haunting doubts, Savannah couldn't help admiring how beautiful Nash's sister looked in the bridal gown. "Oh, Susan, you're lovely."

The young woman viewed herself in the mirror, staring at her reflection for several minutes as if she wasn't sure she could believe what she was seeing.

"I'm going to ask Nash to attend the wedding when we have lunch," she said. Then, biting her lip, she added, "I'm praying he'll agree to that much."

"He should." Savannah didn't want to build up Susan's expectations. She honestly couldn't predict what Nash would say; she only knew what she thought he *should* do.

"He seemed pleased to hear from me," Susan went on to say.

"I'm sure he was." They stood beside each other in front of the mirror. Neither seemed inclined to move. Savannah couldn't speak for Susan, but for her part, the mirror made the reality of her situation all too clear. Her tailored pants might not reveal her scarred and twisted leg, but she remained constantly aware of it, a not-so-gentle reminder of her deficiency.

"Let me know what Nash says," Savannah said impulsively just before Susan left the shop.

"I will." Susan's eyes shone with a childlike enthusiasm as she turned and walked away.

Savannah sat at her desk and wrote down the pertinent facts about the wedding gown she was ordering for Susan, but as she moved the pen across the paper, her thoughts weren't on dress measurements. Instead they flew straight to Nash. If nothing else, he'd given her cause to think over her life and face up to a few uncomfortable truths. That wasn't a bad day's work for a skeptical divorce attorney. It was unfortunate he'd never realize the impact he'd had on her.

Nash was waiting in the booth at quarter after twelve on Thursday, anxiously glancing at his watch every fifteen seconds, convinced Susan wasn't going to show, when she strolled into the restaurant. A smile lit her face when she saw him. It was almost as if they'd never disagreed, and she was a kid again coming to her big brother for advice.

"I'm sorry I'm late," she said, slipping into the vinyl seat across from him. "I'm starved." She reached for a salted chip, weighing it down with spicy salsa.

"It's good to see you," Nash ventured, taking the first step toward reconciliation. He'd missed Susan and he said so.

"I've missed you, too. It doesn't feel right for us to fight, does it?"

"Not at all."

"You're the only real family I have."

"I feel the same way. We've both made mistakes and we should learn from them." He didn't cast blame. There was no point.

The waitress brought their menus. Nash didn't recognize the young woman, which made him consider just how long it was since he'd had lunch with Susan.

Frowning, he realized she'd been the one to approach him about a reconciliation, when as the older, more mature adult, he should've been working toward that end himself.

"I brought you something," Susan said, setting her handbag on the table. She rooted through it until she found what she was looking for. Taking the envelope from her purse, she handed it to him.

Nash accepted the envelope, peeled it open and pulled out a handcrafted wedding invitation, written on antique-white parchment paper in gold letters. He didn't realize his sister knew calligraphy. Although it was obviously handmade, the effort was competent and appealing to the eye.

"I wrote it myself," Susan said eagerly. "Savannah suggested Kurt and I would save money by making our own wedding invitations. It's much more personal this way, don't you think?"

"Very nice."

"The gold ink on the parchment paper was Kurt's idea. Savannah gave me a book on calligraphy and I've been practicing every afternoon."

He wondered how many more times his sister would find an excuse to drag the wedding coordinator's name into their conversation. Each time Susan mentioned Savannah it brought up unwelcome memories of their few short times together. Memories Nash would rather forget.

"Do you like it?" Susan asked eagerly. She seemed to be waiting for something more.

"You did a beautiful job," he said.

"I'm really glad you think so."

Susan was grinning under the warmth of his praise.

The waitress returned and they placed their order, although neither of them had looked at the menu. "We're certainly creatures of habit, aren't we?" his sister teased.

"So," he said, relaxing in the booth, "how are the wedding plans going?"

"Very well, thanks to Savannah." She folded her hands on top of the table, flexing her long fingers against each other, studying him, waiting.

Nash read over the invitation a second time and saw that it had been personally written to him. So this was the purpose of her phone call, the purpose of this lunch. She was asking him if he'd attend her wedding, despite his feelings about it.

"I don't expect you to change your mind about me marrying Kurt," Susan said anxiously, rushing the words together in her eagerness to have them said. "But it would mean the world to me if you'd attend the ceremony. There won't be a lot of people there. Just a few friends and Kurt's immediate family. That's all we can afford. Savannah's been wonderful, showing us how to get the most out of our limited budget. Will you come to my wedding, Nash?"

Nash knew when he was involved in a losing battle. Susan would marry Kurt with or without his approval. His kid sister was determined to do this her way. He'd done his best to talk some sense into her, but to no avail. He'd made the mistake of threatening her, and she'd called his bluff. The past weeks had been miserable for them both.

"I'll come."

"Oh, Nash, thank you." Tears brimmed and spilled over her lashes. She grabbed her paper napkin, holding it beneath each eye in turn. "I can't begin to tell you how much this means to me."

"I know." He felt like crying himself, but for none of the same reasons. He didn't want to see his sister hurt and that was inevitable once she was married. "I still don't approve of your marrying so young, but I can't stop you."

"Nash, you keep forgetting, I'm an adult, over twenty-one. You make me sound like a little kid."

He sighed expressively. That *was* the way he saw her, as his kid sister. It was difficult to think of her married, with a family of her own, when it only seemed a few years back that she was in diapers.

"You'll love Kurt once you get to know him better," she said excitedly, wiping the moisture from her cheek. "Look at what you've done to me," she muttered. Her mascara streaked her face in inky rows.

His hand reached for hers and he squeezed her fingers. "We'll get through this yet, kid," he joked.

Nash suspected, in the days that followed, that it was natural to feel good about making his sister so happy. All he'd agreed to do was attend the ceremony. He hadn't figured out what was going to keep him in his seat when the minister asked anyone who opposed the union to speak now or forever hold their peace. Attending the ceremony itself, regardless of his personal feelings toward marriage, was the least he could do for causing the rift between them.

The card from Savannah that arrived at his office took him by surprise. He stared at the return address on the envelope for a moment before turning it over and opening it with eager fingers. Her message was straightforward: "Thank you." Her elegant signature appeared below.

Nash gazed at the card for several minutes before slapping it down on his desk. The woman was driving him crazy.

He left the office almost immediately, shocking his assistant, who rushed after him, needing to know what she was supposed to do about his next appointment. Nash suggested she entertain him with some law journals and coffee. He promised to be back in half an hour.

Luckily he found a parking spot on the street. Climbing out of his car, he walked purposely toward the bridal shop. Savannah was sitting at her desk intent on her task. When she glanced up and saw him, she froze.

"I got your card," he said stiffly.

"I… It made Susan so happy to know you'd attend her wedding. I wanted to thank you," she said, her eyes following his every move.

He marched to her desk, not understanding even now what force had driven him to her. "How many guests is she inviting?"

"I…believe the number's around sixty."

"Change that," he instructed harshly. "We're going to be inviting three hundred or more. I'll have the list to you in the morning."

"Susan and Kurt can't afford—"

"They won't be paying for it. I will. I want the best for my sister, understand? We'll have a sit-down dinner, a dance with a ten-piece orchestra, real flowers and a designer wedding dress. We'll order invitations because there'll be too many for Susan to make herself. Have you got that?" He motioned toward her pen, thinking she should write it all down.

Savannah looked as if she hadn't heard him. "Does Susan know about all this?"

"Not yet."

"Don't you think you should clear it with her first?"

"It might be too soon, because a good deal of this hinges on one thing."

Savannah frowned. "What's that?"

"If you'll agree to attend the wedding as my date."

Five

"**Y**our *date?*" Savannah repeated as she leapt to her feet. No easy task when one leg was as unsteady as hers. She didn't often forget that, but she did now in her incredulity. "That's emotional blackmail," she cried, before slumping back in her chair.

"You're right, it is," Nash agreed, leaning forward and pressing his hands against the edge of her oak desk. His face was scant inches from her own, and his eyes cut straight through her defenses. "It's what you expect of me, isn't it?" he demanded. "Since I'm so despicable."

"I never said that!"

"Maybe not, but you thought it."

"No, I didn't!" she snapped, then decided she probably had. She'd been shaken by his kiss, and then he'd apologized as if he'd never meant it to happen. And, perhaps worse, maybe he wished it hadn't.

A slow, leisurely smile replaced Nash's dark scowl. "That's what I thought," he said as he raised his hand and brushed a strand of hair from her forehead. His fingertips lingered at her face. "I wish I knew what's happening to us."

"Nothing's happening," Savannah insisted, but her voice lacked conviction even to her own ears. She was fighting the powerful attraction she felt for him for all she was worth, which at the moment wasn't much. "You aren't really going to blackmail me, are you?"

He gently traced the outline of her face, pausing at her chin and tilting it upward. "Do you agree to attend the wedding with me?"

"Yes, only—"

"Then you should know I had no intention of following through with my threat. Susan can have the wedding of her dreams."

Savannah stood, awkwardly placing her weight on her injured leg. "I'm sure there are far more suitable dates for you," she said crisply.

"I want you."

He made this so difficult. "Why me?" she asked. By his own admission, there were any number of other women who'd jump at the chance to date him. Why had he insisted on singling *her* out? It made no sense.

Nash frowned as if he wasn't sure himself, which lent credence to Savannah's doubts. "I don't know. As for this wedding, it seemed to me I could be wrong. It doesn't happen often, but I have been known to make an error in judgment now and again." He gave her a quick, self-deprecating grin. "Susan's my only sister—the only family I've got. I don't want there to be any regrets between us. Your card helped, too, and the way I see it, if I'm going to sit through a wedding, I'm not going to suffer alone. I want you there with me."

"Then I suggest you ask someone who'd appreciate the invitation," she said defiantly, straightening her shoulders.

"I want to be with you," he insisted softly, his eyes revealing his confusion. "Darned if I know why. You're stubborn, defensive and argumentative."

"One would think you'd rather...oh, wrestle a rattle-snake than go out with me."

"One would think," he agreed, smiling boyishly, "but if that's the case, why do I find myself listening for the sound of your voice? Why do I look forward to spending time with you?"

"I...wouldn't know." Except that she found herself in the same situation. Nash was never far from her thoughts; she hadn't been free of him from the moment they'd met.

His eyes, dark and serious, wandered over her face. Before she could protest, he lowered his head and nuzzled her ear. "Why can't I get you out of my mind?"

"I can't answer that, either." He was going to kiss her again, in broad daylight, where they could be interrupted by anyone walking into the shop. Yet Savannah couldn't bring herself to break away, couldn't offer so much as a token resistance.

A heartbeat later, his mouth met hers. Despite her own hesitation, she kissed him back. Nash groaned, drawing her more securely into his embrace.

"Savannah," he whispered as he broke off the kiss. "I can hardly believe this, but it's even better than before."

Savannah said nothing, although she agreed. She was trembling, and prayed Nash hadn't noticed, but that was too much to ask. He slid his fingers into her hair and brought her face close to his. "You're terrified, aren't you?" he asked, his cheek touching hers.

"Don't be ridiculous," she muttered. She felt his smile against her flushed skin and realized she hadn't fooled him any more than she had herself. "I don't know what I am."

"I don't know, either. Somehow I wonder if I ever will. I don't suppose you'd make this process a lot easier and consider just having an affair with me?"

Savannah stiffened, not knowing if he meant what he was saying. "Absolutely not."

"That's what I thought," he said with a lengthy sigh. "It's going to be the whole nine yards with you, isn't it?"

"I have no idea what you mean," she insisted.

"Perhaps not." Pulling away, he checked his watch and seemed surprised at the time. "I've got to get back to the office. I'll give Susan a call this afternoon and the three of us can get together and make the necessary arrangements."

Savannah nodded. "We're going to have to move quickly. Planning a wedding takes time."

"I know."

She smiled shyly, wanting him to know how pleased she was by his change of heart. "This is very sweet of you, Nash."

He gestured weakly with his hands, as if he wasn't sure he was doing the right thing. "I still think she's too young to be married. I can't help thinking she'll regret this someday."

"Marriage doesn't come with guarantees at any age," Savannah felt obliged to tell him. "But then, neither does life. Susan and Kurt have an advantage you seem to be overlooking."

"What's that?"

"They're in love."

"Love." Nash snickered loudly. "Generally it doesn't last more than two or three weeks."

"Sometimes that's true, but not this time," Savannah said. "However, I've worked with hundreds of couples over the years and I get a real sense about the people who come to me. I can usually tell if their marriages will last or not."

"What about Kurt and Susan?"

"I believe they'll have a long, happy life together."

Nash rubbed the side of his face, his eyes intense. He obviously didn't believe that.

"Their love is strong," she said, trying to bolster her argument.

Nash raised his eyebrows. "Spoken like a true romantic."

"I'm hoping the skeptic in you will listen."

"I'm trying."

Savannah could see the truth in that. He *was* trying, for Susan's sake and perhaps hers. He'd come a long way from where he was when they'd first met. But he had a lot farther to go.

Nash had no idea weddings could be so demanding, so expensive or so time-consuming. The one advantage of all this commotion and bother was all the hours he was able to spend with Savannah. As the weeks progressed, Nash came to know Savannah Charles, the businesswoman, as well as he did the lovely, talented woman who'd attracted him from the beginning. He had to admit she knew her stuff. He doubted anyone else could have arranged so large and lavish a wedding on such short notice. It was only because she had long-standing relationships with those involved—the florists, photographers, printers, hotel managers and so on—that Nash was able to give Susan an elaborate wedding.

As the days passed, Nash lost count of how often he asked Savannah out to dinner, a movie, a baseball game. She found a plausible excuse each and every time. A less determined man would have grown discouraged and given up.

But no more, he mused, looking out his office window. As far as she was concerned, he held the trump card in the palm of his hand. Savannah had consented to attend Susan's wedding with him, and there was no way he was letting her out of the agreement.

He sat at his desk thinking about this final meeting scheduled for later that afternoon. He'd been looking forward to it all week. Susan's wedding was taking place Saturday evening, and Savannah had flat run out of excuses.

Nash arrived at the shop before his sister. He was grateful for these few moments alone with Savannah.

"Hello, Nash." Her face lit up with a ready smile when he walked into the shop. She was more relaxed with him now. She stood behind a silver punch bowl, decorating the perimeter with a strand of silk gardenias.

Her knack for making something ordinary strikingly beautiful was a rare gift. In some ways she'd done that with his life these past few weeks, giving him something to anticipate when he got out of bed every morning. She'd challenged him, goaded him, irritated and bemused him. It took quite a woman to have such a powerful effect.

"Susan's going to be a few minutes late," Nash told her. "I was hoping she'd changed her mind and decided to call off the whole thing." He'd hoped nothing of the sort, but enjoyed getting a reaction out of Savannah.

"Give it up. Susan's going to be a beautiful bride."

"Who's going to be working the wedding?" he asked, advancing toward her.

"I am, of course. Together with Nancy. You met her last week."

He nodded, remembering the pleasant, competent young woman who'd come to one of their meetings. Savannah often contracted her to help out at larger events.

"Since Nancy's going to be there, you can attend as my date and leave the work to her."

"Nash, will you please listen to reason? I *can't* be your date…. I know it's short notice but there are plenty of women who'd enjoy—"

"We have an agreement," he reminded her.

"I realize that, but—"

"I won't take no for an answer, Savannah, not this time."

She stiffened. Nash had witnessed this particular reaction on numerous occasions. Whenever he asked her out, her pride exploded into full bloom. Nash was well acquainted with how deeply entrenched that pride was.

"Nash, please."

He reached for her hand and raised it to his lips. His mouth grazed her fingertips. "Not this time," he repeated. "I'll pick you up just before we meet to have the pictures taken."

"Nash…"

"Be ready, Savannah, because I swear I'll drag you there in your nightgown if I have to."

Savannah was in no mood for company, nor was she keen on talking to her mother when Joyce phoned that same evening. She'd done everything she could to persuade Nash to change his plans. But he insisted she be his date for Susan's wedding. Indeed, he'd blackmailed her into agreeing to it.

"I haven't heard from you in ages," her mother said.

"I've been busy with the last-minute details of Susan Davenport's wedding."

"She's Nash's sister, isn't she?"

Her mother knew the answer to that. She was looking for an excuse to bring Nash into the conversation, which she'd done countless times since meeting him. If Savannah had to do that wager over again, she'd handle it differently. Her entire day had been spent contemplating various regrets. She wanted to start over, be more patient, finish what she'd begun, control her tongue, get out of this ridiculous "date" with Nash.

But she couldn't.

"Your father's talking about taking a trip to the ocean for a week or two."

"That sounds like an excellent idea." Savannah had been waiting all summer for them to get away.

"I'm not sure we should go...."

"For heaven's sake, why not?"

"Oh, well, I hate to leave my garden, especially now. And there've been a few break-ins in the neighborhood the last few weeks. I'd be too worried about the house to enjoy myself." The excuses were so familiar, and Savannah wanted to scream with frustration. But her mother had left out the real reason for her uncertainty. She didn't want to leave Savannah. Naturally, her parents had never come right out and said that, but it was their underlying reason for staying close to the Seattle area.

Savannah had frequently tried to discuss this with them. However, both her parents just looked at her blankly as if they didn't understand her concerns. Or they changed the subject. They didn't realize what poor liars they were.

"Have you seen much of Nash lately?" Her mother's voice rose expectantly.

"We've been working together on the wedding, so we've actually been seeing a lot of each other."

"I meant socially, dear. Has he taken you out? He's such a nice young man. Both your father and I think so."

"Mother," Savannah said, hating this, "I haven't been dating Nash."

Her mother's sigh of disappointment cut through Savannah. "I see."

"We're friends, nothing more. I've told you that."

"Of course. Be sure and let me know how the wedding goes, will you?"

Seeing that Nash had spared little expense, it would be gorgeous. "I'll give you a call early next week and tell you all about it."

"You promise?"

"Yes, Mom, I promise."

Savannah replaced the receiver with a heavy heart. The load of guilt she carried was enough to buckle her knees. How could one accident have such a negative impact on so many people for so long? It wasn't fair that her parents should continue to suffer for what had happened to her. Yet they blamed themselves, and that guilt was slowly destroying the best years of their lives.

Nash arrived at Savannah's house to pick her up late Saturday afternoon. He looked tall and distinguished in his black tuxedo and so handsome that for an awkward moment, Savannah had trouble taking her eyes off him.

"What's wrong?" he said, running his finger along the inside of his starched collar. "I feel like a concert pianist."

Savannah couldn't keep from smiling. "I was just thinking how distinguished you look."

His hand went to his temple. "I'm going gray?"

She laughed. "No."

"*Distinguished* is the word a woman uses when a man's entering middle age and losing his hair."

"If you don't get us to this wedding, we're going to miss it, and then you really *will* lose your hair." She placed her arm in his and carefully set one foot in front of the other. She rarely wore dress shoes. It was chancy, but she didn't want to ruin the effect of her full-length dress with flats. Nash couldn't possibly know the time and effort she'd gone to for this one date, which would likely be their first *and* last. She'd ordered the dress from New York, a soft, pale pink gown with a pearl-studded yoke. The long, sheer sleeves had layered pearl cuffs. She wore complementary pearl earrings and a single-strand necklace.

It wasn't often in her life that Savannah felt beautiful, but she did now. She'd worked hard, wanting to make this evening special for Susan—and knowing it would be her only date with Nash. She suspected there was a bit of Cinderella in every woman, the need to believe in fairy tales and happy endings, in true love conquering against impossible odds. For this one night, Savannah longed to forget she was crippled. For this one night, she wanted to pretend she was beautiful. A princess.

Nash helped her across the yard and held open the

door for her. She was inside the car, seat belt buckled, when he joined her. His hands gripped the steering wheel, but when he didn't start the car, she turned to him.

"Is something wrong?"

He smiled at her, but she saw the strain in his eyes and didn't understand it. "It's just that you're so beautiful, I can hardly keep my hands off you."

"Oh, Nash," she whispered, fighting tears. "Thank you."

"For what?"

She shook her head, knowing she'd never be able to explain.

The church was lovely. Savannah had rarely seen a sanctuary decorated more beautifully. The altar was surrounded with huge bouquets of pink and white roses, and their scent drifted through the room. The end of each pew was decorated with a small bouquet of white rosebuds and gardenias with pink and silver bows. The effect was charming.

Seated in the front row, Savannah closed her eyes as the organ music swelled. She stood, and from the rustle of movement behind her, she knew the church was filled to capacity.

Savannah turned to see Nash escort his sister slowly down the center aisle, their steps in tune to the music. They were followed by the bridesmaids and groomsmen, most of them recruited late, every one of them delighted to share in Susan and Kurt's happiness.

Savannah had attended a thousand or more weddings in her years as a coordinator. Yet it was always the same. The moment the music crescendoed, her eyes brimmed with tears at the beauty and emotion of it all.

This wedding was special because the bride was Nash's sister. Savannah had felt a part of it from the beginning, when Susan had approached her, desperate for assistance. Now it was all coming together and Susan was about to marry Kurt, the man she truly loved.

Nash was uncomfortable with love, and a little jealous, too, although she doubted he recognized that. Susan, the little sister he adored, would soon be married and would move to California with her husband.

When they reached the steps leading to the altar, Susan kissed Nash's cheek before placing her hand on Kurt's arm. Nash hesitated as if he wasn't ready to surrender his sister. Just when Savannah was beginning to get worried, he turned and entered the pew, standing next to her. Either by accident or design, his hand reached for hers. His grip was tight, his face strained with emotion.

Savannah was astonished to see that his eyes were bright with tears. She could easily be mistaken, though, since her own were blurred. A moment later, she was convinced she was wrong.

The pastor made a few introductory comments about the sanctity of marriage. Holding his Bible open, he stepped forward. "I'd like each couple who's come to celebrate the union of Susan and Kurt to join hands," he instructed.

Nash took both of Savannah's hands so that she was forced to turn sideways. His eyes delved into hers, and her heart seemed to stagger to a slow, uneven beat at what she read in them. Nash was an expert at disguising his feelings, yes, but also at holding on to his anger and the pain of his long-dead marriage, at keeping that bitterness alive. As he stared down at her, his eyes became bright and clear and filled with an emotion so strong, it transcended anything she'd ever seen.

Savannah was barely aware of what was going on around them. Sounds faded; even the soloist who was singing seemed to be floating away. Savannah's peripheral vision became clouded, as if she'd stepped into a dreamworld. Her sole focus was Nash.

With her hands joined to Nash's, their eyes linked, she heard the pastor say, "Those of you wishing to renew your vows, repeat after me."

Nash's fingers squeezed hers as the pastor intoned the words. "I promise before God and all gathered here this day to take you as my wife. I promise to love and cherish you, to leave my heart and my life open to you."

To Savannah's amazement, Nash repeated the vow in a husky whisper. She could hear others around them doing the same. Once again tears filled her eyes. How easy it would be to pretend he was devoting his life to hers.

"I'll treasure you as a gift from God, to encourage you to be all He meant you to be," Savannah found herself repeating a few minutes later. "I promise to share your dreams, to appreciate your talents, to respect you. I pledge myself to you, to learn from and value our differences." As she spoke, Savannah's heart beat strong and steady and sure. Excitement rose up in her as she realized that what she'd said was true. These were the very things she yearned to do for Nash. She longed for him to trust her enough to allow her into his life, to help him bury the hurts of the past. They were different, as different as any couple could be. That didn't make their relationship impossible. It added flavor, texture and challenge to their attraction. Life together would never be dull for them.

"I promise to give you the very best of myself, to be faithful to you, to be your friend and your partner," Nash whispered next, his voice gaining strength. Sincerity rang through his words.

"I offer you my heart and my love," Savannah repeated, her own heart ready to burst with unrestrained joy.

"You are my friend," Nash returned, "my lover, my wife."

It was as if they, too, were part of the ceremony, as if they, too, were pledging their love and their lives to each other.

Through the minister's words, Savannah offered Nash all that she had to give. It wasn't until they'd finished and Kurt was told to kiss his bride that Savannah remembered this wasn't real. She'd stepped into a dreamworld, the fantasy she'd created out of her own futile need for love. Nash had only been following the minister's lead. Mortified, she lowered her eyes and tugged her trembling fingers free from Nash's.

He, too, apparently harbored regrets. His hands clasped the pew in front of them until his knuckles paled. He formed a fist with his right hand. Savannah dared not look up at him, certain he'd recognize her thoughts and fearing she'd know his. She couldn't have borne the disappointment. For the next several hours they'd be forced to share each other's company, through the dinner and the dance that followed the ceremony. Savannah wasn't sure how she was going to manage it now, after she'd humiliated herself.

Thankfully she was spared having to face Nash

immediately after the ceremony was over. He became a part of the reception line that welcomed friends and relatives. Savannah was busy herself, working with the woman she'd hired to help coordinate the wedding and reception. Together they took down the pew bows, which would serve as floral centerpieces for the dinner.

"I don't think I've ever seen a more beautiful ceremony," Nancy Mastell told Savannah, working furiously. "You'd think I'd be immune to this after all the weddings we attend."

"It…was beautiful," Savannah agreed. Her stomach was in knots, and her heart told her how foolish she'd been; nevertheless, she couldn't make herself regret what had happened. She'd learned something about herself, something she'd denied far too long. She needed love in her life. For years she'd cut herself off from opportunity, content to live off the happiness of others. She'd moved from one day to the next, carrying her pain and disappointment, never truly happy, never fulfilled. Pretending.

This was why Nash threatened her. She couldn't pretend with him. Instinctively he knew. For reasons she'd probably never understand, he saw straight through her.

"Let me get those," Nancy said. "You're a wedding guest."

"I can help." But Nancy insisted otherwise.

When Savannah returned to the vestibule, she found Nash waiting for her. They drove in silence to the high-end hotel, where Nash had rented an elegant banquet room for the evening.

Savannah prayed he'd say something to cut the terrible tension. She could think of nothing herself. A long list of possible topics presented itself, but she couldn't come up with a single one that didn't sound silly or trite.

Heaven help her, she didn't know how they'd be able to spend the rest of the evening in each other's company.

Dinner proved to be less of a problem than Savannah expected. They were seated at a table with two delightful older gentlemen whom Nash introduced as John Stackhouse and Arnold Serle, the senior partners of the law firm that employed him. John was a widower, she gathered, and Arnold's wife was in England with her sister.

"Mighty nice wedding," Mr. Stackhouse told Nash.

"Thank you. I wish I could take credit, but it's the fruit of Savannah's efforts you're seeing."

"Beautiful wedding," Mr. Serle added. "I can't remember when I've enjoyed one more."

Savannah was waiting for a sarcastic remark from Nash, but one never came. She didn't dare hope that he'd changed his opinion, and guessed it had to do with the men who were seated with them.

Savannah spread the linen napkin across her lap. When she looked up, she discovered Arnold Serle watching her. She wondered if her mascara had run or if there was something wrong with her makeup. Her doubts must have shown in her eyes, because he grinned and winked at her.

Savannah blushed. A sixty-five-year-old corporate attorney was actually flirting with her. It took her a surprisingly short time to recover enough to wink back at him.

Arnold burst into loud chuckles, attracting the attention of Nash and John Stackhouse, who glanced disapprovingly at his partner. "Something troubling you, Arnold?"

"Just that I wish I were thirty years younger. Savannah here's prettier than a picture."

"You been at the bottle again?" his friend asked. "He becomes quite a flirt when he has," the other man explained. "Especially when his wife's out of town."

Arnold's cheeks puffed with outrage. "I most certainly do not."

Their salads were delivered and Savannah noted, from the corner of her eye, that Nash was studying her closely. Taking her chances, she turned and met his gaze. To her astonishment, he smiled and reached for her hand under the table.

"Arnold's right," he whispered. "Every other woman here fades compared to you." He paused. "With the exception of Susan, of course."

Savannah smiled.

The orchestra was tuning their instruments in the distance and she focused her attention on the group of musicians, feeling a surge of regret and frustration. "I need to tell you something," she said.

"What?"

"I'm sorry, I can't dance. But please don't let that stop you."

"I'm not much of a dancer myself. Don't worry about it."

"Anything wrong?" Arnold asked.

"No, no," Nash was quick to answer. "Savannah just had a question."

"I see."

"That reminds me," John began. "There's something we've been meaning to discuss with you, Nash. It's about the position for senior partner opening up at the firm," he said.

"Can't we leave business out of this evening?" Arnold asked, before Nash could respond. Arnold frowned. "It's difficult enough choosing another partner without worrying about it day and night."

Nash didn't need to say a word for Savannah to know how much he wanted the position. She felt it in him, the way his body tensed, the eager way his head inclined. But after Arnold's protest, John hadn't continued the discussion.

The dinner dishes were cleared from the table by the expert staff. The music started, a wistful number that reminded Savannah of sweet wine and red roses. Susan, in her flowing silk gown, danced with Kurt as their guests looked on, smiling.

The following number Kurt danced with his mother and Nash with Susan. His assurances that he wasn't much of a dancer proved to be false. He was skilled and graceful.

Savannah must have looked more wistful than she realized because when the next number was announced, Arnold Serle reached for her hand. "This dance is mine."

Savannah was almost too flabbergasted to speak. "I…can't. I'm sorry, but I can't."

"Nonsense." With that, the smiling older man all but pulled her from her chair.

Six

Savannah was close to tears. She couldn't dance and now she was being forced onto the ballroom-style floor by a sweet older man who didn't realize she had a limp. He hadn't even noticed it. Humiliation burned her cheeks. The wonderful romantic fantasy she was living was about to blow up in her face. Then, when she least expected to be rescued, Nash was at her side, his hand at her elbow.

"I believe this dance is mine, Mr. Serle," he said, whisking Savannah away from the table.

Relief rushed through her, until she saw that he was escorting her onto the dance floor himself. "Nash, I can't," she said in a heated whisper. "Please don't ruin this day for me."

"Do you trust me?"

"Yes, but you don't seem to understand…."

Understand or not, he led her confidently onto the crowded floor, turned and gathered her in his arms. "All I want you to do is relax. I'll do the work."

"Nash!"

"Relax, will you?"

"No... Please take me back to the table."

Instead he grasped her hands and raised them, tucking them around his neck. Savannah turned her face away from him. Their bodies fit snugly against each other and Nash felt warm and substantial. His thigh moved against hers, his chest grazed her breasts and a slow excitement began to build within her. After holding her breath, she released it in a long, trembling sigh.

"It feels good, doesn't it?"

"Yes." Lying would be pointless.

"We're going to make this as simple and easy as possible. All you have to do is hold on to me." He held her close, his hands clasped at the base of her spine. "This isn't so bad now, is it?"

"I'll never forgive you for this, Nash Davenport." Savannah was afraid to breathe again for fear she'd stumble, for fear she'd embarrass them both. She'd never been on a dance floor in her life and try as she might, she couldn't make herself relax the way he wanted. This was foreign territory to her, the girl who'd never been asked to a school dance. The girl who'd watched and envied her friends from afar. The girl who'd only waltzed in her dreams with imaginary partners. And not one of them had been anything like Nash.

"Maybe this will help," Nash whispered. He bent his head and kissed the side of her neck with his warm, moist mouth.

"Nash!" She squirmed against him.

"I've wanted to do that all night," he whispered. Goose bumps shivered up her arms as his tongue made lazy circles along one ear. Her legs felt as if they'd collapse, and she involuntarily pressed her weight against him.

"Please stop that!" she said from between clenched teeth.

"Not on your life. You're doing great." He made all the moves and, holding her the way he was, took the weight off her injured leg so she could slide with him.

"I'll embarrass us both any minute," she muttered.

"Just close your eyes and enjoy the music."

Since they were in the middle of the floor, Savannah had no choice but to follow his instructions. Her chance to escape gracefully had long since passed.

The music was slow and easy, and when she lowered her lashes, she could pretend. This was the night, she'd decided earlier, to play the role of princess. Only she'd never expected her Cinderella fantasy to make it all the way to the ballroom floor.

"You're a natural," he whispered. "Why have you waited so long?"

She was barely moving, which was all she could manage. This was her first experience, and although she was loath to admit it, Nash was right; she was doing well. This must be a dream, a wonderful romantic dream. If so, she prayed it'd be a very long time before she woke.

As she relaxed, Nash's arms moved to a more comfortable position. She lowered her own arm just a little, and her fingers toyed with the short hair at his neck. It was a small but intimate gesture, to run her fingers through his hair, and she wondered at her courage. It might be just another facet of her fantasy, but it seemed the action of a lover or a wife.

Wife.

In the church, when they'd repeated the vows, Nash had called her his friend, his lover, his wife. But it wasn't real. But for now, she was in his arms and they were dancing cheek to cheek, as naturally as if they'd been partners for years. For now, she would make it real, because she so badly wanted to believe it.

"Who said you couldn't dance?" he asked her after a while.

"Shh." She didn't want to talk. These moments were much too precious to waste on conversation. This time was meant to be savored and enjoyed.

The song ended, and when the next one started almost without pause, the beat was fast. Her small bubble of happiness burst. Her disappointment must have been obvious because Nash chuckled. "Come on," he said. "If we can waltz, we can do this."

"Nash...I could do the slow dance because you were holding me, but this is impossible."

Nash, however, wasn't listening. He was dancing. Without her. His arms jerked back and forth, and his feet seemed to be following the same haphazard course. He laughed and threw back his head. "Go for it, Savannah!" He shouted to be heard above the music. "Don't just stand there. Dance!"

She was going to need to move—off the dance floor. She was about to turn away when Nash clasped her around the waist, holding her with both hands. "You can't quit now."

"Oh, yes, I can. Just watch me."

"All you need to do is move a little to the rhythm. You don't need to leap across the dance floor."

There was no talking to him, so she threw her arms in the air in abject frustration.

"That's it," he shouted enthusiastically.

"Excuse me, excuse me," Arnold Serle's voice said

from behind her. "Nash, would you mind if I danced with Savannah now?" he shouted.

Nash looked at Savannah and grinned, as cheerful as a six-year-old pulling a prank on his first-grade teacher. "Savannah would love to. Isn't that right?" With that, he danced his way off the floor.

"Ready to rock 'n' roll?" Arnold asked.

Savannah didn't mean to laugh, but she couldn't stop herself. "I'm not very good at this."

"Shall we?" he said, holding out his palm to her.

Reluctantly she placed her hand in his. She didn't want to offend Nash's boss, but she didn't want to embarrass herself, either. Taking Nash's advice, she moved her arms, just a little at first, swaying back and forth, convinced she looked like a chicken attempting flight. Others around her were wiggling and twisting in every which direction. Savannah's movements, or lack of them, weren't likely to be noticed.

To her utter amazement, Mr. Serle began to twist vigorously. His dancing was reminiscent of 1960s teen movies she'd seen on TV. With each jerking motion he sank closer to the floor, until he was practically kneeling. After a moment he stopped moving. He hunkered there, one arm stretched forward, one elbow back.

"Mr. Serle, are you all right?"

"Would you mind helping me up? My back seems to have gone out on me."

Savannah looked frantically around for Nash, but he was nowhere to be seen. She was silently calling him several colorful names for getting her into this predicament. With no other alternative, she bent forward, grabbed the older man's elbow and pulled him into an upright position.

"Thanks," he said, with a bright smile. "I got carried away there and forgot I'm practically an old man. Sure felt good. My heart hasn't beaten this fast in years."

"Maybe we should sit down," she suggested, praying he'd agree.

"Not on your life, young lady. I'm only getting started."

Nash made his way back to the table, smiling to himself. He hadn't meant to embarrass Savannah. His original intent had been to rescue her. Taking her onto the dance floor was pure impulse. All night he'd been looking for an excuse to hold her, and he wasn't about to throw away what might be his only chance.

Beautiful didn't begin to describe Savannah. When he'd first met her, he'd thought of her as cute. He'd dated women far more attractive than she was. On looks alone, she wasn't the type that stood out in a crowd. Nor did she have a voluptuous body. She was small, short and proportioned accordingly. If he was looking for long shapely legs and an ample bust, he wouldn't find either in Savannah. She wasn't a beauty, and yet she was the most beautiful woman he'd ever known.

That didn't make a lot of sense. He decided it was because he'd never met anyone quite like Savannah Charles. He didn't fully understand why she appealed to him so strongly. True, she had a compassionate heart, determination and courage—all qualities he admired.

"Is Arnold out there making a world-class fool of himself?" John Stackhouse asked, when Nash joined the elder of the two senior partners at their table.

"He's dancing with Savannah."

John Stackhouse was by far the most dignified and

reserved of the two. Both were members of the executive committee, which had the final say on the appointment of the next senior partner. Stackhouse was often the most disapproving of the pair. Over the years, Nash had been at odds with him on more than one occasion. Their views on certain issues invariably clashed. Although he wasn't particularly fond of the older man, Nash respected him, and considered him fair-minded.

John Stackhouse sipped from his wineglass. "Actually, I'm pleased we have this opportunity to talk," he said to Nash, arching an eyebrow. "A wedding's not the place to bring up business, as Arnold correctly pointed out, but I believe now might be a good time for us to talk about the senior partnership."

Nash's breath froze in his lungs, and he nodded. "I'd appreciate that."

"You've been with the firm a number of years now, and worked hard. We've won some valuable cases because of you, and that's in your favor."

"Glad to hear that." So Paul Jefferson didn't have it sewn up the way he'd assumed.

"I don't generally offer advice…"

This was true enough. Stackhouse kept his opinions to himself until asked, and it boded well that he was willing to make a few suggestions to Nash. Although he badly wanted the position, Nash still didn't think he had a chance against Paul. "I'd appreciate any advice you care to give me."

"Arnold and a couple of the other members of the executive committee were discussing names. Yours was raised almost immediately."

Nash moved forward, perching on the end of his chair. "What's the consensus?"

"Off the record."

"Off the record," Nash assured him.

"You're liked and respected, but there's a problem, a big one as far as the firm's concerned. The fact is, I'm the one who brought it up, but the others claimed to have noticed it, as well."

"Yes?" Nash's mind zoomed over the list of potential areas of trouble.

"You've been divorced for years now."

"Yes."

"This evening's the first time I've seen you put that failure behind you. I've watched you chew on your bitterness like an old bone, digging it up and showing it off like a prized possession when it suited you. You've developed a cutting, sarcastic edge. That's fine in the courtroom, but a detriment in your professional life as well as your private life. Especially if you're interested in this senior partnership."

"I'm interested," Nash was quick to tell him, too quick perhaps because Stackhouse smiled. That happened so rarely it was worth noting.

"I'm glad to hear you say that."

"Is there anything I could do to help my chances?" This conversation was unprecedented, something Nash had never believed possible.

The attorney hesitated and glanced toward the dance floor, frowning. "How serious are you about this young woman?"

Of all the things Nash had thought he might hear, this was the one he least expected. "Ah…" Nash was rarely at a loss for words, but right now he had no idea how to answer. "I don't know. Why do you ask?"

"I realize it's presumptuous of me, and I do hope

you'll forgive me, but it might sway matters if you were to marry again."

"Marry?" he repeated, as if the word was unfamiliar to him.

"It would show the committee that you've put the past behind you," John continued, "and that you're trying to build a more positive future."

"I...see."

"Naturally, there are no guarantees and I certainly wouldn't suggest you consider marriage if you weren't already thinking along those lines. I wouldn't have said anything, but I noticed the way you were dancing with the young lady and it seemed to me you care deeply for her."

"She's special."

The other man nodded. "Indeed she is. Would you mind terribly if I danced with her myself? I see no reason for Arnold to have all the fun." Not waiting for Nash to respond, he stood and made his way across the dance floor to Savannah and his friend.

Nash watched as John Stackhouse tapped his fellow attorney on the shoulder and cut in. Savannah smiled as the second man claimed her.

Marry!

Nash rubbed his face. A few months earlier, the suggestion would have infuriated him. But a few months earlier, he hadn't met Savannah.

Nor had he stood in a church, held hands with an incredible woman and repeated vows. Vows meant for his sister and the man she loved. Not him. Not Savannah. Yet these vows had come straight from his heart to hers. He hadn't intended it to be that way. Not in the beginning. All he'd wanted to do was show Savannah how far he'd come. Repeating a few words seemed a small thing at the time.

But it wasn't as simple as all that. Because everything had changed from that moment forward. He'd spoken in a haze, not fully comprehending the effect it was having on him. All he understood was that he was tired. Tired of being alone. Tired of pretending he didn't need anyone else. Tired of playing a game in which he would always be the loser. Those vows he'd recited with Savannah had described the kind of marriage she believed in so strongly. It was an ideal, an uncommon thing, but for the first time in years he was willing to admit it was possible. A man and a woman *could* share this loving, mutually respectful partnership. Savannah had made it real to him the moment she'd repeated the vows herself.

Marry Savannah.

He waited for the revulsion to hit him the way it usually did when someone mentioned the word *marriage*. Nothing happened. Of course, that was perfectly logical. He'd spent time in a wedding shop, making a multitude of decisions that revolved around Susan's wedding. He'd become immune to the negative jolt the word always struck in him.

But he expected *some* adverse reaction. A twinge, a shiver of doubt. Something.

It didn't come.

Marriage. He repeated it slowly in his mind. No, he'd never consider anything so drastic. Not for the sole reason of making senior partner. He'd worked hard. It was a natural progression; if he didn't get the appointment now, he would later.

Marriage to Savannah. If there was ever a time the wine was talking, it was now.

Savannah had never experienced a night she'd enjoyed more. She'd danced and drunk champagne, then danced again. Every time she'd turned around, there was someone waiting to dance with her or fill her glass.

"Oh, Nash, I had the most incredible night of my life," she said, leaning against the headrest in his car and closing her eyes. It was a mistake, because the world went on a crazy spin.

"That good, was it?"

"Yes, oh, yes. I hate to see it end."

"Then why should it? Where would you like to go?"

"You'll take me anywhere?"

"Name it."

"The beach. I want to go to the beach." She was making a fool of herself, but she didn't care. She wanted to throw out her arms and sing. Where was a mountaintop when she needed one?

"Your wish is my command," Nash said to her.

She slipped her hand around his upper arm and hugged him, resting her head on his shoulder. "That's how I feel about tonight. It's magical. I could ask for anything and somehow it would be given to me."

"I believe it would."

Excited now that her fantasy had become so real, she lowered the car window and let out a wild whoop of joy.

Nash laughed. "What was that for?"

"I'm so happy! I never dreamed I could dance like that. Did you see me? Did you see all the men who asked me?" She brought her hand to her chest. "Me. I always thought I couldn't dance, and I did, and I owe it all to you."

"I knew you could do it."

"But how…"

"You can walk, can't you?"

"Yes, but I assumed it was impossible to *dance*." The champagne had affected her, but she welcomed the light-headedness it produced. "Oh, did you see Mr. Stackhouse? I thought I'd burst out laughing. I'm convinced he's never done the twist in his life." The memory made her giggle.

"I couldn't believe my eyes," Nash said and she heard the amusement in his voice. "Neither could Arnold Serle. Arnold said they've been friends for thirty-five years and he's never seen John do anything like it, claimed he was just trying to outdo him. That's when he leapt onto the dance floor, too, and the three of you started a conga line."

"There's magic to this night, isn't there?"

"There must be," he agreed.

Her leg should be aching, and would be soon, but she hadn't felt even a twinge. Perhaps later, when adrenaline wasn't pumping through her body and she was back on planet Earth, she'd experience the familiar discomfort. But it hadn't happened yet.

"Your beach," Nash announced, edging into the parking space at Alki Beach in West Seattle. A wide expanse of sandy shore stretched before them. Seattle's lights glittered in the distance like decorations on a gaily lit Christmas tree. Gentle waves lapped the driftwood-strewn sand, and the scents of salt and seaweed hung in the air. "Make all your wishes this easy to fulfill, will you?"

"I'll do my best," she promised. Her list was short, especially for a woman who, on this one night, was a princess in disguise.

"Any other easy requests?" Nash asked. He moved closer and draped his arm across her shoulders.

"A full moon would be nice."

"Will a crescent-shaped one do, instead?"

"It'll have to."

"Perhaps I could find a way to take your mind off the moon," Nash suggested, his voice low and oddly breathless.

"Oh?" *Oh, please let him kiss me,* Savannah pleaded. The night would be perfect if only Nash were to take her in his arms and kiss her….

"Do you know what I'm thinking?" he asked.

She closed her eyes and nodded. "Kiss me, Nash. Please kiss me."

His mouth came down on hers and she thought she was ready for his sensual invasion, since she'd yearned for it so badly. But nothing could have prepared her for the greed they felt for each other. She linked her arms around his neck and gave herself to his touch.

"Why is it," Nash groaned, long minutes later as he breathed kisses across her cheeks, "that we seem to be forever kissing in a car?"

"I…don't know."

His lips toyed with hers. "You're making this difficult."

"I am." Her effect on him made Savannah giddy. It made her feel strong, and for a woman who'd felt weak most of her life, this was a potent aphrodisiac.

"You're so beautiful," Nash whispered, just before he kissed her again.

"Tonight I'm invincible," she murmured. Privately she wondered if Cinderella had spent time like this with her prince before rushing off and leaving him with a single glass slipper. She wondered if her counterpart had the opportunity to experience such unexpected pleasure.

Nash kissed her again and again, until a host of dizzying sensations accosted her from all sides. She broke away and buried her face in his chest in a desperate effort to clear her head.

"Savannah." Taking her by the shoulders, he eased back. "Look at me."

Blindly she obeyed him, running her tongue over lips that were swollen from the urgency of their kisses. "Touch me," she pleaded, gazing at the desire in his eyes, the desire that was a reflection of her own.

Nash went still, his breathing labored. "I can't…. We're on a public beach." He closed his eyes. "That does it," he said forcefully, pulling away from her. "We're going to do this right. We're not teenagers anymore. I want to make love to you, Savannah, and I'm not willing to risk being interrupted by a policeman who'll arrest me for taking indecent liberties." He reached for the ignition and started the car. She saw how badly his hand shook.

"Where are we going?"

"My house."

"Nash…"

"Don't argue with me."

"Kiss me first," she said, not understanding his angry impatience. They had all night. She wouldn't stop being a princess for hours yet.

"I have every intention of kissing you. A lot."

"That sounds nice," she whispered, and with a soft sigh pressed her head against his shoulder.

After several minutes of silence, she said, "I'm not always beautiful." She felt she should remind him of that.

"I hate to argue with you, especially now," he said, planting one last kiss on the corner of her mouth, "but I disagree."

"I'm really not," she insisted, although she thought it was very kind of him to disagree.

"I want you more than I've ever wanted any other woman in my life."

"You do?" It was so nice of him to say such things, but it wasn't necessary. Unexpected tears filled her eyes. "No one's ever said things like that to me before."

"Stupid fools." They stopped at a red light and Nash reached for her and kissed her as if he longed to make up for a lifetime of rejection. Savannah brought her arms around his neck and sighed when he finally broke off the kiss.

"You're not drunk, are you?" Nash demanded, turning a corner sharply. He shot a wary glance at her, as if this was a recent suspicion.

"No." She was, just a little, but not enough to affect her judgment. "I know exactly what I'm doing."

"Right, but do you know what *I* intend on doing?"

"Yes, you're taking me home so we can make love in your bed. You'd prefer that to being arrested for doing it publicly."

"Smart girl."

"I'm not a girl!"

"Sorry, slip of the tongue. Trust me, I know exactly how much of a woman you are."

"No, you don't. You haven't got a clue, Nash Davenport, but that's all right because no one else does, either." Herself included, but she didn't say that.

Nash pulled into his driveway and was apparently going faster than he realized, because when he hit his brakes the car jerked to an abrupt stop. "The way I've been driving, it's a miracle I didn't get a ticket," he mumbled as he leapt out of the car. He opened her door, and Savannah smiled lazily and lifted her arms to him.

"I don't know if I can walk," she said with a tired sigh. "I can dance, though, if anyone cares to ask."

He scooped her effortlessly into his arms and carried her to his front porch. Savannah was curious to see his home, curious to learn everything she could about him. She wanted to remember every second of this incredible night.

It was a bit awkward getting the key in the lock and holding her at the same time, but Nash managed. He threw open the door and walked into the dark room. He hesitated, kicked the door closed and traipsed across the living room, not bothering to turn on the lights.

"Stop," she insisted.

"For what? Savannah, you're driving me crazy."

Languishing in his arms, she arched back her head and kissed his cheek. "What a romantic thing to say."

"Did you want something?" he asked impatiently.

"Oh, yes, I want to see your home. A person can find out a great deal about someone just by seeing the kind of furniture he buys. Little things, too, like his dishes. And books and music and art." She gave a tiny shrug. "I've been curious about you from the start."

"You want to know the pattern of my china?"

"Well, yes…"

"Can it wait until tomorrow? There are other things I'd rather be doing…."

Nash moved expertly down the darkened hallway to his room. Gently he placed her on the mattress and knelt over her. She smiled up at him. "Oh, Nash, you have a four-poster bed. But…tomorrow's too late."

"For what?"

"Us. This—being together—will only work for one night. Then the princess disappears and I go back to being a pumpkin." She frowned. "Or do I mean scullery maid?" She giggled, deciding her fracturing of the fairy tale didn't matter.

Nash froze and his eyes met hers, before he groaned and fell backward onto the bed. "You are drunk, aren't you?"

"No," she insisted. "Just happy. Now kiss me and quit asking so many questions." She was reaching for him when it happened. The pain shot like fire through her leg and, groaning, she fell onto her side.

Seven

Nash recognized the effort Savannah made to hide her agony. It must have been excruciating; it was certainly too intense to disguise. Lying on her back, she squeezed her eyes tightly shut, gritted her teeth and then attempted to manage the pain with deep-breathing exercises.

"Savannah," he whispered, not wanting to break her concentration and at the same time desperately needing to do something, anything, to ease her discomfort. "Let me help," he pleaded.

She shook her head. "It'll pass in a few minutes."

Even in the moonlight, Nash could see how pale she'd become. He jumped off the bed and was pacing like a wild beast, feeling the searing grip of her pain himself. It twisted at his stomach, creating a mental torment unlike anything he'd ever experienced.

"Let me massage your leg," he insisted, and when she didn't protest he lifted the skirt of her full-length gown and ran his hands up and down her thigh. Her skin was hot to the touch and when he placed his chilled hands on her, she groaned anew.

"It'll pass." He repeated her own words, praying he was right. His heart was pounding double-time in his anxiety. He couldn't bear to see Savannah endure this unbearable pain, and stand by and do nothing.

Her whole leg was terribly scarred and his heart ached at the agony she'd endured over the years. Her muscles were tense and knotted but gradually began to relax as he gently worked her flesh with both hands, easing them up and down her thigh and calf. He saw the marks of several surgeries; the scars were testament to her suffering and her bravery.

"There are pills in my purse," she whispered, her voice barely discernible.

Nash quickly surveyed the room, jerking his head from left to right, wondering where she'd put it. He found the small clutch purse on the carpet. Grasping it, he emptied the contents on top of the bed. The brown plastic bottle filled with a prescription for pain medication rolled into view.

Hurrying into his bathroom, he ran her a glass of water, then dumped a handful of the thick chalky tablets into the palm of his hand. "Here," he said.

Levering herself up on one elbow, Savannah took three of the pills. Her hands were trembling, he noted, and he could hardly resist taking her in his arms. Once she'd swallowed the pills, she closed her eyes and laid her head on the pillow.

"Take me home, please."

"In a few minutes. Let's give those pills a chance to work first."

She was sobbing openly now. Nash lay down next to her and gathered her in his arms.

"I'm sorry," she sobbed.

"For what?"

"For ruining everything."

"You didn't ruin anything." He brushed his lips over the crown of her head.

"I…didn't want you to see my leg." Her tears came in earnest now and she buried her face in his shoulder.

"Why?"

"It's ugly."

"You're beautiful."

"For one night…"

"You're wrong, Savannah. You're beautiful every minute of every day." He cradled her head against him, whispering softly in her ear. Gradually he felt her tension diminish, and he knew by the even sound of her breathing that she was drifting off to sleep.

Nash held her for several minutes, wondering what he should do. She'd asked that he take her home, but waking her seemed cruel, especially now that the terrible agony had passed. She needed her sleep, and movement might bring back the pain.

What it came down to, he admitted reluctantly, was one simple fact. He wanted Savannah with him and was unwilling to relinquish her.

Kissing her temple, he eased himself from her arms and crawled off the bed. He got a blanket from the top shelf in his closet and covered her with it, careful to tuck it about her shoulders.

Looking down on her, Nash shoved his hands in his pockets and stared for several minutes.

He wandered into the living room, slumped into his recliner and sat in the dark while the night shadows moved against the walls.

He'd been selfish and inconsiderate, but above all

he'd been irresponsible. Bringing Savannah to his home had been the most recent in a long list of errors in judgment.

He was drunk, but not on champagne. His intoxication was strictly due to Savannah. The idealist. The romantic. Attending his sister's wedding hadn't helped matters any. Susan had been a beautiful bride and if there was ever a time he could believe in the power of love and the strength of vows, it was at her wedding.

It'd started early in the evening when he'd exchanged vows with Savannah as if *they* were the ones being married. It was a moment out of time—dangerous and unreal.

He'd attempted to understand what had happened, offered a litany of excuses, but he wasn't sure he'd ever find one that would satisfy him. He wished there was someone or something he could blame, but that wasn't likely. The best he could hope for was to forget the whole episode and pray Savannah did the same.

Savannah. She was so beautiful. He'd never enjoyed dancing with a woman like he did with her. Smiling to himself, he recalled the way he'd been caught up in the magic of her joy. Being with her, sharing this night with her, was like being drawn into a fairy tale, impossible to resist even if he'd tried. And he hadn't.

Before he knew it, they were parked at Alki Beach, kissing like there was no tomorrow. He'd never desired a woman more.

Wrong. There'd been a time, years earlier, when he'd been equally enthralled with a woman. In retrospect it was easy to excuse his naïveté. He'd been young and impressionable. And because of that, he'd fallen hopelessly in love.

Love. He didn't even like the sound of the word. He'd found love to be both painful and dangerous.

Nash didn't love Savannah. He refused to allow himself to wallow in that destructive emotion a second time. He was attracted to her, but love was out of the question. Denise had taught him everything he needed to know about *that*.

He hadn't thought of her, except in passing, in years. Briefly he wondered if she was happy, and doubted his ex-wife would ever find what she was searching for. Her unfaithfulness continued to haunt him even now, years after their divorce. For too long he'd turned a blind eye to her faults, all in the glorious name of love.

He'd made other mistakes, too. First and foremost he'd married the wrong woman. His father had tried to tell him, but Nash had refused to listen, discrediting his advice, confident his father's qualms about Nash's choice in women were part and parcel of being too old to understand true love. Time had proved otherwise.

Looking back, Nash realized he'd shared only one thing with Denise. Incredible sex. He'd mistaken her physical demands for love. Within a few weeks of meeting, they were living together and their sexual relationship had become addictive.

It was ironic that she'd been the one to bring up the subject of marriage. Until then she'd insisted she was a "free spirit." Not until much later did he understand this sudden need she had for commitment. With his father seriously ill, there was the possibility of a large inheritance.

They'd been happy in the beginning. Or at least Nash had attempted to convince himself of that, and perhaps they were, but their happiness was short-lived.

He'd first suspected something was wrong when he arrived home late one evening after a grueling day in court and caught the scent of a man's cologne. He'd asked Denise and she'd told him he was imagining things. Because he wanted to believe her, because the thought of her being unfaithful was so completely foreign, he'd accepted her word. He had no reason to doubt her.

His second clue came less than a month later when a woman he didn't know met him outside his apartment. She was petite and fragile in her full-length coat, her hands deep in the pockets, her eyes downcast. She hated to trouble him, she said, but could Nash please keep his wife away from her husband. She'd recently learned she was pregnant with their second child and wanted to keep the marriage together if she could.

Nash had been stunned. He'd tried to ask questions, but she'd turned and fled. He didn't say anything to Denise, not that night and not for a long time afterward. But that was when he started to notice the little things that should've been obvious.

Nash hated himself for being so weak. He should have demanded the truth then and there, should have kicked her out of his home. Instead he did nothing. Denial was comfortable for a week and then two, while he wrestled with his doubts.

Savannah's scarred leg was a testament to her bravery, her endless struggle to face life each and every day. His scarred emotions were a testament to his cowardice, to knowing that his wife was cheating on him and accepting it rather than confronting her with the truth.

His wife had been *cheating* on him. What an ineffectual word that was for what he felt. It sounded so...

trivial. So insignificant. But the sense of betrayal was sharper than any blade, more painful than any incision. It had slashed his ego, punctured his heart and forever changed the way he viewed love and life.

Nash had loved Denise; he must have, otherwise she wouldn't have had the power to hurt him so deeply. That love had burned within him, slowly twisting itself into a bitter desire to get even.

The divorce had been ugly. Nash attempted to use legal means to retaliate for what Denise had done to him emotionally. Unfortunately there was no compensation for what he'd endured. He'd learned this countless times since from other clients. He'd wanted to embarrass and humiliate her the way she had him, but in the end they'd both lost.

Following their divorce, Denise had married again almost immediately. Her new husband was a man she'd met three weeks earlier. Nash kept tabs on her for some time afterward and was downright gleeful when he learned she was divorcing again less than a year later.

For a long while Nash was convinced he hated Denise. In some ways he did; his need for revenge had been immature. But as the years passed, he was able to put their short marriage in perspective, and he was grateful for the lessons she'd taught him. Paramount was the complete unreliability of love and marriage.

Denise had initiated him into this kind of thinking, and the hundreds of divorce cases he'd handled since then had reinforced it.

Then he'd met Savannah. In the beginning, she'd irritated him no end. With her head in the clouds, subsisting on the thin air of romance, she'd met each of his arguments as if she alone was responsible for defending the institution of marriage. As if she alone was responsible for changing his views.

Savannah irritated him—that was true enough—but she'd worn down his defenses until he was doing more than listening to her; he was beginning to believe again. It took some deep soul-searching to admit that.

He *must* believe, otherwise she wouldn't be sleeping in his bed. Otherwise they wouldn't have come within a heartbeat of making love.

What a drastic mistake that would have been, Nash realized a second time. He didn't know when common sense had abandoned him, but it had. Perhaps he'd started breathing that impossibly thin air Savannah had existed on all these years. Apparently it had tricked him as it had her.

Nash should have known better than to bring Savannah into his home. He couldn't sleep with her and expect their relationship to remain the same. Everything would change. Savannah wasn't the type of woman to engage in casual affairs and that was all Nash had to offer. A few hours in bed would have been immensely pleasurable, but eventually disastrous to them both.

Savannah woke when dawn light crept through a nearby window. Opening her eyes, she needed a moment to orient herself. She was in a strange bed. Alone. It didn't take long to remember the events of the night before. She was in Nash's home.

Sitting up required an effort. The contents of her purse were strewn across the bed and, gathering them together as quickly as possible, she went in search of her shoes.

Nash was nowhere to be seen. If her luck held, she

could call a cab and be out of his home before he realized she'd gone.

Her folly weighed heavily on her. She'd never felt more embarrassed in her life.

She moved stealthily from the bedroom into the living room. Pausing, she saw Nash asleep in his recliner. Her breath caught in her throat as she whispered a silent prayer of thanksgiving that he was asleep.

Fearing the slightest sound would wake him, she decided to sneak out the back door, find a phone elsewhere and call for a cab. Her cell phone was at home; there hadn't been room for it in the tiny beaded purse she'd brought with her yesterday.

Her hand was on the lock to the back door, a clean escape within her reach, when Nash spoke from behind her.

"I thought you wanted to check out my china pattern."

Savannah closed her eyes in frustration. "You were sleeping," she said without turning around.

"I'm awake now."

Her face was so hot, it was painful. Dropping her hands, she did her best to smile before slowly pivoting around.

"How were you planning on getting home?" he asked.

"A taxi."

"Did you bring your cell?"

He knew perfectly well she hadn't. "No, I was going to locate a phone somewhere and call a cab."

"I see." He began to make a pot of coffee as if this morning was no different from any other. "Why did you find it so important to leave now?" he asked in what she was sure were deceptively calm tones.

"You were sleeping...."

"And you didn't want to disturb me."

"Something like that."

"We didn't make love, so there's no need to behave like an outraged virgin."

"I'm well aware of what we did and didn't do," Savannah said stiffly. He was offended that she was sneaking out of his home. That much was apparent.

Nash was an experienced lover, but she doubted he'd ever dealt with a situation similar to what had happened to them. Most women probably found pleasure in his touch, not excruciating pain. Most women sighed with enjoyment; they didn't sob in agony. Most women lived the life of a princess on a day-to-day basis, while her opportunity came once in a lifetime.

"How's your leg feel?"

"It's fine."

"You shouldn't have danced—"

"Nothing on this earth would have stopped me," she told him, her voice surprisingly strong. "The pain's something I live with every day. It's the price I paid for enjoying myself. I had a wonderful time last night, Nash. Don't take that away from me."

He hesitated, then said, "Sit down and have a cup of coffee. We'll talk and then I'll drive you home." He poured two cups and set them on the round kitchen table. "Cream and sugar?"

She shook her head.

He sat casually in one of the chairs.

"I... I'm not much of a conversationalist in the morning," she said.

"No problem. We can wait until afternoon if you'd rather."

She didn't and he knew that. All she wanted was to escape.

Reluctantly she pulled out the chair opposite his and sat down. The coffee was too hot to drink, but just the right temperature to warm her hands. She cradled the cup between her palms and focused her attention on it. "I want you to know how sorry I am for—"

He interrupted her. "If you're apologizing for last night, don't bother."

"All right, I won't."

"Good."

Savannah took her first tentative sip of coffee. "Well," she said, looking up but avoiding his eyes, "what would you suggest we talk about?"

"What happened."

"Nothing happened," she said.

"It almost did."

"I know that better than you think, Nash. So why are we acting like strangers this morning? Susan's wedding was beautiful. Dancing with you and the two gentlemen from your office was wonderful. For one incredible night I played the glamorous role of a princess. Unfortunately, it ended just a little too soon."

"It ended exactly where it should have. Our making love would have been a mistake."

Savannah was trying to put everything in perspective, but his statement felt like a slap in the face. It shouldn't have hurt so much, but it did. Unwanted tears sprang to her eyes.

"You don't agree?"

"Does it matter?" she asked, refusing to let him know how deeply he'd hurt her.

"I suppose not."

"It doesn't," she said more forcefully. She was having a difficult time holding back the tears. They threatened to spill down her face any second. "I'd like to go home now," she said.

"It wouldn't have worked, you know."

"Of course I know that," she flared.

She felt more than saw Nash's hesitation. "Are you all right?" he asked.

"I've never been better," she snapped. "But I want to go home. Sitting around here in this dress is ridiculous. Now either you drive me or I'm calling a cab."

"I'll drive you."

The ride back to her place was a nightmare for Savannah. Nash made a couple of attempts at conversation, but she was in no mood to talk and certainly in no mood to analyze the events of the night before. She'd been humiliated enough and didn't want to make things worse.

The minute Nash pulled into her driveway, Savannah opened the car door, eager to make her escape. His hand at her elbow stopped her.

Savannah groaned inwardly and froze. But Nash didn't seem to have anything to say.

"Susan's wedding was very nice. Thank you," he finally told her.

She nodded, keeping her back to him and her head lowered.

"I enjoyed our time together."

"I…did, too." Even though that time was over now. It was daylight, and the magic of last night was gone.

"I'll give you a call later in the week."

She nodded, although she didn't believe it. This was probably a line he used often. Just another way of saying goodbye, she figured.

"What about Thursday?" he asked unexpectedly, after he'd helped her out of the car.

"What about it?"

"I'd like to take you out…. A picnic or something."

He couldn't have surprised her more. Slowly she raised her head, studying him, confident she'd misunderstood.

He met her gaze steadily. "What's wrong?"

"Are you asking me out on a date?"

"Yes," he said, taking her house keys from her lifeless hand and unlocking her front door. "Is that a problem?"

"I…I don't know."

"Would you prefer it if we went dancing instead?" he asked, his mouth lifting in a half smile.

Despite their terrible beginning that morning, Savannah smiled. "It'd be nice, but I don't think so."

"I'll see what I can arrange. I'll pick you up around six at the shop. Okay?"

Savannah was too shocked to do anything but nod.

"Good." With that he leaned forward and brushed his lips over hers. It wasn't much as kisses went, but the warmth of his touch went through her like a bolt of lightning.

Savannah stood on her porch, watching him walk away. He was at his car before he turned back. "You were a beautiful princess," he said.

Nash wasn't sure what had prompted the invitation for a picnic for Thursday. It wasn't something he'd given any thought to suggesting. In fact, he felt as surprised as Savannah looked when he'd asked her.

A date. That was simple enough. It wasn't as if he hadn't gone out on dates before, but it had been a long while since he'd formally asked a woman out. He was making more of this than necessary, he decided.

By Wednesday he would have welcomed an excuse to get out of it. Especially after John Stackhouse called him into his office. The minute he received the summons, Nash guessed this was somehow linked to Savannah.

"You wanted to see me?" Nash asked, stepping inside the senior partner's office later that afternoon.

"I hope I'm not calling you away from something important?"

"Not at all," Nash assured him. It might have been his imagination, but Stackhouse's attitude seemed unusually friendly. Although they were always polite to each other, he wasn't John's favorite, not the way Paul Jefferson was. But then, Paul wasn't prone to disagree with anyone who could advance his career.

"I have a divorce I want you to handle," his boss said casually.

These cases were often assigned to him. He'd built his reputation on them. Lately, though, they hadn't held his interest and he was hoping to diversify.

"This man is a friend of mine by the name of Don Griffin. It's a sad case, very sad." John paused, shaking his head.

"Don Griffin," Nash repeated. The name was familiar, but he couldn't place it.

"You might have heard of him. Don owns a chain of seafood restaurants throughout the Pacific Northwest."

"I think I read something about him not long ago."

"You might have," John agreed. "He's mentioned in the paper every now and then. But getting back to the divorce…. Don and Janice have been married a lot of years. They have two college-age children and then Janice learned a few years back that she was pregnant. You can imagine their shock."

Nash nodded sympathetically.

"Unfortunately the child has Down syndrome. This came as a second blow, and Don took it hard. So did Janice."

Nash couldn't blame the couple for that. "They're divorcing?"

"Yes." John's expression was filled with regret. "I don't know all the details, but apparently Janice was devoting all her time and attention to little Amy and well, in a moment of weakness, Don got involved with another woman. Janice found out and filed for divorce."

"I see. And is this what Don wants?"

The senior partner's face tightened with disappointment. "Apparently so. I'm asking you, as a personal favor, to handle this case, representing Don. My late wife and I were good friends with both Don and Janice."

"I'll help in any way I can," Nash said, but without real enthusiasm. Another divorce case, more lives ripped apart. He'd anesthetize his feelings as best he could and struggle to work out the necessary details, but only because John had asked him.

"I'll make an appointment to have Don come in for the initial consultation Friday morning, if that's agreeable?" Once more he made it a question, as if he expected Nash to decline.

This was the first personal favor Stackhouse had ever asked of him.

"I'll be happy to take the case," Nash said again. So he'd been wrong; this had nothing to do with Savannah.

"Good." John reached for his phone. "I'll let Don know I got him the best divorce attorney in town."

"Thank you." Compliments were few and far between from the eldest of the senior partners. Nash suspected he should feel encouraged that the older man trusted him with a family friend.

On his way out of the office, Nash ran into Arnold Serle. "Nash," the other man said, his face lighting up. "I haven't seen you all week."

"I've been in court."

"So I heard. I just wanted you to know how much I enjoyed your sister's wedding."

"We enjoyed having you." So he wasn't going to escape hearing about Savannah after all.

"How's Savannah?" Arnold asked eagerly.

"Very well. I'll tell her you asked about her."

"Please do. My niece is thinking about getting married. I'd like to steer her to Savannah's shop. If your sister's wedding is evidence of the kind of work Savannah does, I'd like to hire her myself." He chuckled then. "I sincerely hope you appreciate what a special woman she is."

"I do."

"Pleased to hear it," Arnold said, grinning broadly.

By Thursday evening, Nash had run through the full range of emotions. Knowing he'd be seeing Savannah later was both a curse and a blessing. He looked forward to being with her and at the same time dreaded it.

He got there right at six. Savannah was sitting at her

desk, apparently working on her computer; she didn't hear him enter the shop because she didn't look up. She was probably entertaining second thoughts of her own.

"Savannah." He said her name lightly, not wanting to frighten her.

She jerked her head up, surprise written on her face. But it wasn't the shock in her eyes that unnerved him, it was the tears.

"It's Thursday," he reminded her. "We have a date."

Nash wondered if she'd forgotten.

"Are you going to tell me what's upset you so much?" he asked.

"No," she said with a warm smile, the welcome in her eyes belying her distress. "I'm glad to see you, Nash. I could do with a friend just now."

Eight

Savannah hadn't forgotten about her date with Nash. She'd thought of little else in the preceding days, wondering if she should put any credence in his asking. One thing she knew about Nash Davenport—he wasn't the type to suggest something he didn't want.

"I had the deli pack us dinner," he told her. "I hope you're hungry."

"I am," she said, wiping the last tears from her face. Nash was studying her with undisguised curiosity and she was grateful he didn't press her for details. She wouldn't have known how to explain, wouldn't have found the words to tell him about the sadness and guilt she felt.

"Where are we going?" she asked, locking the shop. If ever there was a time she needed to get away, to abandon her woes and have fun, it was now.

"Lake Sammamish."

The large lake east of Lake Washington was a well-known and well-loved picnic area. Savannah had been there several times over the years, mostly in the autumn, when she went to admire the spectacular display of fall color. She enjoyed walking along the shore and feeding the ducks.

"I brought a change of clothes," she said. "It'll only take me a minute to get out of this suit."

"Don't rush. We aren't in any hurry."

Savannah moved into the dressing room and replaced her business outfit with jeans and a large sweatshirt with Einstein's image. She'd purchased it earlier in the week with this outing in mind. When she returned, she discovered Nash examining a silk wedding dress adorned with a pearl yoke. She smiled to herself, remembering the first time he'd entered her shop and the way he'd avoided getting close to anything that hinted of romance. He'd come a long way in the past few months, further than he realized, much further than she'd expected.

"This gown arrived from New York this afternoon. It's lovely, isn't it?"

She thought he'd shrug and back away, embarrassed that she'd commented on his noticing something as symbolic of love as a wedding dress.

"It's beautiful. Did one of your clients order it?"

"No. It's from a designer I've worked with in the past and I fell in love with it myself. I do that every once in a while—order a dress that appeals to me personally. Generally they sell, and if they don't, there's always the possibility of renting it out."

"Not this one," he said in a voice so low, she had to strain to hear him. He seemed mesmerized by the dress.

"Why not?" she asked.

"This is the type of wedding gown…" He hesitated.

"Yes?" she prompted.

"When a man sees the woman he loves wearing this dress, he'll cherish the memory forever."

Savannah couldn't believe what she was hearing. This was Nash? The man who'd ranted and raved that love was a wasted emotion? The man who claimed marriage was for the deluded?

"That's so romantic," Savannah murmured. "If you don't object, I'd like to advertise it that way."

Nash's eyes widened and he shook his head. "You want to use that in an ad?"

"If you don't mind. I won't mention your name, unless you want me to."

"No! I mean... Can we just drop this?"

"Of course. I'm sorry, I didn't mean to embarrass you."

"You didn't," he said when it was clear that she had. "I seem to have done this to myself." He made a point of looking at his watch. "Are you ready?"

Savannah nodded. This could prove to be an interesting picnic....

They drove to Lake Sammamish in Nash's car and he seemed extra talkative. "Arnold Serle asked about you the other day," he told her as he wove in and out of traffic.

"He's a darling," Savannah said, savoring the memories of the two older men who'd worked so hard to bolster her self-confidence, vying for her the way they had. "Mr. Stackhouse, too," she added.

"You certainly made an impression on them."

Although the night had ended in disaster, she would always treasure it. Dancing with John and Arnold. Dancing with Nash...

"What's the smile about?" Nash asked, momentarily taking his eyes off the road.

"It's nothing."

"The tears were nothing, too?"

The tears. She'd almost forgotten she'd been crying when he arrived. "I was talking to my parents this afternoon," she said as the misery returned. "It's always the same. They talk about traveling, but they never seem to leave Seattle. Instead of really enjoying life, they smother me with their sympathy and their sacrifices, as if that could bring back the full use of my leg." She was speaking fast and furiously, and not until she'd finished did she realize how close she was to weeping again.

Nash's hand touched hers for a moment. "You're a mature adult, living independently of them," he said. "You have for years."

"Which I've explained so many times, I get angry just thinking about it. Apparently they feel that if something were to happen, no one would be here to take care of me."

"What about other relatives?"

"There aren't any in the Seattle area. I try to reassure them that I'm fine, that no disasters are about to strike and even if one did, I have plenty of friends to call on, but they just won't leave."

"Was that what upset you this afternoon?" he asked.

Savannah dropped her gaze to her hands, now clenched tightly in her lap. "They've decided to stay in Seattle this winter. Good friends of theirs asked if they'd travel with them, leaving the second week of September and touring the South before spending the winter in Arizona. My dad's always wanted to visit New Orleans and Atlanta. They said they'll go another year,"

Savannah muttered, "but I know they won't. They know it, too."

"Your parents love you. I understand their concern."

"How can you say that?" she demanded angrily. "They're doing this because they feel guilty about my accident. Now *I'm* the one who's carrying that load. When will it ever end?"

"I don't know," he said quietly.

"I just wish they loved me enough to trust me to take care of myself. I've been doing exactly that for a long time now."

Nodding, he exited the freeway and took the road leading into Lake Sammamish State Park. He drove around until he found a picnic table close to the parking lot. The gesture was a thoughtful one; he didn't want her to have a long way to walk.

It might not be very subtle, but Savannah didn't care. She was determined to enjoy their outing. She needed this. She knew it was dangerous to allow herself this luxury. She was well aware that Nash could be out of her life with little notice. That was something she'd always taken into account in other relationships, but her guard had slipped with Nash.

He helped her out of the car and carried the wicker basket to the bright blue picnic table. The early evening was filled with a symphony of pleasant sounds. Birds chirped in a nearby tree, their song mingling with the laughter of children.

"I'm starved," Nash said, peering inside the basket. He raised his head and waggled his eyebrows. "My, oh, my, what goodies."

Savannah spread a tablecloth across one end of the

table and Nash handed her a large loaf of French bread, followed by a bottle of red wine.

"That's for show," he said, grinning broadly. "This is for dinner." He took out a bucket of fried chicken and a six-pack of soda.

"I thought you said the deli packed this."

"They did. I made a list of what I wanted and they packed it in the basket for me."

"You're beginning to sound like a tricky defense attorney," she said, enjoying this easy banter between them. It helped take her mind off her parents and their uncomfortable conversation that afternoon.

They sat across from each other and with a chicken leg in front of her mouth, Savannah looked out over the blue-green water. The day was perfect. Not too warm and not too cool. The sun was shining and a gentle breeze rippled off the lake. A lifeguard stood sentinel over a group of preschool children splashing in the water between bursts of laughter. Farther out, a group of teens dived off a large platform. Another group circled the lake in two-seater pedal boats, their wake disrupting the serenity of the water.

"You're looking thoughtful," Nash commented.

Savannah blushed, a little embarrassed to be caught so enraptured with the scene before her. "When I was a teenager I used to dream a boy would ask me to pedal one of the boats with him."

"Did anyone?"

"No…." A sadness attached itself to her heart, dredging up the memories of a difficult youth. "I can't pedal."

"Why not? You danced, didn't you?"

"Yes, but that's different."

"How?"

"Don't you remember what happened after the dance?"

"We could rent a pedal boat and I'll do the work," he said. "You just sit back and enjoy the ride."

She lowered her gaze, not wanting him to see how badly she longed to do what he'd suggested.

"Come on," he wheedled. "It'll be fun."

"We'd go around in circles," she countered. She wasn't willing to try. "It won't work if we don't each do our share of the pedaling. I appreciate what you're doing, but I simply can't hold up my part."

"You won't know that until you try," he said. "Remember, you didn't want to dance, either." His reminder was a gentle one and it hit its mark.

"We might end up looking like idiots."

"So? It's happened before. To me, anyway." He stood and offered her his hand. "You game or not?"

She stared up at him, and indecision kept her rooted to the table. "I don't know if it's a good idea."

"Come on, Savannah, prove to me that you can do this. But more importantly, prove it to yourself. I'm not going to let you overdo it, I promise."

His confidence was contagious. "If you're implying that you could've kept me off the dance floor, think again. I danced every dance."

"Don't remind me. The only way I could dance with you was to cut in on someone else. At least this way I'll have you to myself."

Savannah placed her hand firmly in his, caught up in his smile.

"If anyone else comes seeking the pleasure of your company this time," he said, "they'll have to swim."

Savannah's mood had been painfully introspective

when Nash arrived. Now, for the first time in what seemed like days, she experienced the overwhelming urge to laugh. Hugging Nash was a spontaneous reaction to the lightheartedness she felt with him.

He stiffened when her arms went around him, but recovered quickly, gripping her about her waist, picking her up and twirling her around until she had to beg him to stop. Breathless, she gazed at him, and said, "You make me want to sing."

"You make me want to—"

"What?" she asked.

"Sing," he muttered, relaxing his hold enough for her feet to touch the ground.

Savannah could have sworn his ears turned red. "I make you want to do what?" she pressed.

"Never mind, Savannah," he answered. "It's better that you don't know. And please, just this once, is it too much to ask that you don't argue with me?"

"Fine," she said, pretending to be gravely disappointed. She mocked him with a deep sigh.

They walked down to the water's edge, where Nash paid for the rental of a small pedal boat. He helped her board and then joined her, the boat rocking precariously as he shifted his weight.

Savannah held tightly to her seat. She remained skeptical of this idea, convinced they were going to look like a pair of idiots once they left the shore. She didn't mind being laughed at, but she didn't want *him* laughed at because of her.

"I...don't think we should do this," she whispered, struck by an attack of cowardice.

"I'm not letting you out of this now. We haven't even tried."

"I'll embarrass you."

"Let me worry about that."

"Nash, please."

He refused to listen to her and began working the pedals, making sure the pace he set wasn't too much for her. Water rustled behind them and Savannah jerked around to see the paddle wheel churning up the water. Before she realized it, they were speeding along.

"We're moving," she shouted. "We're actually moving."

It seemed that everyone on the shore had turned to watch them. In sheer delight, Savannah waved her arms. "We're actually moving."

"I think they've got the general idea," Nash teased.

"I could just kiss you," Savannah said, resisting the urge to throw her arms around his neck and do exactly that.

"You'll need to wait a few minutes." His hand reached for hers and he entwined their fingers.

"Let's go fast," she urged, cautiously pumping her feet. "I want to see how fast we can go."

"Savannah...no."

"Yes, please, just for a little bit."

He groaned and then complied. The blades of the paddle behind them churned the water into a frothy texture as they shot ahead. Nash was doing most of the work. Her efforts were puny compared to his, but it didn't seem to matter. This was more fun than she'd dared to dream. As much fun as dancing.

Savannah laughed boisterously. "I never knew," she said, squeezing his upper arm with both hands and pressing her head against his shoulder. "I never thought I could do this."

"There's a whole world out there just waiting to be explored."

"I want to sky-dive next," Savannah said gleefully.

"Sky-dive?"

"All right, roller-skate. I wanted to so badly when I was growing up. I used to skate before the accident, you know. I was pretty good, too."

"I'm sure you were."

"All my life I've felt hindered because of my leg and suddenly all these possibilities are opening up to me." She went from one emotional extreme to the other. First joy and laughter and now tears and sadness. "Meeting you was the best thing that's ever happened to me," she said, and sniffled. "I could cry, I'm so happy."

Nash stiffened and Savannah wondered if she'd offended him. His reaction would have been imperceptible if they hadn't been sitting side by side.

Nash was pedaling harder now; her own feet were set in motion by his efforts. "Where are we going?" she asked, noting that he seemed to be steering the craft toward shore. She didn't want to stop, not when they were just getting started. This was her one fear, that she'd embarrass him, and apparently she had.

"See that weeping willow over on the far side of the bank?" he asked, motioning down the shoreline. She did, noting the branches draped over the water like a sanctuary. It appeared to be on private property.

"Yes."

"We're headed there."

"Why?" she asked, thinking of any number of plausible reasons. Perhaps he knew the people who lived there and wanted to stop and say hello.

"Because that weeping willow offers a little more

privacy than out here on the lake. And I intend to take you up on your offer, because frankly, I'm not going to be able to wait much longer."

Offer, she mused. What offer?

Nash seemed to enjoy her dilemma and raised her hand to his mouth, kissing the inside of her palm. "I seem to remember you saying you wanted to kiss me. So I'm giving you the opportunity."

"Now?"

"In a moment." He steered the boat under the drooping limbs of the tree. The dense growth cut off the sunlight and cooled the late-afternoon air.

Nash stopped and the boat settled, motionless, in the water. He turned to her and his gaze slid across her face.

"Has anyone ever told you how beautiful you are?"

Besides him and her parents? And they *had* to praise her, didn't they? No one. Not ever. "No."

"Is the rest of the world blind?"

His words were followed by silence. A silence that spanned years for Savannah. No man had looked past her flaw and seen the desirable woman she longed to be. No man but Nash.

His mouth came down on hers, shattering the silence with his hungry need, shattering the discipline she'd held herself under all these years. She wrapped herself in his embrace and returned the kiss with the potency of her own need.

Nash moaned and kissed her hard, and she responded with every ounce of her being. She kissed him as if she'd been waiting all her life for this moment, this man. In ways too numerous to count, she had been.

She moaned softly, thinking nothing seemed enough.

Nash made her greedy. She wanted more. More of life. More of laughter. More of *him*.

Dragging his mouth from hers, he trailed a row of moist kisses down her neck. "If we were anyplace but here, do you know what we'd be doing now?"

"I…I think so." How odd her voice sounded.

"We'd be in bed making love."

"I…"

"What?" he prompted. "Were you about to tell me you can't? Because I'll be more than happy to prove otherwise." He directed her mouth back to his…. Then, slowly, reluctantly, as though remembering this was a public place and they could be interrupted at any time, he ended the kiss.

Savannah had more difficulty than Nash in returning to sanity. She needed the solid reality of him close to her. When he eased himself from her arms, his eyes searched out hers.

"If you say that shouldn't have happened, I swear I'll do something crazy," she whispered.

"I don't think I could make myself say it."

"Good," she breathed.

Nash pressed his forehead to hers. "I wish I knew what it is you do to me." She sensed that it troubled him that she could break through that facade of his. She was beginning to understand this man. She was physically handicapped, but Nash was crippled, too. He didn't *want* love, but he couldn't keep himself from needing it, from caring about her, and that worried him. It worried her, too.

"You don't like what I do to you." That much was obvious, but she wanted to hear him admit it.

Nash gave a short laugh. "That's the problem, I like

it too much. There's never been anyone who affects me this way. Not since Denise."

"Your ex-wife?"

"Yes." He regretted mentioning her name, Savannah guessed, because he made a point of changing the subject immediately afterward.

"We should go back to the pier."

"Not yet," Savannah pleaded. "Not so soon. We just got started."

"I don't want you to strain your leg. You aren't accustomed to this much exercise."

"I won't, I promise. Just a little while longer." This was so much fun, she didn't want it to ever end. It wasn't every day that she could turn a dream into reality. It wasn't every day a man kissed her as if she were his cherished love.

Love. Love. Love. The word repeated itself in her mind. She was falling in love with Nash. It had begun weeks earlier, the first time he'd kissed her, and had been growing little by little. Love was a dangerous emotion when it came to Nash. He wouldn't be an easy man to care about.

He steered them away from the tree and into the sunlight. Savannah squinted against the glare, but it didn't seem to affect Nash. He pedaled now as if he was escaping something. The fun was gone.

"I'm ready to go back," Savannah said after several minutes of silence.

"Good." He didn't bother to disguise his relief.

The mood had changed so abruptly that Savannah had trouble taking it all in. Nash couldn't seem to get back to shore fast enough. He helped her out of the boat and placed his arm, grudgingly it seemed, around her waist to steady her. Once he was confident she had her balance, he released her.

"I think we should leave," he said when they returned to the picnic table.

"Sure," she agreed, disappointed and sad. She folded up the tablecloth and handed it to him. He carried the basket to the car and loaded it in the trunk.

Savannah knew what was coming; she'd been through it before. Whenever a man feared he was becoming—or might become—emotionally attached to her, she could count on the same speech. Generally it began with what an exceptional woman she was, talented, gifted, fun, that sort of thing. The conclusion, however, was always the same. Someday a special man would come into her life. She'd never expected her relationship with Nash to get even that far. She'd never expected to see him after Susan's wedding. This outing was an unforeseen bonus.

They were on the freeway, driving toward Seattle, before Savannah found the courage to speak. It would help if she broached the subject first.

"Thank you, Nash, for a lovely picnic."

He said nothing, which was just as well.

"I know what you're thinking," she said, clasping her hands tightly together.

"I doubt that."

She smiled to herself. "I've seen this happen with other men, so you don't need to worry about it."

"Worry about what?"

"You're attracted to me and that frightens you— probably more than the other men I've dated because a woman you once loved has deeply hurt you."

"I said I don't want to talk about Denise."

"I'm not going to ask about her, if that's what concerns you," she said quickly, wanting to relieve him about that. "I'm going to talk about us. You may not realize it now, but I'm saving you the trouble of searching for the right words."

He jerked his head away from traffic and scowled at her. "I beg your pardon?"

"You heard me right. You see, it's all familiar to me, so you needn't worry about it. This isn't the first time."

"It isn't?" The question was heavy with sarcasm.

"I've already explained it's happened before."

"Go on. I'd be interested in hearing this." The hard muscles of his face relaxed and the beginnings of a smile came into play.

"You like me."

"That should be fairly obvious," he commented.

"I like you, too."

"That's a comfort." The sarcastic edge was back, but it wasn't as biting.

"In fact, you're starting to like me a little too much."

"I'm not sure what that means, but go on."

"We nearly made love once."

"Twice," he corrected. "We were closer than you think a few minutes ago."

"Under a tree in a pedal boat?" she asked with a laugh.

"Trust me, honey, where there's a will, there's a way."

Savannah blushed and looked pointedly away. "Let's not get sidetracked."

"Good idea."

He was flustering her, distracting her train of thought. "It becomes a bit uncomfortable whenever a man finds me attractive."

"Why's that?"

"Because…well, because they have to deal with my problem, and most people are more comfortable ignoring it. If you deny that there's anything different, it might go away."

"Have I done that?" This question was more serious than the others.

"No," she admitted. "You've been accepting of my… defect. I'm just not sure—"

"I've never viewed you as defective," he interrupted.

It seemed important to him that she acknowledge that, so she did. "I'm grateful to have met you, Nash, grateful for the fun we've had."

"This is beginning to sound like a brush-off."

"It is," she murmured. "Like I said, I'm saving you the trouble of coming up with an excuse for not seeing me again. This is the better-to-be-honest-now-instead-of-cruel-later scenario."

"Saving me the trouble," he exploded, and then burst into gales of laughter. "So *that's* what this is all about."

"Yes. You can't tell me that isn't what you were thinking. I know the signs, Nash. Things got a bit intense between us and now you're getting cold feet. It happened the night of Susan's wedding, too. We didn't make love and you were grateful, remember?"

He didn't agree or disagree.

"Just now…at the lake, we kissed, and you could feel it happening a second time, and that's dangerous. You couldn't get away from me fast enough."

"That's not entirely true."

"Your mood certainly changed."

"Okay, I'll concede that, but not for the reasons you're assuming. My mood changed because I started thinking about something and frankly it threw me for a loop."

"Thinking about what?" she pressed.

"A solution."

"To what?"

"Hold on, Savannah, because I don't know how you're going to react. Probably about the same way I did."

"Go on," she urged.

"It seems to me…"

"Yes?" she said when he didn't immediately finish.

"It seems to me that we might want to think about getting married."

Nine

"Married," Savannah repeated in a husky whisper.

Nash knew he'd shocked her, but no more than he had himself. The notion of marriage went against the grain. Something was either very wrong—or very right. He hadn't decided yet.

"I don't understand." Savannah shook her head, making a vague gesture with her hands.

"Unfortunately, I don't know if I'll do a decent job of explaining it," Nash said.

"Try." Her hands were at her throat now, fingering the collar of her sweatshirt.

"This could work, Savannah, with a little effort on both our parts."

"Marriage? You hate the very word…. I've never met anyone with a more jaded attitude toward love and romance. Is this some kind of joke?"

"Trust me. I was just as shocked at the idea as you are, but the more I thought about it, the more sense it made. I wish it *was* a joke." Nash's choice of words must have been poor because Savannah recoiled from him. "It would be a marriage of convenience," he added, hoping that might reassure her—or at least not scare her off.

"What?" she cried. "In other words, you intend to take what I consider sacred and make a mockery of it."

It was difficult not to be defensive when Savannah was acting so unreasonable. "If you'll listen, you might see there are advantages for both of us."

"Take me back to my shop," she said in a icy voice.

"I'm going there now, but I was hoping we could talk first."

She said nothing, which didn't bode well. Nash wanted to explain, ease her mind, ease his own, but he wasn't sure he could. He'd spoken prematurely without giving the matter sufficient consideration. It was after they'd kissed under the weeping willow that the idea had occurred to him. It had shocked him so completely that for a time he could barely function. He'd needed to escape and now that they were on their way back into Seattle, he realized he needed to talk this over with her.

"I know this comes as a surprise," he said, looking for a way to broach the subject once again. He exited from the freeway and was within a mile of Savannah's shop.

Savannah looked steadfastly out the window, as if the houses they were passing mesmerized her.

"Say something," Nash demanded. He drove into the alley where her car was parked and turned off the engine. He kept his hands tightly on the steering wheel.

"You wouldn't want to hear what I'm thinking," Savannah told him through clenched teeth.

"Maybe not," he agreed. "But would you listen to what I have to say?"

She crossed her arms and glared at him. "I don't know if I can and keep a straight face."

"Try," he said, just as she had earlier.

"All right, go on, explain." She closed her eyes.

"When I came to pick you up this afternoon, you were upset."

She shrugged, unwilling to acknowledge even that much. It wasn't an encouraging sign. He'd been premature in mentioning marriage. He wasn't sure why he'd considered it so urgent that he couldn't take the night to sleep on it first. Perhaps he was afraid he'd change his mind. Perhaps this was what he'd always wanted, and he needed to salvage his pride with the marriage-of-convenience proposal. Either way, it didn't matter; he'd already shown his hand.

"You love your parents and want them to go after their dream, isn't that right?"

"Would you simply make your point?"

"Fine, I will," he said, his argument gaining momentum. "I'm offering you the perfect solution. You marry me."

"In other words, you're suggesting we mislead my parents into believing this is a love match?"

"I hadn't thought of it in those terms, but, yes, I guess we would be misleading them. If that makes you uncomfortable, tell them the truth. Keep your maiden name if you want. That wouldn't bother me at all. The point is, if you were married, your father and mother would feel free to move south for the winters the way they've always wanted."

"What's in this for you?" she demanded. "Don't try to tell me you're doing it out of the goodness of your heart, either. I know better."

"You're right, there're advantages to me, too."

She snickered softly. "Somehow I thought there would be."

"That's the beauty of my idea," he said, trying to keep his irritation in check. Savannah was treating this like a joke while he was dead serious. A man didn't mention the word *marriage* lightly. Nash had been through this before, but this time marriage would be on his terms.

"Go on," Savannah snapped.

"As I said, there are certain advantages in this marriage for me, as well. The night of Susan's wedding, John Stackhouse pulled me aside and told me that I was being considered for the position of senior partner."

"But it would help if you were married."

Savannah wasn't slow-witted, that was for sure. "Something like that," he admitted. "It seems the other senior partners are afraid that my bitterness about my own divorce has spilled over into other areas of my life."

"Imagine that."

Nash tried to hide his annoyance. Savannah was making this extremely difficult.

"There're no guarantees for either of us, of course. If you agree to the terms of this marriage, that doesn't mean your parents will pack up and head south. If we did go ahead with it, there's nothing to say I'll be made senior partner. There's an element of risk for us both. You might get what you want and I might not. Or vice versa."

"Ah, now I understand," Savannah said in a slow, singsong voice. "That's where the convenience part comes into play. You want an out."

"That has nothing to do with it," Nash flared.

"Do you think I'm stupid, Nash? Of course it does. No one wants a *cripple* for a wife," she said furiously, "and if you can put an escape clause in the marriage contract, all the better."

"That's ridiculous! It has nothing to do with this."

"Would you have proposed marriage to any other woman this way, suggesting a short-term relationship for the sake of convenience? Heaven forbid that you might feel some genuine affection for me!"

It took Nash a moment to compose himself. He'd acted on impulse, which was not only uncharacteristic but a huge mistake, one that had only led to greater confusion. "Maybe this wasn't such a bright idea after all," he began. "I should've ironed out the details before talking to you about it. If you want to find fault with me for that, then I'll accept it with a heartfelt apology, but this business about me using you because I consider you less of a woman—you couldn't be more wrong. Your suggestion insults us both."

"Why do I have a hard time believing that?" Savannah asked. She sounded suspiciously close to tears, which grieved him more than her anger had.

"All I'm looking for here is a way of being fair to us both," Nash argued. "Despite what you think, I didn't mean to insult you."

"I'm sure you didn't. You're probably thinking people will admire you. Imagine Nash Davenport taking pity on that—"

"Savannah, stop." He pressed his lips tightly together. She was making a mockery of his proposal, a mockery of herself.

"Are you saying I'm wrong?"

His self-control was stretched to the limit. "Don't even suggest that," he said.

"I have to go," Savannah whispered. She turned from him, her fingers closing around the door handle. "It'd be best if we didn't see each other again."

Nash knew that the minute she left his car it would be over between them. He couldn't allow that to happen, couldn't let her leave, not without righting the wrong. He needed to do something, anything, to convince her he was sincere.

"Not yet," Nash said, taking her by the shoulder.

"Let go of me."

"Not without this." He locked his arms around her waist and pulled her against him.

She didn't resist, not for a second. Her own arms crept around his neck, and then they were kissing again, with the same passion as before.

He didn't know how long they were in each other's arms—or what brought him back to sanity. Possibly a noise from the street, or Savannah herself. He jerked his head up and buried his face in her shoulder, which was heaving with the strength of her reaction. Her fingers were buried in his hair.

"I find it amazing," she whispered brokenly, "that you're looking for a marriage in name only."

He wasn't sure if she was being humorous or not, but he wasn't taking any chances. "We might need to revise that part of the agreement."

"There won't be any agreement, Nash."

He was afraid of that. "Would you kindly listen to reason, Savannah? I wasn't trying to insult you...I thought you'd *like* the idea."

"Think again." She was breathing deeply, clearly fighting to regain her composure.

"Are you willing to listen to reason?" he asked again, hoping he'd reached her, if on no other level than the physical.

"I've had to deal with a certain amount of cruelty in my life," she said in a low voice. "Children are often brutal with their taunts and their name-calling. It was something I became accustomed to as a child. It hurt. Sticks and stones may break your bones, but words cut far deeper."

"Savannah, stop." That she'd compare his proposal to the ridicule she'd endured as a child was too painful to hear.

She stiffened, her back straight. "I don't want to see you again."

The words hit him hard. "Why not?"

She opened the car door and stepped awkwardly into the alley. Her leg seemed to be bothering her and with some effort she shifted her weight. "I don't trust myself with you...and I don't trust you with me. I've got to take care of myself."

"I want to help you, not hurt you," he insisted.

She hung her head and Nash suspected she did so to hide the fact that she was crying. "Goodbye, Nash. Please don't try to see me again.... Don't make this any more difficult than it already is."

Two weeks later, Nash's sister, Susan, strolled into Savannah's shop. Savannah felt a sense of awe at the happiness that shone from the young woman's eyes.

"What are you doing here?" she asked. "You're supposed to be on your honeymoon."

"We're been back for several days."

Following the wedding, Savannah rarely saw her clients. Whenever someone made the effort to stop in, it was a special treat. More so with Susan because Savannah had been so actively involved in the wedding. Actively involved with Nash, if she was willing to be honest, which at the moment she wasn't.

"You look—" Savannah searched for the right word "—serene." The two women hugged and Savannah held her friend tightly as unexpected tears moistened her eyes. She didn't allow them to fall, not wanting Susan to see how emotional she'd become. "I've missed you," she said. She had, but more than that, she'd missed Nash.

"Nash said the same thing. You both knew before I was married that I'd be moving to California with Kurt. Now you're acting like it's a big shock. By the way, Kurt sends his love."

Savannah eased from Susan's embrace. "What are you doing back in Seattle so soon? Kurt's with you, isn't he?"

"Why I'm here is a long story. As to your second question, Kurt couldn't come. With the wedding and the honeymoon, he couldn't get away. It's the first time we've been apart since the wedding and I miss him dreadfully." A wistful look came over her.

"What brings you to Seattle?"

Susan hesitated just a fraction of a second. "Nash."

So her big brother had sent her. This was exactly what she should have expected from Nash. The man wasn't fair—he'd use any means at his disposal to achieve his purpose.

"He doesn't know I'm here," Susan said as if reading Savannah's thoughts. "He'd be furious if he ever found out. I phoned him when Kurt and I got home from our honeymoon and he said he was having several pieces of furniture shipped to us. Things that belonged to our parents. I was a little surprised, since we're living in a small apartment and don't have much space. Nash knows that. Kurt talked to him, too, and afterward we agreed something was wrong. The best way to handle the situation was for me to visit."

"I see." Savannah made busywork around her desk, turning off her computer, straightening papers, rearranging pens in their holder. "How is Nash?"

"Miserable. I don't know why and he's doing an admirable job of pretending otherwise. He's spending a lot of time at the office. Apparently he's tied up with an important case."

"Divorce?" Savannah asked unnecessarily. That was his specialty—driving a wedge deeper and deeper between two people who'd once loved each other, increasing misery and heartache. Each divorce he handled lent credence to his pessimistic views. That wasn't going to change, and she was a fool if she believed otherwise.

"You might have read about this case. It's the one with Don Griffin, the man who owns all those great seafood restaurants. It's really sad."

Savannah did remember reading something about it. Apparently Mr. Griffin had an affair with a much younger woman. It was a story as old as time. She hadn't realized Nash was involved, but should have. He was Seattle's top divorce attorney, and naturally a man as wealthy and influential as Don Griffin would hire the very best.

"I know the case," Savannah admitted.

"Nash's been working late every night." Susan paused and waited for Savannah to comment.

"He enjoys his work."

"He used to, but I'm not so sure anymore. Something's really bothering him."

Their conversation was making Savannah uncomfortable. "I'm sorry to hear that."

"It's more than what's going on at the law firm, though. Kurt and I both think it has something to do with you, but when I asked him, Nash nearly bit my head off. He wouldn't even talk about you."

Savannah smiled to herself. "Neither will I. Sometimes it's better to leave well enough alone. We both appreciate your love and support, but what's going on between Nash and me is our own business. Leave it at that, please."

"All right." Susan wasn't happy about it, Savannah could tell, but the last thing she and Nash wanted or needed was Susan and Kurt meddling in their lives. Susan looked regretfully at the time. "I have to get back. The movers are coming this afternoon. I'm not taking much—we simply don't have room for it. And with the stuff Nash is shipping... I don't know why he insisted on sending us the rocking horse. Dad built it for him when he was a little kid and it was understood that Nash would hand it down to his own children. It's been in the basement for years. I don't know why he sent it to me. Kurt and I aren't planning to start a family for a couple of years. Men just don't make sense sometimes."

"You're only discovering that now?" Savannah teased.

Susan laughed. "I should know better after living with my brother all those years."

They hugged and Susan left shortly afterward.

The day was exceptionally slow, and with time on her hands, Savannah sat at her desk and drew a design for a flower arrangement. Intent on her task, she worked for several minutes before she saw that it wasn't a flower arrangement that was taking shape, but a child's rocking horse.

"What do you mean Janice turned down our settlement proposal?" Don Griffin shouted. He propelled his large frame from the chair across from Nash's desk and started pacing. His movements were abrupt and disjointed. "It was a fair offer, more than fair. You said so yourself."

"That's how these things work, Mr. Griffin. As I explained earlier, if you'll recall, it was unlikely that your wife and her attorney would accept our first offer. It's just the way the game's played. Your wife's attorney wouldn't be earning his fee if he didn't raise some objections."

"How much longer is this going to drag on?" his client demanded. "I want this over with quickly. Give Janice what she wants. If she insists on taking control of the restaurants, fine, she can have them. She can have the house, the cars, our investments, too, for all I care."

"I can't allow you to do that."

"Why not?" He slammed his hand down on the desk.

"You've hired me to represent you in a court of law, to look after your interests. If you make a decision now based on emotion, you'll regret it later. These matters take time."

"I haven't *got* time," the tall, stocky man said. Don

Griffin was in his fifties, and beginning to show his age.

"Is there a reason we need to rush?" Nash hated surprises. If Don's ex-girlfriend was pregnant, he didn't want to find out about it in the courtroom.

"Yes!" the other man shouted. "There's a very good reason. I hate this constant fighting, hate having my reputation raked over the coals in the press. Twenty-seven years of marriage—and after one indiscretion, Janice makes me look like a serial murderer. The restaurant's receipts actually dropped ten percent after that story was leaked."

Nash didn't know who was responsible for that, but he could make an educated guess. Janice Griffin's attorney, Tony Pound, stirred up controversy whenever possible, especially if it helped his case.

Nash made a note of the lost revenue and decided that when he phoned Tony later this afternoon, he'd tell him Janice's compensation might not be as big as she'd hoped—not if the business failed due to negative publicity.

"If it goes on like this," Don continued, "we may be filing for bankruptcy next."

"I'll make sure Mr. Pound learns this."

"Good, and while you're at it," Don said, waving his finger at Nash, "do what you can about me seeing my daughter. Janice can't keep me away from Amy, and this bull about me being a negative influence on our daughter is exactly that—bull."

"I'll arrange visitation rights for you as soon as I can."

"See if I can have her this weekend. I'm going to the beach and Amy's always loved the beach."

"I'll see what I can do. Is there anything else?"

His client paced, rubbing his hands together. "Have you seen my wife and daughter recently?" he asked.

"No. That would be highly unusual. Is there a reason you're asking?"

"I...I was just wondering how they looked, that's all. If they're well."

It was there in his eyes, Nash saw, the way it always was. The pain, the loneliness, the sense of loss so strong it brought powerful men and women to their knees. Nash thought of these moments when clients realized they were about to lose what they'd once considered their anchor. The chains were broken. With the anchors gone, it became a struggle to keep from drifting. Storms rose up, and that was when Nash learned the truth about his clients. Some weathered these tempests and came out stronger and more confident. Others struggled to stay afloat and eventually drowned.

Sadly, he didn't know which kind of person Don Griffin would prove to be.

The urgency in her father's voice frightened Savannah. His phone call came during her busiest time of day. It took her a moment to decipher what he was saying.

"Mom's in the hospital?" Savannah repeated. Her blood ran cold at the thought.

"Yes." Her father, who was always so calm and collected, was near panic. "She collapsed at home.... I didn't know what to do so I called an aid car and they've brought her to the hospital. The doctors are with her now."

"I'll be there in five minutes," Savannah promised.

Fortunately, Nancy had come in to help her, so she didn't have to close the shop.

She'd always hated the smell of hospitals, she thought as she rushed into the emergency entrance of Northend Memorial. It was a smell that resurrected memories she'd pushed to the back of her mind.

Savannah found her father in the emergency waiting room, his shoulders hunched, his eyes empty. "Daddy," she whispered, "what happened?"

"I...don't know. We were working in the yard when your mother called out to me. By the time I turned around she'd passed out. I was afraid for a moment that she was dead. I nearly panicked."

Savannah sat in the seat beside him and reached for his hand.

"I forgot about you not liking hospitals," her father said apologetically.

"It's all right. I wouldn't want to be anyplace else but here with you."

"I'm scared, sweetheart, really scared."

"I know." Savannah was, too. "Have you talked to the doctors yet?"

He shook his head. "How long will it take? She's been in there for over an hour."

"Anytime now, I'm sure." At the moment, Savannah wasn't sure of anything, least of all how her father would cope without her mother if it turned out that something was seriously wrong....

"Mr. Charles." The doctor approached them, his face revealing concern.

Automatically Savannah and her father got to their feet, bracing themselves for whatever he might say.

"Your wife's suffered a stroke."

* * *

In the past few weeks, Nash had made a habit of staying late at the office. He no longer liked spending time at the house. It'd been nearly a month since Savannah had been inside his home and he swore that whenever he walked inside, he caught a whiff of her perfume. He knew it was ridiculous, but he'd taken to placing air fresheners at strategic points.

His bed was also a problem. Savannah had left her imprint there, as well. When he woke in the morning, he could sense her presence. He could almost hear her breathing, feel her breath, her mouth scant inches from his own. It bothered him that a woman could have this powerful an effect on him.

She'd meant what she said about ending the relationship. Not that he'd expected to hear from her again. He hoped he would, but that was entirely different from *expecting* her to call.

More times than he cared to count, he'd resisted the urge to contact her. He'd considered sending flowers with a humorous note, something to break the ice, to salvage his pride and hers, then decided against it.

She'd made herself clear and he had no option but to abide by her wishes. She didn't want to see him again. So she wouldn't. The next move, if there was one, would have to be hers.

As for that absurd proposal of marriage… Seldom had he regretted anything more. It embarrassed him to think about it, so he avoided doing so whenever possible.

Someone knocked softly on his office door. He checked his watch, surprised to discover he wasn't alone at 10:00 p.m.

"Come in."

The door opened and Savannah stood there. She was pale, her features ashen, her eyes red-rimmed as if she'd recently been crying.

"Savannah," he said, hurrying around his desk. "What's wrong?" He didn't reach for her, much as he wanted to, not knowing if she'd welcome his touch.

"I've come," she said in a voice that was devoid of emotion, "to tell you I've reconsidered. I'll accept your offer of a marriage of convenience…. That is, if it's still open."

Ten

"**Y**ou're sure about this?" Generally Nash wasn't one to look a gift horse in the mouth, but this time was the exception. Something had happened to cause Savannah to change her mind, something drastic. Nash was convinced of that.

"I wouldn't be here if I wasn't sure." Nervously she reached inside her purse and took out a well-creased slip of paper. "I've made up a list of issues we need to discuss first…if you're willing."

"All right." He gestured toward the guest chair and sat down himself. "But first tell me what happened."

"My mother," she began, and paused as her lower lip began to tremble. She needed a moment to compose herself enough to continue speaking. "Mom's in the hospital…. She had a stroke."

"I'm sorry to hear that."

Savannah nodded. "Her prognosis for a complete recovery is excellent, but it frightened me terribly—Dad, too."

"I understand."

"Mom's stroke helped me realize I might not have

my parents much longer. I refuse to allow them to sacrifice their dreams because of me."

"I see."

She unfolded the piece of paper in her hands. "Are
you ready to discuss the details?"

"By all means." He reached for his gold pen and a
fresh legal pad.

"There will be no...lovemaking. You mentioned earlier that you preferred this to be a marriage of convenience, and I'm in full agreement."

That had been a hasty suggestion, certainly not one
he'd carefully thought out. In light of their strong physical attraction, Nash didn't believe this stipulation would
hold up for more than a few days, a week at the most.
The minute he kissed her, or took her in his arms, the
chemistry they shared would return.

"You're sure about this?" he asked.

"Positive."

Suggesting they wouldn't be able to keep their hands
off each other would inevitably trigger a heated argument. Savannah would accuse him of being arrogant.
Nash decided to agree with her for the present and let
time prove him right.

"Do you agree?" Her eyes challenged him to defy
her.

Nash rolled the pen between his palms and relaxed in
his leather chair, not wanting to give her any reason to
suspect that he had reservations or what they were. "If
a marriage in name only is what you want, then naturally I'll agree to those terms."

"Good." She nodded, much too enthusiastically to
suit him.

"Unless we mutually agree otherwise at some point," he added.

Savannah's eyes darted back to his. "I wouldn't count on that if I were you. I'm agreeing to this marriage for one reason and one reason only. I want to be sure you understand that."

"In other words, you don't plan to trick me into falling in love with you." He heard the edge in his own voice and regretted it. Savannah had sacrificed her pride the minute she'd walked through his door; goading wasn't necessary.

"This isn't a game to me, Nash," she said, her voice sharp. "I'm serious. If you aren't, maybe we should call it quits right now."

"I was the one who suggested this," he reminded her, not bothering to mention that it had been a spur-of-the-moment idea he'd deplored ever since. He stared at Savannah, noting the changes in her. He'd always viewed her as delicate, feminine. But there was a hardness to her now, a self-protective shell. She didn't trust him not to hurt her. Didn't trust him not to destroy her once-unshakable faith in love and marriage.

"I'll draw up the papers to read that this will be a marriage of convenience unless we mutually agree otherwise. Does that wording satisfy you?"

"All right, as long we understand each other." Her gaze fell to her list. "The second item I have here has to do with our living arrangements. I'll move in with you for a brief period of time."

"How brief?" This didn't sound any more encouraging than her first stipulation.

"Until my mother's well enough to travel south. That's the reason I'm willing to go through with this, after all. But to be as fair as possible, I'll stay with you until a senior partner's named."

"I'd appreciate that." The announcement would come within the month, Nash was certain, although it was taking much longer than he'd assumed. He'd like nothing better than to pull a fast one on Paul. The pompous ass would likely leave the firm. Nash smiled just thinking about it.

"After that there won't be any need for us to continue this farce. I'll move back to my home and we can have the marriage, such as it is, dissolved. Of course, I'll make no claims on you financially and expect the same."

"Of course," Nash agreed. Yet this talk of divorce so soon after marriage grated on him. It wouldn't look good to John Stackhouse and Arnold Serle if he was only married for a few weeks. And a quick divorce—*any* divorce—was the last thing he wanted. "For propriety's sake, I'd like to suggest we stay married a year," he said.

"A year," she repeated, making it sound as long as a lifetime. She sighed. "Fine. I'll accept that, provided we both adhere to all the other conditions."

"Anything else?" he asked, after making a second notation on the legal pad.

"Yes, as a matter of fact, I have a few more points."

Nash groaned inwardly, but presented a calm exterior.

"While I'm living with you, I insist we sleep in separate bedrooms. The less we have to do with each other, the better. You live your life the same as always and I'll live mine."

Nash wrote this down, as well, but made a point of

hesitating, making sure she was aware of his uneasiness about this latest dictate. This would be the ideal setup if he was looking for a roommate, but Nash was seeking a deeper commitment.

"Since you mention propriety…" Savannah began.

"Yes?" he prompted when she didn't immediately continue.

"Although our marriage will be one of convenience, I feel strongly that we should practice a certain code of ethics." The words were rushed, as if she thought he'd disagree. "I expect you to stop dating other women," she said, speaking more slowly now. "If I were to discover that you'd been seeing someone else, I would consider that immediate grounds for divorce."

"The same would hold true for you," he returned calmly. It made him wonder what kind of man she thought he was. "If I found out you were interested in another man, then I'd see no reason to continue our agreement."

"That isn't likely to happen," she blurted out defensively.

"Any more than it is with me."

She clamped her mouth shut and Nash guessed she didn't believe him. Where had she gotten the impression that he was a playboy? It was true that after his divorce he'd occasionally dated, but there'd never been anyone he was serious about—until Savannah. "We'll need to be convincing," she said next, her voice quavering slightly, "otherwise my parents, especially my father, will see through this whole thing in an instant. They aren't going to be easily fooled, and it's important we persuade them we're getting married because we're in love."

"I can be convincing." He'd gained his reputation swaying twelve-member juries; an elderly couple who wanted to believe he was in love with their daughter would be a piece of cake.

"I'll do my best to be the same," Savannah assured him, relaxing slightly. She neatly folded the sheet of paper, running her fingers along the crease. "Was there anything you wanted to add?"

Without time to think over their agreement, Nash was at a disadvantage. "I might later."

"I...was hoping we could come to terms quickly so I can tell my parents right away."

"We'll tell them together," Nash said. "Otherwise they'll find it odd. What do you want to do about the actual wedding ceremony?"

She looked away, then lowered her gaze. "I wasn't sure you'd agree so I hadn't given it much thought. I guess I should have, since I arrange weddings for a living."

"Don't look so chagrined. This isn't a normal, run-of-the-mill marriage."

"Exactly," she was quick to concur. "I'd like a small gathering. My parents and a few good friends—no more than ten or so. What about you?"

"About that number." He'd make sure Serle and Stackhouse received invitations.

"I'll arrange for the ceremony, then, followed by dinner. Is that agreeable?"

He shrugged, not really caring. Small and private appealed to him far more than the lavish gathering Susan had had. At least Savannah wasn't going to subject him to that, although he felt mildly guilty about cheating her out of a fancy wedding.

"How long do you think you'll need to come up with any further stipulations?" she asked.

"Not long," he promised, but he had one thought that he mentioned before he could censure it. "I'd like us to make a habit of eating dinner together."

"Dinner?" Savannah sounded incredulous.

His sole condition did seem surprising. But he felt that if they were going to the trouble of getting married, they shouldn't remain strangers. "We need to spend some time together, don't you think?"

"I don't see why that's necessary."

"It will be if we're going to create the facade of being married. We'll need to know what's going on in each other's lives."

Her nod was reluctant. "I see your point."

"We can share the housework, so you don't need to worry about me sticking you with the cooking and the cleanup afterward. I want to be fair about this."

"That seems equitable."

"I don't intend to take advantage of you, Savannah." It was important she believe that, although it was obvious she didn't. Even married to Savannah, he didn't hold out much hope of becoming a senior partner. Not when Paul Jefferson was ingratiating himself with anyone and everyone who could advance his career. But if there was the slightest possibility that he might beat out Paul, Nash was willing to risk it. His dislike for the man increased daily, especially since Paul resented that Nash had been given the Don Griffin case and had made his feelings obvious.

"What day should I arrange the wedding for?" Savannah asked, flipping through the pages of a small pocket calendar.

"In a week, if at all possible." He could tell by the way her eyes widened that she expected more time. "Is that too soon?"

"Not really…. A week shouldn't be a problem, although people *are* going to ask questions."

"So? Does that bother you?"

"Not exactly."

"Good." Nash had little success in hiding a smile.

"In that case, I think you should write up the agreement right away," she said. "You can add whatever provisions you want and if I disagree, I'll cross them out."

"Okay. When would you like to tell your parents?"

"As soon as possible. Tomorrow evening?"

Nash stood and replaced his pen in the marble holder. "Is your mother still in the hospital?"

Savannah nodded. "Dad spends almost every minute with her. The nurses told me they tried to send him home the first night, but he refused and ended up sleeping on a cot beside her."

"He's taken this hard, hasn't he?"

Savannah nodded. "He's worried sick…. That's the main reason I decided to accept your proposal. Mom loves the sunshine and I can't think of any place she'd enjoy recuperating more than in Arizona with her friends."

"In that case, we'll do everything we can to be sure that happens."

"Oh, Savannah." Her mother's eyes glistened with the sheen of tears as she sat up in her hospital bed early the next evening. "You're going to be married."

Nash slid his arm around Savannah's waist with familiar ease and smiled down on her. "I know my timing couldn't be worse," he murmured, "but I hope you'll forgive me."

"There's nothing to forgive. We're thrilled, aren't we, Marcus?" Her mother smiled blissfully. Nash was eating up the attention, nuzzling Savannah's neck, planting kisses on her cheek when he was sure her parents would notice. These open displays of affection were unlike him and were fast beginning to irritate Savannah.

"This does seem rather sudden, though, doesn't it?" her father asked. He might have embarrassed her by acting as if Nash was practically her fiancé that first evening, but he was astute about people, and Savannah knew that convincing him would be much more difficult than persuading her mother. Nash must have realized it, too, because he was playing the role as if he expected to earn an award for his performance as the besotted lover.

"Savannah and I've been dating off and on all summer." He brought her close to his side and dropped a quick kiss on the side of her neck. The moment they were alone, she'd tell him to keep his kisses to himself. Every time he touched his lips to her skin, a shiver of awareness raced up her spine. Nash knew it; otherwise he wouldn't take every opportunity to make her so uncomfortable.

"Are you in love?" her father asked her directly.

"Marcus, what a thing to ask," her mother said with a flustered laugh. "Savannah and Nash have come to us wanting to share their wonderful news. This isn't any time to ask a lot of silly questions."

"Would I marry Nash if I didn't love him?" Savannah asked, hoping that would be enough to reassure her father.

"We'd like to have the wedding as soon as possible," Nash added, looking down at her adoringly.

"There's a rush?" her father asked.

His attitude surprised Savannah. She was prepared for a bit of skepticism, but not this interrogation. Once he was convinced Savannah loved Nash—and vice versa—she didn't figure there would be any problems.

"I want Savannah with me," Nash answered. "It took me a long time to decide to marry again and now that I have, each day without her feels like an eternity." He reached for her hand and raised it to his lips, then placed a series of soft kisses on her knuckles. He was overdoing it, making fools of them both, and Savannah fumed.

"You feel the same way about Nash?"

"Yes, Daddy," she returned smoothly.

"I've waited all my life for a woman like Savannah."

Savannah couldn't help it; she stepped on Nash's foot and he yelped, then glared at her accusingly.

"I'm sorry, darling, did I hurt you?" she asked sweetly.

"No, I'm fine." His eyes questioned her, but she ignored the silent entreaty.

Her father stood at the head of the bed, which was angled up so that her mother was in a sitting position. They were holding hands.

"Do you object to Savannah marrying Nash?" her father questioned.

Her mother's sigh was filled with relief and joy. "Savannah's far too old to require our approval, and you know it. She can do as she pleases. I don't understand why you're behaving as if this is some...some tragedy when our little girl is so happy. Isn't this what we've prayed for all these years?"

"I know it's come at you out of the blue, Daddy," Savannah whispered, the words sticking in her throat, "but you know me well enough to know I'd never marry a man I didn't love with all my heart."

"The sooner Savannah's in my life, the sooner I can be complete," Nash added with a dramatic sigh.

Although he was clearly making an effort to sound sincere, it was all Savannah could do not to elbow him in the ribs. Anyone who knew Nash would recognize that he was lying, and doing a poor job of it. Presumably he was more effective in front of a jury.

"I should be out of the hospital by Friday," her mother said excitedly. "That'll give me a couple of days to rest at home before the wedding."

"If you need a few extra days to rest, we don't mind waiting. It's important that you be there, isn't that right, darling?"

Savannah felt him nudging her and quickly nodded. "Of course. Having you both there is more important than anything."

Her father shook his head. "I don't understand why you insist on having the wedding so soon. You've only known each other for a few months."

"We know each other better than you think," Nash said. The insinuation that they were lovers was clear. Savannah bit her tongue to keep from claiming otherwise. If Nash was trying to embarrass her, he'd surpassed his wildest expectations. Her face burned, and she couldn't meet her parents' eyes.

"I don't think we need to question Savannah and Nash any longer," her mother said. "They know their own minds. You have my blessing."

"Daddy?" Savannah whispered, holding her breath.

He didn't say anything, then nodded.

"There are a thousand things to do before Wednesday," Savannah said abruptly, bending over to kiss her mother's pale cheek. "If you don't mind, Nash and I'll leave now."

"Of course," her father said.

"Thank you so much for the wonderful news, sweetheart." Her mother was tiring; their departure came at the opportune moment.

Savannah couldn't wait until they were well outside the hospital room before turning on Nash. "How dare you," she flared, hands clenched at her sides. The man had no sense of decency. She'd told him how important it was to be convincing, but Nash cheerfully went about making fools of them both. His behavior angered her so much she could hardly speak.

"What did I do?" he demanded, wearing a confused, injured look that was meant to evoke sympathy. It wouldn't work—not this time.

"You implied…you—you let my parents believe we were lovers," she sputtered. And that was just for starters.

"So?" Nash asked. "Good grief, Savannah, you're thirty years old. They know you're not a virgin."

She punched the elevator button viciously. The rush of tears was a mingling of outrage and indignation, and she blinked furiously in an effort to keep them from spilling.

Nash exhaled softly and rubbed the back of his neck. "You *are* a virgin, aren't you?"

"Do you mind if we don't discuss such private matters in a public place?" she ground out. The elevator arrived just then, and Savannah eagerly stepped on.

There were a couple of other people who stared at her. Her limp sometimes made her the center of attention, but right now she suspected it was her tears that prompted their curiosity.

She managed to keep quiet until they reached the parking lot. "As for that stupid declaration of being so crazy about me you couldn't wait another minute to make me yours—I wanted to throw up."

"Why? You should be praising me instead of getting all bent out of shape."

"*Praising* you? For what?"

"Convincing your father we're in love."

"Oh, please," Savannah whispered, gazing upward. The sun had begun to set, spreading shades of gold and pink across the sky. It was all so beautiful, when she felt so ugly. Nash was saying the things every woman longs to hear—beautiful words. Only, his were empty. Perhaps that was what troubled her so much, the fact that he didn't mean what he was saying when she wanted it to be true.

"You're not making any sense." His patience was clearly gone as he unlocked the passenger door, then slammed it shut. "Let's have this out right here and now."

"Fine!" she shouted.

"I was doing everything I could think of to convince your parents we're madly in love. Correct me if I'm wrong, but wasn't that the objective?"

"You didn't need to lay it on so thick, did you?"

"What do you mean?"

"Did you have to hold on to me like you couldn't bear to be separated from me for a single second? The kissing has got to stop. I won't have you fawning all over me like…like a lovesick calf."

"Fine. I won't lay another hand on you as long as we're together. Not unless you ask."

"You make that sound like a distinct possibility and trust me, it's not."

He laughed shrewdly, but didn't reply. The look he gave her just then spoke volumes. Savannah found herself getting even angrier.

"You could practice being a bit more subtle, couldn't you?" she went on. "If anyone should know the power of subtlety, it's you. I thought you were this top-notch attorney. Don't you know *anything* about human nature?"

"I know a little." He went strangely quiet for a moment. "You don't think we fooled your father?"

"No, Nash, I don't," she said, calmer now. "The only people we seem capable of fooling are ourselves. I'm afraid this simply isn't going to work."

"You want out already?" he demanded, sounding shocked and surprised. "Our engagement isn't even three hours old and already you're breaking it."

"We don't have any choice," she insisted. "Anyone with sense is going to see through this charade in a heartbeat. If we can't handle announcing the news to my parents, how do you expect to get through the wedding ceremony?"

"We'll manage."

"How can you be so sure of that?"

"We did before, didn't we?" he asked softly. "At Susan's wedding."

He *would* bring that up. The man didn't fight fair. Her behavior at the wedding ceremony had been a slip of judgment and now he was waving it in front of her like a red flag, challenging her to a repeat performance. "But that wasn't real…we weren't the center of attention."

"Like I said, we'll manage very well—just wait and see."

Nash walked around to the front of his car and leaned against the hood, crossing his arms. "Your parents are okay with it, so I suggest we continue as planned. Are you game?"

Savannah nodded, feeling she had no other choice. She suspected she could convince her father that she was in love with Nash; she wasn't sure he'd believe Nash was in love with her.

Nash was busy at his desk, reviewing the latest settlement offer from Don Griffin, when his secretary buzzed him and announced that a Mr. Marcus Charles was there to see him without an appointment.

"Send him in," Nash instructed. He closed the file, set it aside and stood.

Savannah's dad was a gentle, reflective man who reminded him a little of his own father. "Come in, please," Nash said pleasantly. "This is a surprise."

"I should have phoned."

"We all behave impulsively at one time or another," Nash said, hoping Savannah's father would catch his meaning. He'd tried hard to make it sound as if their wedding plans were impulsive, which was more or less the truth. He'd tried to convince her family that he was crazy in love with her and, according to Savannah, he'd overplayed his hand. Perhaps she was right.

"Do you mind if I sit down?"

"Of course not," Nash said immediately, dismayed

by his own lack of manners. Apparently he was more shaken by this unforeseen visit than he'd realized. "Is there anything I can get you? Coffee, tea, a cold drink?"

"No, thanks." He claimed the chair across from Nash's and crossed his legs. "It looks like Joyce will be released from the hospital a day early."

Nash was relieved. "That's wonderful news."

"The news from you and Savannah rivaled that. The doctor seems to think it's what helped Joyce recover so quickly."

"I'm pleased to hear that."

"It's going to take several months before she's fully recovered, but that's to be expected."

Nash nodded, not thinking any comment was necessary. He was rarely nervous, but he felt that way now.

Marcus was silent for a moment. "So you want to marry Savannah."

"Yes, sir." This much was true and his sincerity must have rung clear in his response because it seemed to him that Savannah's father relaxed.

"My daughter's accident damaged her confidence, her self-image, at least in emotional situations." He paused. "Do you know what I mean?"

"Yes," he said honestly.

Marcus stood and walked over to the window. "I'm not going to ask if you love Savannah," he said abruptly. "For a number of reasons that doesn't matter to me as much as it did earlier. If you don't love her, you will soon enough.

"You came to me the other night seeking my blessing and I'm giving it to you." He turned and held out his hand.

The two men exchanged handshakes. When they'd

finished, Marcus Charles reached inside his suit jacket, withdrew a business-size envelope and set it on Nash's desk.

"What's that?"

Marcus smiled. "Savannah's mother and I thought long and hard about what we should give you as a wedding present, then decided the best gift would be time alone. Inside is a map to a remote cabin in the San Juan Islands that we've rented for you. We're giving you one week of uninterrupted peace."

Eleven

"What did you expect me to do?" Nash demanded as they drove off the Washington State ferry. "Refuse your parents' wedding gift?" This marriage was definitely getting off to a rocky start. They'd been husband and wife less than twelve hours and already they were squabbling.

"A remote cabin…alone together," she groaned. "I've never heard of anything more ridiculous."

"Most newlyweds would be thrilled with the idea," he said.

"We're not most newlyweds."

"I don't need you to remind me of that," Nash snapped. "You try to do someone a favor…"

"Are you insinuating that marrying me was a *favor?*" Savannah was huddled close to the door. "That you were doing it out of kindness?"

Nash prayed for patience. So this was what their marriage was going to be like—this constant barrage of insults, nit-picking, faultfinding.

"No, Savannah, I don't consider marrying you a

favor and I didn't do it out of kindness. You're my wife and—"

"In name only," she said in icy tones.

"Does that mean we're enemies now?"

"Of course not."

"Then why have we been at each other's throats from the moment we left the wedding dinner? I'm sorry your family insisted on giving us a honeymoon. I'm well aware that you'd rather spend time with anyone but me. I was hoping we'd make the best of this."

She didn't respond, for which he was grateful. The silence was a welcome contrast to the constant bickering.

"It was a beautiful wedding," she said softly, unexpectedly.

"Yes, it was." Savannah was beautiful in her ivory silk suit with a short chiffon veil decorated with pearls. Nash had barely been able to take his eyes off her. It was a struggle to remember this wasn't a real, till-death-do-us-part marriage.

"I've been acting defensive," she added apologetically. "I'm sorry, Nash, for everything. It isn't your fault we're stuck together like this."

"Well, it was my idea, after all. And our marriage *could* be a good thing in lots of ways."

"You're right," she said, but she didn't sound convinced. "We might find we enjoy each other's company."

Nash was offended by the comment. He'd enjoyed being with Savannah from the beginning, enjoyed goading her, challenging her views on marriage. He'd found himself seeking her out, looking for excuses to be with her, until she'd insisted she didn't want to see him again. He'd abided by her wishes, but he'd missed her, far more than he cared to admit.

"I saw Mr. Serle and Mr. Stackhouse talking to you after the ceremony."

Nash grinned, feeling a sense of satisfaction. Both of the senior partners had been delighted to see Nash marry Savannah. She'd managed to completely captivate those two. Arnold Serle had been acutely disappointed that they'd decided against a wedding dance. He'd been counting on another spin around the floor with Savannah.

"Did they say anything about the senior partnership?" Savannah asked.

He was annoyed that she already seemed eager to get out of their arrangement. "No, but then, a wedding isn't exactly the place to be discussing business." He didn't mention that it was at his sister's reception that John Stackhouse had originally introduced the subject.

"I see." She sounded disappointed, and Nash's hands tightened on the steering wheel. Luckily the drive was a beautiful one through lush green Lopez Island. Although Nash had lived in Washington all his life, he'd never ventured into the San Juan Islands. When they drove off the ferry he was surprised by the quiet coves and breathtaking coastline. In an effort to fill their time, he'd arranged for him and Savannah to take a cruise and explore the northernmost boundary islands of Susia and Patos, which were the closest to the Canadian border. He'd wanted their honeymoon to be a memorable experience; he'd planned a shopping excursion to Friday Harbor for another day. He'd read about the quaint shops, excellent restaurants and a whale museum.

Women liked those sorts of things. It seemed now that his efforts were for naught. Savannah had no intention of enjoying these days together.

"Have your parents said anything about traveling south?"

"Not yet," she said, her voice disheartened.

"They might not, you know." In other words, she could find herself living with him for the next few years, like it or not. The thought didn't appeal to him any more than it did her, especially if she continued with this attitude.

"How much farther is it to the cabin?" she asked stiffly. Nash wasn't sure. He didn't have GPS but he had a detailed map and instructions. However, since he'd never been on Lopez Island, he wasn't any expert. "Soon, I suspect."

"Good."

"You're tired?"

"A little."

It'd been a full day. First the wedding, then the dinner followed by the drive to the ferry and the ride across Puget Sound. Darkness would fall within the hour and Nash had hoped they'd be at the cabin before then.

He reached the turnoff in the road and took a winding, narrow highway for several miles. Savannah was suspiciously silent, clutching her wedding bouquet. He was surprised she'd chosen to bring it with her.

He found the dirt road that led to the cabin and slowly drove down it, grateful he'd rented a four-wheel-drive vehicle. The route was filled with ruts, which didn't lend him much confidence about this remote cabin. If this was any indication of what the house would be like, they'd be lucky to have electricity and running water.

He was wrong and knew it the minute he drove into the clearing. This was no cabin, but a luxurious house, built with a Victorian flair, even to the turret and wraparound porch.

"Oh, my…it's lovely," Savannah whispered.

The house was a sight to behold all on its own, but the view of the water was majestic.

"I'll get the luggage," Nash said, hopping out of the Jeep. He thought better of it, hurried around to Savannah's side and helped her down.

With his hands around her waist, he lifted her onto the ground. He longed to hold her against him, to swing her into his arms and carry her over the threshold like any new husband, but he didn't dare. Savannah would assume he was making a mockery of this traditional wedding custom. That was how she seemed to be dealing with everything lately, distrusting him and his motives. She made marriage feel like an insult. If this attitude lasted much longer, they'd have the shortest marriage on record.

"I'll get the luggage," he said again, unnecessarily. At least if his hands were full, he wouldn't be tempted to reach for Savannah.

"I'll open the door," she said, and for the first time she sounded enthusiastic. She hurried ahead of him and he noticed that she favored her injured leg more than usual. Sitting for any length of time must make movement more difficult. She rarely spoke about her leg—about the accident, her long rehabilitation or the pain she still suffered. He wished he knew how to broach the subject, but every attempt had been met with bristly pride, as if she believed that sharing this imperfect part of herself would make her too vulnerable.

She had the door open when he joined her. Stepping inside the house was like stepping into the nineteenth century. The warmth and beauty of this house seemed to greet them with welcoming arms.

The living room was decorated with a mix of antiques, and huge windows created a room that glowed in the setting sun.

"Oh, Nash," Savannah said, "I don't think I've ever seen anything more beautiful."

"Me, neither."

"Dad must have seen an ad for this house, maybe on a vacation website. He knows how much I love anything Victorian, especially houses."

Nash stashed that away in his storehouse of information about Savannah. When it was time to celebrate her birthday or Christmas, he'd know what to buy her.

"I'll put these in the bedrooms," he said. He didn't like the idea of them sleeping separately, but he didn't have any choice. He'd agreed to do so until she changed her mind, and from the look of things that could be a decade from now—if ever.

The master bedroom was equally attractive, with a huge four-poster mahogany bed. French lace curtains hung from the windows and the walls were papered in pale yellow. He set down Savannah's suitcase and headed for the second bedroom, which would be his. It was originally intended as a children's room, he realized. Instead of spending his wedding night with the woman he'd just married, he was destined to stare at row after row of tin soldiers. So much for romance!

Savannah woke early the next morning. The sunlight spilling in from the window was filtered through the lace curtains until a spidery pattern reflected against the floor. She yawned and sat up in bed. Surprisingly, she'd fallen asleep right away without the sadness or tears she'd expected.

"You're a married woman," she said aloud, thinking she might believe it if she heard herself say it. Her wedding and all that led up to it was still unreal to her. Afterward she'd been awful to Nash.

It took her a long time to understand why she'd behaved in such an uncharacteristic manner. Just before she went to bed, she'd realized what was going on. She was lashing out at him, blaming him for making a farce of what she considered holy. Only, he wasn't to blame; they were in this together. Marriage was advantageous to them both.

She heard him rummaging around in the kitchen. The aroma of coffee urged her out of bed. She threw on her robe and shoved her feet into slippers.

"'Morning," she said when she joined him. He'd obviously been up for hours. His jacket hung on a peg by the back door with a pair of rubber boots on the mat. His hair was wet, and he held a mug of steaming coffee and leaned against the kitchen counter.

"'Morning," he said, grinning broadly.

"You've been exploring." It hurt a little that he'd gone outside without her, but she couldn't really fault him. She hadn't been decent company in the past week or so. And walking along the beach with her wouldn't be much fun, since her gait was slow and awkward.

"I took a walk along the beach. I found you something." He reached behind him and presented her with a perfectly formed sand dollar.

Savannah's hand closed around her prize.

"I'm not sure, but I think I saw a pod of whales. It's a little difficult to tell from this distance."

Savannah made busywork about the kitchen, pouring herself a cup of coffee and checking the refrigerator for milk, all the while struggling to hold back her disappointment. She would've loved to see a pod of whales, even from a distance.

"What would you like for breakfast?" she asked, hoping to get their day off to a better start.

"Bacon, eggs, toast and a kiss."

Savannah froze.

"You heard me right. Come on, Savannah, loosen up. We're supposed to be madly in love, remember? This isn't going to work if you act the part of the outraged virgin."

What he said was true, but that didn't make it any easier. She turned away from him and fought down a confused mixture of anger and pain. She wanted to blame him, and knew she couldn't. She longed to stamp her foot, as she had when she was a little girl, and cry out, "Stop! No more." No more discord. No more silliness. But it wouldn't do any good. She was married but resigned to a life of loneliness. These were supposed to be the happiest days of her life and here she was struggling not to weep.

Nash had moved behind her and placed his hands on her shoulders. "Do you find me so repugnant?" he whispered close to her ear.

His warm breath was moist. She shut her eyes and shook her head.

"Then why won't you let me kiss you?"

She shrugged, but was profoundly aware of the answer. If Nash kissed her, she'd remember how much she enjoyed his touch. It'd been like that from the beginning. He knew it. She knew it. Now he intended to use that against her.

He brought his mouth down to her neck and shivers of awareness moved up and down her spine. Needing something to hold on to, Savannah reached for the kitchen counter.

"One kiss," he coaxed. "Just one."

"Y-you promise?"

"Of course. Anything you say."

She made a small, involuntary movement to turn around. His hands on her shoulders aided the process. She quivered when his mouth met hers and a familiar heat began to warm her. As always, their need for each other was so hot and intense, it frightened her.

Slowly, he lifted his mouth from hers. "Do you want me to stop?" he asked in a husky whisper.

Savannah made an unintelligible sound.

"That's what I thought," he said, claiming her mouth again.

She locked her arms around his neck. Soon the kissing wasn't enough….

Savannah felt as though her body was on fire. She'd been empty and lonely for so long. No man had ever kissed her like this. No man had ever wanted her so badly.

"You don't want me to stop, do you?" he begged. "Don't tell me you want me to stop."

Incapable of a decision, she made a second unintelligible sound.

"If we continue like this, we're going to end up making love on the kitchen floor," Nash whispered.

"I don't know what I want," she whimpered.

"Yes, you do. Savannah. If it gets much hotter, we're both going to explode. Let me make love to you."

She started to protest, but he stopped her, dragging his mouth back to hers. Only she could satisfy him, his kisses seemed to be saying. Savannah didn't know if he was telling her this or if she was hearing it in her mind. It didn't matter; she got the message.

"No," she said with a whimper. She couldn't give him her body. If they made love, he'd own her completely, and she couldn't allow that to happen. Someday he was going to walk away from her. Someday he was going to announce that it was over and she was supposed to go on her merry way without him. She was supposed to pretend it didn't matter.

"You don't mean that," Nash pleaded. "You can't tell me you don't want me." The words were issued in a heated whisper. "Don't do this, Savannah."

She buried her face in his shoulder. "Please…don't. You promised. You said you'd stop…whenever I asked."

He released her then, slowly, her body dragging against his as her feet slid back to the floor. She stepped away from him, anxious to break the contact, desperately needing room to breathe. She pressed her hand to the neckline of her gown and drew in several deep breaths.

Nash's eyes were squeezed shut as he struggled to bring himself under control. When he opened them, Savannah swore they were filled with fire.

Without a word to her, he reached for his jacket, opened the door and walked out.

She was trembling so hard, she had to pull out a chair and sit down. She didn't know how long she was there before she felt strong enough to stand, walk back into the bedroom and dress.

It was a mistake to let him kiss her; she'd known it even as she agreed, known it would be like this between them. Gnawing on her lower lip, she argued with herself. She and Nash had created an impossible situation, drawn up a list of rules and regulations and then insisted on testing each one to the limits of their endurance.

She'd just placed their coffee cups in the dishwasher when the back door opened and Nash appeared. She studied him. He looked calm and outwardly serene, but she wasn't fooled. She could see the angry glint in his eyes.

"If you're looking for an apology, you can forget it," he said.

"I'm…not."

"Good."

Now didn't seem the time to mention that he hadn't helped matters any by suggesting the kiss. Both of them knew what would happen when they started flirting with the physical aspect of their relationship.

Nash poured himself a cup of coffee. "Let's sit down and talk this over."

"I…don't know what there is to say," she said, preferring to avoid the issue completely. "It was a very human thing to happen. You're an attractive, healthy man with…needs."

"And you're a red-blooded woman. You have *needs,* too. But admitting that takes real honesty, doesn't it?"

Savannah found the remark insulting, but then, Nash didn't seem inclined to be generous with her. Since she didn't have an argument to give him, she let it pass.

"I did some thinking while I walked off my frustration."

"Oh?" She was curious about what he'd decided, but didn't want to press him.

"The way I see it, I'm setting myself up for constant frustration if we have any more bouts like this last one. If you want to come out of this marriage as pristine as the freshly fallen snow, then far be it from me to hit my head against a brick wall."

"I'm not sure I understand."

"You don't need to. You have your wish, Savannah. I won't touch you again, not until you ask me, and the way I feel right now, you're going to have to do a whole lot more than ask. You're going to have to beg."

Nash hadn't known it was possible for two human beings to live the way he and Savannah had spent the past two weeks. The so-called honeymoon had been bad enough, but back in civilization, living in his house, the situation had gone from unbearable to even worse. The electricity between them could light up a small city. Yet they continued to ignore their mutual attraction.

They lived as brother and sister. They slept in separate rooms, inquired about each other's day, sat at the dinner table every night and made polite conversation.

In two weeks Nash hadn't so much as held her hand. He dared not for fear he'd get burned. Not by her rejection, but by their need for each other.

Part of the problem was the fact that Savannah was a virgin. She didn't know what she was missing, but she had a fairly good idea, and that added a certain amount of intrigue. He sincerely hoped she was miserable, at least as miserable as he was.

"Mr. Griffin is here to see you," his assistant announced.

Nash stood to greet his client. Don Griffin had lost weight in the past month. Nash had, too, come to think of it. He didn't have much of an appetite and was working out at the gym most nights after dinner.

"Did you hear from Janice's attorney?" Don demanded.

"Not yet."

"Does he normally take this long to return phone calls?" Agitated, Don started to pace.

"He does when he wants us to sweat," he said.

"Raise Janice's monthly allotment by five hundred dollars."

Nash sighed inwardly. This was a difficult case and not for the usual reasons. "Sit down, Mr. Griffin," he said. "Please."

Don complied and sat down. He bounced his fingers against each other and studied Nash as he leaned back in his chair.

"Janice hasn't requested any extra money," Nash said.

"She might need it. Amy, too. There are a hundred unexpected expenses that crop up. I don't want her having to scrimp. It's important to me that my wife and daughter live comfortably."

"You've been more than generous."

"Just do as I say. I'm not paying you to argue with me."

"No, you're paying me for advice and I'm about to give you some, so kindly listen. It doesn't come cheap."

Don snorted loudly. "No kidding. I just got your last bill."

Nash smiled. His clients were often shocked when

they learned how expensive divorce could be. Not only financially, but emotionally. Nash had seen it happen more times than he cared to think about. Once his clients realized how costly a divorce could be, they were already embroiled in bitterness and it was impossible to undo the damage.

"Do you know what you're doing, giving Janice extra money?" he asked.

"Sure I do. I'm attempting to take care of my wife and daughter."

"You're already doing that. Offering them more money is more about easing your conscience. You want to absolve your guilt because you had an affair."

"It wasn't an affair," Don shouted. "It was a one-night thing, a momentary lapse that I've regretted every moment since. Janice would never have found out about it if it hadn't been for—never mind, that doesn't matter now. She found out about it and immediately called an attorney."

"My point is, she learned about your indiscretion and now you want to buy peace of mind. Unfortunately, it doesn't work like that."

"All I'm trying to do is get this divorce over with."

Tony Pound, Janice's attorney, wasn't a fool. He knew exactly what he was doing, dragging the proceedings out as long as possible to prolong the guilt and the agony. To Nash's way of thinking, his client had been punished enough.

"This is one mistake you aren't going to be paying monetarily for the rest of your life," Nash assured him. "And I plan to make sure of it. That's why John Stackhouse asked me to take your case. You've lost your wife, your home, your daughter. You've paid enough. Now go back to your apartment and relax. I'll contact you when I hear from Mr. Pound."

Don Griffin nodded reluctantly. "I don't know how much more of this I can take."

"It shouldn't be much longer," Nash assured him.

He rose slowly from the chair. "You'll be in touch soon?"

Nash said he would. Don left the office and Nash sat down to review his file for the hundredth time. He was missing something, he realized. That cold-blooded instinct for the kill.

He wasn't enjoying this, wasn't even close to experiencing the satisfaction he usually gained from bringing his opponents to their knees. Somewhere along the line he'd changed. He'd sensed things were different shortly after he'd met Savannah. Now there was no hiding his feelings. He'd lost it. Only, he wasn't sure what he'd found in exchange.

"Have you got a moment?" John Stackhouse stuck his head in Nash's office.

"Sure. What can I do for you?"

The senior partner was smiling from ear to ear. "Would you mind coming down to the meeting room?"

Nash's pulse accelerated wildly. The executive committee had been meeting with the other senior partners that afternoon to make their recommendation for new senior partner.

"I got the position?" Nash asked hesitantly.

"I think that would be a fair assessment," the older man said, slapping Nash on the shoulder. "It wasn't a hard decision, Nash. You're a fine attorney and an asset to this firm."

* * *

A half hour later, Nash rushed out of the office and drove directly to Savannah's shop. As luck would have it, she was busy with a customer. He tried to be patient, tried to pretend he was some stranger who'd casually strolled in.

Savannah looked at him with wide, questioning eyes and he delighted in unnerving her by blowing her a kiss.

"When did you say the wedding was?" she asked the smartly dressed businesswoman who was leafing through a book of invitations.

"In December."

"You have plenty of time, but it's a good idea to set your budget now. I'll be happy to assist you in any way I can."

"I appreciate that," Nash heard the woman say.

He wandered over to her desk and sorted through her mail. Without being obvious, Savannah walked over to where he was sitting, took the envelopes from him and gently slapped his hands. "Behave yourself," she said under her breath.

"I have a few extra expenses coming up," he said in a low whisper. "I hope you're doing well. I might need a loan."

"What expenses?" she asked in the same low voice.

"New business cards, stationery and the like."

"New stationery?" she repeated more loudly.

The customer turned around. "I'm sorry," Savannah said apologetically. "I was commenting on something my husband said."

The woman smiled graciously. "I thought you two must be married. I saw the way you looked at each other when he walked in the door."

Neither Nash nor Savannah responded.

Savannah started to walk away, when Nash caught her hand. It was the first time he'd purposely touched her since the morning after their wedding. Apparently it caught her by surprise, because she turned abruptly, her gaze seeking out his.

"I'm the new senior partner."

Savannah's eyes lit up with undisguised delight. "Nash, oh, Nash." She covered her mouth with both hands and blinked back tears. "Congratulations."

"If you don't mind, I'll come back another time with my fiancé," Savannah's customer said.

"I'm sorry," Savannah said, limping toward the woman.

"Don't apologize. Celebrate with your husband. You both deserve it." When she reached the front door, she turned the sign to "Closed," winked at Nash and walked out of the store.

"When did you find out?" Savannah asked, rubbing her index finger beneath her eye.

"About half an hour ago. I thought we'd go out to dinner and celebrate."

"I...don't know what to say. I'm so happy for you."

"I'm happy, too." It was difficult not to take her in his arms. He stood and walked away from her rather than break his self-imposed restriction.

"Where are you going?" Savannah asked, sounding perplexed.

"I need to keep my distance from you."

"Why?"

"Because I want to hold you so much, my arms ache."

Savannah broke into a smile. "I was just thinking the same thing," she said, opening her arms to him.

Twelve

Nash checked his watch for the time, set aside the paper and hurried into the kitchen. It was his night to cook and he'd experimented with a new recipe. If anyone had told him he'd be hanging around a kitchen, fretting over elaborate recipes, he would've stoutly denied such a thing could even happen.

Marriage had done this to him, and to his surprise Nash wasn't complaining. He enjoyed their arrangement, especially now that they were on much friendlier terms. The tension had lessened considerably following the evening they'd celebrated his appointment as senior partner. It felt as if the barriers were gradually being lowered.

He was bent over the oven door when he heard Savannah come into the house. She'd called him at the office to let him know she'd be late, which had become almost a nightly occurrence.

"I'm home," she said, entering the kitchen. She looked pale and worn-out. He'd never have guessed September would be such a busy month for weddings. Savannah had overbooked herself and spread her time and energy much too thin. He'd resisted the urge to lecture her, although it'd been difficult.

"Your timing couldn't be better," he said, taking the sausage, cabbage and cheese casserole out of the oven and setting it on the counter. The scent of spicy meat filled the kitchen.

"That smells delicious," Savannah said, and Nash beamed proudly. He'd discovered, somewhat to his surprise, that he enjoyed cooking. Over the years he'd learned a culinary trick or two, creating a small repertoire of dinners. Nothing, however, that required an actual recipe. Now he found himself reading cookbooks on a regular basis.

"I've got the table set if you're ready to eat," he told her.

"You must've known I was starving."

"Did you skip lunch again today?" he asked, using oven mitts to carry the glass casserole dish to the table. Once again he had to stop himself from chastising her. Their peace was too fragile to test. "Sit down and I'll bring you a plate."

It looked as if Savannah was in danger of falling asleep as he joined her at the table.

"Nash," she said after the first taste, "this is wonderful!"

"I'm glad you approve."

"Keep this up and you can do all the cooking," she teased, smiling over at him.

Nash set his fork aside and folded his hands. He couldn't keep silent any longer. "You're working too hard."

She lowered her gaze and nodded. "I know. I scheduled the majority of these weddings soon after our own.

I…I thought it would be a good idea if I spent as much time at the shop as possible."

In other words, less time with him. "I hope you've changed your mind."

"I have." Her hand closed around her water glass. "I assumed our…arrangement would be awkward, but it hasn't been, not since the beginning."

"I've enjoyed spending time with you." It frustrated him, living as they did, like polite strangers, but that, too, had changed in the past couple of weeks. Their relationship had become that of good friends. Their progress was slow but steady, which gave Nash hope that eventually Savannah would be comfortable enough with him to make love. He realized his attitude was shortsighted. Breaching that barrier had been a challenge from the first, but he hadn't thought beyond it. He didn't want to think about it now.

When they finished eating, Savannah carried their plates to the sink. They had an agreement about cleanup, one of many. When one of them did the cooking, the other washed the dishes.

"Sit down," Nash ordered, "before you collapse."

"This will only take a couple of minutes," she insisted, opening the dishwasher.

Nash took her by the hands and led her into the living room. Pushing her down on the sofa, he said, "I want you to relax."

"If I do that, I'll fall asleep, and I need to go back to the shop later to finish up a few things."

"Don't even think about it, Savannah." Those were fighting words, but he counted on her being too tired to argue with him. "You're exhausted. I'm your husband,

and I may not be a very good one, but I refuse to allow you to work yourself this hard."

She closed her eyes and leaned her head against the sofa cushion. She gave him a small smile. "You are a good husband, Nash. Thoughtful and considerate."

"Right." He hoped she wasn't expecting an argument. As it was, he should be awarded some kind of medal.

He reached for her legs and placed them on his lap. "Just relax," he urged again when she opened her eyes, silently questioning him. He removed her shoes and massaged her tired feet. She sighed with pleasure and wiggled her toes.

"I haven't been to my place in a week," she said, and Nash found that an odd comment until he thought about it. She was admitting how comfortable she'd gotten living with him. It was a sign, a small one, that she was willing to advance their relationship. Nash didn't intend to waste it.

"I've moved nearly all my clothes here," she continued in sleepy tones.

"That's very good, don't you think?" he asked, not expecting her to reply.

"Hmm."

He continued to rub her feet and ankles, marveling at the delicate bone structure. He let his hands venture upward over her calves. She sighed and nestled farther down in the sofa. Gaining confidence, Nash risked going higher, where her skin was silky warm and smooth. He wasn't sure how this was affecting Savannah, but it was having a strong effect on him. His breathing went shallow and his heart started to thunder in his ears. He'd promised himself that he wouldn't ask her to make love again. She'd have to come to him. He wanted her to beg—but if anyone was going to do any begging, it was him.

"It's very relaxing," Savannah murmured with a sigh.

Funny, it wasn't relaxing for him….

"Nash." His name was released on a harshly indrawn breath.

His hands froze. His heart went still and his breath caught. "Yes?" He struggled to sound expressionless, although that was nearly impossible. The less she recognized how critical his need was for her, the better.

"I think I should stop, don't you?" Where he dredged up the strength to suggest that was beyond him.

"It feels good."

"That's the problem. It feels *so* good."

"For you, too?"

Sometimes he forgot what an innocent she was. "For me, too."

Her head was propped against the back of the sofa, her eyes closed. Her mouth was slightly parted and she moistened her lips with the tip of her tongue. Nash groaned inwardly and forced himself to look away.

"Maybe we should kiss," she whispered.

Nash wasn't interested in a repeat performance of what had taken place earlier, but at the same time he wasn't about to turn down her offer. She wasn't begging, but this was close enough.

He shifted his weight and brought her into his arms.

Perspiration broke out on his forehead and he held his breath while he reined in his desire. "If we start kissing, we might not be able to stop."

"I know."

"You know that?" Something was wrong with him.

He should be carrying her into the bedroom and not asking questions until afterward. A long time afterward.

"We can follow through with our agreement, can't we?" she asked. Her eyes fluttered open.

"What agreement?" His mind could only hold one thing at the moment, and that was his painful physical need for her.

"We'll separate once my parents decide to travel," she said, and it sounded more like a reassurance. "In the meantime, I'm not going to be trapped in a loveless marriage. As per the contract, we can initiate divorce proceedings when the year's up."

"Fine," he said, willing to agree to any terms. "Whatever you want."

"Do you think it would be a mistake to make love?" she asked.

"No." He sounded as if he'd choked on something. "That seems like a good idea to me," he said a couple of seconds later. He got off the sofa, reached down and scooped her into his arms.

She gave a small cry of surprise when he lifted her up and marched down the darkened hallway. He walked into his bedroom and placed her on his bed.

He was afraid of going too fast—and of not going fast enough. Afraid of not lasting long enough, of cheating her out of what lovemaking should be for her first time. His fears managed to make him feel indecisive.

"Is something wrong?" she asked, staring up at him, her eyes wide and questioning.

Unable to answer, he shook his head.

She smiled then, softly, femininely, and stretched her arms up, bringing him down next to her. He noticed that her breathing was as quick and shallow as his own.

Carefully he peeled open the front of her shirt and eased it from her shoulders. Her bra and everything else soon followed….

They fell asleep afterward, their arms and legs intertwined, their bodies joined in the most elemental of ways. Nash had never known such peace, never experienced such serenity, and it lulled him into a deep sleep.

It was after midnight when he woke. The lights were still on in the living room and the kitchen. Carefully, so as not to wake Savannah, he crawled out of the bed and reached for his robe. Shuffling barefoot out of the bedroom, he yawned.

He felt good. Like he could run a marathon or swim a mile in world-record time. He finished the dinner dishes and was turning off the kitchen light when he looked up and saw Savannah standing inside the living room. Her hair was tousled, yet he'd never seen her look more beautiful. She'd donned her blouse, which covered precious little of her body.

"I woke up and you were gone," she said in a small voice.

"I was coming back to bed."

"Good." She led him back, not that he required any coaxing. The room was dark, but streaks of moonlight floated against the wall as they made their way to the bed.

Nash held back the covers and Savannah climbed in. He followed, gathering her in his arms, cradling her head against his shoulder.

He waited for her to speak, wondering what she was thinking, afraid to ask. With utter contentment he kissed her hair. She squirmed against him, nestling in as close as possible, and breathed out a long, womanly sigh.

Although he was an experienced lover, Nash had never heard a woman sigh the way Savannah did just then. It seemed to come from deep inside her, speaking of pleasure and the surprise of mutual satisfaction.

"Thank you," he whispered.

"No," she said. "Thank you." And then she snuggled up to him again, as if she needed this closeness as much as he did. As if she craved these peaceful moments, too.

He waited a few more minutes, wanting to be sure she hadn't drifted off to sleep. "We should talk."

"I know," she whispered. "I thought about that, too."

"And?"

"I planned on discussing things with you, reassessing the issues, that sort of thing."

"Why didn't you?" He couldn't help being curious.

He felt her lips move in a smile. "When the time came, all I wanted was you."

His chest rose with an abundance of fierce male pride. "I wanted you, too."

Serenity surrounded him and he sank into its warmth.

"Should we talk now?" Savannah asked after a while.

The last thing Nash wanted right this minute was a lengthy conversation about their marriage. Words would destroy the tranquillity, and these moments were too precious to waste.

"This doesn't have to change anything, if you don't want it to," he murmured, rubbing his chin over her head, loving the silky feel of her hair.

Savannah went still, and he wondered if he'd said something wrong. "You're content with our arrangement the way it is?" she asked.

"For now I am. We don't have to make any decisions tonight, do we?"

"No," she agreed readily.

"Then relax and go back to sleep." His eyes drifted shut as he savored this closeness.

"Nash."

"Hmm?"

"It was nothing like I expected," she told him.

"Better, I hope."

"Oh, yes." And then she kissed him.

Don and Janice Griffin's meeting before Judge Wilcox was scheduled for two in the afternoon. Nash was well prepared for this final stage of the divorce proceedings.

Don Griffin arrived at his office an hour early and—in what was fast becoming a habit—started pacing the room.

"I'm ready anytime you are," his client said.

"If we leave now, we'll end up sitting outside in the hallway," Nash told him.

"I don't care. I want this over with as quickly and cleanly as possible, understand?"

"That message came through loud and clear," Nash assured him. "Settle down and relax, will you?"

Don thrust both hands into his hair. "*Relax?* Are you crazy, man? You might've gone through this a thousand times, but it's almost thirty years of my life we're throwing out the window. The stress is getting to me."

"What's this I hear about putting a divorce special on your restaurants' menu?" Nash asked in an effort to take the older man's mind off the coming proceedings.

"Anyone who comes into any of your restaurants the day his divorce is final eats for free."

"That's right, and I'd rather you didn't say anything derogatory about it. I've met a number of men just like me. Some of 'em married twenty, thirty years and all of a sudden it's gone. Poof. Suddenly they're lost and alone and don't know what to do with the rest of their lives."

"I'm not going to say anything negative. I think it's a generous thing you're doing."

Don Griffin eyed him as if he wasn't sure he should believe that.

When they arrived at the courtroom, Mr. Griffin and Nash took their seats behind one table. Janice Griffin and Tony Pound sat behind the other. Nash noticed the way Don stole a look at his almost ex-wife. Next, he caught a glimpse of Janice looking at Don. It wasn't anything he hadn't seen countless times before. One last look, so to speak, before the ties were severed. A farewell. An acceptance that it was soon to be over—the end was within sight. This marriage was about to breathe its last breath.

Judge Wilcox entered the room and everyone stood. In a crisp, businesslike manner, he asked a series of questions of each party. Janice responded, her voice shaking. Don answered, sounding like a condemned man. They sat back down and the final decree was about to be pronounced when Nash vaulted out of his seat.

For a moment he didn't know what had forced him into action. "If you'll pardon me, Your Honor," he said, with his back to his client, "I'd like to say a few words."

He could hear Tony begin to object. Nash didn't give him the opportunity.

"My client doesn't want this divorce, and neither does his wife."

A string of hot words erupted behind him as Tony Pound flew out of his chair. The judge's gavel pounded several times, the noise deafening.

"Your Honor, if you'll indulge me for just a moment."

No one was more surprised than Nash when he was given permission. "Proceed."

"My client has been married for almost thirty years. He made a mistake, Your Honor. Now, he'll be the first to admit it was a foolish, stupid mistake. But he's human and so is his wife. They've both paid dearly for this blunder and it seems to me they've paid enough."

He turned to face Janice Griffin, who was shredding a tissue in her hand. "You've made mistakes in your life, too, haven't you, Mrs. Griffin?"

Janice lowered her gaze and nodded.

"You can't cross-examine my client," Pound yelled.

Nash ignored him, and thankfully so did Judge Wilcox.

"My client has loved his wife and family for nearly thirty years. He still loves her. I saw the way he looked at Mrs. Griffin when she walked into the courtroom. I also saw the way she looked at him. These two people care deeply for each other. They've been driven apart by their pain and their pride. Thirty years is a very long time out of a person's life, and I don't believe anyone should be in a rush to sign it away."

"Your Honor, I find this outburst extremely unprofessional," Tony Pound protested.

Nash didn't dare turn around.

"Don Griffin has suffered enough for his indiscretion. Mrs. Griffin has been through enough agony, too.

It's time to think about rebuilding lives instead of destroying them."

There wasn't a sound in the courtroom. Having had his say, Nash returned to his seat.

Judge Wilcox held his gavel with both hands. "Is what Mr. Davenport said true, Mr. Griffin? Do you love your wife?"

Don Griffin rose slowly to his feet. "A thousand times more than I thought possible."

"Mrs. Griffin?"

She, too, stood, her eyes watering, her lips trembling. "Yes, Your Honor."

The judge glared at them both and set down the gavel. "Then I suggest you try to reconcile your differences and stop wasting the court's time."

Nash gathered together the papers he'd removed from his briefcase and slipped them back inside. Don Griffin walked behind him and was met halfway by his wife. From his peripheral vision, Nash watched as Janice Griffin, sobbing, walked into her husband's arms. They held on to each other, weeping and laughing and kissing all at once.

Not bad for an afternoon's work, Nash decided.

He picked up his briefcase and walked out of the courtroom. He hadn't taken two steps when Tony Pound joined him.

"That was quite a little drama you put on just now."

"I couldn't see two people who were obviously in love end their marriage," Nash said. They marched side by side through the halls of justice.

"It's true, then," Tony commented.

"What is?"

"That you've lost your edge, that killer instinct you're

famous for. I have to admit I'm glad to see it. People said it'd happen when they learned you were married, but no one expected it to be this soon. Whoever took you on as a husband must be one heck of a woman."

Nash smiled to himself. "She is."

"It doesn't look like I'll be seeing you in court all that often."

"Probably not. I'm not taking on any new divorce cases."

"Dad, what an unexpected surprise," Savannah said, delighted that her father had decided to drop in at her store. He didn't visit often and his timing was perfect. She was about to take a break, sit down and rest her leg. "How's Mom?"

"Much better," he said, pulling out a chair as Savannah poured him a cup of coffee.

"Good."

"That's what I've come to talk to you about."

Savannah poured herself a cup and joined him. Her mother had made impressive progress in the past six weeks. Savannah called and visited often, and several times Nash had accompanied her. Joyce was growing stronger each day. She was often forgetful and that frustrated her, but otherwise she was recuperating nicely.

"I thought it'd be a good idea if I talked to you first," her father said.

"About what?"

"Your mother and I traveling."

It was the welcome news she'd been waiting to hear. At the same time it was the dreaded announcement that would end the happiest days of her life.

"I think you *should* travel. I always have."

"I was hoping to take your mother south. We might even look for a place to buy."

"Arizona," she suggested, raising the cup to her lips. "Mom's always loved the Southwest."

"The sunshine will do her good," her father agreed.

Savannah didn't know how she'd be able to pull this off, when she felt like she was dying on the inside. Over the years she'd become proficient at disguising her pain. Pain made others uncomfortable, so she'd learned to live with it.

"You wouldn't object to our going?" Her father didn't often sound hesitant but he did now.

"Of course I don't! I want you to travel and enjoy your retirement years. I've got Nash now, so there's no need to worry about me. None whatsoever."

"You're sure?"

"Dad! Go and enjoy yourselves," Savannah said and managed to laugh.

Three hours later, she sat in the middle of Nash's living room, staring aimlessly into space. All that was left now was the waiting—that, and telling him….

Nash got home shortly after six. His eyes were triumphant as he marched into the house. "Savannah," he said, apparently delighted to see her. "You didn't work late tonight."

"No," she responded simply.

He lifted her off the sofa as if she weighed nothing and twirled her around. "I had the most incredible day."

"Me, too."

"Good. We'll celebrate." Tucking his arm beneath her knees, he started for the bedroom. He stopped abruptly when he saw her suitcase sitting at the end of the hallway. His eyes were filled with questions as they met hers.

"Are you going somewhere?"

She nodded. "My parents have decided to take an extended trip south."

"So?"

"So, according to the terms of our marriage agreement, I'm moving back into my own home."

Thirteen

"You're moving out just like that?" Nash asked, lowering her feet to the ground. He stepped away from her as if he needed to put some distance between them. His eyes narrowed and he studied her, his expression shocked.

Savannah hadn't expected him to look at her like that. This was what they'd decided in the beginning, it was what he said he wanted after the first time they'd made love. She'd asked, wanting to be clear on exactly what her role in his life was to be, and Nash had said that making love changed nothing.

"This shouldn't come as a surprise," she said, struggling to keep her voice as even as possible.

"Is it what you want?" He thrust his hands deep inside his pockets and glared at her icily.

"Well?" he demanded when she didn't immediately answer.

"It doesn't matter what I think. I'm keeping my end of the bargain. What do you want me to do?"

Nash gave a nonchalant shrug of his shoulders. "I'm

not going to hold you prisoner here against your wishes, if that's what you're asking."

That *wasn't* what she was asking. She wanted some indication that he loved her and wanted her living with him. Some indication that he intended to throw out their stupid prenuptial agreement and make this marriage real. Apparently Nash wasn't interested.

"When are your parents leaving?"

"Friday morning, at dawn."

"So soon?"

She nodded. "Dad wanted to wait until Mom was strong enough to travel comfortably…and evidently she is now."

"I see." Nash wandered into the kitchen. "So you're planning to move out right away?"

"I…thought I'd take some clothes over to my house this evening."

"You certainly seem to be in a rush."

"Not really. I've managed to bring quite a few of my personal things here. I…imagine you'll want me out as quickly as possible." The smallest sign that he loved her would be enough to convince her to stay. A simple statement of need. A word. A look. Anything.

Nash offered nothing.

He opened the refrigerator and took out a cold soda, popping it open.

"I started dinner while I was waiting for you," she said. "The casserole's in the oven."

Nash took a long swallow of his soda. "I appreciate the effort, but I don't seem to have much of an appetite."

Savannah didn't, either. Calmly she walked over and turned off the oven. She stood with her back to Nash and bit her lip.

What a romantic fool she was, hoping the impossible would happen. She'd known when she agreed to marry him that it would be like this. He was going to break her heart. She'd tried to protect herself from exactly this, but it hadn't worked.

These past few weeks had been the happiest of her life and nothing he said now would take them away from her. He loved her, she knew he did, as much as it was possible for Nash to love anyone. He'd never said the words, but he didn't need to. She felt them when she slept in his arms. She experienced them each time they made love.

Her heart constricted with fresh pain. She didn't want to leave Nash, but she couldn't stay, not unless he specifically asked, and it was clear he had no intention of doing so.

She heard him leave the room, which was just as well since she was having a hard time not breaking into tears.

She was angry then. Unfortunately there wasn't a door to slam or anything handy to throw. Having a temper tantrum was exactly what she felt like doing.

Dinner was a waste. She might as well throw the whole thing in the garbage. Opening the oven door, she reached inside and grabbed the casserole dish.

Intense, unexpected pain shot through her fingers as she touched the dish.

She cried out and jerked her hand away. Stumbling toward the sink, she held her fingers under cold running water.

"Savannah?" Nash rushed into the kitchen. "What happened?"

"I'm all right," she said, fighting back tears by taking

deep breaths. If she was lucky, her fingers wouldn't blister, but she seemed to be out of luck lately.

"What happened?" Nash demanded again.

"Nothing." She shook her head, not wanting to answer him because that required concentration and effort, and all she could think of at the moment was pain. Physical pain. Emotional agony. The two were intermingled until she didn't know where one stopped and the other started.

"Let me look at what you've done," he said, moving close to her.

"No," Savannah said, jerking her arm away from him. "It's nothing."

"Let me be the judge of that."

"Leave me alone," she cried, sobbing openly now, her shoulders heaving. "Just leave me alone. I can take care of myself."

"I'm your husband."

She whirled on him, unintentionally splashing him with cold water. "How can you say that when you can hardly wait to be rid of me?"

"What are you talking about?" he shouted. "*I* wasn't the one who packed my bags and casually announced I was leaving. If you want to throw out questions, then you might start by asking yourself what kind of wife *you* are!"

Savannah rubbed her uninjured hand beneath her nose. "You claimed you didn't want a wife."

"I didn't until I married you." Nash opened the freezer portion of the refrigerator and brought out a tub of ice cubes. "Sit down," he said in tones that brooked no argument. She complied. He set the tub on the table and gently placed her burned fingers inside it. "The first couple of minutes will be uncomfortable, but after that you won't feel much," he explained calmly.

Savannah continued to sob.

"What did you do?" he asked.

"I was taking out the baking dish."

Nash frowned. "Did the oven mitt slip?"

"I forgot to use one," she admitted.

He took a moment to digest this information before kneeling down at her feet. His eyes probed hers and she lowered her gaze. Tucking his finger beneath her chin, he leveled her eyes to his.

"Why?"

"Isn't it obvious? I…was upset."

"About what?"

She shrugged, not wanting to tell him the truth. "These things happen and…"

"Why?" he repeated softly.

"Because you're an idiot," she flared.

"I know you're upset about me not wanting dinner, but—"

"Dinner?" she cried, incredulous. "You think this is because you didn't want dinner? How can any man be so dense?" She vaulted to her feet, her burned fingers forgotten. "You were just going to let me walk out of here."

"Wrong."

"Wrong? And how did you plan to stop me?"

"I figured I'd move in with you."

She blinked. "I beg your pardon?"

"You heard me. The agreement, as originally written, states that you'll move out of my premises after your parents decide to travel and you—"

"I know what that stupid piece of paper says," Savannah said, frowning.

"If you don't want to live with me, then it makes perfect sense for me to—"

"I *do* want to live with you, you idiot," she broke in. "I was hoping you'd do something—anything—to convince me to stay."

Nash was quiet for a few seconds. "Let me see if I have this straight. You were going to move out, although you didn't want to. Is that right?"

She nodded.

"Why?"

"Because I wanted you to *ask* me to stay."

"Ah, I understand now. You do one thing, hoping I'll respond by asking you to do the opposite."

She shrugged, realizing how silly it sounded in the cold light of reason. "I…guess so."

"Let this be a lesson to you, Savannah Davenport," Nash said, taking her in his arms. "If you want something, all you need to do is ask for it. If you'd simply sought my opinion, you'd have learned an important fact."

"Oh?"

"I'm willing to move heaven and earth to make sure we're together for the rest of our natural lives."

"You are?"

"In case you haven't figured it out yet, I'm in love with you." A surprised look must have come over her because he added, "You honestly didn't know?"

"I…prayed you were, but I didn't dare hope you'd admit it. I've been in love with you for so long I can't remember when I didn't love you."

He kissed her gently, his mouth coaxing and warm.

"Promise you won't ever stop loving me. I need you so badly. It wasn't until you were in my life that I saw how jaded I'd become. Taking on so many divorce cases didn't help my attitude any. I've made a decision that's due to your influence on me. When I graduated from law school, I specialized in tax and tax laws. I'm going back to that."

"Oh, Nash, I'm so pleased."

He kissed her with a hunger that left her weak and clinging.

"I can ask for anything?" she murmured between kisses.

"Anything."

"Throw away that stupid agreement."

He smiled boyishly and pressed his forehead against hers. "I already have…. The first night, after we made love."

"You might have told me!"

"I intended to when the time was right."

"And when did you calculate that to be?" she asked, having difficulty maintaining her feigned outrage.

"Soon. Very soon."

She smiled and closed her eyes. "But not soon enough."

"I had high hopes for us from the first. I opened my mouth and stuck my foot in it at the beginning by suggesting that ludicrous marriage-of-convenience idea. Marriage, the second time around, is a lot more frightening because you've already made one mistake."

"Our marriage isn't a mistake," she assured him. "I won't let it be."

"I felt that if I had control of the situation, I might

be able to control my feelings for you, but after Susan's wedding I knew that was going to be impossible."

"Why didn't you follow your own advice and ask how *I* felt?" she said, thinking of all the weeks they'd wasted.

"We haven't been on the best of terms, have we?" he murmured.

Savannah was embarrassed now by what a shrew she'd been. She slid her arms around his neck and kissed him soundly in an effort to make up for those first weeks.

"You said I can ask for anything I want?" she said against his lips.

"Hmm…anything," he agreed.

"I'd like a baby."

Nash's eyes flew open with undisguised eagerness. "How soon?"

"Well…I was thinking we could start on the project tonight."

A slow, lazy smile came into place. "That's a very good idea. Very good indeed."

Three years later…

"I can't believe the changes in Nash," Susan commented to Savannah. She and Kurt had flown up from California to spend the Christmas holiday with them this year. The two women were working in the kitchen.

"He's such a good father to Jacob," Savannah said, blinking back tears. She cried so easily when she was pregnant, and she was entering her second trimester with this baby. If the ultrasound was accurate, they were going to have a little girl.

"Nash is doing so well and so are you. But don't you miss working at the shop?"

"No, I've got a wonderful manager and you can imagine how busy a fourteen-month-old keeps me. I've thought about going back part-time and then decided not to, not yet at any rate. What about you? Will you continue teaching?" Savannah softly patted Susan's slightly distended stomach.

"No, but I'll probably work on a substitute basis to keep up my credentials so when our family's complete, I can return without a lot of hassle."

"That's smart."

"She's my sister, isn't she?" Nash said, walking into the kitchen, cradling his son in his arms. Jacob babbled happily, waving his rattle in every direction. He'd been a contented baby from the first. Their joy.

Kurt's arms surrounded his wife and he flattened his hands over her stomach. "We've decided to have our two close together, the same way you and Savannah planned your family."

Savannah and Nash exchanged smiles. "Planned?" she teased her husband.

"The operative word there is *two,*" Nash said, eyeing her suspiciously.

"Sweetheart, we've been over this a hundred times. I really would like four."

"Four!" Nash cried. "The last time we talked you said three."

"I've changed my mind. Four is a nice even number."

"Four children is out of the question," Nash said with a disgruntled look, then seemed to notice Kurt and Susan staring at him. "We'll talk about this later, all right? But we will talk."

"Of course we will," Savannah promised, unable to hold back a smile.

"She's going to do it," Nash grumbled to his sister and brother-in-law. "Somehow, before I've figured out how she's managed it, we'll be a family of six."

"You'll love it, Nash, I promise." The oven timer rang and Savannah glanced at the clock. "Oh, dear, I've got to get busy. Mr. Serle and Mr. Stackhouse will be here any minute."

"This is something else she didn't tell me before we were married," Nash said, his eyes shining with love. "She charms the most unexpected people...."

"They love Jacob," Savannah reminded him.

"True," Nash said wryly. "I've never seen two old men more taken with a toddler."

"And I've never seen a man more taken with his wife," Susan added. "I could almost be jealous, but there's no need." She turned to her husband and put her arms around his neck. "Still, it doesn't do any harm to keep him on his toes."

"No, it doesn't," Savannah agreed. And they all laughed.

* * * * *

LAUGHTER IN THE RAIN

One

"I'm so late. I'm so late."

The words were like a chant in Abby Carpenter's mind with every frantic push of the bike pedals. She was late. A worried glance at her watch when she paused at the traffic light confirmed that Mai-Ling would already be in Diamond Lake Park, wondering where Abby was. Abby should have known better than to try on that lovely silk blouse, but she'd seen it in the store's display window and couldn't resist. Now she was paying for the impulse.

The light turned green and Abby pedaled furiously, rounding the corner to the park entrance at breakneck speed.

Panting, she stopped in front of the bike stand and secured her lock around a concrete post. Then she ran across the lush green lawn to the picnic tables, where she normally met Mai-Ling. Abby felt a rush of relief when she spotted her.

Mai-Ling had recently immigrated to Minneapolis from Hong Kong. As a volunteer for the World Literacy

Movement, Abby was helping the young woman learn to read English. Mai-Ling caught sight of her and waved eagerly. Abby, who'd been meeting her every Saturday afternoon for the past two months, was impressed by her determination to master English.

"I'm sorry I'm late," Abby apologized breathlessly.

Mai-Ling shrugged one shoulder. "No problem," she said with a smile.

That expression demonstrated how quickly her friend was adapting to the American way of speaking—and life.

Mai-Ling started to giggle.

"What's so funny?" Abby asked as she slid off her backpack and set it on the picnic table.

Mai-Ling pointed at Abby's legs.

Abby looked down and saw one red sock and one that was blue. "Oh, dear." She sighed disgustedly and sat on the bench. "I was in such a rush I didn't even notice." No wonder the salesclerk had given her a funny look. Khaki shorts, mismatched socks and a faded T-shirt from the University of Minnesota.

"I am laughing with you," Mai-Ling said in painstaking English.

Abby understood what she meant. Mai-Ling wanted to be sure Abby realized she wasn't laughing *at* her. "I know," she said as she zipped open the backpack and took out several workbooks.

Mai-Ling sat opposite Abby. "The man's here again," she murmured.

"Man?" Abby twisted around. "What man?"

Abby couldn't believe she'd been so unobservant. She felt a slight twinge of apprehension as she looked at the stranger. There was something vaguely familiar about him, and that bothered her. Then she remembered—he was the same man she'd seen yesterday afternoon at the grocery store. Had he been following her?

The man turned and leaned against a tree not more than twenty feet away, giving her a full view of his face. His tawny hair gleamed in the sunshine that filtered through the leaves of the huge elm. Beneath dark brows were deep-set brown eyes. Even from this distance Abby could see their intense expression. His rugged face seemed to be all angles and planes. He was attractive in an earthy way that would appeal to a lot of women and Abby was no exception.

"He was here last week," Mai-Ling said. "And the week before. He was watching you."

"Funny, I don't remember seeing him," she murmured, unable to disguise her discomfort.

"He is a nice man, I think. The animals like him. I am not worried about him."

"Then I won't worry, either," Abby said with a shrug as she handed Mai-Ling the first workbook.

In addition to being observant, Mai-Ling was a beautiful, sensitive and highly intelligent woman. Sometimes she became frustrated with her inability to communicate, but Abby was astonished at her rapid progress. Mai-Ling had mastered the English alphabet in only a few hours and was reading Level Two books.

A couple of times while Mai-Ling was reading a story about a woman applying for her first job, Abby's attention drifted to the stranger. She watched in astonishment as he coaxed a squirrel down the trunk of the tree. He pulled what appeared to be a few peanuts from his pocket and within seconds the squirrel was eating out of his hand. As if aware of Abby's scrutiny, he stood up and sauntered lazily to the nearby lakeshore. The instant he appeared, the ducks squawked as though recognizing an old friend. The tall man took bread crumbs from a sack he carried and fed them. Lowering himself to a crouch, he threw back his head and laughed.

Abby found herself smiling. Mai-Ling was right; this man had a way with animals—and women, too, if her pounding heart was anything to judge by.

A few times Mai-Ling faltered over a word, and Abby paused to help her.

The hour sped by, and soon it was time for the young woman to meet her bus. Abby walked Mai-Ling to the busy street and waited until she'd boarded, cheerfully waving to Abby from the back of the bus.

Pedaling her bicycle toward her apartment, Abby's thoughts again drifted to the tall, good-looking stranger. She had to admit she was enthralled. She wondered if he was attracted to her, too, since apparently he came to the park every week while she was there. But maybe she wasn't the one who attracted him; perhaps it was Mai-Ling. No, she decided. Mai-Ling had noticed the way the handsome stranger studied Abby. He was interested in *her*. Great, she mused contentedly; Logan Fletcher could do with some competition.

Abby pulled into the parking lot of her low-rise apartment building and climbed off her bike. Automatically she reached for her backpack, which she'd placed on the rack behind her, to get the apartment keys. Nothing. Surprised, Abby turned around to look for it. But it wasn't there. Obviously she'd left it at the park. Oh, no! She exhaled in frustration and turned, prepared to go and retrieve her pack.

"Looking for this?" A deep male voice startled Abby and her heart almost dropped to her knees. The bike slipped out from under her and she staggered a few steps before regaining her balance.

"Don't you know better than to sneak up on someone like that? I could have…" The words died on her lips as she whirled around to face the stranger. With her mouth hanging half open she stared into the deepest brown eyes she'd ever seen—the man from the park.

Her tongue-tied antics seemed to amuse him, but then it could have been her mismatched socks. "You forgot this." He handed her the backpack. Speechless, Abby took it and hugged it to her stomach. She felt grateful…and awkward. She started to thank him when another thought came to mind.

"How'd…how'd you know where I live?" The words sounded slightly scratchy, and she cleared her throat.

He frowned. "I've frightened you, haven't I?"

"How'd you know?" She repeated the question less aggressively. He hadn't scared her. If anything, she felt a startling attraction to him, to the sheer force of his masculinity. Logan would be shocked. For that matter, so was she. But up close, this man was even more appealing than he'd been at a distance.

"I followed you," he said simply.

"Oh." A thousand confused emotions dashed through her mind. He was so good-looking that Abby couldn't manage another word.

"I didn't mean to scare you," he said, regret in his voice.

"You didn't," she hurried to assure him. "I have an overactive imagination."

Shaking his head, he thrust his hands into his pants pockets. "I'll leave before I do any more damage."

"Please don't apologize. I should be thanking you. There's a Coke machine around the corner. Would you like to—"

"I've done enough for one day." Abruptly he turned to go.

"At least tell me your name." Abby didn't know where the request came from; it tumbled from her lips before she'd even formed the thought.

"Tate." He tossed it over his shoulder as he stalked away.

"Bye, Tate," she called as he opened his car door. When he glanced her way, she lifted her hand. "And thanks."

A smile curved his mouth. "I like your socks," he returned.

Pointedly she looked down at the mismatched pair. "I'm starting a new trend," she said with a laugh.

Standing beside her bike, Abby waited until Tate had driven away.

Later that night, Logan picked her up and they had hamburgers, then went to a movie. Logan's obligatory good-night kiss was…pleasant. That was the only way Abby could describe it. She had the impression that Logan kissed her because he always kissed her good-night. To her dismay, she had to admit that there'd never been any driving urgency behind his kisses. They'd been dating almost a year and the mysterious Tate was capable of stirring more emotion with a three-minute conversation than Logan had all evening. Abby wasn't even sure why they continued to date. He was an accountant whose office was in a building near hers. They had many of the same friends, and did plenty of things together, but their relationship was in a rut. The time had come to add a little spice to her life and Abby knew exactly where that spice would be coming from....

After Logan had left, Abby settled into the overstuffed chair that had once belonged to her grandfather, and picked up a new thriller she'd bought that week.

Dano, her silver-eyed cat, crawled into her lap as Abby opened the book. Absently she stroked the length of his spine. Her hand froze in midstroke as she discovered the hero's name: Logan. Slightly unnerved, she dropped the book and jumped up from her chair to look for the remote. Turning on the TV, she told herself she shouldn't feel guilty because she felt attracted to another man. The first thing she saw on the screen was a commercial for Logan Furniture's once-a-year sofa sale. Abby stared at the flashing name and hit the off button. This was crazy! Logan wouldn't care if she was interested in someone else. He might even be grateful. Their relationship was based on friendship and had progressed to romance, a romance that was more about routine than passion. If Abby *was* attracted to another man, Logan would be the first to step aside. He was like that—warm, unselfish, accommodating.

Her troubled thoughts on Saturday evening were only the beginning. Tate dominated every waking minute, which just went to prove how limited her social life really was. She liked Logan, but Abby longed for some excitement. He was so staid—yes, that was the word. *Staid.* Solid as a rock, and about as imaginative.

Logan came over to her apartment on Sunday afternoon, which was no surprise. He always came over on Sunday afternoons. They usually did something together, but never anything very exciting. More often than not Abby went over to his house and made dinner. Sometimes they watched a DVD. Or they played a game of backgammon, which he generally won. During the summer they'd ride their bikes, some of their most pleasant dates had been spent in Diamond Lake Park. Logan would lie on the grass and rest his head in her lap while she read whatever thriller or mystery she was currently devouring.

They'd been seeing each other so often that the last time they had dinner at her parents', Abby's father had suggested it was time they thought about getting married. Abby had been mortified. Logan had laughed and changed the subject. Later, her mother had tactfully reminded Abby that he might not be the world's most exciting man, but he was her best prospect. However, Abby couldn't see any reason to rush into marriage. At twenty-six, she had plenty of time.

"I thought we'd bike around the park," Logan said.

The day was gloriously sunny and although Abby wished Logan had proposed something more inventive, the idea *was* appealing. She enjoyed the feel of the breeze in her hair and the sense of exhilaration that came with rapid movement.

"Hi!" Abby and Logan were greeted by Patty Martin just inside the park's boundaries. "How's it going?"

"Fine," Logan answered for them as they braked to a stop. "How about you?"

Patty had recently started to work in the same office building as Logan, which was how Abby had met her. Although Abby didn't know her well, she'd learned that Patty was living with her sister. They'd talked briefly at lunch one day, and Abby had invited her to join an office-league softball team she and Logan had played in last summer.

"I'm fine, too," Patty answered shyly and looked away.

In some ways she reminded Abby of Mai-Ling, who hadn't said more than a few words to her the first couple of weeks they'd worked together. Only as they came to know each other did Mai-Ling blossom. Abby herself had never been shy. The world was her friend, and she felt certain Patty would soon be comfortable with her, too.

"I can't talk now. I saw you and just wanted to say hello. Have fun, you two," Patty murmured and hurried away.

Confused, Abby watched her leave. The girl looked like a frightened mouse as she scurried across the grass. The description was more than apt. Patty's drab brown hair was pulled back from her face and styled unattractively. She didn't wear makeup and was so shy it was difficult to strike up a conversation.

After biking around the lake a couple of times, they stopped to get cold drinks. As they rested on a park bench, Logan slipped an affectionate arm around

Abby's shoulders. "Have I told you that you look lovely today?"

The compliment astonished Abby; there were times she was convinced Logan didn't notice anything about her. "Thank you. I might add that you're looking very good yourself," she said with twinkling eyes, then added, "but I won't. No need for us both to get conceited."

Logan smiled absently as they walked their bikes out of the park. His expression was oddly distant; in some ways he hadn't been himself lately, but she couldn't put her finger on anything specific.

"Do you mind if we cut our afternoon short?" he asked unexpectedly.

He didn't offer an explanation, which surprised Abby. They'd spent most Sunday afternoons together for the past year. More surprising—or maybe not, considering her recent boredom with Logan—was the fact that Abby realized she didn't care. "No, that shouldn't be any problem. I've got a ton of laundry to do anyway."

Back at her apartment, Abby spent the rest of the afternoon doing her nails, feeling lazy and ignoring her laundry. She talked to her mother on the phone and promised to stop by sometime that week. Abby had been on her own ever since college. Her job as receptionist at an orthopedic clinic had developed with time and specialized training into a position as an X-ray technician. The advancement had included a healthy pay increase—enough to start saving for a place of her own. In the meanwhile, she relished her independence, enjoying her spacious ground-floor apartment, plus the satisfactions of her job and her volunteer work.

* * *

Several times over the next few days, Abby discovered herself thinking about Tate. Their encounter had been brief, but had left an impression on her. He was the most exciting thing that had happened to her in months.

"What's the matter with you?" Abby admonished herself. "A handsome man gives you a little attention and you don't know how to act."

Dano mewed loudly and weaved between her bare legs, his long tail tickling her calves. It was the middle of June and the hot summer weather had arrived.

"I wasn't talking to you." She leaned over to pet the cat. "And don't tell me you're hungry. I know better."

"Meow."

"You've already had your dinner."

"Meow. Meow."

"Don't you talk to me in that tone of voice. You hear?"

"Meow."

Abby tossed him the catnip mouse he loved to hurl in the air and chase madly after. Logan had gotten it for Dano. With his nose in the air, the cat ignored his toy and sauntered into Abby's room, jumping up to sit on the windowsill, his back to her. He ignored Abby, obviously pining after whatever he could see outside. In some obscure way, Abby felt that she was doing the same thing to Logan and experienced a pang of guilt.

Since it was an older building, the apartments didn't have air-conditioning, so Abby turned on her large fan. Then, settling in the large overstuffed chair, she draped one leg over the arm and munched on an apple as she read. She was so engrossed in her thriller that when she glanced at her watch, she gasped in surprise. Her Tuesday evening painting class was in half an hour and Logan would arrive in less than fifteen minutes. He was always punctual, and although he seldom said anything, she could tell by the set of his mouth that he disliked it when she was behind schedule.

The "I'm late, I'm late" theme ran through her mind as she vaulted out of the chair, changed pants and rammed her right foot into her tennis shoe without untying the lace. Whipping a brush through her long brown hair, she searched frantically for the other shoe.

"It's got to be here," she told the empty room frantically. "Dano," she cried out in frustration. "Did you take my shoe?"

She heard a faint indignant "meow" from the bedroom.

On her knees she crawled across the carpet, desperately tossing aside anything in her path—a week-old newspaper, a scarf, a CD case, the mismatched pair of socks she'd worn last Saturday and a variety of other unimportant things.

She bolted to her feet when her apartment buzzer went off. Logan must be early.

She automatically let him into the building, threw open her door—and saw *Tate* standing in the hallway.

Abby felt the hot color seep up from her neck. He *would* come now, when she wasn't prepared and looking her worst.

He approached her apartment. "Hello," he said, staring down at her one bare foot. "Missing something?"

"Hello again." Her voice sounded unnaturally high. She bit her lip and tried to smile. "My shoe's gone."

"Walked away, did it?"

"You might say that. It was here a few minutes ago. I was reading and…" She dropped to her knees and lifted the skirting around the chair. There, in all its glory, was the shoe.

"Find it?" He was still in the doorway.

"Yes." She sat on the edge of the cushion and jerked her foot into the shoe.

"It might help if you untied the laces," he said, watching her with those marvelous eyes.

"I know, but I'm in a hurry." With her heel crushing the back of the shoe, Abby hobbled over to the door. "Come on in." She closed it behind him. "I'm—"

"Abby."

"Yes. How did you know?"

"I heard your friend say it at the park. And when I got to the lobby, I asked one of your neighbors." He frowned. "You should identify your guests before you let them in, you know."

"I know. I will. But I—was expecting someone else and…" Her words drifted off.

Smiling, he offered her his hand. "Tate Harding," he said.

A tingling sensation slipped up her arm at his touch.

Tate's hand was callused and rough from work. She successfully restrained her desire to turn it over and examine the palm. His handsome face was tanned from exposure to the elements. Tate was handsome, compellingly so.

"It looks as if I came at an inconvenient time."

"Oh, no," she hurried to assure him. She noticed that he'd released his grip, although she continued to hold her hand in midair. Self-consciously she lowered it to her side. "Sit down," she said, motioning toward her favorite chair. The hot color in her face threatened to suffocate her with its intensity.

Tate sat and lazily crossed his legs, apparently unaware of the effect he had on her.

Abby was shocked by her own reaction. She'd dated a number of men. She was neither naive nor stupid. "Would you like something to drink?" she asked as she hastily retreated to the kitchen, not waiting for his answer. Pausing, she frantically prayed that for once, just once, Logan would be late. No sooner had the thought formed than she heard the apartment buzzer again. This time she listened to her speaker.

"Abby?"

Logan. Abby hesitated, but let him in.

Tate had stood and opened the door by the time she turned around. Logan had arrived. When he stepped inside, the two men eyed each other skeptically. A slight scowl drew Logan's brows together.

"Logan, this is Tate Harding. Tate, Logan Fletcher." Abby flushed uncomfortably and darted an apologetic look at them both.

"I thought we had a class tonight." Logan spoke somewhat defensively.

"This is my fault," Tate said, his gaze resting on Abby's face and for one heart-stopping moment on her softly parted lips. "I dropped by unexpectedly."

Logan's mouth thinned with displeasure and Abby pulled her eyes from Tate's. Logan had never been the jealous type, but then he'd never had reason or opportunity to reveal that side of his nature. Still, it surprised her. Abby hadn't considered this a *serious* relationship. It was more of a companionable one. Logan had understood and accepted that, or so she'd thought.

"I'll come back another time," Tate suggested. "You've obviously got plans with Logan."

"We're taking classes together," Abby rushed to explain. "I'm taking painting and Logan's studying chess. We drive there together, that's all."

Tate's smile was understanding. "I won't keep you, then."

"Nice to have met you," Logan stated, sounding as if he meant exactly the opposite.

Tate turned back and nodded. "Perhaps we'll meet again."

Logan nodded briskly. "Perhaps."

The minute Tate left Abby whirled around to face Logan. "That was so rude," she whispered fiercely. "For heaven's sake—you were acting like you owned me... like I was your property."

"Think about it, Abby," Logan said just as forcefully, also in a heated whisper. His dark eyes narrowed as he stalked to the other side of the room. "We've been dating exclusively for almost a year. I assumed that you would've developed some loyalty. I guess I was mistaken."

"Loyalty? Is that all our relationship means to you?" she demanded.

Logan didn't answer her. He walked to the door and held it open, indicating that if she was coming she needed to do it now. Silently Abby followed him through the lobby and into the parking lot.

The entire way to the community center they sat

without speaking. The hard set of Logan's mouth indicated the tight rein he had on his temper. Abby forced her expression to remain haughtily cold.

They parted in the hallway, Logan taking the first left while Abby continued down the hall. A couple of the women she'd become friends with greeted her, but Abby had difficulty responding. She took twice as long as normal setting up her supplies.

The class, which was on perspective, didn't go well, since Abby's attention kept returning to the scene with Logan and Tate. Logan was obviously jealous. He'd revealed more emotion in those few minutes with Tate than in the past twelve months. Logan tended to be serious and reserved, while she was more emotional and adventurous. They were simply mismatched. Like her socks—one red, one blue. Logan had become too comfortable in their relationship these last months, taking too much for granted. The time had come for a change, and after tonight he had to recognize that.

After class they usually met in the coffee shop beside the center. Logan was already in a booth when she arrived there.

Wordlessly, Abby slipped into the seat across from him. Folding her hands on the table, she pretended to study her nails, wondering if Logan was ever going to speak.

"Why are you so angry?" Abby finally asked. "I hardly know Tate. We only met a few days ago."

"How many times have you gone out with him?"

"None," Abby said righteously.

"But not because you turned him down." Logan shook his head grimly. "I saw the way you looked at him, Abby. It was all you could do to keep from drooling."

"That's not true," she denied vehemently—and realized he was probably right. She'd never been good at hiding her feelings. "I admit I find him attractive, but—"

"But what?" Logan taunted softly. "But you had this old boyfriend you had to get rid of first?" The hint of a smile touched his mouth. "And I'm not referring to my age." He was six years older than Abby. "I was pointing out that we've been seeing each other two or three times a week and suddenly you're not so sure how you feel about me."

Abby opened, then closed her mouth. She couldn't argue with what he'd said.

"That's it, isn't it?"

"Logan." She said his name on a sigh. "I like you. You know that. Over the past year I've grown very... fond of you."

"Fond?" He spat the word at her. "One is *fond* of cats or dogs—not men. And particularly not me."

"That was a bad choice of words," Abby agreed.

"You're not exactly sure what you feel." Logan said, almost under his breath.

Abby's fingers knotted until she could feel the pain in her hands. Logan was right; she *didn't* know. She was attracted to Tate, but she knew nothing about him. The problem was that she liked what she saw. If her feelings for Logan were what they should be after a year, she wouldn't want Tate to ask her out so badly.

"You aren't sure, are you?" Logan said again.

She hung her head so that her face was framed by her dark hair. "I don't want to hurt you," she murmured.

"You haven't." Logan's hand reached across the table and squeezed her fingers reassuringly. "Beyond anything else, we're friends and I don't want to do anything to upset that friendship because it's important to me."

"That's important to me, too," she said and offered him a feeble smile. Their eyes met as the waitress came and turned over the beige cups and filled them with coffee.

"Do you want a menu?"

Abby couldn't have eaten anything and shook her head.

"Not tonight. Thanks, anyway," Logan answered for both of them.

"I don't deserve you," Abby said after the waitress had moved to the next booth.

For the first time all night Logan's lips curved into a genuine smile. "That's something I don't want you to forget."

For a few minutes they sipped their coffee in thoughtful silence. Holding the cup with both hands, she studied him. Logan's eyes were as brown as Tate's. Funny she hadn't remembered how brown they were. Tonight the color was intense, deeper than ever. They made quite a couple; she was so emotional—and he wasn't. Abby noticed that Logan's jaw was well-defined. Tate's jaw, although different, revealed that same quality— determination. With Logan, Abby recognized there was nothing he couldn't do if he wanted. Instinctively she knew the same was true of Tate.

She sensed that there were definite similarities

between Logan and Tate, and yet she was reacting to them in different ways.

It seemed unfair that a man she'd seen only a couple of times could affect her like this. If she fell madly in love with someone, it should be Logan.

"What are you thinking about?" His words broke into her troubled thoughts.

Abby shrugged. "Oh, this and that," she said vaguely.

"You didn't even add sugar to your coffee."

Abby grimaced. "No wonder it tastes so awful."

Chuckling, he handed her the sugar canister.

Pouring some onto her spoon, Abby stirred it into her coffee. Logan had a nice mouth, she reflected. She couldn't remember thinking that in a long time. She had when they'd first met, but that was nearly two years ago. She watched him for a moment, trying to figure him out. Logan was so—Abby searched for the right word—sensible. Nothing ever seemed to rattle him. There wasn't an obstacle he couldn't overcome with cool reason. For once, Abby wanted him to do something crazy and nonsensical and fun.

"Logan." She spoke softly, coaxingly. "Let's drive to Des Moines tonight."

He looked at her as if she'd lost her mind. "Des Moines, Iowa?"

"Yes. Wouldn't it be fun just to take off and drive for hours—and then turn around and come home?"

"That's not fun, that's torture. Anyway, what's the point?"

Abby pressed her lips together and nodded. She shouldn't have asked. She'd known his answer even before he spoke.

The ride home was as silent as the drive to class. The tension wasn't nearly as great, but it was still evident.

"I have the feeling you're angry," Logan said as he parked in front of her building. "I'm sorry that spending the whole night on the road doesn't appeal to me. I've got this silly need for sleep. From what I understand, it affects older people."

"I'm not angry," Abby said firmly. She felt disappointed, but not angry.

Logan's hand caressed her cheek, curving around her neck and directing her mouth to his. Abby closed her eyes, expecting the usual feather-light kiss. Instead, Logan pulled her into his arms and kissed her soundly. Deeply. Passionately. Surprised but delighted, Abby groaned softly, liking it. Her hands slipped over his shoulders and joined at the base of his neck.

Logan had never kissed her with such intensity, such unrestrained need. His mouth moved over hers, and Abby sucked in a startled breath as pure sensation shot through her. When he released her, she sighed longingly and rested her head against his chest. Involuntarily, a picture of Tate entered her mind. This was what she'd imagined kissing *him* would be like....

"You were pretending I was Tate, weren't you?" Logan whispered against her hair.

Two

"Oh, Logan, of course I wasn't," Abby answered somewhat guiltily. She *had* thought of Tate, but she hadn't pretended Logan's kiss was Tate's.

He brushed his face along the side of her hair. Abby was certain he wanted to say something more, but he didn't, remaining silent as he climbed out of the car and walked around to her side. She smiled weakly as he offered her his hand. Logan could be such a gentleman. She was perfectly capable of getting out of a car by herself, but he always wanted to help. Abby supposed she should be grateful—but she wasn't. Those old-fashioned virtues weren't the ones that really mattered to her.

Lightly, he kissed her again outside her lobby door. Letting herself in, Abby was aware that Logan waited on the other side until he heard her turn the lock.

After changing into her long nightgown, Abby went into the kitchen and poured a glass of milk. She sat at the small round table and placed her feet on the edge of a chair, pulling her gown over her knees. Did she love Logan? The answer came almost immediately. Although he'd taken offense, "fond" had aptly described her feelings. She liked Logan, but Tate had aroused far more emotion during their short acquaintance. Downing the milk, Abby turned off the light and miserably decided to go to bed. Dano joined her, purring loudly as he arranged himself at her feet.

Friday evening, she begged off when Logan invited her to a movie, saying she was tired and didn't feel well. He seemed to accept that quite readily. And, in fact, she watched a DVD at home, by herself, and was in bed by ten, reading a new mystery novel, with Dano stretched out at her side.

Saturday afternoon, Abby arrived at the park a half-hour early, hoping Tate would be there and they'd have a chance to talk. She hadn't heard from him and wondered if he'd decided Logan had a prior claim to her affection. However, Tate didn't seem the type who'd be easily discouraged. She found him in the same spot as last week and waved happily.

"I was hoping you'd be here," she said eagerly and sat on the grass beside him, leaning her back against the massive tree trunk.

"My thoughts exactly," Tate replied, with a warm smile that elevated Abby's heart rate.

"I'm sorry about Logan," she told him, weaving her fingers through the grass.

"No need to apologize."

"But he was so rude," Abby returned, feeling guilty for being unkind. But she'd said no less to Logan himself.

Tate sent her a look of surprise. "He didn't behave

any differently than I would have, had the circumstances been reversed."

"Logan doesn't own me," she said defiantly.

A smile bracketed the edges of his mouth. "That's one piece of news I'm glad to hear."

Their eyes met and he smiled. Abby could feel her bones melt. It was all she could do to smile back.

"Do you like in-line skating?"

"I love it." She hadn't skated since she was a teen at the local roller rink, but if Tate suggested they stand on their heads in the middle of the road, Abby probably would have agreed.

"Would you like to meet me here tomorrow afternoon?"

"Sure," she said without hesitating. "Here?" she repeated, sitting up.

"You *have* skated?" He gave her a worried glance.

"Oh, sure." Her voice squeaked, embarrassing her. "Tomorrow? What time?"

"Three," Tate suggested. "After that we'll go out for something to eat."

"This is sounding better all the time," Abby teased. "But be warned, I do have a healthy appetite. Logan says—" She nearly choked on the name, immediately wishing she could take it back.

"You were saying something about Logan," Tate prompted.

"Not really." She gave a light shrug, flushing involuntarily.

Mai-Ling stepped off the bus just then and walked toward them. Abby stood up. Brushing the grass from her legs, she smiled warmly at her friend.

"Why do you meet her every week?" Tate asked. The teasing light vanished from his eyes

"I do volunteer work with the World Literacy Movement. Mai-Ling can read perfectly in Chinese, but she's an American now so I'm helping her learn to read and write English."

"Have you been a volunteer long?"

"A couple of years. Why? Would you like to help? We're always looking for volunteers."

"Me?" He looked stunned and a little shocked. "Not now. I've got more than I can handle helping at the zoo."

"The zoo?" Abby shot back excitedly. "Are you a volunteer?"

"Yes," Tate said as he stood and glanced at his watch. "I'll tell you more about it tomorrow. Right now I've got to get back to work before the boss discovers why I've taken extended lunch breaks the past four Saturdays."

"I'll look forward to tomorrow," Abby murmured, thinking she'd never known anyone as compelling as Tate.

"You met the man?" Mai-Ling asked as she came over to Abby's side and followed her gaze to the retreating male figure.

"Yes, I met him," Abby answered wistfully. "Oh, Mai-Ling, I think I'm in love!"

"Love?" Mai-Ling frowned. "The American word for love is bad."

"Bad?" Abby repeated, not comprehending.

"Yes. In English one word means many kinds of love."

Abby turned her attention from Tate to her friend and asked, "What do you mean?"

"In America, love for a husband is the same as...
as love for chocolate. I heard a lady on the bus say she
loves chocolate, then say she is in love with a new man."
Mai-Ling shook her head in astonishment and disbelief.
"In Chinese it is much different. Better."

"No doubt you're right," Abby said with a bemused
grin. "I guess it's all about context."

Mai-Ling ignored that. "You will see the man again?"

"Tomorrow," Abby said dreamily. Suddenly her eyes
widened. Tomorrow was Sunday, and Logan would
expect her to do something with him. Oh dear, this
was becoming a problem. Not only hadn't she skated
in years, but she was bound to have another uncomfortable confrontation with Logan. Her eager anticipation
for tomorrow was quickly replaced by a sinking feeling
in the pit of her stomach.

Abby spent another miserable night. She'd attempted
to phone Logan and make up another excuse about not
being able to get together, but he hadn't been home. She
didn't feel it was right to leave a message, which struck
her as cowardly. Consequently her sleep was fitful and
intermittent. It wasn't as if Logan called and arranged
a time each week; they had a simple understanding that
Sundays were *their* day. Arrangements for most other
days were more flexible. But Abby couldn't remember
a week when they hadn't gotten together on a Sunday.
Her sudden decision would be as readable as the morning headlines. Logan would know she was meeting Tate.

Abby's first inclination was not to be there when he
arrived, but that was even more cowardly. In addition,
Abby knew Logan well enough to realize that her attempts to dodge him wouldn't work. Either he'd go to

the park and look for her or he'd drive to her parents' house and worry them sick.

By the time he did arrive, Abby's stomach felt as if a lead balloon had settled inside.

"Beautiful afternoon, isn't it?" Logan came over to her and slipped an arm around her waist, drawing her close to his side. "Are you feeling better?" he asked in a concerned voice. So often in the past year, Abby had longed for him to hold her like this. Now when he did, she wanted to scream with frustration.

"Yes, I'm…okay."

"What would you like to do?" he asked, nuzzling her neck and holding her close.

"Logan." Abby hesitated, and cleared her throat, feeling guilty. "I've got other plans this afternoon." Her voice didn't even sound like her own as she squeezed her eyes shut, afraid to meet his hard gaze.

A grimness stole into his eyes as his hand tightened. "You're seeing Tate, aren't you?"

Abby caught her breath at the ferocity of his tone. "Of course not!" She couldn't look at him. For the first time in their relationship, Abby was blatantly lying to Logan. No wonder she was experiencing this terrible guilt. For one crazy minute, Abby felt like bursting into tears and running out of the apartment.

"Tell me what you're doing then," he demanded.

Abby swallowed at the painful lump in throat. "Last week you cut our time together short," she said. "I didn't ask where you were going. I don't feel it's too much to expect the same courtesy."

Logan's grip on her waist slackened, but he didn't

release her. "What about later? Couldn't we meet for dinner? There's something I wanted to discuss."

"I can't," she said quickly. Too quickly. Telltale color warmed her face.

Logan studied her for a long moment, then dropped his arm. She should've been glad. Instead she felt chilled and suddenly bereft.

"Let me know when you're free." His words were cold as he moved toward the door.

"Logan," Abby called out to him desperately. "Don't be angry. Please."

When he paused and turned around, his eyes flickered over her. She couldn't quite read his expression but she knew it wasn't flattering. Wordlessly, he turned again and left.

Abby wanted to crawl into a hole, curl up and die. Logan deserved so much better than this. Any number of women would call her a fool—and they'd be right.

Dressed in white linen shorts and a red cotton shirt, Abby studied her reflection in the full-length mirror on the back of the bedroom door. Her hair hung in a long ponytail, practical for skating, she figured. Makeup did little to disguise the doubt and unhappiness in her eyes. With a jagged breath, Abby tied the sleeves of a sweater around her neck and headed out the door.

Tate was standing by the elm tree waiting for her. He was casually dressed in jeans and a V-neck sweater that hinted at curly chest hair. Even across the park, Abby recognized the quiet authority of the man. His virile look attracted the attention of other women in the vicinity, but Tate didn't seem to notice.

He started walking toward her, his smile approving as he surveyed her long legs.

"You look like you've lost your best friend," Tate said as he slid a casual arm around her shoulder.

Abby winced; his comment might be truer than he knew.

"Problem?" he asked.

"Not really." Her voice quavered, but she managed to give him a broad smile. "I'm hoping we can rent skates. I don't have a pair."

"We can."

It didn't take long for Tate's infectious good mood to brighten Abby's spirits. Soon she was laughing at her bungling attempts to skate. A concrete pathway was very different from the smooth, polished surface of the rink. Either that, or it'd been longer than she realized since her last time on skates.

Tate tucked a hand around her hip as his movements guided hers.

"You're doing great." His eyes were smiling as he relaxed his grasp.

Laughing, Abby looked away from the pathway to answer him when her skate hit a rut and she tumbled forward, wildly thrashing her arms in an effort to remain upright. She would have fallen if Tate hadn't still been holding her. His hand tightened, bringing her closer. She faltered a bit from the effect of his nearness.

"I'm a natural," she said with a grin.

"A natural klutz," he finished for her.

They skated for two hours. When Tate suggested they stop, Abby glanced at her watch and was astonished by the time.

"Hungry?" Tate asked next.

"Famished."

The place Tate took her to was one of those relatively upscale restaurants that charged a great deal for its retro diner atmosphere, but where the reputation for excellent food was well-earned. Abby couldn't imagine Logan bringing her someplace like this. Knowing that made the outing all the more enticing.

When the waitress came, Abby ordered an avocado burger with a large stuffed baked potato and strawberry shortcake for dessert.

Tate smiled. "I'll have the same," he told the waitress, who wrote down their order and stepped away from the table.

"So you do volunteer work at the zoo?" Abby was interested in learning the details he'd promised to share with her.

"I've always loved animals," he began.

"I could tell from the way you talked to the ducks and the squirrels," Abby inserted, recalling the first time she'd seen Tate.

He acknowledged her statement with a nod. "Even as a child I'd bring home injured animals—rabbits, raccoons, squirrels—and do what I could to make them well."

"Why didn't you become a veterinarian?"

Tate ignored the question. "The hardest part was setting them free once they were well. I might have been a veterinarian if things in my life had gone differently, but I'm good with cars, too."

"You're a mechanic?" Abby asked, already knowing

the answer. The callused hands told her that her guess couldn't be far off.

"I work at Bessler's Auto Repair."

"Sure. I know it. That's across the street from the Albertsons' store."

"That's it."

So it *had* just been a coincidence that she'd seen Tate in the store; he worked in the immediate vicinity.

"I've been working there since I was seventeen," Tate added. "Jack Bessler is thinking about retirement these days."

"What'll happen to the shop?"

"I'm hoping to buy it," Tate said as he held his fork, nervously rotating it between two fingers.

Tate was uneasy about something. He ran his fingers up and down the fork, not lifting his gaze from his silverware.

Their meal was as delicious as Abby knew it would be. Whatever had bothered Tate was soon gone and the remainder of the evening was spent talking, getting to know each other with an eagerness that was as strong as their mutual attraction. They talked nonstop for hours, sauntering lazily along the water's edge and laughing, neither of them eager to bring their time together to a close.

When Abby finally got home it was nearly midnight. She floated into the apartment on a cloud of happiness. Even as she readied for bed, she couldn't forget how wonderful the night had been. Tate was a man she could talk to, really talk to. He listened to her and seemed to understand her feelings. Logan listened, too, but Abby had the impression that he sometimes felt impatient with her. But perhaps that wasn't it at all. Maybe she was looking for ways to soothe her conscience. His reaction today still shocked her; as far as she was concerned, they hadn't made any commitment to each other beyond that of friendship. Sometimes Abby wondered if she really knew Logan.

The phone rang fifteen minutes after she was in the door.

Assuming it was Tate, Abby all but flew across the room to answer it, not bothering to check call display. "Hello," she said in a low, sultry voice.

"Abby, is that you? You don't sound right. Are you sick?"

It was Logan.

Instantly, Abby stiffened and sank into the comfort of her chair. "Logan," she said in her normal voice. "Hi. Is something wrong?" He wouldn't be phoning this late otherwise.

"Not really."

"I just got in…I mean…" She faltered as her thoughts tripped over each other. "I thought you might be in bed, so I didn't call," she finished lamely. He was obviously phoning to find out what time she got home.

Deftly Logan changed the subject to a matter of no importance, confirming Abby's suspicions. "No," he said, "I was just calling to see what time you wanted me to pick you up for class on Tuesday."

Of all the feeble excuses! "Next time I go somewhere without you, do you want me to phone in so you'll know the precise minute I get home?" she asked crisply, fighting her temper as her hand tightened around the receiver.

His soft chuckle surprised her. "I guess I wasn't very original, was I?"

"No. This isn't like you, Logan. I've never thought of you as the jealous type."

"There's a lot you don't know about me," he answered on a wry note.

"I'm beginning to realize that."

"Do you want me to pick you up for class this week, or have you…made other arrangements?"

"Of course I want you to pick me up! I wouldn't want it any other way." Abby meant that. She liked Logan. The problem was she liked Tate, too.

Logan hesitated and the silence stretched between them. Abby was sure he could hear her racing heart over the phone. But she hoped he couldn't read the confusion in her mind.

After work on Monday afternoon, instead of heading back to her apartment and Dano, Abby stopped off at her parents' house.

"Hi, Mom." She sauntered into the kitchen and kissed her mother on the cheek. "What's there to eat?" Opening the refrigerator door, Abby surveyed the contents with interest.

"Abby," her mother admonished, "what's wrong?"

"Wrong?" Abby feigned ignorance.

"Abby, I'm your mother. I know you. The only time you show up in the middle of the week is if something's bothering you."

"Honestly, aren't I allowed an unexpected visit without parental analysis?"

"Did you and Logan have a fight?" her mother persisted.

Glenna Carpenter's chestnut hair was as dark as Abby's but streaked with gray, creating an unusual color a hairdresser couldn't reproduce. Glenna was a young sixty, vivacious, outgoing and—like Abby—a doer.

"What makes you say that? Logan and I never fight." Abby chewed on a stalk of celery and closed the refrigerator. Taking the salt from the cupboard beside the stove she sprinkled some on it.

"Salt's bad for your blood pressure." Glenna took the shaker out of Abby's hand and replaced it in the cupboard. "Are you going to tell me what's wrong?" She spoke in a warning tone that Abby knew better than to disregard.

"Honest, Mom, there's nothing."

"Abby." Sapphire-blue eyes snapped with displeasure.

Abby couldn't hold back a soft laugh. Her mother had a way of saying more with one glare than some women did with a tantrum.

Holding the celery between her teeth, Abby placed both hands on the counter and pulled herself up, sitting beside the sink.

"Abby," her mother said a second time.

"It's Logan." She gave a frustrated sigh. "He's become so possessive lately."

"Well, thank goodness. I'd have thought you'd be happy." Glenna's smiling eyes revealed her approval. "I was wondering how long it would take him."

"Mother!" Abby wanted to cry. Deep in her heart,

she'd known her mother would react like this. "It's too late—I've met someone else."

Glenna froze and a shocked look came over her. "Who?"

"His name is Tate Harding."

"When?"

"A couple of weeks ago."

"How old is he?"

Abby wanted to laugh at her mother's questions. She sounded as if Abby was fifteen again and asking for permission to date. "He's twenty-seven and a hardworking, respectable citizen. I don't know how to explain it, Mom, but I was instantly attracted to him. I think I'm falling in love."

"Falling in love," Glenna echoed, reheating the day's stale coffee and pouring herself a cup. Her hand shook as she lifted the mug to her mouth a couple of minutes later.

Abby knew her mother was taking her seriously when she drank coffee, which she usually reserved for mornings. A smile tugged at Abby's mouth, but she successfully restrained it.

"I know what you must be thinking," Abby said. "You don't even have to say it because I've already chided myself a thousand times. Logan's the greatest man in the world, but Tate is—"

"The ultimate one?"

The suppressed smile came to life. "You could say that."

"Does Logan know?"

"Of all the luck, they ran into each other at my apartment last week. It would've helped if they hadn't met like that."

"I think having Logan and Tate stumble into each other was more providential than you realize," Glenna murmured with infuriating calm. "I've always liked Logan. I think he's perfect for you."

"How can you *say* that?" Abby demanded indignantly. "We aren't anything alike. We don't even enjoy the same things. Logan can be such a stuffed shirt. And you haven't even met Tate."

"No." Her mother ran the tip of one finger along the rim of her mug. "To be honest, I could never understand why Logan puts up with you. I love you, Abby, but I know your faults as well as your strengths. Apparently Logan sees the same potential in you that I do."

"I can't believe my own mother would talk to me like this." Abby spoke to the ceiling, venting her irritation. "I come to her to pour out my heart and seek her advice and end up being judged."

Glenna laughed. "I'm not judging you," she declared. "Just giving you some sound, motherly advice." An ardent light glowed from her eyes. "Logan loves you. He—"

"Mother," Abby interrupted. "How can you be so sure? If he does, which I sincerely doubt, then he's never told me."

"No, I don't imagine he has. Logan is waiting."

"Waiting?" Abby asked sarcastically. "For what? A blue moon?"

"No," Glenna said sharply and took a long, deliberate sip of her coffee, which must have tasted foul. "He's been waiting for you to grow up. You're impulsive and quick-tempered, especially when it comes to relationships. You expect him to take the lead and yet you resent him for it."

Abby gasped; she couldn't help it. Rarely had her mother spoken this candidly to her. Abby opened her mouth to deny the accusations, then closed it again. The words hurt, especially coming from her own mother, and she lowered her gaze to hide the onrush of emotional pain. Tears gathered in her eyes.

"I'm not saying these things to hurt you," Glenna continued softly.

"I know that." Abby grimaced. "You're right. I should be more honest, but I don't want to hurt Logan."

"Then tell him what you're feeling. Stringing him along would be unkind."

"But it's hard," Abby protested, wiping her eyes. "If I told him yesterday that I was going out with Tate he would've been angry. And miserable."

"And do you suppose he wasn't? I know Logan. If you said anything to him, he'd immediately step aside until you've settled things in your own mind."

"I know," Abby breathed in frustration. "But I'm not sure I want that either."

"You mean you want to have your cake and eat it, too," Glenna said. "As the old cliché has it…"

"I never have understood that saying."

"Then maybe you'd better think about it, Abby."

"In other words you're telling me I should let Logan know how I feel about Tate."

"Yes. You can't have it both ways. You can't keep Logan hanging if you want to pursue a romance with this other man."

The seriousness of her mother's look, her words, transferred itself to Abby.

"Today," Glenna insisted. "Now, before you change your mind."

Slowly Abby nodded. She hopped down from the counter, prepared to talk to Logan. "Thanks, Mom."

Glenna Carpenter gave Abby a motherly squeeze. "I'll be thinking about you."

"You'll like Tate."

"I'm sure I will. You always did have excellent taste."

Abby's smile was tentative.

She knew Logan was working late tonight, so she drove straight to his accounting firm, which was situated half a block from her own office. Karen, his assistant, had gone home, and Abby knocked at the outer office. Almost instantly the door opened and Logan gestured her inside.

"Abby." He beamed her a warm smile. "What a nice surprise. Come in, won't you."

Abby took the leather chair opposite his desk.

"Logan." Her fingers had knotted into a tight fist in her lap. "Can we talk?"

He looked down at his watch.

"It won't take long, I promise," she added hurriedly.

Leaning against the side of his desk, he crossed his arms. "What is it, Abby? You never look this serious about anything."

"I think you have a right to know that I was with Tate Harding yesterday." Her heart was hammering wildly as she said this.

"Abby, you're as readable as a child. I was aware

from the beginning who you were with," he told her. "I only wish that you'd been honest with me."

"Oh, Logan, I do apologize for that."

"Fine. It's forgotten."

How could he be so generous? So forgiving? Just when she was about to explain that she wanted to continue seeing Tate, Logan reached for her, drawing her into his embrace. As his mouth settled over hers, he drew from her a response so complete that Abby was left speechless and all the more confused. He kissed her as if he couldn't get enough of her mouth, of *her*.

"I've got a client meeting in five minutes," Logan whispered as he massaged her shoulders. "But believe me, holding you is far more appealing. Promise me you'll drop by the office again."

Then he let her go, and she sank back into the chair.

Three

Abby punched the pillow and determinedly shut her eyes. She shouldn't be having so much trouble falling asleep, she thought, fighting back a loud yawn. Ten minutes later, she wearily raised one eyelid and glared at the clock radio. Two-thirty! She groaned audibly. Logan was responsible for this. He should've taken the time to listen to her. Now she didn't know when she'd work up the courage to talk to him about Tate.

And speaking of Tate… He'd phoned after dinner and suggested going to the zoo that weekend. Abby couldn't refuse him. Now she was paying the price—remorse and self-recrimination. Worse, it was all Logan's fault that she hadn't been able to explain the situation to him. She didn't mean to do anything behind his back. She liked both men, but the attraction she felt toward Tate was far more intense than the easy camaraderie she shared with Logan.

Bunching the pillow, Abby forced her eyes to close. She'd gone to Logan to tell him she wanted to date other men. She'd tried, really tried. What else could she do?

When the radio went off at six, Abby wanted to scream. Sleep had eluded her the entire night. The few hours she'd managed to catch wouldn't be enough to see her through the day. Her eyes burned as she tossed aside the covers and sat on the edge of the bed.

More from habit than anything, Abby brushed her teeth and dressed. Coffee didn't help. And the tall glass of orange juice tasted like tomato, but she didn't open her eyes to investigate.

Half an hour later, she let herself into the clinic. The phone was already ringing.

"Morning." Cheryl Hansen, the receptionist, smiled at Abby before answering the call.

Abby returned the friendly gesture with a weak smile of her own.

"You look like the morning after a wild and crazy night," Cheryl said as Abby hung her jacket in the room off the reception area.

"It was wild and crazy, all right," Abby said after an exaggerated yawn. "But not the way you think."

"Another late night with Logan?"

Abby's eyes widened. "No!"

"Tate then?"

"No. Unfortunately."

"I'm telling you, Ab, keeping track of your love life is getting more difficult all the time."

"I haven't got a love life," she murmured, unable to stop yawning. Covering her mouth, Abby moved to the end of the long hallway.

The day didn't get any better. By noon, she recognized that she couldn't possibly attend tonight's class with Logan. For one thing, she was too tired to concentrate on painting theory and technique. For another, as soon as he saw her troubled expression, he'd know immediately that she was deceiving him and seeing Tate again. And something she didn't need today was another confrontation with Logan. She didn't want to hurt him. But more than that—she didn't want to lie to him.

On her way back from lunch, Abby decided to call his office. Her guilt grew heavier at the pleasure in his voice.

"Abby! What's up?"

"Hi, Logan." She groaned inwardly. "I hope you don't mind me phoning you like this."

"Not at all."

"I'm not feeling well." She paused, her hand tightening around the receiver. "I was thinking that maybe it'd be best if I skipped class tonight."

"What's wrong?" His genuine concern was nearly her undoing. "You weren't well on Friday, either."

Did he really believe her excuse of Friday evening, which had been nothing but a way of avoiding him?

"You must be coming down with something," he said.

"I think so." *Like a terminal case of cowardice,* her mind shot back.

"Have you seen a doctor?"

"It isn't necessary. Not yet. But I thought I'd stay home again tonight and go to bed early," Abby mumbled, feeling more wretched every second.

"Do you need me to do anything for you?" His voice was laced with gentleness.

"No," she assured him quickly. "I'm fine. Really.

I just thought I'd nip this thing in the bud and take it easy."

"Okay. But promise me that if you need anything, you'll call."

"Oh, sure."

Abby felt even worse after making that phone call. By the time she returned to her apartment late that afternoon her excuse for not attending her class had become real. Her head was throbbing unmercifully; her throat felt dry and scratchy and her stomach was queasy.

With her fingertips pressing her temple, Abby located the aspirin in the bathroom cabinet and downed two tablets. Afterward she lay on the sofa, the phone beside her, head propped up with a soft pillow, and closed her eyes. She didn't open them when the phone rang and she scrabbled around for it blindly.

"Hello." Her reluctant voice was barely above a whisper.

"Abby, is that you?"

She breathed easier. It was her mother.

"Hi, Mom."

"What's wrong?"

"I've got a miserable headache."

"What's bothering you?"

"What makes you think anything's bothering me?" Her mother displayed none of the sympathy Logan had.

"Abby, I know you. When you get a headache it's because something's troubling you."

Breathing deeply, Abby glanced at the ceiling with wide-open eyes, unable to respond.

"Did you talk to Logan yesterday?" Her mother resumed the interrogation.

"Only for a little while. He was on his way to a meeting."

"Did you tell him you want to continue seeing Tate?"

"I didn't get the chance," Abby said more aggressively than she'd intended. "Mom, I tried, but he didn't have time to listen. Then Tate phoned me and asked me out this weekend and...I said yes."

"Does Logan know?"

"Not yet," she mumbled.

"And you've got a whopper of a headache?"

"Yes." The word trembled on her lips.

"Abby." Her mother's voice took on the tone Abby knew all too well. "You've *got* to talk to Logan."

"I will."

"Your headache won't go away until you do."

"I know."

Dano strolled into the room and leaped onto the sofa, settling in Abby's lap. Grateful to have one friend left in the world, Abby stroked her cat.

It took her at least twenty minutes to work up enough fortitude to call Logan's home number. His phone rang six times, and Abby sighed, not leaving a message. She assumed he'd gone to class on his own, that he was on his way, so she didn't bother trying his cell. She'd talk to him tomorrow.

She closed her eyes again, wondering how—if— she could balance her intense attraction to Tate with her feelings of friendship for Logan. Friendship that sometimes hinted at more. His ardent kiss yesterday had taken her by surprise. But she *had* to tell him about Tate....

The apartment buzzer woke Abby an hour later. She sat up and rubbed the stiff muscles of her neck. Dano remained on her lap and meowed angrily when she stood, forcing the cat to leap to the floor.

"Yes?" she said into the speaker.

"It's Logan."

Abby buzzed him in. Her hand was shaking visibly as she unlocked the door. "Hi," she said in a high-pitched voice.

Logan stepped inside. "How are you feeling?"

"I don't know." She yawned, stretching her arms. "Better, I guess." Her attention was drawn to a white sack Logan was holding. "What's that?"

A crooked smile slanted his mouth. "Chicken soup. I picked some up at the deli." He handed her the bag. "I want to make sure you're well enough for the game tomorrow night."

Abby's head shot up. "Game? What game?"

"I wondered if you'd forgotten. We signed up a couple of weeks ago for the softball team. Remember?"

This was the second summer they were playing in the office league. With her recent worries, softball had completely slipped Abby's mind. "Oh, *that* game." Abby wanted to groan. She'd *never* be able to avoid Logan. Too many activities linked them together—work, classes and now softball.

She took the soup into the kitchen, removing the large plastic cup from the sack. The aroma of chicken and noodles wafted through the small room. Logan followed her in and slipped his arms around her waist from behind. His chin rested on her head as he spoke. "I woke you up, didn't I?"

She nodded, resisting the urge to turn and slip her arms around his waist and bury her face in his chest. "But it's probably a good thing you did. I've gotten a crick in my neck sleeping on the couch with Dano on my lap."

Logan's breath stirred the hair at the top of her head. The secure feeling of his arms holding her close was enough to bring tears to her eyes.

"Logan." She breathed his name in a husky murmur. "Why are you so good to me?"

He turned her to face him. "I would've thought you'd have figured it out by now," he said as he slowly lowered his mouth to hers.

A sweetness flooded Abby at the tender possession of his mouth. She wanted to cry and beg him *not* to love her. Not yet. Not until she was sure of her feelings. But the gentle caress of his lips prevented the words from ever forming. Her hands moved up his shirt and over his shoulders, reveling in his strength.

His hands, at the small of her back, arched her closer as he inhaled deeply. "I've got to go or I'll be late for class. Will you be all right?"

Speaking was impossible and it was almost more than Abby could do to simply nod her head.

He straightened, relaxing his grip. "Take care of yourself," he said as his eyes smiled lovingly into hers.

Again it was all Abby could do to nod.

"I'll pick you up tomorrow at six-thirty, if you're up to it. We can grab a bite to eat after the game."

"Okay," she managed shakily and walked him to the door. "Thanks for the soup."

Logan smiled. "I've got to take care of the team's first-base player, don't I?" His mouth brushed hers and he was gone.

Leaning against the door, Abby looked around her grimly. If she felt guilty before, she felt wretched now.

Shoving the baseball cap down on her long brown hair, which she'd tied back in a loose ponytail, Abby couldn't stifle a sense of excitement. She did enjoy softball. And Logan was right—she was the best first-base player the team was likely to find. Not to mention her hitting ability.

Logan wasn't as good a player but enjoyed himself as much as she did. He just didn't have the same competitive edge. More than once he'd been responsible for an error. But no one seemed to mind and Abby didn't let it bother her.

As usual he was punctual when he came to pick her up. "Hi. I can see you're feeling better."

"Much better."

The game was scheduled to be played in Diamond Lake Park, and Abby was half-afraid Tate would stumble across them. She wasn't sure how often he went into the park and— She reined in her worries. There was no reason to assume he'd show up or that he'd even recognize her.

Most of the team had arrived by the time Abby and Logan sauntered onto the field. The Jack and Jill Softball League was recreational. Of all their team members, Abby was the one who took the game most seriously. The team positions alternated between men and women. Since Abby played first base, a man was at second. Logan was in the outfield.

The team they were playing was from a local church that Abby remembered having beaten last summer.

Dick Snyder was their office team's coach and strategist. "Hope that arm's as good as last year," Dick said to Abby, who beamed at him. It was gratifying to be appreciated.

After a few warm-up exercises and practice pitches, their team left the field. Logan was up at bat first. Abby cringed at the stiff way he held himself. He wasn't a natural athlete, despite his biking prowess.

"Logan," she shouted encouragingly, "flex your knees."

He did as she suggested and swung at the next pitch. The ground ball skidded past the shortstop and Logan was safe on first.

Abby breathed easier and sent him a triumphant smile.

Patty Martin was up at bat next. Abby took one look at the shy, awkward young woman and knew she'd be an immediate out. Patty was new to the team this year, and Abby hoped she'd stick with it.

"Come on, Patty," she called out, hoping to instill some confidence, "you can do it!"

Patty held the bat clumsily and bit her lip as she glared straight ahead at the pitcher. She swung at the first three balls and missed each one.

Dick pulled Patty aside and gave her a pep talk before she took her place on the bench.

Abby hurried over to Patty and patted her knee. "I'm

glad you decided to play with us." She meant that honestly. She suspected Patty could do with some friends.

"But I'm terrible." Patty stared at her clenched hands and Abby noticed how white her knuckles were.

"You'll improve," Abby said with more certainty than she felt. "Everyone has to learn, and believe me, every one of us strikes out. Don't worry about it."

By the time Abby was up to bat, there were two outs and Logan was still at first. Her standup double and a home run by the hitter following her made the score 3-0.

It remained the same until the bottom of the eighth. Logan was playing the outfield when a high fly ball went over his head. He scrambled to retrieve it.

Frantically jumping up and down at first base, Abby screamed, "Throw the ball to second! Second." She watched in horror as Logan turned and faced third base. "Second!" she yelled angrily.

The woman on third base missed the catch, and the batter went on to make it home, giving his team their first run.

Abby threw her glove down and, with her hands placed defiantly on her hips, stormed into the outfield and up to Logan. "I told you to throw the ball to second."

He gave her a mildly sheepish look. "Sorry, Abby. All your hysterics confused me."

Groaning, Abby returned to her position.

They won the game 3-1 and afterward gathered at the local restaurant for pizza and pitchers of beer.

"You're really good," Patty said, sitting beside Abby.

"Thanks," she said, smiling into her beer. "I was on

the high-school team for three years, so I had lots of practice."

"I don't know if I'll ever learn."

"Sure you will," Logan insisted. "Besides, we need you. Didn't you notice we'd be one woman short if it wasn't for you?"

Abby hadn't noticed that, but was pleased Logan had brought it up. This quality of making people feel important had drawn Abby to him on their first date.

"I'm awful, but I really like playing. And it gives me a chance to know all of you better," Patty added shyly.

"We like having you," Abby confirmed. "And you *will* improve." Patty seemed to want the reassurance that she was needed and appreciated, and Abby didn't mind echoing Logan's words.

They ate their pizzas and joked while making plans for the game the following Wednesday evening.

Dick Snyder and his wife gave Patty a ride home. Patty hesitated in the parking lot. "Bye, Abby. Bye, Logan," she said timidly. "I'll see you soon."

Abby smiled secretly to herself. Patty was attracted to Logan. She'd praised his skill several times that evening. Abby didn't blame her. Logan was wonderful. True, he wasn't going to be joining the Minnesota Twins any year soon—or ever. But he'd made it to base every time he was up at bat.

Logan dropped Abby off at her apartment, but didn't accept her invitation to come in for a glass of iced tea. To be honest, Abby was grateful. She didn't know how much longer she could hide from Logan that she was continuing to see Tate. And she refused to lie if he asked her. She planned to tell him soon…as soon as an appropriate opportunity presented itself.

The remainder of the week went smoothly. She didn't talk to Logan, which made things easier. Abby realized that Sunday afternoon with him would be difficult after spending Saturday with Tate, but she decided to worry about it then.

She woke Saturday morning with a sense of expectation. Tate was taking the afternoon off and meeting her in the park after she'd finished tutoring Mai-Ling. From there they were driving out to Apple Valley and the Minnesota Zoo where he did volunteer work.

She wore a pale pink linen summer dress and had woven her long brown hair into a French braid. A glance in the mirror revealed that she looked her best.

Mai-Ling met her and smiled knowingly. "You and Tate are seeing each other today?"

"We're going to the zoo."

"The animal place, right?"

"Right."

Abby's attention drifted while Mai-Ling did her lesson. The woman's ability was increasing with every meeting. Judging by the homework Mai-Ling brought for Abby to examine, the young woman wouldn't be needing her much longer.

They'd finished their lesson and were laughing when Abby looked up and saw Tate strolling across the lawn toward her.

Again she was struck by the sight of this ruggedly appealing male. He was dressed in jeans, a tight-fitting T-shirt and cowboy boots.

His rich brown eyes seemed to burn into hers. "Hello,

Abby." He greeted Mai-Ling, but his eyes left Abby's only for a second.

"I'll catch my bus," said Mai-Ling, excusing herself, but Abby barely noticed.

"You're looking gorgeous today," Tate commented, taking her hand in his.

A tingling sensation shot up her arm at his touch. Her nerves felt taut just from standing beside him. Abby couldn't help wondering what kissing Tate would be like. Probably the closest thing to heaven this side of earth.

"You seem deep in thought."

Abby smiled up at him. "Sorry. I guess I was."

They chatted easily as Tate drove toward Apple Valley. Abby learned that he'd been a volunteer for three years, working at the zoo as many as two days a week.

"What animals do you care for?"

Tate answered her without taking his eyes off the road. "Most recently I've been working with a llama for the Family Farm, but I also do a lot of work with birds. In fact, I've been asked to assist in the bird show."

"Will you?" Abby remembered seeing Tate that first day with the ducks....

"Yes."

"What other kinds of things do you do?"

Tate's returning smile was quick. "Nothing that glamorous. I help at feeding time and I clean the cages. Sometimes I groom and exercise the animals."

"What are you doing with the llama?"

"Mostly I've been working to familiarize him with people. We'd like Larry to join his brother in giving children rides."

Tate parked the car and came around to her side to open the passenger door. He kept her hand tucked in his as he led the way to the entrance.

"You love it here, don't you?" Abby asked as they cleared the gates.

"I do. The zoo gives us a rare opportunity to discover nature and our relationship to other living things. We have a responsibility to protect animals, as well as their habitats. Zoos, good zoos like this, are part of that." A glint of laughter flashed in his eyes as he turned toward her. "I didn't know I could be so profound."

Someone called out to Tate, and Abby watched him respond with a brief wave.

"Where would you like to start?"

The zoo was divided into five regions and Abby chose Tropics Trail, an indoor oasis of plants and animals from Asia.

As they walked, Tate explained what they were seeing, regaling her with fascinating bits of information. She'd been to the zoo before, but she'd never had such a knowledgeable guide.

Three hours later, it was closing time.

"Promise you'll bring me again," Abby begged, her eyes held by Tate's with mesmerizing ease.

"I promise," he whispered as he led her toward his car.

The way he said it made her feel weak in the knees, made her forget everything and everyone else. She lapsed into a dreamy silence on the drive home.

Tate drove back to Minneapolis and they stopped at a Mexican restaurant near Diamond Lake Park. Abby had passed it on several occasions but never eaten there.

A young Hispanic waitress smiled at them and led them to a table.

Tate spoke to the woman in Spanish. She nodded her head and turned around.

"What did you ask?" Abby whispered.

"I wanted to know if we could eat outside. You don't mind, do you? The evening is lovely."

"No, that sounds great." But she did mind. Because it immediately occurred to her that Logan might drive past and see her eating there with Tate. Abby managed to squelch her worries as she sat down at a table on the patio and opened her menu. She studied its contents, but her appetite had unexpectedly disappeared.

"You've got that thoughtful look again," Tate remarked. "Is everything okay, Abby?"

"Oh, sure," she said.

Abby decided what she'd order and took the opportunity to watch Tate as he reviewed the menu. His brow was creased, his eyes narrowed in concentration. When he happened to glance up and found her looking at him he set the menu aside.

An awkwardness followed. It continued until the waitress finally stopped at their table. Abby ordered cheese enchiladas and a margarita; Tate echoed her choice but asked for a Corona beer. "I had a good time today," Abby said in an attempt to breach the silence after the waitress left.

"I did, too." Tate sounded stiff, as if he suddenly felt uneasy.

"Is something wrong?" Abby asked after another silence.

It could have been Abby's imagination, but she sensed that Tate was struggling within himself.

"Tate?" she prompted.

He leaned forward and pinched the bridge of his nose before exhaling loudly. "No...nothing."

Long after he'd dropped her off at the apartment, Abby couldn't shake the sensation that something was troubling him. Twice he'd seemed about to speak, but both times he'd stopped himself.

Abby's thoughts were heavy as she drifted into sleep. Tomorrow she'd be spending the afternoon with Logan. She had to tell him she'd decided to see Tate; delaying it any longer was a grave disservice to them both—to Logan *and* to Tate.

Sunday afternoon, Logan sat on the sofa beside Abby and reached for her hand. She had to force herself not to snatch it away. So often in the past Abby had wanted Logan to be more demonstrative. And now that he was, it caused such turmoil inside her that she wanted to cry.

"You're looking pale, Abby. Are you sure you're feeling all right?" he asked her, his voice concerned.

"Logan, I've got to talk to you," she blurted out miserably. "I need to—"

"What you need is to get out of this stuffy apartment." He stood up, bringing her with him. Slipping an arm around her waist, Logan directed her out of the apartment and to his car.

Abby didn't have time to protest as he opened the door. She climbed inside and he leaned across to fasten her seat belt.

"Where are we going?" she asked, confused and unhappy as he backed out of the parking area.

"For a drive."

"I don't want to go for a drive."

Logan glanced away from the road long enough to narrow his eyes slightly at her. "Abby, what is it? You look like you're about to cry."

"I am." She swallowed convulsively and bit her bottom lip. "I want to go back to the apartment."

Logan pulled over and cut the engine. "Abby, what's wrong?" he asked solicitously.

Abby got out and leaned against the side of the car. The blood was pounding wildly in her ears. She hugged her waist with both arms.

"Abby?" he prompted softly as he joined her.

"I tried to tell you on Monday evening," she said. "I even went to your office, but you had some stupid meeting."

He didn't argue with her. "Is this about Tate?"

"Yes!" she shouted. "I went to the zoo with him yesterday. All week I've felt guilty because I know you don't want me to see anyone except you."

Abby chanced a look at him. He displayed no emotion, his eyes dark and unreadable. "Do you want to continue seeing him?" he asked carefully.

"I like Tate. I've liked him from the time we met," Abby admitted in a low whisper. "I don't know him all that well, but—"

"You want to get to know him better?" His eyes seemed to draw her toward him like a magnet.

"Yes," she whispered, gazing up at him.

"Then you should," he said evenly.

"Oh, Logan," she breathed. "I was hoping you'd understand."

"I do, Abby." He placed his hands deep inside his pants pockets and walked around the car, opening the passenger door.

"Where are we going?"

He looked mildly surprised. "I'm taking you home."

The smile that touched the corners of his mouth didn't reach his eyes. "Abby, if you're seeing Tate, you won't be seeing me."

Four

Shocked, Abby stared at him, and her voice trembled slightly. "What do you mean?"

"Isn't it obvious?" Logan turned toward her. His eyes had darkened and grown more intense. There was an almost imperceptible movement along his jaw. "Remind me. How long have we been dating?" he asked, but his voice revealed nothing.

"You know how long we've been dating. About a year now. What's that got to do with anything?"

Logan frowned. "If you don't know how you feel about me in that length of time, then I can't see continuing a relationship."

Abby clenched her fist, feeling impotent anger well up within her. "You're trying to blackmail me, aren't you?"

"Blackmail you?" Logan snapped. He paused and breathed in deeply. "No, Abby, that isn't my intention."

"But you're saying that if I go out with Tate, then I can't see you," she returned with a short, bitter laugh.

"You're not being fair. I like you both. You're wonderful, Logan, but…but so is Tate."

"Then decide. Which one of us do you want?"

Logan made it sound so simple. "I can't." She inhaled a shaky breath and raked a weary hand through her hair. "It's not that easy."

"Do you want Tate and me to slug it out? Is that it? Winner takes the spoils?"

"No!" she cried, shocked and angry.

"You've got the wrong man if you think I'll do that."

Tears spilled from Abby's eyes. "That's not what I want, and you know it."

"Then what *do* you want?" The low question was harsh.

"Time. I…I need to sort through my feelings. When did it become a crime to feel uncertain? I barely know Tate—"

"Time," Logan interrupted, but the anger in his tone didn't seem directed at her. "That's exactly what I'm giving you. Take as long as you need. When you've decided what you feel, let me know."

"But you won't see me?"

"Seeing you will be unavoidable. Our offices are half a block apart—and we have the softball team."

"Classes?"

"No. There's no need for us to go together or to meet each other there."

Tilting her chin downward, Abby swiped at her tears, trying to quell the rush of hurt. Logan could remove her from his life so effortlessly. His apparent indifference pierced her heart.

Without a word, he drove her back to the apartment building and parked, but didn't shut off the engine.

"Before you go," Abby said, her voice quavering, "would you hold me? Just once?"

Logan's hand tightened on the steering wheel until his knuckles were strained and white. "Do you want a comparison? Is that it?" he asked in a cold, stiff voice.

"No, that wasn't what I wanted." She reached for the door handle. "I'm sorry I asked."

Logan didn't move. They drew each breath in unison. Unflinching, their eyes held each other until Logan, his clenched jaw, hard and proud, became a watery blur and Abby lowered her gaze.

"Call me, Abby. But only when you're sure." The words were meant as a dismissal and the minute she was out of his car, he drove away.

Abby's knees felt so weak, she sat down as soon as she got inside her apartment. She was stunned. She'd expected Logan to be angry, but she'd never expected *this*—that he'd refuse to see her again. She'd only tried to be fair. Hurting Logan, or Tate for that matter, was the last thing she wanted. But how could she possibly know what she felt toward Tate? Everything was still so new. As she'd told Logan, they barely knew each other. They hadn't so much as kissed. But she and Logan were supposed to be friends....

She moped around the house for a couple of hours, then thought she'd pay her parents a visit. Her mother would be as shocked at Logan's reaction as she'd been. Abby needed reassurance that she'd done the right thing, especially since nothing had worked out as she'd hoped.

The short drive to her parents' house was accomplished

in a matter of minutes. But there was no response to her knock; her parents appeared to be out. Belatedly, Abby recalled her mother saying that they were going camping that weekend.

Abby slumped on the front steps, feeling enervated and depressed. Eventually she returned to her car, without any clear idea of where she should go or what she should do.

Never had a Sunday been so dull. Abby drove around for a time, picked up a hamburger at a drive-in and washed her car. Without Logan, the day seemed empty.

Lying in bed that night, Dano at her feet, Abby closed her eyes. If she'd missed Logan, he must have felt that same sense of loss. This could work both ways. Logan would soon discover how much of a gap she'd left in *his* life.

The phone rang Monday evening and Abby glanced at it anxiously. It had to be Logan, she thought hopefully. Who else would be calling? She didn't recognize the number, so maybe he had a new cell, she told herself.

"Hello," she said cheerfully. If it *was* Logan, she didn't want him to get the impression that she was pining away for him.

"Abby, it's Tate."

Tate. An unreasonable sense of disappointment filled her. What was the matter with her? This whole mess had come about because she wanted to be with Tate.

"How about a movie Friday evening?"

"I'd like that." She exhaled softly.

"You don't sound like yourself. Is something wrong?"

"No," she denied quickly. "What movie would you like to see?"

They spoke for a few more minutes and Abby managed to steer the conversation away from herself. For those few minutes, Tate helped her forget how miserable she was, but the feelings of loss and frustration returned the moment she hung up.

Tuesday evening, Abby waited outside the community center hoping to see Logan before class. She planned to give him a regal stare that would show how content she was without him. Naturally, if he gave any hint of his own unhappiness, she might succumb and speak to him. But either he'd arrived before her or after she'd gone into the building, because Abby didn't catch a glimpse of him anywhere. Maybe he'd even skipped class, but she doubted that. Logan loved chess.

The painting class remained a blur in her mind as she hurried out the door to the café across the street. She'd met Logan there after every class so far. He'd come; Abby was convinced of it. She pictured how their eyes would meet and intuitively they'd know that being apart like this was wrong for them. Logan would walk to her table, slip in beside her and take her hand. Everything would be there in his eyes for her to read.

The waitress gave Abby a surprised glance and asked if she was sitting alone tonight as she handed her the menu. Dejectedly Abby acknowledged that she was alone…at least for now.

When Logan entered the café, Abby straightened, her heart racing. He looked as good as he always did. What she didn't see was any outward sign of unhappiness…or relief at her presence. But, she reminded herself, Logan wasn't one to display his emotions openly. Their eyes met and he gave her an abrupt nod before sliding into a booth on the opposite side of the room.

So much for daydreams, Abby mused. Well, fine, he could sit there all night, but she refused to budge. Logan would have to come to her. Determinedly she studied the menu, pretending indifference. When she couldn't stand it any longer, she glanced at him from the corner of her eye. He now shared his booth with two other guys and was chatting easily with his friends. Abby's heart sank.

"I'm telling you, Mother," Abby said the next afternoon in her mother's kitchen. "He's blown this whole thing out of proportion."

"What makes you say that?" Glenna Carpenter closed the oven door and set the meat loaf on top of the stove.

"Logan isn't even talking to me."

"It doesn't seem like there's been much opportunity. But I wouldn't worry. He will tonight at the game."

"What makes you so sure of that?" Abby hopped down from her position on the countertop.

Glenna straightened and wiped her hands on her ever-present terry cloth apron. "Things have a way of working out for the best, Abby," she continued nonchalantly.

"Mom, you've been telling me that all my life and I've yet to see it happen."

Glenna chuckled, slowly shaking her head. "It happens every day of our lives. Just look around." Deftly she turned the meat loaf onto a platter. "By the way, didn't you say your game's at six o'clock?"

Abby nodded and glanced at her watch, surprised that the time had passed so quickly. "Gotta rush. Bye, Mom." She gave her mother a peck on the cheek. "Wish me well."

"With Logan or the game?" Teasing blue eyes so like her own twinkled merrily.

"Both!" Abby laughed and was out the door.

Glenna followed her to the porch, and Abby felt her mother's sober gaze as she hurried down the front steps and to her car.

Almost everyone was on the field warming up when Abby got there. Immediately her gaze sought out Logan. He was in the outfield pitching to another of the male players. Abby tried to suppress the emotion that charged through her. Who would've believed she'd feel so lost and unhappy without Logan? If he saw that Abby had arrived, he gave no indication.

"Hi, Abby," Patty called, waving from the bench.

Abby smiled absently. "Hi."

"Wait until you see me bat." Patty beamed happily, pretending to swing at an imaginary pitch. Then, placing her hand over her eyes as the fantasy ball flew into left field, she added, "I think I'll be up for an award by the end of the season."

"Good." Abby was preoccupied as she stared out at Logan. He looked so attractive. So vital. Couldn't he have the decency to develop some lines at his eyes or a few gray hairs? He *had* to be suffering. She was, although it wasn't what she'd wanted or expected.

"Logan took me to see the Twins play on Monday night and he gave me a few pointers afterward," Patty continued.

Abby couldn't believe what she was hearing. *A few pointers? I'll just bet he did!* Logan and Patty?

The shock must have shown in her eyes because Patty added hurriedly, "You don't mind, do you? When Logan phoned, I asked him about the two of you and he said you'd both decided to start seeing other people."

"No, I don't mind," Abby returned flippantly, remembering her impression last week—that Patty had a crush on him. "Why should I?"

"I…I just wanted to be sure."

If Patty thought she'd get an award for baseball, Abby was sure someone should nominate *her* for an Oscar. By the end of the game her face hurt from her permanent smile. She laughed, cheered, joked and tried to suggest that she hadn't a care in the world. At bat she was dynamite. Her pain was readily transferred to her swing and she didn't hit anything less than a double and got two home runs.

Once, Logan had patted her affectionately on the back to congratulate her, Abby had shot him an angry glare. It'd taken him only one day. *One day* to ask Patty out. That hurt.

"Abby?" Logan's dark brows rose questioningly. "What's wrong?"

"Wrong?" Although she gave him a blank look, she realized her face must have divulged her feelings. "What could possibly be wrong? By the way, Tate said hello. He wanted to be here tonight, but something came up." Abby knew her lie was childish, but she couldn't help her reaction.

She didn't speak to him again.

Gathering the equipment after the game, Abby tried not to remember the way Patty had positioned herself next to Logan on the bench during the game and how she made excuses to be near him at every opportunity.

"You're coming for pizza, aren't you?" Dick asked Abby for the second time.

Abby wanted to go. The get-togethers after the game were often more fun than the game itself. But she couldn't bear the curious stares that were sure to follow when Logan sat next to Patty and started flirting with her.

"Not tonight," Abby responded, opening her eyes wide to give Dick a look of false candor. "I've got other plans." Abby noticed the way Logan's mouth curved in a mirthless smile. He'd heard that and come to his own conclusions. Good!

Abby regretted her hasty refusal later. The apartment was hot and muggy. Even Dano, her temperamental cat, didn't want to spend time with her.

After a cool shower, Abby fixed a meal of scrambled eggs, toast and a chocolate bar. She wasn't the least bit hungry, but eating was at least a distraction.

She couldn't concentrate on her newest suspense novel, so she sat on the sofa and turned on the TV. A rerun of an old situation comedy helped block out the image of Patty in Logan's arms. Abby didn't doubt that Logan had kissed Patty. The bright, happy look in her eyes had said as much.

Uncrossing her legs, Abby released a bitter sigh. She

shouldn't care if Logan kissed a hundred women. But she did. It bothered her immensely—regardless of her own hopes and fantasies about Tate. She recognized how irrational she was being, and her confusion only increased.

With the television blaring to drown out the echo of Patty's telling her about the fun she'd had with Logan, Abby reached for the chocolate bar and peeled off the wrapper. The sweet flavor wouldn't ease the discomfort in her stomach, because Abby knew it wasn't chocolate she wanted, it was Logan. Feeling wretched again, she set the candy bar aside and leaned her head back, closing her eyes.

By Friday evening, Abby was convinced all the contradictory feelings she had about Logan could be summed up in one sentence: The grass is always greener on the other side of the fence. It was another of those clichés her mother seemed so fond of and spouted on a regular basis. She was surprised Glenna hadn't dragged this one into their conversations about Logan and Tate. The idea of getting involved with Tate had been appealing when she was seeing Logan steadily. It stood to reason that the reverse was also true—that Logan would miss her and lose interest in Patty. At least that was what Abby told herself repeatedly as she dressed for her date.

With her long brown hair a frame around her oval face, she put on more makeup than usual. With a secret little smile she applied an extra dab of perfume. Tate wouldn't know what hit him! The summer dress was one of her best—a pale blue sheath that could be dressed up or down, so she was as comfortable wearing it to a movie as she would be to a formal dinner.

When Tate arrived, he had on a pair of cords and a cotton shirt, open at the neck, sleeves rolled up. It was undeniably a sexy look.

"You're stunning," he said appreciatively, kissing her lightly on the cheek.

"Thank you." Abby couldn't restrain her disappointment. He'd looked at her the way one would a sister and his kiss wasn't that of a lover—or someone who intended to be a lover.

Still, they joked easily as they waited in line for the latest blockbuster action movie and Abby was struck by their camaraderie. It didn't take her long to realize that their relationship wasn't hot and fiery, sparked by mutual attraction. Instead, it was…friendly. Warm. Almost lacking in imagination. Ironically, that had been exactly her complaint about Logan.…

Tate bought a huge bucket of popcorn, which they shared in the darkened theater. But Abby noted that he appeared restless, often shifting his position, crossing and uncrossing his legs. Once, when he assumed she wasn't watching, he laid his head against the back of the seat and closed his eyes. Was Tate in pain? she wondered.

Abby's attention drifted from the movie. "Tate," she whispered. "Are you okay?"

He immediately opened his eyes. "Of course. Why?"

Rather than refer to his restlessness, she simply shook her head and pretended an interest in the screen.

When they'd finished the popcorn, Tate reached for her hand. But Abby noted that it felt tense. If she didn't know better, she'd swear he was nervous. But Abby couldn't imagine what possible reason Tate would have to be nervous around her.

The evening was hot and close when they emerged from the theater.

"Are you hungry?" Tate asked, taking her hand, and again, Abby was struck by how unnaturally tense he seemed.

"For something cold and sinful," she answered with a teasing smile.

"Beer?"

"No," Abby said with a laugh. "Ice cream."

Tate laughed, too, and hand in hand they strolled toward the downtown area where Tate assured her he knew of an old fashioned ice-cream place. The Swanson Parlor was decorated in pink—pink walls, pink chairs, pink linen tablecloths and pink-dressed waitresses.

Abby decided quickly on a banana split and mentioned it to Tate.

"That does sound good. I'll have one, too."

Abby shut her menu and set it aside. This was the third time they'd gone for something to eat, and each time Tate had ordered the same thing she did. He didn't seem insecure. But maybe she was being oversensitive. Besides, it didn't make any difference.

Their rapport made conversation comfortable and lighthearted. They talked about the movie and other films they'd both seen. Abby discussed some of her favorite mystery novels and Tate described animal behavior he'd witnessed. But several times Abby noted that his laughter was forced. His gaze would become intent and his sudden seriousness would throw the conversation off stride.

"I love Minneapolis," Abby said as they left the ice-cream parlor. "It's such a livable city."

"I agree," Tate commented. "Do you want to go for a walk?"

"Yes, let's." Abby tucked her hand in the crook of his elbow.

Tate looked at her and smiled, but again Abby noted the sober look in his eyes. "I was born in California," he began.

"What's it like there?" Abby had been to New York but she'd never visited the West Coast.

"I don't remember much. My family moved to New Mexico when I was six."

"Hot, I'll bet," Abby said.

"It's funny, the kinds of things you remember. I don't recall what the weather was like. But I have a very clear memory of my first-grade teacher in Alburquerque, Ms. Grimes. She was pretty and really tall." Tate chuckled. "But I suppose all teachers are tall to a six-year-old. We moved again in the middle of that year."

"You seem to have moved around quite a bit," Abby said, wondering why Tate had started talking about himself so freely. Although they had talked about a number of different subjects, she knew little about his personal life.

"We moved five times in as many years," Tate continued. "We had no choice, really. My dad couldn't hold down a job, and every time he lost one we'd pack up and move, seeking another start, another escape." Tate's face hardened. "We came to Minneapolis when I was in the eighth grade."

"Did your father finally find his niche in life?" Abby sensed that Tate was revealing something he rarely shared with anyone. She felt honored, but surprised. Their relationship was promising in some ways and disappointing in others, but the fact that he trusted her with his pain, his difficult past, meant a lot. She wondered why he'd chosen her as a confidante.

"No, Dad died before he ever found what he was looking for." There was no disguising the anguish in his voice. "My feelings for my father are as confused now as they were then." He turned toward Abby, his expression solemn. "I hated him and I loved him."

"Did your life change after he was gone?" Abby's question was practically a whisper, respecting the deep emotion in Tate's eyes.

"Yes and no. A couple of years later, I dropped out of school and got a job as a mechanic. My dad taught me a lot, enough to persuade Jack Bessler to hire me."

"And you've been there ever since?"

His mouth quirked at one corner. "Ever since."

"You didn't graduate from high school then, did you?"

"No."

That sadness was back in his voice. "And you resent that?" Abby asked softly.

"I may have for a time, but I never fit in a regular classroom. I guess in some ways I'm a lot like my dad. Restless and insecure. But I'm much more content working at the garage than I ever was in a classroom."

"You've worked there for years now," Abby said,

contradicting his assessment of himself. "How can you say you're restless?"

He didn't acknowledge her question. "There's a chance I could buy the business. Jack's ready to retire and wants out from under the worry."

"That's what you really want, isn't it, Tate?"

"The business is more than I ever thought I'd have."

"But something's stopping you?" Abby could sense this more from his tension than from what he said.

"Yes." The stark emotion in his voice startled her.

"Are you worried about not having graduated from high school? Because, Tate, you can now. There's a program at the community center where I take painting classes. You can get what they call a G.E.D.—General Education Diploma, I think is what it means. Anyway, all you need to do is talk to a counselor and—"

"That's not it." Tate interrupted her harshly and ran a hand across his brow.

"Then what is it?" Abby asked, her smile determined.

Tate hesitated until the air between them was electric, like a storm ready to explode in the muggy heat.

"Where are you going with this discussion? What can I do to help? I don't understand." One minute Tate was exposing a painful part of his past, and the next he was growling at her. What was it with men? Something had been bothering him all evening. First he'd been restless and uneasy, then brooding and thoughtful, now angry. Nothing made sense.

And it wasn't going to. Abruptly he asked her if she was ready to leave.

He hardly said a word to her when he dropped her off at her apartment.

For a moment, Abby was convinced he'd never ask her out again.

"What about Sunday?" he finally said. "We can bring a picnic."

"Okay." But after this evening, Abby wasn't sure. He didn't sound as if he really wanted her company. "How about three o'clock?"

"Fine." His response was clipped.

Again he gave her a modest kiss, more a light brushing of their mouths than anything passionate or intense. Not a real kiss, in her opinion.

She leaned against the closed door of her apartment, not understanding why Tate was bothering to take her out. It seemed apparent that his interest in her wasn't romantic—although she didn't know what it actually was, didn't know what he wanted or needed from her. And for that matter, the bone-melting effect she'd experienced at their first meeting had long since gone. Tate was a handsome man, but he wasn't what she'd expected.

Maybe the grass wasn't so green after all.

After a restless Sunday morning, Abby decided that she'd go for a walk in the park. Logan often did before he came over to her place, and she hoped to run into him. She'd make a point of letting him know that their meeting was pure coincidence. They'd talk. Somehow she'd inform him, casually of course, that things weren't working out as she'd planned. In fact, yesterday, during her lesson with Mai-Ling, Tate hadn't come to the park, and she'd secretly been relieved. Despite today's picnic, she suspected that their romance was over before it could really start. And now she had doubts about its potential, anyway. Hmm. Maybe she'd hint to Logan that she missed his company. That should be enough to break the ice without either of them losing their pride. And that was what this came down to—pride.

The park was crowded by the time Abby arrived. Entering the grounds, she scanned the lawns for him and released a grateful sigh to find that he was sitting on a park bench reading. By himself. To her relief, Patty wasn't with him.

Deciding on her strategy, Abby stuck her hands in her pockets and strolled down the paved lane, hoping to look as if she'd merely come for a walk in the park. Their meeting would be by accident.

Abby stood about ten feet away, off to one side, watching Logan. She was surprised at the emotion she felt just studying him. He looked peaceful, but then he always did. He was composed, confident, in control. Equal to any situation. They'd been dating for almost a year and Abby hadn't realized that so much of her life was interwoven with Logan's. She'd taken him for granted until he was gone, and the emptiness he'd left behind had shocked her. She'd been stupid and insensitive. And heaven knew how difficult it was for her to admit she'd been wrong.

For several minutes Abby did nothing but watch him. A calm settled over her as she focused on Logan's shoulders. They weren't as broad or muscular as Tate's, but somehow it didn't matter. Not now, not when she was hurting, missing Logan and his friendship. Without giving it much thought, she'd been looking forward to Sunday all week and now she knew precisely why:

Sundays had always been special because they were spent with Logan. It was Logan she wanted, Logan she needed, and Abby desperately hoped she wasn't too late.

Abby continued to gaze at him. After a while her determination to talk to him grew stronger. Never mind her pride—Logan had a right to know her feelings. He'd been patient with her far longer than she deserved. Her stomach felt queasy, her mouth dry. Just when she gathered enough courage to approach him, Logan closed his book and stood up. Turning around he looked in her direction, but didn't hesitate for a second. He glanced at his watch and walked idly down the concrete pathway toward her until he was within calling distance. Abby's breath froze as he looked her way, blinked and looked in the opposite direction. She couldn't believe he'd purposely avoid her and she doubted he would've been able to see her standing off to the side.

The moment she was ready to step forward, Logan stopped to chat with two older men playing checkers. From her position, Abby saw them motion for him to sit down, which he did. He was soon deep in conversation with them. The three were obviously good friends, although she'd never met the other men before.

Abby loitered as long as she could. Half an hour passed and still Logan stayed.

Defeated, Abby realized she'd have to hurry or be late for her picnic with Tate. Silently she slipped from her viewing position and started across the grounds. When she glanced over her shoulder, she saw that Logan was alone on a bench again and watching a pair of young lovers kissing on the grass. Even from this distance, she saw a look of such intense pain cross his face, she had to force herself not to run to his side. He dropped his head in his hands and hunched forward as if a heavy burden was weighing on him.

Abby's throat clogged with tears until it was painful to breathe. They filled her eyes. Logan loved her and had loved her from the beginning, but she'd carelessly thrown his love aside. It had taken only a few days' separation to know with certainty that she loved him, too.

Tears rolled down her face, but Abby quickly brushed them aside. Logan wouldn't want to know she'd seen him. She'd stripped him of so much, it wouldn't be right to take his pride, as well. Today she'd tell Tate she wouldn't be seeing him again. If that was all Logan wanted, it would be a small price to pay. She'd run back to his arms and never leave him again.

By the time she got to her building, Tate was at the front door. They greeted each other and Tate told her about a special place he wanted to show her near Apple Valley.

She ran into her apartment to get a few things, then joined him in the car.

Both seemed preoccupied during the drive. Abby helped him unload the picnic basket, her thoughts racing at breakneck speed. She folded the tablecloth she'd brought over a picnic table while Tate spread out a blanket under a shady tree. They hardly spoke.

"Abby—"

"Tate—"

They both began together.

"You first," Abby murmured and sat down, drawing up her legs and circling them with both arms, then resting her chin on her bent knees.

Tate remained standing, hands in his pockets as he paced. Again, something was obviously troubling him.

"Tate, what is it?"

"I didn't know it would be so hard to tell you," he said wryly and shook his head. "I meant to explain weeks ago."

What was he talking about?

His gaze settled on her, then flickered to the ground. "I tried to tell you Friday night after the movie, but I couldn't get the words out." He ran a weary hand over his face and fell to his knees at her side.

Abby reached for his hand and held it.

"Abby." He released a ragged breath. "*I can't read. I'll pay you any amount if you'll teach me.*"

Five

In one brilliant flash everything about Tate fell into place. He hadn't been captivated by her charm and natural beauty. He'd overheard her teaching Mai-Ling how to read and knew she could help him. That was the reason he'd sought her out and cultivated a friendship. She could help him.

Small things became clear in her mind. No wonder Tate ordered the same thing she did in a restaurant. Naturally their date on Friday night had been awkward. He'd been trying to tell her then. How could she have been so blind?

Even now he studied her intently, awaiting her response. His eyes glittered with pride, insecurity and fear. She recognized all those emotions and understood them now.

"Of course I'll teach you," she said reassuringly.

"I'll pay you anything you ask."

"Tate." Her grip on his hand tightened. "I wouldn't take anything. We're friends."

"But I can afford to pay you." He took a wad of bills

from his pocket and breathed in slowly, glancing at the money in his hand.

Again Abby realized how difficult admitting his inability to read had been. "Put that away," Abby said calmly. "You won't be needing it."

Tate stuffed the bills back in his pocket. "You don't know how relieved I am to have finally told you," he muttered hoarsely.

"I don't think I could have been more obtuse," she said, still shocked at her own stupidity. "I'm amazed you've gotten along as well as you have. I was completely fooled."

"I've become adept at this. I've done it from the time I was in grade school."

"What happened?" Abby asked softly, although she could guess.

A sadness stole into his eyes. "I suppose it's because of all those times I was pulled out of school so we could move," he said unemotionally. "We left New Mexico in the middle of first grade and I never finished the year. Because I was tall for my age my mother put me in second grade the following September. The teacher wanted to hold me back but we moved again. And again and again." A bitterness infected his voice. "By the time I was in junior high and we'd moved to Minneapolis, I had devised all kinds of ways to disguise the fact that I couldn't read. I was the class clown, the troublemaker, the boy who'd do anything to get out of going to school."

"Oh, Tate." Her heart swelled with compassion.

Sitting beside her, Tate rubbed his hand across his

face and smiled grimly. "But the hardest part was getting up the courage to tell you."

"You've never told anyone else, have you?"

"No. It was like admitting I have some horrible disease."

"You don't. We can fix this," she said. She was trying to reassure him and felt pathetically inadequate.

"Will you promise me that you'll keep this to yourself? For now?"

She nodded. "I promise." She understood how humiliated he felt, why he wanted his inability to read to remain a secret, and felt she had to agree.

"When can we start? There's so much I want to learn. So much I want to read. Books and magazines and computer programs…" He sounded eager, his gaze level and questioning.

"Is tomorrow too soon?" Abby asked.

"I'd say it's about twenty years too late."

Tate brought Abby back to her apartment two hours later. Tomorrow she'd call the World Literacy Movement and have them email the forms for her to complete regarding Tate. He looked jubilant, excited. Telling her about his inability to read had probably been one of the most difficult things he'd ever done in his life. She understood how formidable his confession had felt to him because now she had to humble herself and call Logan. And that, although major to her, was a small thing in comparison.

Abby wasn't unhappy at Tate's confession. True, her pride was stung for a moment. But overall she was relieved. Tate was the kind of man who'd always attract women's attention. For a brief time she'd been caught up in his masculine appeal. And if it hadn't been for Tate, it would have taken her a lot longer to recognize how fortunate she was to have Logan.

The thought of phoning him and admitting that she was wrong had been unthinkable a week ago. Had it only been a week? In some ways it felt like a year.

Abby glanced at the ceiling and prayed that Logan would answer her call. There was so much stored in her heart that she wanted to tell him. Her hand trembled as she lifted the receiver and tried to form positive thoughts. *Everything's going to work out. I know it will.* She repeated that mantra over and over as she dialed.

She was so nervous her fingers shook and her stomach churned until she was convinced she was going to be sick. Inhaling, Abby held her breath as his phone rang the first time. Her lungs refused to function. Abby closed her eyes tightly during the second ring.

"Hello."

Abby took a deep breath.

"Logan, this is Abby."

"Abby?" He sounded shocked.

"Can we talk? I mean, I can call back if this is inconvenient."

"I'm on my way out the door. Would you like me to come over?"

"Yes." She was surprised at how composed she sounded. "That would be great." She replaced the phone and tilted her head toward the ceiling. "Thank you," she murmured gratefully.

Looking down, Abby realized how casually she was

dressed. When Logan saw her again, she wanted to bowl him over.

Racing into her room, she ripped the dress she'd worn Friday night off the hanger, then decided it wouldn't do. She tossed it across her bed. She tried on one outfit and then another. Never had she been more unsure about what she wanted to wear. Finally she chose a pair of tailored black pants and a white blouse with an eyelet collar. Simple, elegant, classic.

Abby was frantically brushing her hair when the buzzer went. *Logan.* She gripped the edge of the sink and took in a deep breath. Then she set down the brush, practiced her smile and walked into the living room.

"Hello, Abby," Logan said a moment later as he stepped into the apartment.

Her first impulse was to throw her arms around him and weep. A tightness gripped her throat. Whatever poise she'd managed to gather was shaken and gone with one look from him.

"Hello, Logan. Would you like to sit down?" She gestured toward the chair. Her gaze was fixed on his shoulders as he walked across the room and took a seat.

"And before you ask," he interjected sternly, "no, I don't want anything to drink. Sit down, Abby."

She complied, grateful because she didn't know how much longer her knees would support her.

"You wanted to talk?" The lines at the side of his mouth deepened, but he wasn't smiling.

"Yes." She laced her hands together tightly. "I was wrong," she murmured. Now that the words were out, Abby experienced none of the calm she'd expected. "I'm—I'm sorry."

"It wasn't a question of my being right or your being wrong," Logan said. "I'm not looking for an apology."

Abby's lips trembled and she bit into the bottom corner. "I know that. But I felt I owed you one."

"No." He stood and with one hand in his pocket paced the width of the carpet. "That's not what I wanted to hear. I told you to call me when you were sure it was me you wanted and not Tate." His eyes rested on her, his expression hooded.

Abby stood, unable to meet his gaze. "I *am* sure," she breathed. "I know it's you I want."

His mouth quirked in what could have been a smile, but he didn't acknowledge her confession.

"You have every right to be angry with me." She couldn't look at him, afraid of what she'd see. If he were to reject her now, Abby didn't think she could stand it. "I've missed you so much," she mumbled. Her cheeks flamed with color, and she couldn't believe how difficult this was. She felt tears in her eyes as she bowed her head.

"Abby." Logan's arms came around her shoulders, bringing her within the comforting circle of his arms. He lifted her chin and lovingly studied her face. "You're sure?"

The growing lump in her throat made speech impossible. She nodded, letting all the love in her eyes say the words.

"Oh, Abby…" He claimed her lips with a hungry kiss that revealed the depth of his feelings.

Slipping her arms around his neck, Abby felt him shudder with a longing he'd suppressed all these months.

He buried his face in the dark waves of her hair and held her so tightly it was difficult to breathe.

"I've been so wrong about so many things," she confessed, rubbing her hands up and down his spine, reveling in the muscular feel of him.

Lowering himself to the sofa, Logan pulled Abby onto his lap. His warm breath was like a gentle caress as she wound her arms around his neck and kissed him, wanting to make up to him for all the pain she'd caused them both. The wild tempo of her pulse made clear thought impossible.

Finally, Logan dragged his mouth from hers. "You're sure?" he asked as if he couldn't quite believe it.

Abby pressed her forehead against his shoulder and nodded. "Very sure. I was such a fool."

His arm held her securely in place. "Tell me more. I'm enjoying this."

Unable to resist, Abby kissed the side of his mouth. "I thought you would."

"So you missed me?"

"I was miserable."

"Good!"

"Logan," she cried softly. "It wouldn't do you any harm to tell me how lonely *you* were."

"I wasn't," he said jokingly.

Involuntarily Abby stiffened and swallowed back the hurt. "I know. Patty mentioned that you'd taken her to the Twins game."

Logan smiled wryly. "We went with several other people."

"It bothers me that you could see someone else so soon."

"Honey." His hold tightened around her waist, bringing her closer. "It wasn't like you're thinking."

"But…you said you weren't lonely."

"How could I have been? I saw you Tuesday and then at the game on Wednesday."

"I know, but—"

"Are we going to argue?"

"A thousand kisses might convince me," she teased and rested her head on his shoulder.

"I haven't got the willpower to continue kissing you without thinking of other things," he murmured in her ear as his hand stroked her hair. "I love you, Abby. I've loved you from the first time I asked you out." His breathing seemed less controlled than it had been a moment before.

"Oh, Logan." Fresh tears sprang to her eyes. She started to tell him how much she cared for him, but he went on, cutting off her words.

"As soon as I saw Tate I knew there was no way I could compete with him. He's everything I'll never be. Tall. Movie-star looks." He shook his head. "I don't blame you for being attracted to him."

Abby straightened so she could look at this man she loved. Her hands framed his face. "You're a million things Tate could never be."

"I know this has been hard on you."

"But I was so stupid," Abby inserted.

He kissed her lightly, his lips lingering over hers. "I can't help feeling grateful that you won't be seeing him again."

Abby lowered her eyes. She *would* be seeing Tate, but not in the way Logan meant.

A stillness filled the room. "Abby?"

She gave him a feeble smile.

"You aren't seeing Tate, are you?"

She couldn't reveal Tate's problem to anyone. She'd promised. And not for the world would she embarrass him, especially when admitting he couldn't read had been so difficult. No matter how much she wanted to tell Logan, she couldn't.

"I'd like to explain," Abby replied, her voice trembling.

Logan stiffened and lightly pushed her from his lap. "I don't want explanations. All I want is the truth. Will you or will you not be seeing Tate?"

"Not romantically," she answered, as tactfully and truthfully as possible.

Logan's eyes hardened. "What other explanation could there be?"

"I can't tell you that," she said forcefully and stood up.

"Of course you can." A muscle worked in his jaw. "We're right back where we started, aren't we, Abby?"

"No." She felt like screaming at him for being so unreasonable. Surely he recognized how hard it had been for her to call him and admit she was wrong?

"Will you stop seeing Tate, then?" he challenged.

"I can't." Her voice cracked in a desperate appeal for him to understand. "We live in the same neighborhood..." she said, stalling for time as her mind raced for an excuse. "I'll probably run into him.... I mean, it'd be only natural, since he's so close and all."

"Abby," Logan groaned impatiently. "That's not what

I mean and you know it. Will you or will you not be *seeing* Tate?"

She hesitated. Knowing what her promise was doing to her relationship with Logan, Tate would want him to know. But she couldn't say anything without clearing it with him first.

"Abby?"

"I'll be seeing him, but please understand that it's not the way you assume."

For an instant, Abby saw pain in Logan's eyes. The pain she witnessed was the same torment she was experiencing herself.

They stood with only a few feet separating them and yet Abby felt they'd never been further apart. Whole worlds seemed to loom between them. Logan's ego was at stake, his pride, and he didn't want her to continue seeing Tate, no matter what the reason.

"You won't stop seeing him," Logan challenged furiously.

"I can't," Abby cried, just as angry.

"Then there's nothing left to say."

"Yes," Abby said, "there is, but you're in no mood to hear it. Just remember that things aren't always as they appear."

"Goodbye, Abby," he responded. "And next time don't bother calling me unless—"

Abby stalked across the room and threw open the door. "Next time I won't," she said with a cutting edge.

Reaction set in the minute the door slammed behind him. Abby was so angry that pacing the floor did little to relieve it. How could Logan say he loved her in one breath and turn around and storm out the next? Yet, he'd done exactly that.

Once the anger dissipated, Abby began to tremble and felt the tears burning for release. Pride demanded that she forestall them. She wouldn't allow Logan to reduce her to that level. She shook her head and kept her chin raised. She wouldn't cry, she wouldn't cry, she repeated over and over as one tear after another slid down her cheeks.

"Who did you say was responsible for the literacy movement?" Tate asked, leafing respectfully through the first book.

"Dr. Frank Laubach. He was a missionary in the Philippines in the 1920s. At that time some of the island people didn't have a written language. He invented one and later developed a method of teaching adults to read."

"Sounds like he accomplished a lot."

Abby nodded. "By the time he died in 1970, his work had spread to 105 countries and 313 languages."

Tate continued leafing through the pages of the primary workbook. Abby wanted to start him at the most fundamental skill level, knowing his progress would be rapid. At this point, Tate would need all the encouragement he could get and the speed with which he completed the lower-level books was sure to help.

Abby hadn't underestimated Tate's enthusiasm. By the end of the first lesson he had relearned the alphabet and was reading simple phrases. Proudly he took the book home with him.

"Can we meet again tomorrow?" he asked, standing near her apartment door.

"I've got my class tomorrow evening," Abby explained, "but if you like, we could meet for a half hour before—or after if you prefer."

"Before, I think."

The following afternoon, Tate showed up an hour early, just after she got home from work, and seemed disappointed that Abby would be occupied with softball on Wednesday evening.

"We could get together afterward if you want," she told him.

Affectionately, Tate kissed her on the cheek. "I want."

Again she noted that his fondness for her was more like that of a brother—or a pupil for his teacher. She was grateful for that, at least. And he was wonderful to her. He brought over takeout meals and gave her small gifts as a way of showing his appreciation. The gifts weren't necessary, but they salvaged Tate's pride and that was something she was learning more about every day—male pride.

Abby was dressing for the game Wednesday evening when the phone rang. No longer did she expect or even hope it would be Logan. He'd made his position completely clear. Fortunately, call display told her it was her parents' number.

"Hello, Mom."

"Abby, I've been worried about you."

"I'm fine!" She forced some enthusiasm into her voice.

"Oh, dear, it's worse than I thought."

"What's worse?"

"Logan and you."

"There is no more Logan and me," she returned.

A strained silence followed. "But I thought—"

"Listen, Mom," Abby cut in, unwilling to listen to her mother's postmortem. "I've got a game tonight. Can I call you later?"

"Why don't you come over for dinner?"

"Not tonight." Abby hated to turn down her mother's invitation, but she'd already agreed to see Tate for his next lesson.

"It's your birthday Friday," Glenna reminded her.

"I'll come for dinner then," Abby said with a feeble smile. Her birthday was only two days away and she wasn't in any mood to celebrate. "But only if you promise to make my favorite dish."

"Barbecued chicken!" her mother announced. "You bet."

"And, Mom," Abby continued, "you were right about Logan."

"What was I right about?" Her mother's voice rose slightly.

"He does love me, and I love him."

Abby thought she heard a small, happy sound.

"What made you realize that?" her mother asked.

"A lot of things," Abby said noncommittally. "But I also realized that loving someone doesn't make everything perfect. I wish it did."

"I have the feeling there's something important you're not telling me, Abby," Glenna said on a note of puzzled sadness. "But I know you will in your own good time."

Abby couldn't disagree with her mother's observation. "I'll be at your place around six on Friday," she murmured. "And thanks, Mom."

"What are mothers for?" Glenna teased.

The disconnected phone line droned in Abby's ear before she hung up, suddenly surprised to see that it was time to head over to the park. For the first time that she could remember, she didn't feel psyched up for the game. She wasn't ready to see Logan, which would be more painful than reassuring. And if he paid Patty special attention, Abby didn't know how she'd handle that. But Logan wouldn't do anything to hurt her. At least she knew him well enough to be sure of that.

The first thing Abby noticed as she walked onto the diamond was that Patty Martin had cut and styled her hair. The transformation from straight mousy-brown hair to short, bouncy curls was astonishing. The young woman positively glowed.

"What do you think?" Patty asked in a hurried voice. "Your hair is always so pretty and…" She let the rest of what she was going to say fade.

Abby held herself motionless. Patty had made herself attractive for Logan. She desperately wanted Logan's interest, and for all Abby knew, she was getting it. "I think you look great," Abby commented, unable to deny the truth or to be unkind.

"I was scared out of my wits," Patty admitted shyly. "It's been a long time since I was at the hairdresser's."

"Hey, Patty, they're waiting for you on the field," the team's coach hollered. "Abby, you, too."

"Okay, Dick," Patty called back happily, her eyes shining. "I've gotta go. We'll talk later, okay?"

"Fine." Softening her stiff mitt against her hand with unnecessary force, Abby ran to her position at first base.

Logan was practicing in the outfield.

"Abby," he called, and when she turned, she found his gaze level and unwavering. "Catch."

Nothing appeared to affect him. They'd suffered through the worst four days of their relationship and he looked at her as coolly and unemotionally as he would a…a dish of potato salad. She didn't respond other than to catch the softball and pitch it to second base.

The warm-up period lasted for about ten minutes. Abby couldn't recall a time she'd felt less like playing, and it showed.

"What's the matter, Ab?" Dick asked her at the bottom of the fifth after she'd struck out for the third time. "You're not yourself tonight."

"I'm sorry," she said with a frustrated sigh. Her eyes didn't meet his. "This isn't one of my better nights."

"She's got other things on her mind." Logan spoke from behind her, signaling that he was sitting in the bleachers one row above. "Her boyfriend just showed up, so she'll do better."

Abby whirled around to face Logan. "What do you mean by that?"

Logan nodded in the direction of the parking lot. Abby's gaze followed his movement and she wanted to groan aloud. Tate was walking toward the stands.

"Tate isn't my boyfriend," Abby's voice was taut with impatience.

"Oh, is that terminology passé?" Logan returned.

Stunned at the bitterness in him, Abby found no words to respond. They were both hurting, and in their pain they were lashing out at each other.

Logan slid from the bleachers for his turn at bat. Abby focused her attention on him, deciding she didn't want to make a fuss over Tate's unexpected arrival.

Logan swung wildly at the first pitch, hitting the ball with the tip of his bat. Abby could hear the wood crack as the ball went flying over the fence for a home run. Logan looked as shocked as Abby. He tossed the bat aside and ran around the bases to the shouts and cheers of his teammates. Abby couldn't remember Logan ever getting more than a single.

"Hi." Tate slid into the row of seats behind her. "You don't mind if I come and watch, do you?" he asked as he leaned forward with lazy grace.

"Not at all," Abby said blandly. It didn't make any difference now. She stared at her laced fingers, attempting to fight off the depression that seemed to have settled over her. She was so caught up in her own sorrows that she didn't see the accident. Only the startled cries of those around her alerted her to the fact that something had happened.

"What's wrong?" Abby asked frantically as the bench cleared. Everyone was running toward Patty, who was clutching her arm and doubled over in pain.

Logan's voice could be heard above the confusion. "Stand back. Give her room." Gently he aided Patty into a sitting position.

Even to Abby's untrained eye it was obvious that Patty's arm was broken. Logan tore off his shirt and tied it around her upper body to create a sling and support the injured arm.

The words *hospital* and *doctor* were flying around, but everyone seemed stunned and no one moved. Again it was Logan who helped Patty to her feet and led her to his car. His calm, decisive actions imparted confidence to both teams. Only minutes before, Abby had been angry because he displayed so little emotion.

"What happened?" Abby asked Dick as they walked off the field.

"I'm not sure." Dick looked shaken himself. "Patty was trying to steal a base and collided with the second baseman. When she fell, she put out her arm to catch herself and it twisted under her."

"Will she be all right?"

"Logan seemed to think so. He's taking her to the emergency room. He said he'd let us know her condition as soon as possible."

The captain of the opposing team crossed the diamond to talk to Dick and it was decided that they'd play out the remainder of the game.

But without Logan the team was short one male player.

"Do you think your friend would mind filling in?" Dick asked somewhat sheepishly, glancing at Tate.

"I can ask."

"No problem," Tate said, smiling as he picked up Logan's discarded mitt and ran onto the field.

Although they'd decided to finish the game, almost everyone was preoccupied with the accident. Abby's team ended up winning, thanks to Tate, but only by a slight margin.

The group as a whole proceeded to the pizza parlor to wait for word about Patty.

Tate sat across the long wooden table from Abby, chatting easily with her fellow teammates. Only a few slices of the two large pizzas had been eaten. Their conversation was a low hum as they recounted their versions of the accident and what could have been done to prevent it.

Abby was grateful for Logan's clear thinking and quick actions. He wasn't the kind of skilled softball player who'd stand out, but he gave of himself in a way that was essential to every member of the team. Only a few days earlier she'd found Logan lacking. Compared to the muscular Tate, he'd seemed a poor second. Now she noted that his strengths were inner ones. Again she was reminded that if given the chance, she would love this man for the rest of her life.

Abby didn't see Logan enter the restaurant, but the immediate clamor caused her to turn. She stood with the others.

"Patty's fine," he assured everyone. "Her arm's broken, but I don't think that's news to anyone."

"When will she be back?"

"We want to send flowers or something."

"When do you think she'll feel up to company?"

Everyone spoke at once. Calmly Logan answered each question and when he'd finished, the mood around the table was considerably lighter.

A tingling awareness at the back of her neck told

Abby that Logan was near. With a sweeping action he swung his foot over the long bench and joined her.

He focused on Tate, sitting across from Abby. "I wish I could say it's good to see you again," he said with stark unfriendliness.

"Logan, please!" Abby hissed.

The two men eyed each other like bears who'd violated each other's territory. Tate had no romantic interest in her, Abby was convinced of that, but Logan was openly challenging him and Tate wouldn't walk away from such blatant provocation.

Unaware of the dangerous undercurrents swirling around the table, Dick Snyder sauntered over and slapped Logan on the back.

"We owe a debt of thanks to Tate here," he informed Logan cheerfully. "He stepped in for you when you were gone. He batted in the winning run."

Logan and Tate didn't so much as blink. "Tate's been doing a lot of that for me lately, isn't that right, Abby?"

Wrenching her gaze from him, Abby stood and, with as much dignity and pride as she could muster, walked out of the restaurant and went home alone.

The phone was ringing when she walked into the apartment. Abby let it ring. She didn't want to talk to anyone. She didn't even want to know who'd called.

"Abby, would you take the bread out of the oven?" her mother asked, walking out to the patio.

"Okay." Abby turned off the broiler and pulled out the cookie sheet, on which slices of French bread oozed with melted butter and chopped garlic. Her enthusiasm for this birthday celebration was nil.

The doorbell caught her by surprise. "Are you expecting anyone?" she asked her mother, who'd returned to the kitchen.

"Not that I know of. I'll get it."

Abby was placing the bread slices in a warming basket when she heard her mother's surprised voice.

Turning, Abby looked straight at Logan.

Six

A shocked expression crossed Logan's face. "Abby." He took a step inside the room and paused.

"Hello, Logan." A tense silence ensued as Abby primly folded her hands.

"I'll check the chicken," Glenna Carpenter murmured discreetly as she hurried past them.

"What brings you to this neck of the woods?" Abby forced a lightness into her voice. He looked tired, as if he hadn't been sleeping well. For that matter, neither had Abby, but she doubted either would admit as much.

Logan handed her a wrapped package. "I wanted your mother to give you this. But since you're here—happy birthday."

A small smile parted her trembling lips as Abby accepted the brightly wrapped gift. He had come to her parents' home to deliver this, but he hadn't expected her to be there.

"Thank you." She continued to hold it.

"I, uh, didn't expect to see you." He stated the obvious, as though he couldn't think of anything else to say.

"Where else would I be on my birthday?"

Logan shrugged. "With Tate."

Abby released a sigh of indignation. "I thought I'd explained that I'm not involved with Tate. We're friends, nothing more."

She shook her head. They'd gone over this before. Another argument wouldn't help. Abby figured she'd endured enough emotional turmoil in the past few weeks. She still hadn't spoken to Tate about telling Logan the truth. But she couldn't, not with Tate feeling as sensitive as he did about the whole thing.

"Abby." Logan's voice was deadly quiet. "Don't you see what's happening? You may not think of Tate in a romantic light, but I saw the way he was looking at you in the pizza place."

"You openly challenged him." Abby threw out a few challenges of her own. "How did you expect him to react? You wouldn't have behaved any differently," she said. "And if you've come to ruin my birthday…then you can just leave. I've had about all I can take from you, Logan Fletcher." She whirled around, not wanting to face him.

"I didn't come for that." The defeat was back in his voice again.

Abby's pulse thundered in her ears as she waited for the sounds of him leaving—at the same time hoping he wouldn't.

"Aren't you going to open your present?" he said at last.

Abby turned and wiped away a tear that had escaped from the corner of her eye. "I already know what it is," she said, glancing down at the package. "Honestly, Logan, you're so predictable."

"How could you possibly know?"

"Because you got me the same perfume for my birthday last year." Deftly she removed the wrapping paper and held up the small bottle of expensive French fragrance.

"I like the way it smells on you," Logan murmured, walking across the room. He rested his hands on her shoulders. "And if I'm so predictable, you'll also recall that there's a certain thank-you I expect."

Any resistance drained from her as Logan pulled her into his embrace. Abby slid her arms around his neck and tasted the sweetness of his kiss. A wonderful languor stole through her limbs as his mouth brushed the sweeping curve of her lashes and burned a trail down her cheek to her ear.

"I love you, Logan," Abby whispered with all the intensity in her.

Logan went utterly still. Gradually he raised his head so he could study her. Unflinching, Abby met his gaze determined that he see for himself what her eyes and heart were saying.

"If you love me, then you'll stop seeing Tate," he said flatly.

"And if you love *me,* you'll trust me."

"Abby." Logan dropped his hands and stepped away. "I—"

"Oh, Logan." Glenna Carpenter moved out of the kitchen. "I'm glad to see you're still here. We insist you stay for dinner. Isn't that right, Abby?"

Logan held her gaze with mesmerizing simplicity.

"Of course we do. If you don't have another appointment," Abby said meaningfully.

"You know I don't."

Abby knew nothing of the kind, but didn't want to argue. "Did you see the gift Logan brought me?" Abby asked her mother and held out the perfume.

"Logan is always so thoughtful."

"Yes, he is," Abby agreed and slipped an arm around his waist, enjoying the feel of him at her side. "Thoughtful, but not very original." Her eyes smiled into his, pleading with him that, for tonight, they could forget their differences.

Logan's arms slid just as easily around her. "But with that kind of thank-you, what incentive do I have for shopping around?"

Abby laughed and led the way to the back patio.

Frank Carpenter, Abby's father, was busy standing in front of the barbecue, basting chicken.

"Logan," he exclaimed and held out a welcoming hand. "This is a pleasant surprise. Good to see you."

Logan and her father had always gotten along and had several interests in common. For a time that had irked Abby. Defiantly she'd wanted to make it clear that she wouldn't marry a man solely because her parents thought highly of him. Her childish attitude had changed dramatically these past weeks.

Abby's mother brought another place setting from the kitchen to add to the three already on the picnic table. Abby made several more trips into the kitchen to carry out the salad, toasted bread and a glass of wine for Logan.

Absently, Logan accepted the glass from her and

smiled, deep in conversation with her father. Happiness washed over Abby as she munched on a potato chip. Looking at the two of them now—Abby busy helping her mother and Logan chatting easily with her father— she figured there was little to distinguish them as un-married.

Dinner and the time that followed were cheerful. Frank suggested a game of cards while they were eating birthday cake and ice cream. But Abby's mother im-mediately rejected the idea.

"I think Glenna's trying to tell me to keep my mouth shut because it's obvious you two want some time alone," Abby's father complained.

"I'm saying no such thing," Glenna denied instantly as an embarrassed flush brightened her cheeks. "We were young once, Frank."

"Once!" Frank scolded. "I don't know about you, but I'm not exactly ready for the grave."

"We'll play cards another time," Logan promised, ending a friendly argument between her parents.

"Double-deck pinochle," Frank prompted. "Best card game there is."

Glenna pretended to agree but rolled her eyes dra-matically when Frank wasn't looking.

"Shall we?" Logan successfully contained a smile and held out his open palm to Abby. She placed her hand in his, more contented than she could ever remember being. After their farewells to her parents, Logan fol-lowed her back to her apartment, parking his car beside hers. He took a seat while Abby hurried into the next room.

"Give me a minute to freshen up," Abby called out

as she ran a brush through her hair and studied her reflection in the bathroom mirror. She looked happy. The sparkle was back in her eyes.

She dabbed some of the perfume Logan had given her to the pulse points at her throat and wrists. Maybe this would garner even more of a reaction. He wasn't one to display a lot of emotion, but he seemed to be coming along nicely in that area. His kisses had produced an overwhelming physical response in Abby, and she was aware that his feeling for her ran deep and strong. It had been only a matter of weeks ago that she'd wondered why he bothered to kiss her at all.

"I suppose you're going to suggest we drive to Des Moines and back," Logan teased when she joined him a few minutes later.

"Logan!" she cried, feigning excitement. "That's a wonderful idea."

He rolled his eyes and and laid the paper on the sofa. "How about a movie instead?"

Abby gave a fake groan. "So predictable."

"I've been wanting to see this one." He pointed at an ad for the movie she'd seen with Tate.

"I've already been," Abby tossed back, not thinking.

"When?"

Abby could feel the hostility exuding from Logan. He knew. Without a word he'd guessed that Abby had been to the movie with Tate.

"Not long ago." She tried desperately to put the evening back on an even keel. "But I'd see it again. The film's great."

The air between them became heavy and oppressive.

"Forget the movies," Logan said and neatly folded

the paper. He straightened and stalked to the far side of the room. "In fact, why don't we forget everything."

Hands clenched angrily at her side, Abby squared her shoulders. "If you ruin my birthday, Logan Fletcher, I don't think I'll ever forgive you."

His expression was cold and unreadable. "Yes, but there's always Tate."

A hysterical sob rose in her throat, but Abby managed to choke it off. "I…I told you tonight that I loved you." Her voice wobbled treacherously as her eyes pleaded with his. "Doesn't that mean anything to you? Anything at all?"

Logan's gaze raked her from head to foot. "Only that you don't know the meaning of the word. You want both Tate *and* me, Abby. But you can't decide between us so you'd prefer to keep us both dangling until you make up your mind." His voice gained volume with each word. "But I won't play that game."

Abby breathed in sharply as a fiery anger burned in her cheeks. Once she would have ranted, cried and hurled her own accusations. Now she stood stunned and disbelieving. "If you honestly believe that, then there's nothing left to say." Her voice was calmer than she dared hope. Life seemed filled with ironies all of a sudden. Outwardly she presented a clearheaded composure while on the inside she felt a fiery pain. Perhaps for the first time in her life she was acting completely selflessly, and this was her reward—losing Logan.

Without another word, Logan walked across the room and out the front door.

Abby watched him leave with a sense of unreality. This couldn't be happening to her. Not on her birthday.

Last year Logan had taken her to dinner at L'Hôtel Sofitel and given her—what else—perfume. A hysterical
bubble of laughter slipped from her. He was predictable, but so loving and caring. She remembered how
they'd danced until midnight and gone for a stroll in
the moonlight. Only a year ago, Logan had made her
birthday the most perfect day of her life. But this year
he was ruining it.

Angry, hurt and agitated, Abby paced the living-
room carpet until she thought she'd go mad. Dano had
wandered into the living room when she and Logan
came in, but had disappeared into her bedroom once
he sensed tension. Figured. Not even her cat was interested in comforting her. Usually when she was upset
she'd ride her bike or do something physical. But bike
riding at night could be dangerous, so she'd go running
instead. She changed into old jeans and a faded sweatshirt that had a picture of a Disneyland castle on the
front. She had trouble locating her second tennis shoe,
then threw it aside in disgust when the rainbow-colored
lace snapped in two.

She sighed. Nothing had gone right today. Tate had
been disappointed that she wasn't able to meet him.
Because of that, she'd been fighting off a case of guilt
when she went to her parents'. Then Logan had shown
up, and everything had steadily and rapidly gone down-
hill.

Ripping a lace from one of her baseball shoes, Abby
had to wrap it around the sole of the shoe several times.
On her way out the door, she paused and returned to the
bathroom. If she was going to go running, then she'd do
it smelling better than any other runner in Minneapolis

history. She'd dabbed perfume on every exposed part of her body when she stepped out the door.

A light drizzle had begun to fall. Terrific. A fitting end to a rotten day.

The first block was a killer. She couldn't be that badly out of shape, could she? She rode her bike a lot. And wasn't her running speed the best on the team?

The second block, Abby forced her mind off how out of breath she was becoming. Logan's buying her perfume made her chuckle. *Predictable. Reliable. Confident.* They were all words that adequately described Logan. But so were *unreasonable* and *stubborn*—traits she'd only seen recently.

The drizzle was followed by a cloudburst and Abby's hair and clothes were plastered against her in the swirling wind and rain. She shouldn't be laughing. But she did anyway as she raced back to her apartment. It was either laugh or cry, and laughing seemed to come naturally. Laughing made her feel better than succumbing to tears.

By the time Abby returned to her building, she was drenched and shivering. With her chin tucked under and her arms folded around her middle, she fought off the chill and hurried across the parking lot. She was almost at her building door when she realized she didn't have the keys. She'd locked herself out!

What more could go wrong? she wondered. Maybe the superintendent was home. She stepped out in the rain to see if the lights were on in his apartment, which was situated above hers. His place was dark. Of course. That was how everything else was going.

Cupping one hand over her mouth while the other

held her stomach, Abby's laughter was mixed with sobs of anger and frustration.

"Abby?" Logan's urgent voice came from the street. Hurriedly he crossed it, took one look at her and hauled her into his arms.

"Logan, I'll get you wet," she cried, trying to push herself free.

"What happened? Are you all right?"

"No. Yes. I don't know," she murmured, sniffling miserably. "What are you doing here?"

Logan brought her out of the rain and stood with his back blocking the wind, trying to protect her from the storm. "Let's get you inside and dry and I'll explain."

"Why?" she asked and wrung the water from the hem of her sweatshirt. "So you can hurl insults at me?"

"No," he said vehemently. "I've been half-crazy wondering where you were."

"I'll just bet," Abby taunted unmercifully. "I'm surprised you didn't assume I was with Tate."

A grimace tightened his jaw, and Abby knew she'd hit her mark. "Are you going to be difficult or are we going inside to talk this out reasonably?"

"We can't go inside," she said.

"Why not?"

"Because I forgot my keys."

"Oh, Abby," Logan groaned.

"And the manager's gone. Do you have any more bright ideas?"

"Did you leave the bedroom window open?" he asked with marked patience.

"Yes, just a little, but—" A glimmer of an idea sparked and she smiled boldly at Logan. "Follow me."

"Why do I have the feeling I'm not going to like this?" he asked under his breath as Abby pulled him by the hand around to the back of the building.

"Here," she said, bending her knee and lacing her fingers together to give him a boost upward to the slightly open window.

"You don't expect to launch me through there, do you?" Logan glared at her. "I won't fit."

Rivulets of rain trickled down the back of Abby's neck. "Well, I can't do it. You know I'm afraid of heights."

"Abby, the window's barely five feet off the ground."

"I'm standing here, drenched and miserable," she said, waving her hands wildly. "On my birthday, no less," she added sarcastically, "and you don't want to rescue me."

"I'm not in the hero business," Logan muttered as he hunched his shoulders to ward off the rain. "Try Tate."

"Fine, I'll do that." She stalked off to the side of the building.

"Abby?" He sounded unsure as she dragged over an aluminum garbage can.

"Go away!" she shouted. "I don't need you."

"What's the difference between going through the window using a garbage can or having me lift you through?"

"Plenty." She wasn't sure what, but she didn't want to take the time to figure it out. All she wanted was a hot bath and ten gallons of hot chocolate.

"You're being totally irrational."

"I've always been irrational. It's never bothered you before." Her voice trembled as she balanced her weight on the lid of the garbage can. She reached the window and pushed it open enough to crawl through when she felt the garbage can lid give way. "Logan!" she screamed, terror gripping her as she started to fall.

Instantly he was there. His arms gripped her waist as she tumbled off the aluminum container. Together they went crashing to the ground, Logan twisting so he took the worst of the fall.

"Are you okay?" he asked frantically, straightening and brushing the hair from her face.

Abby was too stunned and breathless to speak, so she just nodded.

"Now listen," he whispered angrily. "I'm going to lift you up to the windowsill and that's final. Do you understand?"

She nodded again.

"I've had enough of this arguing. I'm cold and wet and I want to get inside and talk some reason into you." He stood and wiped the mud from his hands, then helped her up. Taking the position she had earlier, he crouched and let her use his knee as a step as his laced fingers boosted her to the level of the window.

Abby fell into the bedroom with a loud thud, knocking the lamp off her nightstand. Dano howled in terror and dashed under the bed.

"Are you okay?" Logan yelled from outside.

Abby stuck her head out the window. "Fine. Come around to the front and I'll let you in."

"I'll meet you at your door."

"Logan." She leaned forward and smiled at him provocatively. "You *are* my hero."

He didn't look convinced. "Sure. Whatever you say."

Abby had buzzed open the front door and unlocked her own by the time he came around the building. His wet hair was dripping water down his face, and his shirt was plastered to his chest, revealing a lean, muscular strength. He looked as drenched and miserable as she felt.

"You take a shower while I drive home and change out of these." He looked down ruefully at his mud-spattered beige pants and rain-soaked shirt.

Abby agreed. Logan had turned and was halfway out the door when Abby called him back. "Why are you here?" she asked, wanting to delay his leaving.

He shrugged and gave her that warm, lazy smile she loved. "I don't know. I thought there might be another movie you wanted to see."

Abby laughed and blew him a kiss. "I'm sure there is."

When Logan returned forty minutes later, Abby's hair was washed and blown dry and hung in a long French braid down the middle of her back. She'd changed into a multicolored bulky sweater and jeans.

Abby smiled. "We're not going to fight, are we?"

"I certainly hope not!" he exclaimed. "I don't think I can take much more of this. When I left here the first time I was thinking…" He paused and scratched his head. "I was actually entertaining the thought of driving to Des Moines and back."

"That's crazy." Abby tried unsuccessfully to hide her giggles.

"You're telling me?" He sat on the sofa and held out his arm to her, silently inviting her to join him.

Abby settled on the sofa, her head resting on his chest while his hand caressed her shoulder.

"Do you recall how uncomplicated our lives were just a few weeks ago?" Logan asked her.

"Dull. Ordinary."

"What changed all that?"

Abby was hesitant to bring Tate's name into the conversation. "Life, I guess," she answered vaguely. "I know you may misunderstand this," she added in a husky murmur, "but I don't want to go back to the way our relationship was then." He hadn't told her he loved her and she hadn't recognized the depth of her own feelings.

He didn't move. "No, I don't suppose you would."

Abby repositioned her head and placed the palm of her hand on his jaw, turning his face so she could study him. Their eyes met. The hard, uncompromising look in his dark eyes disturbed her. She desperately wanted to assure him of her love. But she'd realized after the first time that words were inadequate. She shifted and slid her hands over his chest to pause at his shoulders.

The brilliance of his eyes searched her face. "Abby." He groaned her name as he fiercely claimed her lips. His hand found its way to the nape of her neck, his fingers gently pulling dark strands free from the braid so he could twine them through his fingers.

His breathing deep, he buried his face in the slope of her neck. "Just let me hold you for a while. Let's not talk."

She agreed and settled into the warm comfort of his embrace. The staccato beat of his heart gradually returned to a normal pace and Abby felt content and loved. The key to a peaceful relationship was to bask in their love for each other, she thought, smiling. That, and not saying a word.

"What's so amusing?" Logan asked, his breath stirring the hair at the side of her face.

"How do you know I'm smiling?"

"I can feel it."

Abby tilted her head so she could look into his eyes. "This turned into a happy birthday, after all," she said.

Now he smiled, too. "Can I see you tomorrow?"

"If you weren't going to ask me, then I would've been forced to make some wild excuse to see *you*." Lovingly Abby rubbed her hand along the side of his jaw, enjoying the slightly prickly feel of his beard.

"What would you like to do?"

"I don't care as long as I'm with you."

"My, my," he whispered, taking her hand. Tenderly he kissed her palm. "You're much easier to please than I remember."

"You don't know the half of it," she teased.

Logan stiffened and sat upright. "What's tomorrow?"

"The tenth. Why?"

"I can't, Abby. I've got something scheduled."

She felt a rush of disappointment but knew that if she was frustrated, so was Logan. "Don't worry, I'll survive," she assured him, then smiled. "At least I think I will."

"But don't plan anything for the day after tomorrow."

"Of course I'm planning something."

"Abby." He sounded tired and impatient.

"Well, it's Sunday, right? Our usual day. So I'm planning to spend it with you. I thought that was what you wanted."

"I do."

The grimness about his mouth relaxed.

Almost immediately afterward, Logan appeared restless and uneasy. Later, as she dressed for bed, she convinced herself that it was her imagination.

The lesson with Mai-Ling the following afternoon went well. It was the last reading session they'd have, since Mai-Ling was now ready to move on. She'd scheduled one with Tate right afterward, deciding that what Logan didn't know wouldn't hurt him. Tate was still painfully self-conscious and uncomfortable about telling anyone else, although his progress was remarkable and he advanced more quickly than any student she'd ever tutored, including the talented Mai-Ling. From experience, she could tell he was spending many hours each evening studying.

On her way back to her apartment late Saturday afternoon, Abby decided on the spur of the moment to stop at Patty's and see how she was recuperating. She'd sent her an email wishing her a rapid recovery and had promised to stop over some afternoon. Patty needed friends and Abby was feeling generous. Her topsy-turvy world had been righted.

She went to a drugstore first and bought half a dozen glossy magazines as a get-well gift, then drove to Patty's home.

Her sister answered the doorbell.

"Hi, you must be from the baseball team. Patty's gotten a lot of company. Everyone's been wonderful."

Abby wasn't surprised. Everyone on the team was warm and friendly.

"This must be her day for company. Come on in. Logan's with her now."

Seven

Abby was dismayed as the sound of Patty's laughter drifted into the entryway, but she followed Patty's sister into the living room.

Patty's broken arm was supported by a white linen sling and she sat opposite Logan on a long sofa. Her eyes were sparkling with undisguised happiness. Logan had his back to Abby, and it was all she could do not to turn around and leave. Instead she forced a bright smile and made an entrance any actress would envy. "Hello, everyone!"

"Hi, Abby!" Patty had never looked happier or, for that matter, prettier. Not only was her hair nicely styled, but she was wearing light makeup, which added color to her pale cheeks and accented her large brown eyes. She wore a lovely summer dress, a little fancy for hanging around the house, and shoes that were obviously new.

"How are you feeling?" Abby prayed the phoniness in her voice had gone undetected.

Logan stood up and came around the couch, but his eyes didn't meet Abby's probing gaze.

"Hello, Logan, good to see you again."

"Hello, Abby."

"Sit down, please." Patty pointed to an empty chair. "We've got a few minutes before dinner." Patty seemed oblivious to the tension between her guests.

"No, thanks," Abby murmured, faking another smile. "I can only stay a minute. I just wanted to drop by and see how you were doing. Oh, these are for you," she said, handing over the magazines. "Some reading material…"

"Thank you! And I'm doing really well," Patty said enthusiastically. "This is the first night I've been able to go out. Logan's taking me to dinner at the Sofitel."

Abby breathed in sharply and clenched her fist until her nails cut into her hand. Logan had taken her there only once, but Abby considered it their special restaurant. He could've taken Patty anyplace else in the world and it would've hurt, but not as much as this.

"Everyone's been great," Patty continued. "Dick and his wife were over yesterday, and a few others from the team dropped by. Those flowers—" she indicated several plants and bouquets "—are from them."

"We all feel terrible about the accident." Abby made her first honest statement of the visit.

"But it was my own fault," Patty said as Logan hovered stiffly on the other side of the room.

Abby lowered her eyes, unable to meet the happy glow in Patty's. A crumpled piece of wrapping paper rested on the small table at Patty's side. It was the same paper Logan had used to wrap Abby's birthday gift the day before. He *couldn't* have gotten Patty perfume. He wouldn't dare.

"You look so nice," Abby said. Her pulse quickened. What *had* Logan brought Patty? She thought she recognized that scent.… "Is that a new perfume you're wearing?"

"Yes, as a matter of fact, Logan—"

"Hadn't we better be going?" Logan said as he made a show of glancing at his watch.

Patty looked flustered. "Is it time already?"

Following her cue, Abby glared at Logan and took a step in retreat. "I should go, too." A contrived smile curved her mouth. "Have a good time."

"I'll walk you to your car," Logan volunteered.

Walking backward Abby gestured with her hands, swinging them at her sides to give a carefree impression. "No, that isn't necessary. Really. I'm capable of finding my own way out."

"Abby," Logan said under his breath.

"Have a wonderful time, you two," Abby continued, her voice slightly high-pitched. "I've only been to the Sofitel once. The food was fantastic, but I can't say much for my date. But I no longer see him. A really ordinary guy, if you know what I mean. And so predictable."

"I'll be right back." Logan directed his comment to Patty and gripped Abby by the elbow.

"Let me go," she seethed.

Logan's grip relaxed once they were outside the house. "Would you let me explain?"

"Explain?" She threw the word in his face. "What could you possibly say? No." She waved her hand in front of his chest. "Don't say a word. I don't want to hear it. Do you understand? Not a word."

"You're being irrational again," Logan accused, apparently having difficulty keeping his rising temper in check.

"You're right," she agreed. "I've completely lost my sense. Please forgive me for being so closed-minded." Her voice was surprisingly even but it didn't disguise the hurt or the feeling of betrayal she was experiencing.

"Abby."

"Don't," she whispered achingly. "Not now. I can't talk now."

"I'll call you later."

She consented with an abrupt nod, but at that point, Abby realized, she would have agreed to anything for the opportunity to escape.

Her hand was shaking so badly that she had trouble sliding the key into the ignition. This was crazy. She felt secure in his love one night and betrayed the next.

Abby didn't go home. The last thing she wanted to do was sit alone on a Saturday night. To kill time, she visited the Mall of America and did some shopping, buying herself a designer outfit that she knew Logan would hate.

The night was dark and overcast as she let herself into the apartment. Hanging the new dress in her closet, Abby acknowledged that spending this much money on one outfit was ridiculous. Her reasons were just as childish. But it didn't matter; she felt a hundred times better.

The phone rang the first time at ten. Abby ignored it. Logan. Of course. When it started ringing at five-minute intervals, she simply unplugged it. There was nothing she had to say to him. When they spoke again, she wanted to feel composed. Tonight was too soon. She wasn't ready yet.

Calm now, she changed into her pajamas and sat on the sofa, brushing her long hair in smooth, even strokes. Reaction would probably set in tomorrow, but for now she was too angry to think.

Half an hour later, someone pressed her buzzer repeatedly. Annoying though it was, she ignored that, too.

When there was a banging at her door, Abby hesitated, then continued with her brushing.

"Come on, Abby, I know you're in there." Logan shouted.

"Go away. I'm not dressed," she called out sweetly.

"Then get dressed."

"No!" she yelled back.

Logan's laugh was breathless and bitter. "Either open up or I'll tear the stupid door off its hinges."

Just the way he said it convinced Abby this wasn't an idle threat. And to think that only a few weeks ago she'd seen Logan as unemotional. Laying her brush aside, she walked to the door and unlatched the safety chain.

"What do you want? How did you get into the building? And for heaven's sake, keep the noise down. You're disturbing the neighbors."

"Some guy from the second floor recognized me and opened the lobby door. And if you don't let me in to talk to you, I'll do a lot more than wake the neighbors."

Abby had never seen Logan display so much passion. Perhaps she should've been thrilled, but she wasn't.

"Did you and Patty have a nice evening?" she asked with heavy sarcasm.

Logan glanced briefly at his hands. "Reasonably nice."

"I apologize if I put a damper on your *date*," she returned with smooth derision. "Believe me, had I known about it, I would never have visited Patty at such an inopportune time. My timing couldn't have been better—or worse, depending on how you look at it."

"Abby," he sighed. "Let me in. Please."

"Not tonight, Logan."

Frustration furrowed his brow. "Tomorrow, then?"

"Tomorrow," she agreed and started to close the door. "Logan," she called and he immediately turned back. "Without meaning to sound like I care a whole lot, let me ask you something. Why did you give Patty the same perfume as me?" Some perverse part of herself had to know.

His look was filled with defeat. "It seemed the thing to do. I knew she'd enjoy it, and to be honest, I felt sorry for her. Patty needs someone."

Abby's chin quivered as the hurt coursed through her. Pride dictated that she maintain a level gaze. "Thank you for not lying," she said and closed the door.

Tate was waiting for her when Abby entered the park at eleven-thirty Sunday morning. Since her Saturday sessions with Mai-Ling had come to an end, Abby was now devoting extra time on weekends to Tate.

"You look like you just stepped out of the dentist's chair," Tate said, studying her closely. "What's the matter? Didn't you sleep well last night?"

She hadn't.

"You work too hard," he told her. "You're always helping others. Me and Mai-Ling…"

Abby sat on the blanket Tate had spread out on the grass and lowered her gaze so that her hair fell forward, hiding her face. "I don't do nearly enough," she disagreed. "Tate," she said, raising her eyes to his. "I've never told anyone the reason we meet. Would you mind if I did? Just one person?"

Unable to sleep, Abby had considered the various reasons Logan might have asked Patty out for dinner. She was sure he hadn't purposely meant to hurt her. The only logical explanation was that he wanted her to experience the same feelings he had, since she was continuing to see Tate. And yet he'd gone to pains to keep her from knowing about their date. Nothing made sense anymore. But if she could tell Logan the reason she was meeting Tate, things would be easier.…

Tate rubbed a weary hand over his eyes. "This is causing problems with you and—what's-his-name—isn't it?"

Abby didn't want to put any unnecessary pressure on Tate so she shrugged her shoulders, hoping to give the impression of indifference. "A little. But I don't think Logan really understands."

"Is it absolutely necessary that he know?"

"No, I guess not." Abby had realized it would be extremely difficult for Tate to let anyone else learn about his inability to read—especially Logan.

"Then would it be too selfish of me to ask that you don't say anything?" Tate asked. "At least not yet?" A look of pain flashed over his face, and Abby understood anew how hard it was for him to talk about his problem. "I suppose it's a matter of pride."

Abby's smile relaxed her tense mouth. The relationship among the three of them was a mixed-up matter of pride, and she didn't know whose was the most unyielding.

"No, I don't mind," she replied, and opened her backpack to take out some books. "By the way, I want to give you something." She handed him three of her favorite Dick Francis books. "These are classics in the mystery genre. They may be a bit difficult for you in the beginning, but I think you'll enjoy them."

Tate turned the paperback copy of *The Danger* over and read the back cover blurb. "His business is kidnapping?" He sounded unsure as he raised his eyes to hers.

"Trust me. It's good."

"I'll give it a try. But it looks like it'll take me a while."

"Practice makes perfect."

Tate laughed in the low, lazy manner she enjoyed so much. "I've never known anyone who has an automatic comeback the way you do." He took a cold can of soda and tossed it to her. "Let's drink to your wit."

"And have a celebration of words." She settled her back against the trunk of a massive elm and closed her eyes as Tate haltingly read the first lines of the book she'd given him. It seemed impossible that only a few weeks before he'd been unable to identify the letters of the alphabet. But his difficulty wasn't attributed to any learning disability, such as she'd encountered in the past with others. He was already at a junior level and advancing so quickly she had trouble keeping him in material, which was why she'd started him on a novel. Unfortunately, his writing and spelling skills were advancing at a slower pace. Abby calculated that it wouldn't take more than a month or two before she could set him on his own with the promise to help when he needed it. Already he'd voiced his concerns about an application he'd be filling out for the bank to obtain a business loan. She'd assured him they'd go over it together.

Abby hadn't been home fifteen minutes when Logan showed up at her building. She buzzed him in and opened the door, but for all the emotion he revealed, his face might have been carved in stone.

"Are you going to let me inside today?" he asked, peering into her apartment.

"I suppose I'll have to."

"Not necessarily. You could make a fool of me the way you did last night."

"Me?" she gasped. "You don't need *me* to make you look like a fool. You do a bang-up job of it yourself."

His mouth tightened as he stepped into her apartment and sank down on the sofa.

Abby sat as far away from him as possible. "Well?" She was determined not to make this easy.

"Patty was in a lot of pain when I drove her to the hospital the night of the accident," he began.

"Uh-huh." She sympathized with Patty but didn't know why he was bringing this up.

Logan's voice was indifferent. "I was talking to her, trying to take her mind off how much she was hurting. It seems that in all the garble I rashly said I'd take her to dinner."

"I suppose you also—rashly—suggested the Sofitel?" She felt chilled by his aloofness and she wasn't going to let him off lightly.

An awkward silence followed. "I don't remember that part, but apparently I did."

"Apparently so," she returned with forced calm. "Maybe I could forget the dinner date, but not the perfume. Honestly, Logan, that was a rotten thing to do."

Impatience shadowed his tired features. "It's not what you think. I got her cologne. Not perfume."

"For heaven's sake," she said, exasperated. "Can't you be more original than that?"

"But it's the truth."

"I know that. But you can't go through life giving women perfume and cologne every time the occasion calls for a gift. And, even worse, you chose the same scent!"

"It's the only one I know." He shook his head. "All right, the next time I buy a woman a gift, I'll take you along."

"The next time you buy a woman a gift," she interrupted in a stern voice, "it had better be me."

He ignored her statement. "Abby, how could you believe I'm attracted to Patty?"

She opened her mouth and closed it again. "Maybe I can believe that you really do care about me. But I've seen the way Patty looks at you. It wouldn't take more than a word to have her fall in love with you. I don't want to see her hurt." Or any of them for that matter, Abby mused. "I don't believe you're using Patty to make me jealous," she said honestly. "I mean, I wondered about it but then decided you weren't."

"I'm glad you realize that much." He breathed out in obvious relief.

"But I recognize the looks she's giving you, Logan. She wants you."

"And Tate wants you!"

Abby's shoulders sagged. "Don't go bringing him into this discussion. It's not right. We were talking about you, not me."

"Why not? Isn't turnabout fair play?" The contempt in his expression made her want to cry.

"That's tiddlywinks, not love," she said saucily.

"But if Patty looks at me with adoring eyes, it only mirrors the way Tate looks at you."

"Now you're being ridiculous," she said, annoyed by his false logic.

Slowly Logan rubbed his chin. "It's always amazed me that you can twist a conversation any way you want."

"That's not true," she said, hating the fact that he'd turned the situation around to suit himself.

"All right, let's put it like this—if you mention Patty Martin, then I mention Tate Harding. That sounds fair to me."

"Fine." She flipped a strand of hair over her shoulder. "I won't mention Patty again."

"Are you still seeing him?"

"Who?" Abby widened her eyes innocently.

Logan's jaw tightened grimly. "I want you to promise me that you won't date Harding again."

Abby stared at him.

"A simple yes or no. That's all I want."

The answer wasn't even difficult. She *wasn't* dating him. "And what do I get in return?"

He bent his head to study his hands. "Something that's been yours for over a year. My heart."

At his words, all of Abby's defensive anger melted. "Oh, Logan," she whispered, emotion bringing a misty happiness to her eyes.

"I've loved you so long, Abby, I can't bear to lose you." There could be no doubt of his sincerity.

"I love you, too."

"Then why are you on the other side of the room when all I want to do is hold you and kiss you?"

The well of tenderness inside her overflowed. She rose from her sitting position. "In the interests of fairness, I think we should meet halfway. Okay?"

He chuckled as he stood, coming to her, but his eyes revealed a longing that was deep and intense. A low groan rumbled from his throat as he swept her into his arms and held her as if he never wanted to let her go. He kissed her eyes, her cheeks, the corner of her mouth until she moaned and begged for more.

"Abby." His voice was muffled against her hair. "You're not going to sidestep my question?"

"What question?" She smiled against his throat as she gave him nibbling, biting kisses.

His hands gripped her shoulders as he pulled her slightly away from him so he could look into her face. "You won't be seeing Tate again?"

She decided not to make an issue of semantics. He *meant* date, not see. What she said in response was the truth. "I promise never to date anyone else again. Does that satisfy you?"

He linked his hands at the small of her back and

smiled deeply into her eyes. "I suppose it'll have to," he said, echoing her remark when she'd let him in.

"Now it's your turn."

"What would you like?"

"No more dating Patty, okay?"

"I agree," he replied without hesitation.

"Inventive gift ideas."

He hesitated. "I'll try."

"You're going to have to do better than that."

"All right, all right, I agree."

"And—"

"There's more?" he interrupted with mock impatience.

"And at some point in our lives I want to drive to Des Moines."

"Fine. Shall we seal this agreement with a kiss?"

"I think it would be only proper," Abby said eagerly as she slid her arms around his waist and fit her body to his.

His large hands framed her face, lifting her lips to meet his. It lacked the urgency of their first kiss, but was filled with promise. His breathing was ragged when he released her, but Abby noted that her own wasn't any calmer.

Not surprisingly, their truce held. Maybe it was because they both wanted it so badly. The next Sunday they met at her place for breakfast, which Abby cooked. Later, they drove over to her parents' house and during their visit Frank Carpenter speculated that the two of them would be married by the end of the year. A few not-so-subtle questions about the "date" popped up here and there in the conversation. But neither of them seemed to mind. Logan was included in Abby's every thought. This was the way love was supposed to be, Abby mused as they returned to her apartment.

After changing clothes, they rode their bikes to the park and ate a picnic lunch. After that, with Logan's head resting in her lap, Abby leaned against an elm tree and closed her eyes. This was the same tree that had supported her back during more than one reading session with Tate. A guilty sensation attacked the pit of her stomach, but she successfully fended it off.

"Did you hear that Dick Snyder wants to climb Mount Rainier this summer?" Logan asked unexpectedly, as he chewed lazily on a long blade of grass.

In addition to softball, Dick's passion was mountains. She'd heard rumors about his latest venture, but hadn't been all that interested.

"Yeah, I heard that," she murmured. "So?"

"So, what do you think?"

"What do I think about what?" Abby asked.

"They need an extra man. It sounds like the expedition will be cancelled otherwise." Logan frowned as he looked up at her.

"Climbing the highest mountain in Washington State should be a thrill—for some people. They won't have any trouble finding someone. Personally, I have trouble making it over speed bumps," she teased, leaning forward to kiss his forehead. "What's wrong?"

He smiled up at her and raised his hands to direct her mouth to his. "What could possibly be wrong?" he whispered as he moved his mouth onto her lips for a kiss that left her breathless.

The next week was the happiest of Abby's life. Logan

saw her daily. Monday they went to dinner at the same
Mexican restaurant Tate had taken her to weeks before.
The food was good, but Abby's appetite wasn't up to
par. Again, Abby dismissed the twinge of guilt. Tuesday he picked her up for class, but they decided to skip
school. Instead they sat in the parking lot and talked
until late. From there they drove until they found a café
where they could enjoy their drinks outside. The communication between them had never been stronger.

Tate phoned Abby at work on Wednesday and asked
her to meet him at the park before the softball game.
He wanted to be sure his application for the business
loan had been filled out correctly. Uneasy about being
in public with him, for fear Logan would see or hear
about it, Abby promised to stop off at his garage.

Later, when Logan picked her up for the game she
was short-tempered and restless.

"What's the matter with you tonight?" he complained
as they reached the park. "You're as jumpy as a bank
robber."

"Me?" She feigned innocence. "Nervous about the
game, I guess."

"You?" He looked at her with disbelief. "Ms. Confidence? You'd better tell me what's really bothering you.
Fess up, kid."

She felt her face heat with a guilty blush. "Nothing's
wrong."

"Abby, I thought we'd come a long way recently.
Won't you tell me what's bothering you?"

Logan was so sincere that Abby wanted to kick herself. "Nothing. Honest," she lied and tried to swallow

the lump in her throat. She hated this deception, no matter how minor it really was.

"Obviously you're not telling the truth," he insisted, and a muscle twitched in his jaw.

"What makes you say that?" She gave him a look of pure innocence.

"Well, for one thing, your face is bright red."

"It's just hot, that's all."

He released a low breath. "Okay, if that's the way you want it."

Patty was in the bleachers when they arrived, and waved eagerly when she saw Logan. Abby doubted she'd noticed that Abby was with him.

"Your girlfriend's here," Abby murmured sarcastically.

"My girlfriend is walking beside me," Logan said. "What's gotten into you lately?"

Abby sighed. "Don't tell me we're going over all of that again?" She didn't wait for him to answer. Instead she ran onto the field, shouting for Dick to pitch her the ball.

The game went smoothly. Patty basked in the attention everyone was giving her and had the team sign her cast. Abby readily agreed to add her own comment, eager to see what Logan had written on the plaster. But she couldn't locate it without being obvious. Maybe he'd done that on purpose. Maybe he'd written Patty a sweet message on the underside of her arm, where no one else could read it. The thought was so ridiculous that Abby almost laughed out loud.

They lost the game by a slim margin, and Abby realized she hadn't been much help. During the get-together at the pizza place afterward she listened to the others joke and laugh. She wanted to join in, but tonight she simply didn't feel like partying.

"Are you feeling all right?" Logan sat beside her, holding her hand. He studied her with worried eyes.

"I'm fine," she answered and managed a halfhearted smile. "But I'm a little tired. Would you mind taking me home?"

"Not at all."

They got up and, with Logan's hand at the small of her back, they made their excuses and left.

The silence in the car was deafening, but Abby did her best to ignore the unspoken questions Logan was sending her way.

"How about if I cook dinner tomorrow?" Abby said brightly. "I've been terrible tonight and I want to make it up to you."

"If you're not feeling well, maybe you should wait."

"I'm fine. Just don't expect anything more complicated than hot dogs on a bun." She was teasing and Logan knew it.

He parked outside her building and kissed her gently. Abby held on to him compulsively as if she couldn't bear to let him go. She felt caught in a game of cat and mouse between Tate and Logan—a game in which she was quickly becoming the loser.

The following evening, Abby was putting the finishing touches on a salad when Logan came over.

"Surprise," he said as he held out a small bouquet of flowers. "Is this more original than perfume?" he asked with laughing eyes.

"Hardly." She gave him a soft brushing kiss across his freshly shaven cheek as she took the carnations from his hand. "Mmm, you smell good."

Logan picked a tomato slice out of the salad and popped it into his mouth. "So do you."

"Well, if you don't like the fragrance, you have only yourself to blame."

"Me? You smell like pork chops." He slipped his arms around her waist from behind and nuzzled her neck. "You know I could get used to having dinner with you every single night." The teasing quality left his eyes.

Abby dropped her gaze as her heart went skyrocketing into space. She knew what he was saying. The question had entered her mind several times during the past few days. These feelings they were experiencing were the kind to last a lifetime. Abby wanted to share Logan's life. The desire to wake up with him at her side every morning, to marry him and have his children, was stronger than any instinct. She loved this man and wanted to be with him always.

"I think I could get used to that, too," she admitted softly.

Someone knocked at the door, breaking into their conversation. Impatiently Logan glanced at it. "Are you expecting anyone? One of your neighbors?"

"You," she said. "Here, turn these. I'll see who it is and get rid of them." She handed him the spatula.

Abby's hand was shaking as she grasped the knob, praying it wouldn't be Tate. If she was lucky, she could ask him to leave before Logan knew what was happening.

Her worst fears were realized when she pulled the door open halfway.

"Hi. Someone let me into the lobby."

"Hello, how are you?" she asked in a hushed whisper.

"I'm returning the books you lent me. I really enjoyed them." Tate gave her a funny look. "Is this a bad time or something?"

"You might say that," she breathed. "Could you come back tomorrow?"

"Sure, no problem. Is it Logan?"

Abby nodded, and as she did, the door was opened all the way.

"Hello, Tate," Logan greeted him stiffly. "I've been half-expecting you. Why don't you come inside where we can all visit?"

Eight

The two men regarded each other with open hostility.

Glancing from one to the other, Abby paused to swallow a lump of apprehension. Her worst fears had become reality. She wanted to blurt out the truth, explain to Logan exactly why she was seeing Tate. But one look at the two of them standing on either side of the door and Abby recognized the impossibility of making any kind of explanation. Like rival warlords, the two blatantly dared each other to make the first move.

Logan loomed at her side exuding bitterness, surprise, hurt and anger. He held himself still and rigid.

"I'll see you tomorrow, Abby?" Tate spoke at last, making the statement a question.

"Fine." Abby managed to find her voice, which was low and urgent. She wanted to scream at him to leave. If pride wasn't dominating his actions, he'd recognize what a horrible position he was putting her in. Apparently maintaining his pride was more important than the problem he was causing her. Abby's eyes pleaded with

Tate, but either he chose to ignore the silent entreaty or he didn't understand what she was asking.

The enigmatic look on Tate's face moved from Logan to Abby. "Will you be all right? Do you want me to stay?"

"Yes. No!" She nearly shouted with frustration. He'd read the look in her eyes as a plea for help. This was crazy. This whole situation was unreal.

"Tomorrow, then," Tate said as he took a step in retreat.

"Tomorrow," Abby confirmed and gestured with her hand, begging him to leave.

He turned and stalked away.

Immobile, Abby stood where she was, waiting for Logan's backlash.

"How long have you been seeing each other?" he asked with infuriating calm.

If he'd shouted and decried her actions, Abby would have felt better; she could have responded the same way. But his composed manner relayed far more adequately the extent of his anger.

"How long, Abby?" he repeated.

Her chin trembled and she shrugged.

His short laugh was derisive. "Your answer says quite a bit."

"It's not what you think," she said hoarsely, desperately wanting to set everything straight.

His jaw tightened forbiddingly. "I suppose you're going to tell me you and Tate are just good friends. If that's the case, you can save your breath."

"Logan." Fighting back tears of frustration, Abby

moved away from the door and turned to face him. "I need you to trust me in this."

"Trust you!" His laugh was mocking. "I asked you to decide which one of us you wanted. You claimed you'd made your decision. You even went so far as to assure me you wouldn't be seeing Tate again." The intense anger darkened the shadows across his face, making the curve of his jaw look sharp and abrupt.

"I said I wouldn't *date* him again," she corrected.

"Don't play word games with me," he threw back at her. "You knew what I meant."

She merely shook her head, incapable of arguing. Why *couldn't* he trust her? Why hadn't Tate just *told* him? Why, why, why.

"I suspected something yesterday at the game," Logan continued wryly. "That guilty look was in your eyes again. But I didn't want to believe what I was seeing."

Abby lowered her gaze at the onrush of pain. This deception hadn't been easy for her. But she was bound by her promise to Tate. She couldn't explain the circumstances of their meetings to Logan; only Tate's permission would allow her to do that. But Tate couldn't risk his pride to that extent and she wouldn't ask him to.

Logan's short laugh was bitter with irony. "Yet, when the doorbell rang, I knew immediately it was Tate. To be honest, I was almost glad, because it clears away the doubts in my mind."

Determinedly he started for the door, but Abby's hand delayed him. "Don't go," she whispered. "Please." Her fingers tightened around his arm, wanting to bind him to her forever, beginning with this moment. "I love you and…and if you love me, then you'll trust me."

"Love?" he repeated in a contemptuous voice. "You don't know the meaning of the word."

Stunned, Abby dropped her hand and with a supreme effort met his gaze without emotion. "If that's what you think, maybe it would be better if you did leave."

Logan paused, his troubled expression revealing the inner storm raging within him.

"I may be wrong, but I was brought up to believe that love between two people required mutual trust," Abby added.

One corner of his mouth quirked upward. "And I assumed, erroneously it seems, that love required honesty."

"I…I bent the truth a little."

"Why?" he demanded. "No." He stopped her from explaining. "I don't want to know. Because it's over. I told you before that I wouldn't be kept dangling like a schoolboy while you made up your mind."

"But I *can't* explain now! I may never be able to tell you why."

"It doesn't matter, Abby, it's over," Logan said starkly, his expression impassive.

Abby's stomach lurched with shock and disbelief. Logan didn't mean that. He wouldn't do that to them.

Without another word he walked from the room. The door slammed as he left the apartment. He didn't hesitate or look back.

Abby held out her hand in a weak gesture that pleaded with him to turn around, to trust her. But he couldn't see her, and she doubted it would've had any effect on him if he had. Unshed tears were dammed in her throat, but Abby held her head up in a defiant gesture of pride. The pretense was important for the moment, as she calmly moved into the kitchen and turned off the stove.

Only fifteen minutes before, she had stared lovingly into Logan's eyes, letting her own eyes tell him how much she wanted to share his life. Now, swiftly and without apparent concern, Logan had rejected her as carelessly and thoughtlessly as he would an old pair of shoes. Yet Abby knew that wasn't true. He *did* love her. He couldn't hold her and kiss her the way he did without loving her. Abby knew him as well as he knew her. But then, Abby mused, she had reason to doubt that Logan knew her at all.

Even worse was the fact that Abby recognized she was wrong. Logan deserved an explanation. But her hands were bound by her promise to Tate. And Tate had no idea what that pledge was doing to her and to her relationship with Logan. She couldn't believe he'd purposely do this, but Tate was caught in his own trap. He viewed her as his friend and trusted teacher. He felt fiercely protective of her, wanting in his own way to repay her for the second chance she was giving him by teaching him to read.

Logan and Tate had disliked each other on sight. The friction between them wasn't completely her fault, Abby realized. The ironic part was that for all their outward differences they were actually quite a bit alike.

When Abby had first met Tate that day in the park she'd found him compelling. She'd been magnetically drawn to the same strength that had unconsciously bound her to Logan. This insight had taken Abby weeks to discover, but it had come too late.

The weekend arrived in a haze of emotional pain. Tate phoned Friday afternoon to tell her he wouldn't be able to meet her on Saturday because he was going to the bank to sign the final papers for his loan. He invited her to dinner in celebration, but she declined. Not meeting him gave Abby a reprieve. She wasn't up to facing anyone right now. But each minute, each hour, the hurt grew less intense and life became more bearable. At least, that was what she tried to tell herself.

She didn't see Logan on Sunday, and forced herself not to search for him in the crowded park as she took a late-afternoon stroll. This was supposed to be their day. Now it looked as if there wouldn't be any more lazy Sunday afternoons for them.

Involved in her melancholy thoughts, Abby wandered the paths and trails of the park, hardly noticing the people around her.

Early that evening, as the sun was lowering in a purple sky, Abby felt the urge to sit on the damp earth and take in the beauty of the world around her. She needed the tranquillity of the moment and the assurance that another day had come and gone and she'd made it through the sadness and uncertainty. She reflected on her feelings and actions, admitting she'd often been headstrong and at times insensitive. But she was learning, and although the pain of that growth dominated her mind now, it, too, would fade. Abby stared at the darkening sky and, for the first time in several long days, a sense of peace settled over her.

Sitting on the lush grass, enjoying the richness of the park grounds, Abby gazed up at the sky. These rare, peaceful minutes soothed her soul and quieted her troubled heart. If she were never to see Logan again, she'd always be glad for the good year they'd shared. Too late she'd come to realize all that Logan meant to her. She'd carelessly tossed his love aside—with agonizing consequences.

The following afternoon Abby called Dick Snyder about Wednesday's softball game. Although she was dying for the sight of Logan, it would be an uncomfortable situation for both of them.

"Dick, it's Abby," she said when he answered. She suddenly felt awkward and uneasy.

"Abby," Dick greeted her cheerfully. "It's good to hear from you. What's up?"

An involuntary smile touched the corners of her mouth. No-nonsense Dick. He climbed mountains, coached softball teams, ran a business with the effectiveness of a tycoon and raised a family; it was all in a day's work, as he often said. "Nothing much, but I wanted you to know I won't be able to make the game on Wednesday."

"You, too?"

"Pardon?" Abby didn't know what he meant.

"Logan phoned earlier and said he wouldn't be at the game, either. Are you two up to something we should know about?" he teased. "Like running off and getting married?"

Abby felt the color flow out of her face, and her heart

raced. "No," she breathed, hardly able to find her voice. "That's not it at all."

Her hand was trembling when she replaced the receiver a couple of minutes later. So Logan had decided not to play on Wednesday. If he was quitting softball, she could assume he'd also stop attending classes on Tuesday nights. The possibility of their running into each other at work was still present, since their offices were only half a block apart, but he must be going out of his way to avoid any possible meeting. For that matter, she was doing the same thing.

Soon Abby's apartment began to feel like her prison. She did everything she could to take her mind off Logan, but as the weeks progressed, it became more and more difficult. Much as she didn't want to talk to anyone or provide long explanations about Logan's absence, Abby couldn't tolerate another night alone. She had to get out. So after work the following Wednesday, she got in her car and started to drive.

Before she realized where she was headed, Abby pulled into her parents' driveway.

"Hi, Mom," Abby said as she let herself in the front door.

Her father was reading the paper, and Abby paused at his side. She placed her hand on his shoulder, kissing him lightly on the forehead. "What's that for?" Frank Carpenter grumbled as his arm curved around her waist. "Do you need a loan?"

"Nope," Abby said with forced cheer. "I was just thinking that I don't say *I love you* nearly enough." She glanced up at her mother. "I'm fortunate to have such good parents."

"How sweet," Glenna murmured softly, but her eyes were clouded with obvious worry. "Is everything all right?"

Abby restrained the compulsion to cry out that *nothing* was right anymore. Not without Logan. She left almost as quickly as she'd come, making an excuse about hurrying home to feed Dano. That weak explanation hadn't fooled her perceptive mother. Abby was grateful Glenna didn't pry.

Another week passed and Abby didn't see Logan. Not that she'd expected to. He was avoiding her as determinedly as she did him. Seeing him would only mean pain. She lost weight, and the dark circles under her eyes testified to her inability to sleep.

Sunday morning, Abby headed straight for the park, intent on finding Logan. Even a glimpse would ease the pain she'd suffered without him. She wondered if his face would reveal any of the same torment she had endured. Surely he regretted his lack of trust. He must miss her—perhaps even enough to set aside their differences and talk to her. And if he did, Abby knew she'd readily respond. She imagined the possible scenes that might play out—from complete acceptance on his part to total rejection.

There was a certain irony in her predicament. Tate had been exceptionally busy and she hadn't tutored him at all that week. He was doing so well now that it wouldn't be more than a month before he'd be reading and writing at an adult level. Once he'd completed the lessons, Abby doubted she'd see him very often, despite the friendship that had developed between them. They had little in common and Tate had placed her on such a high pedestal that Abby didn't think he'd ever truly see her as a woman. He saw her as his rescuer, his salvation—not a position Abby felt she deserved.

She sat near the front entrance of the park so she wouldn't miss Logan if he showed up. She made a pretense of reading, but her eyes followed each person entering the park. By noon, she'd been waiting for three hours and Logan had yet to arrive. Abby felt sick with disappointment. Logan came to the park every Sunday morning. Certainly he wouldn't change that, too— would he?

Defeated, Abby closed her book and meandered down the path. She'd been sitting there since nine, so she was sure she hadn't missed him. As she strolled through the park, Abby saw several people she knew and paused to wave but walked on, not wanting to be drawn into conversation.

Dick Snyder's wife was there with her two school-aged children. She called out Abby's name.

"Hi! Come on over and join me. It'll be nice to have an adult to talk to for a while." Betty Snyder chatted easily, patting an empty space on the park bench. "I keep telling Dick that one of these days *I'm* going mountain climbing and leaving him with the kids." Her smile was bright.

Abby sat on the bench beside Betty, deciding she could do with a little conversation herself. "Is he at it again?" she asked, already knowing the answer. Dick thrived on challenge. Abby couldn't understand how anyone could climb anything. Heights bothered her too much. She remembered once—

"Dick and Logan."

"Logan?" His name cut into her thoughts and a tightness twisted her stomach. "He's not climbing, is he?" She didn't even try to hide the alarm in her voice. Logan was no mountaineer! Oh, he enjoyed a hike in the woods, but he'd never shown any interest in conquering anything higher than a sand dune.

Betty looked at her in surprise. She'd obviously assumed Abby would know who Logan was with and what he was up to.

"Well, yes," Betty hedged. "I thought you knew. The Rainier climb is in two weeks."

"No, I didn't." Abby swallowed. "Logan hasn't said anything."

"He was probably waiting until he'd finished learning the basics from Dick."

"Probably," Abby replied weakly, her voice fading as terror overwhelmed her. Logan climbing mountains? With a dignity she didn't realize she possessed, Abby met Betty's gaze head-on. It would sound ridiculous to tell Betty that this latest adventure had slipped Logan's mind. The fact was, Abby knew it hadn't. She recalled Logan's telling her that Dick was looking for an extra climber. But he hadn't said it as though he was considering it *himself.*

Betty continued, apparently trying to fill the stunned silence. "You don't need to worry. Dick's a good climber. I'd go crazy if he weren't. I have complete and utter confidence in him. You shouldn't worry about Logan. He and Dick have been spending a lot of time together preparing for this. Rainier is an excellent climb for a first ascent."

Abby heard almost nothing of Betty's pep talk and

her heart sank. This had to be some cruel hoax. Logan was an accountant. He didn't have the physical endurance needed to ascend fourteen thousand feet. He wasn't qualified to do any kind of climbing, let alone a whole mountain. Someone else should go. Not Logan.

Not the man she loved.

Betty's two rambunctious boys returned and closed around the women, chatting excitedly about a squirrel they'd seen. The minute she could do so politely, Abby slipped away from the family and hurried out of the park. She had to get to Logan—talk some sense into him.

Abby returned to her apartment and got in her car. She drove around, dredging up the nerve to confront Logan. If he was out practicing with Dick, he wouldn't be back until dark. Twice she drove by his place, but his parking space was empty.

After a frustrating hour in a shopping mall, Abby sat through a boring movie and immediately drove back to Logan's. For the third time she saw that he hadn't returned. She drove around again—for how long she was unsure.

Abby couldn't comprehend what had made him decide to do this. A hasty decision wasn't like him. She wondered if this crazy mountain-climbing expedition was his way of punishing her; if so, he'd succeeded beyond his expectations. The only thing left to do was confront him.

Abby drove back to Logan's building, telling herself that the sooner they got this settled, the better. Relief washed over her at the familiar sight of his car.

She pressed his apartment buzzer, but Logan didn't

respond. She tried again, keeping her finger on it for at least a minute. And still Logan didn't answer.

Abby decided she could sit this out if he could. Logan wasn't fooling her. He was there.

When he finally answered and let her into the building lobby, Abby ran in, rushing up to his third-floor apartment. He'd opened the door and she stumbled ungracefully across the threshold. Regaining her balance—and her breath—she turned to glare angrily at him.

"Abby." Logan was holding a pair of headphones. "Were you waiting long?" He closed the door, placing the headset on a shelf. "I'm sorry I didn't hear you, but I was listening to a CD."

Regaining her composure, Abby straightened. "Now listen here, Logan Fletcher." She punctuated her speech with a finger pointed at him. "I know why you're doing this, and I won't let you."

"Abby, listen." He murmured her name in the soft way she loved.

"No," she cried. "I *won't* listen!"

He held her away from him, one hand on each shoulder. Abby didn't know if this was meant to comfort her or to keep her out of his arms. Desperately she wanted his arms around her, craved the comfort she knew was waiting for her there.

"You don't need to prove anything to me," she continued, her voice gaining in volume and intensity. "I love you just the way you are. Logan, you're more of a hero than any man I know, and I can't—no," she corrected emotionally, "I *won't* let you do this."

"Do what?"

She looked at him in stunned disbelief. "Climb that stupid mountain."

"So you did hear." He sighed. "I was hoping none of this would get back to you."

"Logan," she gasped. "You weren't planning to let me know? You're doing this to prove some egotistical point to me and you weren't even going to let me know until it was too late? I can't believe you'd do that. I simply can't believe it. You've always been so logical and all of a sudden you're falling off the deep end."

Now it was his turn to look flabbergasted. "Abby, sit down. You're becoming irrational."

"I am not," she denied hotly, but she did as he suggested. "Logan, please listen to me. You can't go traipsing off to Washington on this wild scheme. The whole idea is ludicrous. Crazy!"

He knelt beside her and she framed his face with both hands, her eyes pleading with his.

"Don't you understand?" she said. "You've never climbed before. You need experience, endurance and sheer nerve to take on a mountain. You don't have to prove anything to me. I love you just the way you are. Please don't do this."

"Abby," Logan said sternly and pulled her hand free, holding her fingers against his chest. "This decision is mine. You have nothing to do with it. I'm sorry this upsets you, but I'm doing something I've wanted to do for years."

"Haven't you listened to a word I've said?" She yanked her hands away and took in several deep breaths. "You could be killed!"

"You seem to be confusing the issues. My desire to

make this climb with Dick and his friends has nothing to do with you."

"Nothing to do with me?" she repeated frantically. Had Logan gone mad? "If you think for one instant that I'm going to let you do this, then you don't know me, Logan Fletcher."

He stood up, and smoothed the side of his hair with one hand as he regarded her quizzically. "You seem to be under the mistaken impression that I'm doing this to prove something to you."

"You may not have admitted it to yourself, but that's exactly the reason you are." She shook her head frantically. "You're climbing this crazy mountain because you want to impress me."

Logan's short laugh was filled with amusement. "I'm doing this, Abby, because I want to. My reasons are as simple as that. You're making it sound like I'm going in front of a firing squad. Dick's an experienced climber. I expect to be perfectly safe," he said matter-of-factly.

"I don't believe you could be so naive," she told him flatly, "about the danger of mountain-climbing *or* about your own motivations."

"Then that's your problem."

"But…you could end up dead!"

"I could walk across the street and be hit by a car tomorrow," Logan replied with infuriating calm.

Abby couldn't stand his quiet confidence another second. She leaped to her feet and stalked across the floor, gesturing wildly with her hands, unable to clarify her thoughts enough to reason with him. Pausing, she took a moment to compose herself. "If this is something you always wanted to do, how come I've never heard about it before?"

"Because I knew what your reaction would be—and I was right. I—"

"You're so caught up in the excitement of this adventure, you can't see how crazy it is," Abby interrupted, not wanting him to argue with her. He *had* to listen.

Logan took her gently by the shoulders and turned her around. "I think you should realize that nothing you say is going to change my mind."

"I drove you to this—" Her voice throbbed painfully.

"No," he cut in abruptly and brushed a hand across his face. "As I keep telling you, this is something I've always wanted to do, whether you like it or not."

"I don't like it and I don't believe it."

"That's too bad." Logan breathed in harshly. "But unlike certain people I know, I don't bend the truth. It's true, Abby."

Abby's mouth twisted in a smile. "And you weren't even going to tell me."

His look was grudging. "I think you can understand why."

Abby shut her eyes and groaned inwardly.

"Now if you'll excuse me, I really do need to get back to the audio book I'm listening to. It's on climbing. Dick recommended it."

"I thought you were smarter than this. I've never heard of anything so stupid in my life," she said waspishly, lashing out at him in her pain.

His smile was mirthless as if he'd expected that kind of statement from her.

"I'm sorry," she mumbled as she studied the

scuffed-up toe of her shoe. The entire day had been crazy. "I didn't mean that."

A finger under her chin lifted her eyes to his. "I know you didn't." For that instant all time came to a halt. His eyes burned into hers with an intensity that stole her breath.

Seemingly of their own volition, her hands slid over his chest. She wound her arms around his neck and stood on the tips of her toes as she fitted her mouth over his. The slow-burning fire of his kiss melted her heart. Every part of her seemed to be vibrantly alive. Her nerves tingled and flared to life.

Angrily Logan broke the kiss. "What's this?" he said harshly. "My last kiss before I face the firing squad?"

"Hardly. I expect you to come back alive." She paused, frowning at him. "If you don't, I swear I'll never forgive you."

He rammed his hands into his pants pockets. Then, as if he couldn't bear to look at her, he stalked to the other side of the room. "If I don't come back, why would it matter? We're not on speaking terms as it is."

From somewhere deep inside her, Abby found the strength to swallow her pride and smile. "That's something I'd like to change."

"No," he said without meeting her gaze.

"You're not leaving for two weeks. During that time you won't be able to avoid seeing me," she went on. "I don't mind telling you that I plan to use every one of those days to change your mind."

"It won't work, Abby," he murmured.

"I can try. I—"

"What I mean is that I have two weeks before the

climb, but we're flying in early to explore several other mountains in the Cascade Range."

"The Cascades?" From school, Abby remembered that parts of the Cascade mountain range in Washington State had never been explored. This made the whole foolish expedition even more frightening.

"My flight leaves tomorrow night."

"No," she mumbled miserably, the taste of defeat filling her.

"There's a whole troop who'll be seeing us off. If you're free, you might want to come, too."

Abby noted that he didn't ask her to come, but merely informed her of what was happening. Sadly she shook her head. "I don't think so, Logan. I refuse to be a part of it. Besides, I'm not keen on tearful farewells and good wishes."

"I won't ask anything from you anymore, Abby."

"That's fine," she returned more flippantly than she intended. Involuntary tears gathered in her eyes. "But you'd better come back to me, Logan Fletcher. That's all I can say."

"I'll be back," he told her confidently.

Not until Abby was halfway home did she realize that Logan hadn't said he was coming back *to her*.

Later that night Abby lay in bed while a kaleidoscope of memories went through her mind. She recalled the most memorable scenes of her year-long relationship with Logan. One thing was clear: she'd been blind and stupid not to have appreciated him, or recognized how much she loved him.

Staring at the blank ceiling, she felt a tear roll from

the corner of her eye and fall onto the pillow. Abby was intensely afraid for Logan.

The following afternoon, when Abby let herself into her apartment, the phone was ringing.

Abby's heart hammered in her throat. Maybe Logan was calling to say goodbye. Maybe he'd changed his mind and would ask her to come to the airport after all.

But it was her mother.

"Abby." Glenna's raised voice came over the line. "I just heard that Logan's joining Dick Snyder on his latest climb."

"Yes," Abby confirmed in a shaky voice, wondering how her mother had found out about it. "His plane's leaving in—" she paused to check her watch "—three hours and fifteen minutes. Not that I care."

"Oh, dear, I was afraid of that. You're taking this hard."

"Me? Why would I?" Abby attempted to sound cool and confident. She didn't want her mother to worry about her. But her voice cracked and she inhaled a quivering breath before she was able to continue. "He's in Dick's capable hands, Mother. All you or I or anyone can do is wait."

The hesitation was only slight. "Sometimes you amaze me, Ab."

"Is that good or bad?" Some of her sense of humor was returning.

"Good," her mother whispered. "It's very good."

The more Abby told herself she wouldn't break down and go to the airport, the more she realized there was nothing that could stop her.

A cold feeling of apprehension crept up her back and extended all the way to the tips of her fingers as Abby drove. Her hands felt clammy, but that was nothing compared to her stomach. The churning pain was almost more than she could endure. Because she hadn't been able to eat all day, she felt light-headed now.

Abby arrived at the airport and the appropriate concourse in plenty of time to see the small crowd of well-wishers surrounding Dick, Logan and company. They obviously hadn't checked in for their flight. Standing off to one side, Abby chose not to involve herself. She didn't want Logan to know she'd come. Almost everyone from the softball team was there, including Patty. She seemed more quiet and subdued than normal, Abby noted, and was undoubtedly just as worried about Logan's sudden penchant for danger as she herself was.

Once Abby thought Logan was looking into the crowd as if seeking someone. Desperately she wanted to run to him, hold him and kiss him before he left. But she was afraid she'd burst into tears and embarrass them both. Logan wouldn't want that. And her pride wouldn't allow her to show her feelings.

When it came time for Logan and the others to check in and go through security, there was a flurry of embraces, farewells and best wishes. Then almost everyone departed en masse.

Abby waited, studying the departures board until she knew his plane had left.

Nine

Abby rolled out of bed, stumbled into the kitchen and turned on the radio, anxious to hear the weather report. They were in the midst of a July heatwave.

Cradling a cup of coffee in her hands, Abby eyed the calendar. In a few days Logan would be home. Each miserable, apprehensive day brought him closer to her.

Betty Snyder continued to hear regularly from Dick about the group's progress as they trekked over some of the most difficult of the Cascade mountains. Trying not to be obvious, Abby phoned Betty every other day or so, to hear whatever information she could impart. Abby still didn't know the true reasons Logan had joined this venture, but believed they were the wrong ones.

The first week after his departure, Abby received a postcard. She'd laughed and cried and hugged it to her breast. An email would've been nice. Or a phone call. But she'd settle—happily—for a postcard. Crazy, wonderful Logan. Anyone else would have sent her a scene of picturesque Seattle or at least the famous mountain he was about to climb. Not Logan. Instead he sent her a picture of a salmon.

His message was simple:

How are you? Wish you were here. I saw you at the airport. Thank you for coming. See you soon.

Love, Logan

Abby treasured the card more than the bottles of expensive French perfume he'd given her. Even when several other people on the team received similar messages, it didn't negate her pleasure. The postcard was tucked in her purse as a constant reminder of Logan. Not that Abby needed anything to jog her memory; Logan was continually in her thoughts. And although the message on the postcard was impersonal, Abby noted that he'd signed it with his love. It was a minor thing, but she held on to it with all her might. Logan did love her, and somehow, some way, they were going to overcome their differences because what they shared was too precious to relinquish.

"Disturbing news out of Washington State for climbers on Mount Rainier..." the radio announced.

Abby felt her knees go weak as she pulled out a kitchen chair and sat down. She immediately turned up the volume.

"An avalanche has buried eleven climbers. The risk of another avalanche is hampering the chances of rescue. Six men from the Minneapolis area were making a southern ascent at the time of the avalanche. Details at the hour."

A slow, sinking sensation attacked Abby as she placed a trembling hand over her mouth.

During the news, the announcer related the sketchy details available about the avalanche and fatalities and concluded the report with the promise of updates as they became available. Abby ran for the TV and turned it to an all-news channel. She heard the same report over and over. Each word struck Abby like a body blow, robbing her lungs of oxygen. Pain constricted her chest. Fear, anger and a hundred emotions she couldn't identify were all swelling violently within her. When the telephone rang, she nearly tumbled off the chair in her rush to answer it.

Please, oh, please don't let this be a call telling me Logan's dead, her mind screamed. *He promised he'd come back.*

It was Betty Snyder.

"Abby, do you have your radio or TV on?" she asked urgently. Her usual calm manner had evaporated.

"Yes…I know," Abby managed shakily. "Have you heard from Dick?"

"No." Her soft voice trembled. "Abby, the team was making a southern ascent. If they survived the avalanche, there's a possibility they'll be trapped on the mountain for days before a rescue team can reach them." Betty sounded as shocked as Abby.

"We'll know soon if it's them."

"It's not them," Betty continued on a desperate note, striving for humor. "And if it isn't, I'll personally kill Dick for putting me through this. We should hear something soon."

"I hope so."

"Abby," Betty asked with concern, "are you going to be all right?"

"I'll be fine." But hearing the worry in her friend's voice did little to reassure her. "Do you want me to come over? I can take the day off..."

"Dick's mother is coming and she's a handful. You go on to work and I'll call you if I hear from Dick—or anyone."

"Okay." Her friends at the clinic and on the team would need reassurance themselves and Abby could quickly relay whatever messages came through. She'd check her computer regularly for any breaking news.

"Everything's going to work out fine." Betty's tone was low and wavering and Abby realized her friend expected the worst.

The day was a living nightmare; every nerve was stretched taut. With each ring of the office phone her pulse thundered before she could bring it under control and react normally.

Keeping busy was essential for her sanity those first few hours. But by quarter to five she'd managed to settle her emotions. The worst that could've happened was that Logan was dead. The worst. But according to the news, no one from the Minneapolis area was listed among those missing and presumed dead. Abby decided to believe they were fine; there was no need to face any other possibility until necessary.

After work Abby drove directly to Betty's. She hadn't realized how emotionally and physically drained she was until she got there. But she forced herself to relax before entering her friend's home, more for Betty's sake than her own.

"Have you heard anything?" she asked calmly as Betty let her in the front door. She could hear the TV in the background.

"Not a word." Betty studied Abby closely. "Just what's on the news. The hardest part is not knowing."

Abby nodded and bit her bottom lip. "And the waiting. I won't give up my belief that Logan's alive and well. He must be, because *I'm* alive and breathing. If anything happened to Logan, I'd know. My heart would know if he was dead." Abby recognized that her logic was questionable, but she expected her friend to understand better than anyone else exactly what she was saying.

"I feel the same thing," Betty confirmed.

Dick's mother had gone home and Abby stayed for a while to keep Betty and the kids company. Then she went to her apartment to change clothes and watch the latest update on TV. The television reporter wasn't able to relate much more than what had been available that morning.

Tate was waiting for her at the little Mexican restaurant where they met occasionally and raised his hand when she entered. They'd arranged this on the weekend, and Abby had decided not to change their plans. She needed the distraction.

Her relationship with Tate had changed in the past weeks. *He'd* changed. Confident and secure now, he often came to her with minor problems related to the business material he was reading. She was his friend as well as his teacher.

"I didn't know if you'd cancel," Tate said as he pulled

out a chair for her. "I heard about the accident on Mount Rainier."

"To be honest, I wasn't sure I should come. But I would've gone crazy sitting at home brooding about it," Abby admitted.

"Any news about Logan?"

Abby released a slow, agonizing breath. "Nothing."

"He'll be fine," Tate said. "If anyone could take care of himself, I'd say it was Logan. He wouldn't have gone if he didn't know what to expect and couldn't protect himself."

Abby was surprised by Tate's insights. She wouldn't have thought that Tate would be so generous in his comments.

"I thought you didn't like Logan." She broached the subject boldly. "It seemed that every time you two were around each other, fireworks went off."

Tate lifted one shoulder in a dismissive shrug. "That's because I didn't like his attitude toward you."

"How's that?"

"You know. He acted like he owned you."

The problem was that he held claim to her heart and it had taken Tate to show Abby how much she loved Logan. Her fingers circled the rim of the glass and she smiled into her water. "In a way he does," she whispered. "Because I love him, and I know he loves me."

Tate picked up the menu and studied it. "I'm beginning to realize that...." he murmured. "Look, I'll try to talk to him, if that'll help."

Abby reached across the table and squeezed his hand "Thanks, Tate."

The waitress approached them. "Are you ready to order?"

Abby glanced at the menu and nodded. "I'll have the cheese enchiladas."

"Make that two," Tate said absently. "No." He paused. "I've changed my mind. I'll have the pork burrito."

Abby tried unsuccessfully to disguise her amusement.

"What's so funny?" Tate asked.

"You. Do you remember the first few times we went out to eat? You always ordered the same thing I did. I'm pleased to see you're not still doing it."

"It became a habit." He paused. "I owe you a great deal, Abby, more than I'll ever be able to repay."

"Nonsense." They were friends, and their friendship had evolved from what it had been in those early days, but his gratitude sometimes made her uncomfortable.

"Maybe this will help show a little of my appreciation." Tate pulled a small package from inside his pocket and handed it to her.

Abby was stunned, her fingers numb as she accepted the beautifully wrapped box. She raised her eyes to his. "Tate, please. This isn't necessary."

"Hush and open your gift," he instructed, obviously enjoying her surprise.

When she pulled the paper away, Abby was even more astonished to see the name of a well-known and expensive jeweler embossed across the top of the case. Her heart was in her throat as she shook her head disbelievingly. "Tate," she began. "I—"

"Open it." An impish light glinted in his eyes.

Slowly she raised the lid to discover a lovely

intricately woven gold chain on a bed of blue velvet. Even with her untrained eye, Abby recognized that the chain was of the highest quality. A small cry of undisguised pleasure escaped before she could hold it back.

"Tate!" She could hardly take in its beauty. For the first time in months she found herself utterly speechless.

"Abby?"

"I…I can't believe it. It's beautiful."

"I knew you'd like it."

"Like it! It's the most beautiful necklace I've ever seen. Thank you." Abby smiled at him. "But you shouldn't have. You know that, don't you?"

"If you say so."

"*Now* he's agreeable." Abby smiled as she spoke to the empty chair beside her. "Here, help me put it on."

Tate stood and came around to her side of the table. He took the chain from its plush bed and laid it against the hollow of her throat. Abby bowed her head and lifted the hair from the back of her neck to make it easier for Tate to fasten the necklace.

When he returned to his chair, Abby felt a warm glow. "I still think you shouldn't have done this, but to be honest, I'm glad you did."

"I knew the minute I saw it in the jeweler's window that it was exactly what I was looking for. If you want the truth, I'd been searching for weeks for something special to give you. I want to thank you for everything you've done for me."

Abby didn't think Tate realized what a small part she'd played in his tutoring. He'd done all the real work himself. He was the one who'd sought her out with a need and admitted that need—something he'd never been able to do before, having always hidden his inability. Abby doubted Tate recognized how far he'd come from the day he'd followed her home from the park.

Later, when Abby undressed for bed, she fingered the elegant chain, remembering Tate's promise. Maybe now he'd be willing to explain to Logan why Abby had met with him. The chain represented his willingness to help repair her relationship with Logan. That would be the most significant gift he could possibly give her.

Before leaving for work the next morning, Abby checked the news. Nothing. Then she phoned Betty in case there'd been any calls during the night. There hadn't been, and discouragement sounded in Betty's voice as she promised to phone Abby's office if she heard anything.

At about ten that morning, Abby had just finished updating the chart on a young teen who'd visited the clinic, when she glanced up and saw Betty in the doorway.

Abby straightened and stood immobile, her heart pumping at a furious rate. Suddenly, she went cold with fear. She couldn't move or think. Even breathing became impossible. Betty would've come to the office for only one reason, she thought. Logan was dead.

"Betty," she pleaded in a tortured whisper, "tell me. What is it?"

"He's fine! Everyone is. They were stuck on the slopes an extra night, but made it safely to camp early this morning. I just heard—Dick called me."

Abby closed her eyes and exhaled a breath of pure

release. Her heart skipped a beat as she moved across the room. The two women hugged each other fiercely as tears of happiness streaked their faces.

"They're on their way home. The flight will land sometime tomorrow evening. Everyone's planning to meet them at the airport. You'll come, won't you?"

In her anger and pain Abby had refused to see him off with the others…until the last minute. She wouldn't be so stubborn about welcoming him home. Abby doubted she'd be able to resist hurling herself into his arms the instant she saw him. And once she was in his arms, Abby defied anyone to tear her away.

"Abby? You'll come, won't you?" Betty's soft voice broke into her musings.

"I'll be there," Abby replied, as the image of their reunion played in her mind.

"I thought you'd want to be." Her friend gave her a knowing look.

Logan was safe and coming home. Abby's heart leaped with excitement and she waited until it resumed its normal pace before returning to her desk.

"Tonight," Abby explained to Tate at lunch on Thursday. She swallowed a bite of her pastrami sandwich. "Their flight's arriving around nine-thirty. The team's planning a get-together with him and Dick on Friday night. You're invited to attend if you'd like."

"I just might come."

Tate surprised her with his easy acceptance. Abby had issued the invitation thoughtlessly, not expecting Tate to take her up on it. For that matter, it might even have been the wrong thing to do, since Logan would almost certainly be offended.

"I was beginning to wonder if you were ever going to invite me to any of those social functions your team's always having."

"Tate." Abby glanced up in surprise. "I had no idea you wanted to come. I wish you'd said something earlier." Now she felt guilty for having excluded him in the past.

"Sure," Tate chimed in defensively. "They'll take one look at a mechanic and decide they've got something better to do."

"Tate, that's simply not true." And it wasn't. He'd be accepted as would anyone who wished to join them. Plenty of friends and coworkers attended the team's social events.

"It might turn a few heads." Tate expelled his breath as if he found the thought amusing.

"Oh, hardly."

"You don't think so?" he asked hopefully.

Tate's lack of self-confidence was a by-product of his inability to read. Now that reading was no longer a problem, he would gain that new maturity. She was already seeing it evolve in him.

Moonlight flooded the ground. The evening was glorious. Not a cloud could be seen in the crystal-blue sky as it darkened into night. Slowly, Abby released a long, drawn-out sigh. Logan would land in a couple of hours and the world had never been more beautiful. She paused to hum a love ballad playing on the radio, thrilled by the romantic words.

She must have changed her clothes three times, but everything had to be perfect. When Logan saw her at the airport, she wanted to look as close to an angel as anything he would find this side of heaven.

She spent half an hour on her hair and makeup. Nothing satisfied her. Tight-lipped, Abby realized she couldn't suddenly make herself into an extraordinarily beautiful woman. Sad but true. She could only be herself. She dressed in a soft, plum-colored linen suit and a pink silk blouse. Dissatisfied with her hair, Abby pulled it free of the confining pins and brushed it until it shimmered and fell in deep natural waves down the middle of her back. Logan had always loved her hair loose....

A quick glance at her watch showed her that she was ten minutes behind schedule. Grabbing her purse, Abby hurried out to her car—and she noticed that it was running on empty. Everything seemed to be going wrong....

Abby pulled into a service station, splurging on full service for once instead of pumping her own. *Hurry*, she muttered to herself as the teenager took his time.

"Do you want me to check your oil?"

"No, thanks." Abby handed him the correct change, plus a tip. "And don't bother washing the window."

Inhaling deep breaths helped take the edge off her impatience as she merged onto the freeway. A mile later an accident caused a minor slowdown.

By the time she arrived at the airport, her heart was pounding. Checking the arrivals board revealed that Logan's flight was on schedule.

Abby ran down the concourse. Within minutes the

team, as well as Karen, Logan's assistant, came into sight.

Warmth stole over Abby as she saw Logan, a large backpack slung over one shoulder. His face was badly sunburned, the skin around his eyes white from his protective eye gear. He looked tanned and more muscular than she could remember. His eyes searched the crowd and paused on her, his look thoughtful and intense.

Abby beamed, wearing her brightest smile. He was so close. Close enough to reach out and touch if it weren't for the people crowding around. Abby's heart swelled with the depth of her love. His own eyes mirrored the longing she was sure he could see in hers. These past weeks were all either of them would need to recognize that they should never be apart again.

Abby edged her way toward him and Dick. The others who'd come to greet Logan were chatting excitedly, but Abby heard none of their conversation. Logan was back! Here. Now. And she loved him. After today he'd never doubt the strength of her feelings again.

In her desire to get to Logan quickly, Abby nearly stumbled over an elderly man. She stopped and apologized profusely, making sure the white-haired gentleman wasn't hurt. As she straightened, she heard someone call out Logan's name.

In shocked disbelief, Abby watched as Patty Martin ran across the room and threw herself dramatically into Logan's arms. He dropped his pack. Sobbing, she clung to him as if he'd returned from the dead. Soon the others gathered around, and Dick and Logan were completely blocked from Abby's view.

The bitter taste of disappointment filled her mouth.

Logan should have pushed the others aside and come to her. *Her* arms should be the ones around him. *Her* lips should be the ones kissing his.

Proudly Abby decided she wouldn't fight her way through the throng of well-wishers. If Logan wanted her, then she was here. And he knew it.

But apparently he didn't care. Five minutes later, the small party moved out of the airport and progressed to the parking lot. As far as Abby could tell, Logan hadn't so much as looked around to see where she was.

After all the lonely days of waiting for Logan, Abby had a difficult time deciding if she should attend the party being held at a local buffet restaurant in his and Dick's honor the following evening. If he hadn't come to her at the airport, then what guarantee did she have that he wouldn't shun her a second time? The pain lingered from his first rejection. Abby didn't know if she could bear another one.

To protect her ego on Friday night Abby dressed casually in jeans and a cotton top. She timed her arrival so she wouldn't cause a stir when she entered the restaurant. As she'd expected, and as was fitting, Logan and Dick were the focus of attention while they relived their tales of danger on the high slopes.

Abby filled her plate and took a seat where she could see Logan. She knew she wouldn't be able to force down any dinner; occasionally she rearranged the food in front of her in a pretence of eating.

Sitting where she was, Abby could observe Logan covertly. Every once in a while he'd glance up and search the room. He seemed to be waiting for someone.

Abby would've liked to believe he was looking for her, but she could only speculate. The tension flowed out of her as she witnessed again the strength and vitality he exuded. That experience on the mountain had changed him, just as it had changed her.

Unable to endure being separated any longer, Abby pushed her plate aside and crossed the room to his table. Logan's eyes locked with hers as she approached. Someone was speaking to him, but Abby doubted that Logan heard a word of what was being said.

"Hello, Logan," she said softly. Her arms hung nervously at her sides. "Welcome home."

"It's good to see you, Abby." His gaze roamed her face lovingly. He didn't need to pull her into his arms for Abby to know what he was feeling. It was all there for her to read. Her doubts, confusion and anxiety were all wiped out in that one moment.

"I'm sorry about what happened at the airport." His hand clasped hers. "There wasn't anything I could do."

Their eyes held as she studied his face. Every line, every groove, was so familiar. "Don't apologize. I understand." Who would've believed a simple touch could cause such a wild array of sensations? Abby felt shaky and weak just being this close to him. A tingling warmth ran up the length of her arm as he gently enclosed her in his embrace.

"Can I see you later?"

"You must be exhausted." She wanted desperately to be with him, but she could wait another day. After all this time, a few more hours wouldn't matter.

"Seeing you again is all the rest I need."

"I'll be here," she promised.

Dick Snyder tapped Logan on the shoulder and led him to the front row of tables. After a few words from Dick about their adventure, Logan stood and thanked everyone for their support. He relayed part of what he'd seen and the group's close brush with death.

The tables of friends and relatives listened enthralled as Logan and Dick spoke. Hearing him talk so casually about their adventures was enough to make Abby's blood run cold. She'd come so close to losing him.

Abby stood apart from Dick and Logan while they shook everyone's hand as they filed out the door and thanked them for coming. When the restaurant began to empty Logan hurried across the room and brought Abby to his side. She wasn't proud of feeling this way, but she was glad Patty hadn't come. Abby was also grateful that Tate had called to say he couldn't make it. In an effort to assure him he'd be welcome another time, Abby invited him to the team picnic scheduled that Sunday in Diamond Lake Park. Tate promised to be there if possible.

Logan led her into the semidarkened parking lot and turned Abby into his arms. There was a tormented look in his eyes as he gazed down on her upturned face.

"Crazy as it sounds, the whole time we were trapped on that mountain, I was thinking that if I didn't come back alive you'd never forgive me." With infinite tenderness he kissed her.

"I wouldn't have forgiven you," she murmured and smiled up at him in the dim light.

"Abby, I love you," he said. "It took a brush with death to prove how much I wanted to come home to you."

His mouth sought hers and with a joyful cry, Abby wrapped her arms around him and clung. Tears of happiness clouded her eyes as Logan slipped his hands into the length of her hair. He couldn't seem to take enough or give enough as he kissed her again and again. Finally he buried his face in the slope of her neck.

He held her face as he inhaled a steadying breath. "When I saw you across the restaurant tonight, it was all I could do to be polite and stay with the others."

Abby lowered her eyes. "I wasn't sure you wanted to see me."

"You weren't sure?" Logan said disbelievingly. He slid his hands down to rest on the curve of her shoulders. His finger caught on the delicate gold chain and he pulled it up from beneath her blouse.

Abby went completely still. Logan seemed to sense that something wasn't right as his eyes searched hers.

"What's wrong?"

"Nothing."

His eyes fell on the chain. "This is lovely and it's far more expensive than you could afford. Who gave it to you, Abby? Tate?"

Ten

Abby pressed her lips so tightly together that they hurt. "Yes, Tate gave me the necklace."

"You're still seeing him, aren't you?" Logan dropped his hands to his sides and didn't wait for her to respond. "After everything I've said, you still haven't been able to break off this relationship with Tate, have you?"

"Tate has nothing to do with you and me," she insisted, inhaling deeply to hide her frustration. After the long, trying days apart, they *couldn't* argue! Abby wanted to cry out that she loved him and nothing else should matter. She should be able to be friends with a hundred men if she loved only him. Her voice shaking, she attempted to salvage their reunion. "I know this is difficult for you to understand. To be honest, I don't know how I'd feel if you were to continue seeing Patty Martin."

His mouth hardened. "Then maybe I should."

Abby realized Logan was tired and impatient, but an angry retort sprang readily to her lips. "You certainly seem to have a lot in common with Patty—far more than you do with me."

"The last thing I want to do is argue."

"I don't, either. My intention in coming tonight wasn't to defend my actions while you were away. And yes—" she paused to compose herself, knowing her face was flushed "—I did see Tate."

The area became charged with an electricity that seemed to spark and crackle. The atmosphere was heavy and still, pressing down on her like the stagnant air before a thunderstorm.

"I think that says everything I need to know," he said with quiet harshness.

Abby nodded sharply, forcing herself to meet his piercing gaze. "Yes, I suppose it does." She took a step backward.

"It was kind of you to come and welcome me back this evening." A muscle twitched in his jaw. "But as you can imagine, the trip was exhausting. I'd like to go home and sleep for a week."

Abby nodded, trying to appear nonchalant. "Perhaps we can discuss this another time."

Logan shook his head. "There won't be another time, Abby."

"That decision is yours," she said calmly, although her voice trembled with reaction. "Good night, Logan."

"Goodbye, Abby."

Goodbye! She knew what he was saying as plainly as if he'd screamed it at her. Whatever had been between them was now completely over.

"I expect you'll be seeing a lot more of Logan now that he's back," Tate commented from her living room the following afternoon.

Abby brought out a sandwich from the kitchen and handed it to him before taking a seat. "We've decided to let things cool between us," she said with as much aplomb as she could manage. "Cool" was an inadequate word. Their relationship was in Antarctica. They'd accidentally run into each other that morning while Abby was doing some grocery shopping and had exchanged a few stilted sentences. After a minute Abby could think of nothing more to say.

"You know what I think, Tate?" Abby paid an inordinate amount of attention to her sandwich. "I've come to the belief that love is a highly overrated emotion."

"Why?"

Abby didn't need to glance up to see the amusement in Tate's face. Instead she took the first bite of her lunch. How could she explain that from the moment she realized how much she loved Logan, all she'd endured was deep emotional pain. "Never mind," she said at last, regretting that she'd brought it up.

"Abby?" Tate's look was thoughtful.

She leaped to her feet. "I forgot the iced tea." She hurried into the kitchen, hoping Tate would let the subject drop.

"Did I tell you the bank approved my loan?"

Returning with their drinks, Abby grinned. "That's great!"

"They phoned yesterday afternoon. Bessler's pleased, but not half as much as I am. I have a lot to thank you for, Abby."

"I'm so happy for you," Abby said with a quick nod. "You've worked hard and deserve this." Abby knew how relieved Tate was that the loan had gone through.

He'd called Abby twice out of pure nerves, just to talk through his doubts.

Tomorrow afternoon they were going to attend the picnic together and although Abby was grateful for Tate's friendship, she didn't want to give her friends the wrong impression. Logan had already jumped to conclusions. There was nothing to say the others wouldn't, too. Tate was a friend—a special friend—but their relationship didn't go beyond that. It couldn't, not when she was in love with Logan.

"Abby," Tate said quietly. "I'm going to talk to him."

Sunday afternoon Abby was preoccupied as she dressed in shorts and a Twins T-shirt for the picnic. She was glad Tate was going with her, glad he'd promised to explain, but she hoped Logan didn't do or say anything to make him uncomfortable.

Logan. The unhappiness weighed down on her heart. Her thoughts were filled with him every waking minute. Even her dreams involved him. This misunderstanding, this lack of trust, had to stop once and for all. From the moment Logan had left for Washington, Abby had longed for Tate to explain the situation and heal her relationship with Logan. She'd assumed that as time went on they'd naturally get back together. Now, just the opposite was proving to be true. With every passing hour, Logan was drifting further and further out of her life. Yet her love was just as strong. Perhaps stronger. Whether Tate went through with his confession and whether it changed things remained to be seen.

Since Tate was meeting her at the park, Abby got there early and found a picnic table for them. When

Logan came, he claimed the table directly across from hers and Abby felt the first bit of encouragement since they'd last spoken. As quickly as the feeling came, it vanished. Logan set out a tablecloth and unpacked his cooler without so much as glancing her way. Only a few feet separated her from him, but it felt as if their distance had never been greater. He gave no indication that he'd seen her. Even her weak smile had gone unacknowledged.

Soon they were joined by the others, chatting and laughing. A few men played horseshoes while the women sat and visited. The day was glorious, birds trilled their songs from the tree branches and soft music came from someone's CD player. Busy putting the finishing touches on a salad, Abby sang along with the music. The last thing in the world she felt like doing was singing, but if she didn't, she'd start crying.

Tate arrived and Abby could see by the way he walked that he was nervous. He'd met some of the people at the softball game. Still, he looked surprised when one of the guys called out a greeting. The two men talked for a minute and Tate joined her soon afterward.

"Hi."

"There's no need to be nervous," she said, smiling at him.

"What? Me nervous?" he joked. "They're nice people, aren't they?"

"The best."

"Even Logan?"

"Especially Logan."

Tate was silent for a moment. "Like I said, I'll see what I can do to patch things up between you two."

Unhurriedly, she raised her gaze to his. "I'd appreciate that."

His returning smile told her how difficult revealing his past would be. Abby hated to ask him to do it, but there didn't seem to be any other way.

As he wandered off, Abby laced her fingers tightly and sat there, searching for Logan. He was standing alone with his back to her, staring out over the still, quiet lake.

Abby spread out a blanket between the two picnic tables and lay down on it, pretending to sunbathe. She must have drifted off, because the low-pitched voices of Tate and Logan were what stirred her into wakefulness.

"Seems to me you've got the wrong table," Logan was saying. "Your girlfriend's over there."

"I was hoping we could talk."

"I can't see that there's much to talk about. Abby's made her decision."

The noises that followed suggested that Logan was arranging drinks on the table and ignoring Tate as much as possible. Abby resisted the urge to roll over and see exactly what was happening.

"Abby's a friend," Tate said next. "No more and no less."

"You two keep saying that." Logan sounded bored.

"It's the truth."

"Sure."

There was a rustling sound and faintly Abby could hear Tate stumbling over the awkward words in the list of ingredients on the side of a soda can.

"What are you doing?" Logan asked.

"Reading," Tate explained. "And for me that's some kind of miracle. You see, until I met Abby here in the park helping Mai-Ling, I couldn't read."

A shocked silence followed his announcement.

"For a lot of reasons, I never properly learned," Tate continued. "Then I found Abby. Until I met her, I didn't know there were good people like her who'd be willing to teach me."

"Abby taught you to read?" Logan was obviously stunned.

"I asked her not to tell anyone. I suppose that was selfish of me in light of what's happened between you two. I don't have any excuse except pride."

Someone called Logan's name and the conversation was abruptly cut off. Minutes later someone else announced that it was time to eat. Abby joined the others, helping where she could. She and Tate were sitting with Dick and Betty when she felt Logan's eyes on her. The conversation around her faded away. The space between them seemed to evaporate as she turned and boldly met his look. In his eyes she read anger, regret and a great deal of inner pain.

When it came time to pack up her things and head home, Abby found Tate surrounded by a group of single women. He glanced up and waved. "I'll call you later," he told her cheerfully, clearly enjoying the attention he was receiving.

"Fine," she assured him. She hadn't gotten as far as the parking lot when Logan caught up with her.

He grabbed her shoulder as he turned her around. The anger she'd thought had been directed inward was now focused on her.

"Why didn't you tell me?" he demanded.

"I couldn't," she said simply. "Tate asked me not to."

"That's no excuse," he began, then paused to inhale a shuddering breath. "All the times I questioned you about meeting Tate, you were tutoring him. The least you could've done was tell me!"

"I already told you Tate was uncomfortable with that. Even now, I don't think you appreciate what it took for him to admit it to you," she explained slowly, enunciating each word so there'd be no misunderstanding. "I was the first person he'd ever told about this problem. It was traumatic for him and I couldn't go around telling others. Surely you can understand that."

"What about me? What about *us?*"

"My hands were tied. I asked you to trust me. A hundred times I pleaded with you to look beyond the obvious."

Logan closed his eyes and emitted a low groan. "How could I have been so stupid?"

"We've both been stupid and we've both learned valuable lessons. Isn't it time to put all that behind us?" She wanted to tell him again how much she loved him, but something stopped her.

Hands buried deep in his pockets, Logan turned away from her, but not before Abby saw that his eyes were narrowed. The pride in his expression seemed to block her out.

Abby watched in disbelief. The way he was behaving implied that *she'd* been the unreasonable, untrusting one. The more Abby thought about their short conversation as she drove home, the angrier she got.

Pacing her living room, she folded her arms around

her waist to ward off a sudden chill. "Of all the nerve," she snapped at Dano who paraded in front of her. The cat shot into her bedroom, smart enough to know when to avoid his mistress.

Yanking her car keys out of her purse, Abby hurried outside. She'd be darned if she'd let Logan end things like this.

His car was in its usual space, and he'd just opened the driver's door. She marched over, standing directly in front of him.

Logan frowned. "What's going on?"

She pointed her index finger at his chest until he backed up against the car.

"Now listen here, Logan Fletcher. I've had about all I can take from you." Every word was punctuated with a jab of her finger.

"Abby? What's the problem?"

"You and that stubborn pride of yours."

"Me?" he shouted in return.

"When we're married, you can bet I won't put up with this kind of behavior."

"Married?" he repeated incredulously. "Who said anything about marriage?"

"I did."

"Doesn't the man usually do the asking?" he said in a sarcastic voice.

"Not necessarily." Some of her anger was dissipating and she began to realize what a fool she was making of herself. "And...and while we're on the subject, you owe me an apology."

"You weren't entirely innocent in any of this."

"All right. I apologize. Does that make it easier on your fragile ego?"

"I also prefer to make my own marriage proposals."

Abby paled and crossed her arms. She wouldn't back down now. "Fine. I'm waiting."

Logan squared his shoulders and cleared his throat. "Abby Carpenter." His voice softened measurably. "I want to express my sincere apology for my behavior these past weeks."

"Months," she inserted with a low breath.

"All right, months," Logan amended. "Although you seem to be rushing the moment, I don't suppose it would do any harm to give you this." He pulled a diamond ring from his pocket.

Abby nearly fell over. Her mouth dropped open and she was speechless as he lifted her hand and slipped the solitaire diamond on her ring finger. "I was on my way to your place," he explained as he pulled her into his embrace. "I've loved you for a long time. You know that. I hadn't worked out a plan to steal your heart away from Tate. But you can be assured I wasn't going to let you go without a struggle."

"But I love—"

His lips interrupted her declaration of love. Abby released a small cry of wonder and wound her arms around his neck, giving herself to the kiss as his mouth closed over hers.

Gradually Logan raised his head, and his eyes were filled with the same wonder she was experiencing. "I talked to Tate again after you left the park," Logan said in a husky murmur. "I was a complete fool."

"No more than usual." Her small laugh was breathless.

"I'll need at least thirty years to make it up to you."

"Change that to forty and you've got yourself a deal."

His eyes smiled deeply into hers. "Where would you like to honeymoon?"

Abby's eyes sparkled. "Des Moines—where else?"

* * * * *

Celebrate Christmas
with #1 *New York Times* bestselling author Debbie Macomber!

$2.00 OFF DEBBIE MACOMBER'S CHRISTMAS COOKBOOK

NEW!
October 2011

FAVORITE RECIPES *and* **HOLIDAY TRADITIONS** *from* **DEBBIE MACOMBER'S HOME TO YOURS!**

$2.00 OFF DEBBIE MACOMBER'S CHRISTMAS COOKBOOK

Offer valid from Sept. 27, 2011, till Nov. 30, 2011.
Redeemable at participating retail outlets. Limit one coupon per purchase.
Valid in the U.S.A. and Canada only.

52609998

5 65373 00082 3 (8100)0 11760

® and TM are trademarks owned and used by the trademark owner and/or its licensee.

© 2011 Harlequin Enterprises Limited

HNFDMCCCP11MM

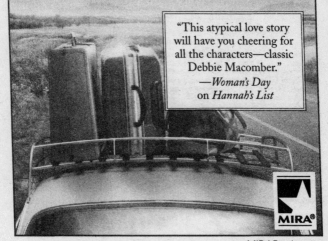

New York Times and USA TODAY Bestselling Author

SHERRYL WOODS

After being unceremoniously dumped two weeks before
getting hitched to a man even her *mother* approves of,
Maggie Forsythe has officially given up. But when her
friends suggest she help them build a house for a needy
family, it's hard for her to resist. Especially when sparks
begin to fly between Maggie and the project foreman....

Flirting with Disaster

"Woods…is noted for appealing, character-driven stories."
—*Library Journal*

"Sherryl Woods gives her characters depth, intensity, and the right
amount of humor." —*RT Book Reviews*

Available wherever books are sold.

REQUEST YOUR FREE BOOKS!

2 FREE NOVELS
FROM THE ROMANCE COLLECTION
PLUS 2 FREE GIFTS!

YES! Please send me 2 FREE novels from the Romance Collection and my 2 FREE gifts (gifts are worth about $10). After receiving them, if I don't wish to receive any more books, I can return the shipping statement marked "cancel." If I don't cancel, I will receive 4 brand-new novels every month and be billed just $5.99 per book in the U.S. or $6.49 per book in Canada. That's a saving of at least 25% off the cover price. It's quite a bargain! Shipping and handling is just 50¢ per book in the U.S. and 75¢ per book in Canada.* I understand that accepting the 2 free books and gifts places me under no obligation to buy anything. I can always return a shipment and cancel at any time. Even if I never buy another book, the two free books and gifts are mine to keep forever.

194/394 MDN FELQ

Name _____ (PLEASE PRINT) _____

Address _____ Apt. #

City _____ State/Prov. _____ Zip/Postal Code

Signature (if under 18, a parent or guardian must sign)

Mail to the **Reader Service**:
IN U.S.A.: P.O. Box 1867, Buffalo, NY 14240-1867
IN CANADA: P.O. Box 609, Fort Erie, Ontario L2A 5X3

Not valid for current subscribers to the Romance Collection
or the Romance/Suspense Collection.

Want to try two free books from another line?
Call 1-800-873-8635 or visit www.ReaderService.com.

* Terms and prices subject to change without notice. Prices do not include applicable taxes. Sales tax applicable in N.Y. Canadian residents will be charged applicable taxes. Offer not valid in Quebec. This offer is limited to one order per household. All orders subject to credit approval. Credit or debit balances in a customer's account(s) may be offset by any other outstanding balance owed by or to the customer. Please allow 4 to 6 weeks for delivery. Offer available while quantities last.

Your Privacy—The Reader Service is committed to protecting your privacy. Our Privacy Policy is available online at www.ReaderService.com or upon request from the Reader Service.

We make a portion of our mailing list available to reputable third parties that offer products we believe may interest you. If you prefer that we not exchange your name with third parties, or if you wish to clarify or modify your communication preferences, please visit us at www.ReaderService.com/consumerschoice or write to us at Reader Service Preference Service, P.O. Box 9062, Buffalo, NY 14269. Include your complete name and address.

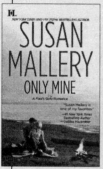
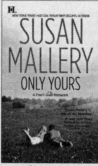
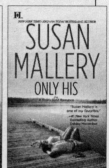

DEBBIE MACOMBER

89213	DEBBIE MACOMBER'S CEDAR COVE COOKBOOK	___ $29.95 U.S.	___ $32.95 CAN.
32988	OUT OF THE RAIN	___ $7.99 U.S.	___ $9.99 CAN.
32983	A TURN IN THE ROAD	___ $24.95 U.S.	___ $27.95 CAN.
32971	92 PACIFIC BOULEVARD	___ $7.99 U.S.	___ $9.99 CAN.
32970	8 SANDPIPER WAY	___ $7.99 U.S.	___ $9.99 CAN.
32969	74 SEASIDE AVENUE	___ $7.99 U.S.	___ $9.99 CAN.
32968	6 RAINIER DRIVE	___ $7.99 U.S.	___ $9.99 CAN.
32967	44 CRANBERRY POINT	___ $7.99 U.S.	___ $9.99 CAN.
32946	311 PELICAN ROAD	___ $7.99 U.S.	___ $9.99 CAN.
32929	HANNAH'S LIST	___ $7.99 U.S.	___ $9.99 CAN.
32918	AN ENGAGEMENT IN SEATTLE	___ $7.99 U.S.	___ $9.99 CAN.
32911	THE MANNING SISTERS	___ $7.99 U.S.	___ $9.99 CAN.
32883	TWENTY WISHES	___ $7.99 U.S.	___ $9.99 CAN.
32880	A GOOD YARN	___ $7.99 U.S.	___ $9.99 CAN.
32861	204 ROSEWOOD LANE	___ $7.99 U.S.	___ $9.99 CAN.
32840	THURSDAYS AT EIGHT	___ $14.95 U.S.	___ $17.95 CAN.
32828	ORCHARD VALLEY BRIDES	___ $7.99 U.S.	___ $9.99 CAN.
32822	CHRISTMAS IN CEDAR COVE	___ $7.99 U.S.	___ $9.99 CAN.
32819	CALL ME MRS. MIRACLE	___ $16.95 U.S.	___ $19.95 CAN.
32806	1022 EVERGREEN PLACE	___ $7.99 U.S.	___ $9.99 CAN.
32783	THE MAN YOU'LL MARRY	___ $7.99 U.S.	___ $9.99 CAN.
32743	THE SOONER THE BETTER	___ $7.99 U.S.	___ $9.99 CAN.
32702	FAIRY TALE WEDDINGS	___ $7.99 U.S.	___ $9.99 CAN.
32701	WYOMING BRIDES	___ $7.99 U.S.	___ $8.99 CAN.
32682	THE PERFECT CHRISTMAS	___ $16.95 U.S.	___ $19.95 CAN.
32679	MARRIED IN SEATTLE	___ $7.99 U.S.	___ $7.99 CAN.
32602	THE MANNING GROOMS	___ $7.99 U.S.	___ $7.99 CAN.
32569	ALWAYS DAKOTA	___ $7.99 U.S.	___ $7.99 CAN.
32474	THE MANNING BRIDES	___ $7.99 U.S.	___ $7.99 CAN.
32362	COUNTRY BRIDES	___ $7.99 U.S.	___ $9.50 CAN.
20000	THE MATCHMAKERS	___ $4.99 U.S.	___ $5.99 CAN.

(limited quantities available)

TOTAL AMOUNT	$	_____
POSTAGE & HANDLING	$	_____
($1.00 for 1 book, 50¢ for each additional)		
APPLICABLE TAXES*	$	_____
TOTAL PAYABLE	$	_____

(check or money order—please do not send cash)

To order, complete this form and send it, along with a check or money order for the total above, payable to MIRA Books, to: **In the U.S.:** 3010 Walden Avenue, P.O. Box 9077, Buffalo, NY 14269-9077; **In Canada:** P.O. Box 636, Fort Erie, Ontario, L2A 5X3.

Name: _____
Address: _____ City: _____
State/Prov.: _____ Zip/Postal Code: _____
Account Number (if applicable): _____
075 CSAS

*New York residents remit applicable sales taxes.
*Canadian residents remit applicable GST and provincial taxes.

MIRA   **H HARLEQUIN®**
www.Harlequin.com

MDM0811BL